Accolades for America's greatest hero Mack Bolan

D0001399

Treason!

First there was the *Challenger* disaster, then the bizarre series of fatal "accidents" that wiped out a small, select group of the world's foremost scientists. Suddenly Mack Bolan is thrust into the middle of a deadly internal war raging deep within the U.S. power structure—a war that could usher in doomsday.

DON PENDLETON's
MACK BOLAN

FIRE IN THE SKY

A GOLD EAGLE BOOK FROM
WORLDWIDE®

TORONTO · NEW YORK · LONDON · PARIS
AMSTERDAM · STOCKHOLM · HAMBURG
ATHENS · MILAN · TOKYO · SYDNEY

First edition February 1988

ISBN 0-373-61410-1

Special thanks and acknowledgment to
Mike McQuay for his contribution to this work.

Determination will carry the soldier only
as far as the place where he dies, and few
soldiers care to go that far.

> —A. J. Liebling, Oct. 19, 1963

Fight the good fight with all thy might.

> —J. S. A. Monsell, 1863

It was my destiny, all those miles ago, to resolve
to stand firm against America's enemies, whoever they
may be. I'll defend her to my last breath.

> —Mack Bolan

To those who pledge to uphold the
principles of democracy

Prologue

Nobody watched the launches anymore. Nobody took them seriously. As Jerry Butler sat, mesmerized, in front of his nine-inch black-and-white TV screen, he thought that if familiarity didn't breed contempt, it certainly bred easy acceptance.

And therein lay the danger.

He sat in the small, trashed-out bungalow that he'd rented just weeks before, the easy roar of the Atlantic coast surf just barely reaching through his closed and shuttered windows. He wore only pajama bottoms, his unkempt hair falling wildly into his eyes. Half-eaten TV dinners, rotting in their aluminum containers, were scattered around the small living room. His six-day growth of beard had reached the itching stage, and he'd developed a rash on his neck from continual, absentminded scratching.

Normally a neat, fastidious man, Jerry Butler had lately discovered that the mind could easily and rapidly create new realities for itself if given the proper stimulus. In his case fear was the key. His doctor would perhaps call it paranoia.

Where was McMasters? He should be here by now.

On the small, flickering screen, *Challenger* sat on its pad like a squat frog, ready to leap, pure white smoke bleeding from the solid fuel boosters that would kick it, screaming, from Earth's atmosphere and into orbit. It was chilly outside, and cloudy. Butler desperately hoped that the inclement weather would scrub the mission for at least one more day.

But it wasn't to be. Bureaucratic priorities would win out over intelligence and common sense every time, and the space shuttle program had to hurry and show its commercial value in order to justify more congressional bureaucratic dollars being spent on its survival. He thought bitterly of the term, "commercial value." The profit motive, plus easy acceptance, were at the moment threatening the entire planet, and Jerry Butler felt himself the only man capable of stopping it.

"The countdown is continuing at T minus 60 seconds and counting," came the voice of the NASA spokesman over the television.

"Damn," Butler muttered. This thing could be handled even if the shuttle was in orbit, but it would be infinitely more difficult.

Out of the corner of his eye, he saw a shadow flit past the side window. He jumped up and ran to the window, parting the curtains. Through the shutter slats he could see a normal, if cool, Florida morning. The snowbirds who had rented these beachfront cottages to escape the northern winter were getting a taste of it anyway. The sky was slate, palm trees swaying in the stiff wind.

He closed the curtains and returned to the television. Supply trucks were racing away from the launch platform and large, billowing clouds of smoke were now filling the screen.

"T minus 30 seconds and counting."

Another shadow flitted past the window. But he ignored it this time, his eyes fixed on the excitement of the launch.

At T minus 10 seconds there was pounding on the back door, Butler jerking his head to the sound. McMasters. Finally.

He jumped up, listening to the sounds of the lift-off as he pulled the door open. Glen McMasters stood before him, weaving slightly, like a drunk. The man's eyes were glassy, a strange look of perturbed confusion twisting his pale, fleshy face.

"Wha..." Butler began, then his eyes took in the spreading pool of red that wet the man's sport shirt. Blood and fatty tissue were oozing from several wounds on McMasters's chest and stomach.

"Oh God!"

Butler tried to back away, but McMasters fell into his arms, his lips sputtering soundlessly. Butler supported the man's weight for a second, then the bulk of it took both of them slowly to the floor.

Wrenching away, Butler slid out from under the dead-weight, his mind numbed by fear and confusion. He got to his feet—McMasters's blood all over him—and clenched his fists, trying to force his mind to calm long enough to think of a course of action.

He took several deep breaths. The first thing he had to do was to get help for McMasters. The next thing he had to do was get the hell out of there. Had he looked more closely, he would have discovered that McMasters was already dead.

His knees were weak, almost buckling, as he hurried to the phone. He picked up the receiver just in time to watch the space shuttle on the TV screen explode in a huge fire-ball seventy-three seconds into the flight.

"No!" he screamed. "Those bastards! Those bastards!"

And through the anger and the fear, a small truth made its way into his tortured, reeling brain: the phone he held up to his ear was soundless—dead.

The receiver slipped from his grasp, his whole body numb. He thought to try to run for the bedroom window, but heard a loud crashing back there. He turned toward the front door, unable to look at the body that lay near the back way out.

He took one faltering step, then another, his body responding sluggishly, as in a dream, unable to hurry. Then he saw the door burst open, a man in a Security Police-man's uniform filling the doorway.

No words were exchanged as the SP slowly raised the M-16 he carried at his side. Butler gave up then, resigned himself to the end of his world. In his last seconds he saw things with a crystal clarity that was almost frightening, and wondered, given the opportunity to live it over again, if he'd be willing to condemn the rest of the world to extend his own existence just a little longer. Then it struck him that he was getting the better end of the deal after all.

The SP grinned broadly and pulled the trigger.

Jerry Butler never heard the sound of the weapon or felt even the slightest twinge of pain. His body simply accepted what his mind had already embraced.

Chapter One

The fog in Mississippi was the worst Bolan had ever seen anywhere. He drove the big, old Cadillac through dense impenetrable patches of it, thick like delta cotton, that rolled aggressively along the twisting blacktop and extended visibility no farther than the end of the hood. It hung suspended in the thick stands of woods that butted all the way up to the road on both sides and turned what was already a dark and foreboding landscape into a surreal nightmare.

He was tired and irritable from the intense concentration demanded by the fog, his mood not helped by the constant bickering of the two people sharing the front seat with him. Husband and wife, they seemed a physical and emotional mismatch, drawn together by mutual scientific interest and nothing else. At the moment they were arguing loudly.

"Skinner was right," Dr. Harry Arnold said. "Control the environment and you control the man. Control the environment positively and you have a happy man."

"But *who* controls, Harry, who controls?" Julie Arnold replied, turning and leaning against the passenger-side door to stare at him. She pointed. "And who controls the controllers? Somebody's got to be in charge."

"Don't be a fool," the man replied wearily. "My theory implies first and foremost that benign, intelligent direction would institute the control. That would be the first step."

"You're living in a test tube," she replied, her eyes bright fire in the darkness of the car. "Even your given is an impossibility. Power corrupts."

"Stop!" Bolan ordered, rubbing a hand across his face. "Between the fog and the arguing, I'm getting a headache. We've only got another hour on the road. Let's spend it peacefully."

Dr. Arnold looked at him over the top of his wire-frame glasses. "Your job is to drive," he said coldly.

Bolan hit the brakes, hard, the car jerking to a stop in the middle of the dark, lonely road. He turned a stern face to the Arnolds. "Look, you'd better keep quiet," he said, menace in his voice.

Julie Arnold started to speak, but stopped herself. Throwing Bolan an amused look, she straightened up in the seat and looked out the windshield.

Bolan sighed and drove on, reaching out to hit the wipers long enough to clear the moisture that had accumulated. He hadn't wanted this job, hadn't wanted any part of it, but here he was. The Arnolds were classified, even from him, but he did know that they were government research scientists who were being escorted to a safehouse in the Mississippi delta and that the Justice Department didn't want to take it through regular channels.

And Mack Bolan was definitely not regular channels.

Hal Brognola, Bolan's friend and contact at Justice, had asked him as a personal favor to handle the transport. It had seemed like a waste of time, but Hal had been insistent. And to Mack Bolan, real friendships ran deep and true. He had taken the job, and from the moment he had climbed into the vehicle with the Arnolds in Langley, Virginia, he'd regretted every minute of it.

Of the Arnolds, Bolan knew very little. They had been on the road together for nearly eighteen hours, most of them spent in disagreement. Both were scientists, Julie working as her husband's assistant. There was, perhaps, a twenty- to twenty-five-year difference in their ages. He was rumpled suits; she was blue jeans and sweaters. Beyond that, they were strangers to him. It seemed best to keep it that way.

Bolan looked at his watch, the luminous dial telling him that another day had begun. He'd been at the wheel the entire time, stopping only for food and gas. The roads were the safest, least predictable means of conveyance, and, according to procedure, he'd changed routes frequently and changed cars twice. His hardware weighed heavily against him in the humid air—a Beretta 93-R and a .44 AutoMag—hidden from view in a combat harness concealed beneath a light windbreaker. He'd nearly stowed them in the trunk before the start of the trip, and now, as he sweated profusely under the leather of the harness, he wished he had.

The safehouse, near Hattiesburg, was a converted plantation that had survived the Civil War. Southern Mississippi was rife with these antebellum dinosaurs of a bygone era. They were tucked away in the incredible, dense forests that blanketed two-thirds of the state, many of them redecorated and opened to a public curious to see the remnants of American aristocracy.

To the dreamer in Bolan, the pristine conservation of such natural wonders as the forests and the ghosts of the memory they protected was a romantic legacy of a unique and delicate past, but to the soldier in Bolan, this was the worst possible place in the world. The two-lane blacktop snaked its way through uncountable miles of totally impenetrable forests. The road had been deserted for hours. He longed for open country, for visibility. Anything, any-*one* could disappear from these roads and never be seen again. The forests held secrets, and the forests remained silent.

Bolan suddenly slowed the Cadillac to a crawl. "There's something up ahead."

They peered intently through the windshield. The fog glowed brightly in the distance, then receded, back and forth.

"What is it?" Harry Arnold asked.

"Maybe a police car," Bolan offered, "with its cherry turned on."

"Maybe there was a wreck," Julie Arnold said.

"Yeah...maybe," Bolan said, but it didn't feel right. He looked in the rearview mirror. The fog behind was glowing brightly—headlights. There was no reason for there *not* to be a car behind them, but to see so much activity after so much solitude just didn't sit right.

"Something's starting to take shape," Dr. Arnold said.

"A car?" the woman said.

"A jeep," Bolan replied, bringing the Cadillac to a complete stop perhaps thirty feet from the blue Security Police jeep that had been parked across the road. He could make out a larger form behind the vehicle, perhaps an armored carrier, that blocked what the jeep didn't. A man, wraithlike in the fog, stepped out of the vehicle. He wore a colonel's uniform.

Bolan checked the rearview mirror again. The dark hulk of a two-and-a-half-ton canvas-covered truck—also with Air Force markings—had pulled up twenty feet behind. Engine idling, it just sat there, headlights lighting the area around the Cadillac.

"He's coming this way," Julie Arnold said, pointing at the colonel who moved, smiling, toward them.

Bolan eased the Beretta out of its holster.

"What are you doing?" Dr. Arnold asked. "Those are *our* people."

Bolan said nothing as he primed the weapon. He rolled down the window and called out, "That'll be far enough, Colonel. I want to ask you a few questions."

The man smiled broadly and raised his hands. "Quite understandable, Mr. Bolan," he called back. "Sorry to have engaged you in such an...unorthodox manner. You've been out of contact, however, and it couldn't be helped."

Bolan tensed. There was no way this man could have known his name. Brognola was the only one who knew he was the escort. The operation had been compromised.

"My name's Kit Givan, Colonel, United States Air Force. You are transporting Drs. Harry and Julie Arnold to our safehouse in Hattiesburg. I have been sent to escort you."

The Arnolds sighed in unison, then chuckled in relief. Bolan felt no better. The man once again started to walk toward the car.

"Stop!" Bolan said, and the smile finally disappeared from Givan's face. "Why are you intercepting us? This is an undercover operation."

"We have received reports that KGB agents might try something at the house," Givan called. "We are here to protect you."

"If KGB agents know about the safehouse," Bolan replied, "then that's the last place I want to take my charges."

"This is not a request, Bolan," Givan returned. "These are orders...yours, as well as ours."

"I don't take orders from you," Bolan said, his eyes scanning the surrounding trees. Had he caught movement? "I want you to remove your vehicles from the roadway so I may proceed with my mission. I'll make my own contacts with Justice and determine at that time the proper course of action in this matter."

"What are you saying?" Julie Arnold asked, angry. "This is the Air Force. We work for them."

"I don't," Bolan replied. "And from where I sit, this whole setup stinks."

He saw them again, maddeningly brief glimpses of shadows with rifles running between the pine trees. They were close enough to be visible only because they wanted to be close enough to get off a shot.

"I'm ordering you to stand out of the vehicle!" Givan called, his hands resting on his gun belt. "I am now in command of this operation!"

"Give me a minute to discuss this with my people," Bolan returned.

The colonel looked at his watch. "You have thirty seconds."

Julie Arnold was fiddling with the lock on her door. "This is foolish," she told Bolan. "I don't know who or what you are, but you're making a lot of trouble with the government."

"Don't get out yet," Bolan ordered.

"Go to hell," the woman answered, pushing the door partway open.

Bolan leveled a penetrating look at her. "You'll be dead when your foot touches the ground. Wait until I give you the word."

She looked at him, her eyes narrowing. "Who are you?"

"You're nearly out of time!" Givan called.

"Listen," Bolan told the Arnolds. "The woods around us are filled with men with guns, and they're not the good guys. Whoever these people are, they're here to kill us. We're going to have to break for the woods. The darkness and fog will hide us as well as it's hiding them."

"You're crazy!" Harry Arnold said.

"Time's up!" Givan shouted.

"Okay," Bolan said. "Out your side and don't stop running. For anything. Go!"

"No!" Julie Arnold said. "I can't just jump—"

"Go!" Bolan rasped. "Go!"

He saw Colonel Givan turn and run back to his jeep at the same instant that muzzle-flashes lit up the night on the opposite side of the roadway.

Bolan ducked instinctively to the chain-saw rattle of automatic weapons, glass shattering all around them. Harry Arnold yelled once, a scream that caught in his throat and died abruptly, his body slumping onto Bolan.

As small-arms fire ate away at the Cadillac, Bolan pulled free of Arnold's body to look at the woman. She was down, too, staring in horrified fascination at the mass of red, quivering flesh that had once been her husband's face.

"Julie!" Bolan called loudly, and her vacant eyes found his. "Run! Now, or we're dead!"

She bit her lower lip, mind reeling. Then she kicked open the unlatched door and rolled out in a crouch. Bolan followed, scrambling over the body to fall headfirst from the vehicle and somersault to his feet.

Julie was at the edge of the woods by the time he got his feet, the ground kicking up death all around her. Bolan ignored the action behind him, firing from instinct at shadows in the forest.

He heard a groan; a body slumped from the tree line and fell directly behind him as he made the woods. As he ran through the darkness, he tried to keep his attention on the woman, saving his peripheral vision for the enemy, not wanting to confuse the two.

He fired twice at a muzzle-flash on his right, and was rewarded by a piercing scream. They were twenty feet into the thicket now, voices loud behind them. The enemy fire had become more sporadic; it appeared that the forces were regrouping.

They had broken through the front line, and Bolan caught up to Julie a hundred feet into the Piney Woods of the national forest. He grabbed her, pulling her behind a longleaf pine.

She was panting, her face streaked with tears.

"What do they want?" she whispered harshly.

"Us," Bolan said. "Dead."

"Why?"

"I was hoping you could tell me."

"Could they be KGB?"

He shrugged, pulling the AutoMag out of his harness. "Seems like they wanted you two alive," he said.

Her lower lip started to tremble, and she looked at the ground. "Harry was so damned...hard-assed—" she sobbed "—but he was a good..."

"Stow it," Bolan snapped. "We'll talk about him later. Right now we've got to save our own hides. Do you know how to fire one of these?" He held the automatic out to her.

She took the weapon, her face hardening. "The government made us all take training," she said. "I can get by."

"Great," he replied, straining past her to try to see through the fog. "If anyone other than me gets anywhere near you, don't even think, just shoot it."

She nodded grimly and primed the gun.

"Bolan!" Givan's amplified voice shouted from a distance. "Mack Bolan! We don't want you! We couldn't care less about you! Send us the woman, or shoot her yourself! We don't care! Do it and leave. You have my word that you're free!"

Julie Arnold looked up at him, her eyes frightened.

He smiled in return. "Let's move," he said. "They're going to make a sweep of the area."

"Move where?" she asked.

"I want to try to flank them and get back to the roadway," he replied, taking her by the arm and moving off again. "Maybe we can take some of their transport."

"That sounds dangerous."

"You're already winded from the short run we've made," he replied. "You'd never survive a firefight out here."

"Why is this happening?" she asked, voice strained.

"Stick close," he said, ignoring her question. "Think about nothing but making that roadway. This isn't going to be easy."

He moved out at a jog, angling at what he hoped was a parallel to the road. The opposing force was undoubtedly fanning out at this point, preparing their sweep. He wanted to get beyond them, then cut back.

As they ran, keeping their arms up in front of their faces to ward off branches, they could hear voices calling out, setting up their free-fire zone. Time was running out.

All at once the fog lit up brilliantly around them, trees standing out in stark contrast to the brightness of the light.

"Flares!" Bolan called. "Hurry!"

Flares began going off everywhere, magnesium burning the brightest white, as voices yelled orders. Then an explosion shook the ground, and a large limb crashed into the brush. Grenades.

"They've spotted us!" Bolan said, taking the woman by the arm. "Come on!"

Silhouettes backlit by the bright lights charged the fleeing couple, small fires crackling where the flares had set the undergrowth ablaze. Bolan turned and fired at one of the silhouettes, the body punched hard backward before slamming into the ground.

They were going to have to make their move. Bolan dropped to a crouch, pulling the woman down with him. He encompassed the area around them with a wide sweep of his arm. "Lay down a pattern of fire," he said. "Empty the gun. When you're finished, we take off."

The woman complied without question, firing at any movement, while Bolan aimed more carefully. They would only have a few seconds before Givan figured out what they were up to and took countermeasures. Every shot had to count.

Bolan took out a silhouette at the legs, then another chest high, knocking the man into one of the brush fires, his screams reverberating loudly through the forest.

The fires were growing in intensity, threatening to get out of control.

"Empty!" Julie Arnold shouted, just as another explosion drove them flat to the ground.

Bolan jumped up and dragged her to her feet. "This is it! Let's go!"

They cut straight back, charging in the direction that they had cleared with their own fire—the weak link in the chain. The fires helped. Large and bright now, they blended pluming black smoke with the fog.

And Bolan was through the line, taking advantage of Givan's tactical blunder. They gained the roadway fifty feet beyond the roadblock. The fires were huge now, burning out of control and, farther down the blacktop, men were straggling out of the woods coughing and gagging.

"Almost there," Bolan told the woman, who was bent over, wheezing, out of breath. "Come on. We need wheels."

She nodded, straightened and took a deep breath. They charged toward the armored carrier, a manned M-60 atop it; the gunner watched the fires, oblivious to their approach.

Ten feet from the carrier, Bolan stopped, drawing down on the gunner with the Beretta. The man saw him too late. He hurried to swivel the M-60 around, but Bolan already had him nailed, lacing him across the chest with an automatic burst.

There were other trucks parked in the area, personnel carriers and supply vehicles. Bolan spotted an Air Force pickup half on, half off the road. He and Julie raced toward it, reaching the vehicle just as they were spotted.

They jumped in the truck and Bolan turned the key—which was already in the ignition—and fired the machine to life. He jammed into reverse, the wheels screeching, rubber burning as he jerked the vehicle back onto the road. He hit the brakes so hard that they were thrown violently against the seat. Then he pulled the stick into gear and drove out of there, the sounds of gunfire fading behind them.

He drove fast, plunging blindly into the thick fog, hoping against hope that no one was coming from the other direction while he was driving down the middle of the road. Within minutes, the warrior found a side road and took it, then another, and with every passing mile he felt a bit more relaxed.

The woman had been looking out the back window since their escape. Two bullet holes had spiderwebbed the glass neatly, forcing her to peer through the small, intact sections. Finally she turned around and slumped down in the seat. "Thanks," she said wearily, her expression shocked as the events of the previous ten minutes fully sank in. "I don't know what..."

"We're not out of it yet," Bolan said. "We're both as hot as pistols."

She nodded and leaned her head back against the seat.

"What are you researching, anyway?" he asked finally, unable to keep it in any longer.

She looked at him with wide, innocent eyes. "Electricity," she said with a shrug. "Just electricity."

"Electricity," he repeated, shaking his head. Amazing.

Chapter Two

Julie Arnold sat nursing a cup of tea in the Vicksburg Holiday Inn coffee shop, watching as the man who had saved her life talked heatedly on the phone attached to the wall near the entrance. Who he was exactly, she didn't know. More than just a driver, surely, but beyond that things just got too complicated.

She was dirty, grimy, her good clothes torn and smelling of sweat. They had stopped at a gas station's rest rooms to clean the soot and filth from their faces and arms, but it hadn't done much good. Even here, in the restaurant, people were staring at her with narrowed eyes. Unconsciously she reached up and tried unsuccessfully to straighten her hair.

She thought of Harry and shivered at the memory of her last glimpse of him. She was still numb on the subject of Harry. The grief would have to come, but when, and how much? It wasn't as if she had loved him—his death brought a freedom that she had longed for—but he had been a vital part of her life for many years. His death was going to leave a void that would be hard to fill. So, her sorrow, then, would be more for herself than for Harry. She took a sip of the lukewarm brew. Wasn't that what all sorrow was, though?

So, Harry Arnold was dead, killed, apparently, by the government he had worked so long and hard for. He was dead on the eve of the breakthrough that would have earned the respect and admiration of his colleagues, which he had craved. A few ounces of lead stuck in the right places had stilled that great mind; and here she sat, her life in the hands of a man she knew nothing about. Scientist to fugitive, the brim to the dregs, all in a few hours' time. She was frightened, and would have been more frightened if it wasn't for the numbness.

All around Julie waitresses in frilly aprons hurried between the tables, refilling coffee mugs for businessmen in a rush to get back on the road and make their presentations. She felt so removed from all that, so distant from the routines of life. She wanted to shout at them, to tell them that everything wasn't fine and good, that something dark and nasty had gone down in the Mississippi woods. But she didn't dare.

She didn't know whom she could trust.

Her eyes drifted once more to the question mark at the telephones.

Bolan had an eye trained on Julie Arnold. So far she had held up better than he could have hoped, but he knew that much of that could simply be shock. She was an amateur caught up in something prickly and professional, and once she cracked, Bolan's job was going to be difficult. He wanted her off his hands fast, because the people who had pulled the ambush in the woods were connected, powerful and obviously motivated. Julie Arnold was going to need more protection than he could provide.

"Okay," Hal Brognola said on the other end of the line. "We're secured."

"Are you sure?" Bolan asked, irritation evident in his voice. "We're in no shape here to—"

"We're secured," Brognola said, his voice rising slightly. "What the hell's going on out there?"

Bolan glanced quickly around, making sure no one was listening. Then he cupped the receiver and spoke low. "We were stopped in the middle of the night by an Air Force convoy. They knew me, and they knew my cargo."

"Good God . . ."

"Yeah, good God. When they couldn't get us out of the car, they blasted us while we were in it. Dr. Arnold's dead. His wife and I managed to get away in one of their trucks."

"Where are you now?" Brognola asked.

"You sure this line is clear?" Bolan returned.

"Striker..."

Bolan drew a breath. "We drove most of the night and ran out of gas outside of Vicksburg. We made it in on foot, staying off the roads. The woman's holding up all right. What's this all about?"

There was a slight hesitation on the line. "I honestly don't know," the man finally answered.

"You know more than you're telling me," Bolan said.

"Yes. I want to get as much together on this thing as I can before we talk about it." There was another silence, the shuffling of papers. "I'm looking at a report about a fire in the Bienville National Forest," Brognola said.

"That's where they hit us," Bolan answered.

"The reports are clean. The fire was brought under control by one Colonel Kit Givan with some loss of Air Force personnel. It doesn't mention Harry Arnold, but the reports treat this Colonel Givan like some sort of hero for putting out the fire."

"Great. They've taken care of the evidence," Bolan said, and wondered how Julie Arnold would react to the disappearance of her husband's body. "Hal, we've got to get out of here."

"I don't trust regular channels at this point," Brognola replied. "Someone in my department is obviously in on this, and I can't take the chance of tipping them. I'm going to take a plane out to where you are. Sit tight for today. We'll meet tomorrow."

"Where?"

"I've been to Vicksburg. The city was under siege during the Civil War. The battlefield is a national park. Let's meet tomorrow morning at ten in the battlefield cemetery. It commands a wide view from high ground. Is there any chance that they'll find the abandoned truck?"

"I ditched it in the thick woods," Bolan replied. "I think we're all right for now."

"Get a room there under an assumed name. We're going to bottle you up right now until we know what we're up against. Fair enough?"

"It suits," Bolan growled. "It has to."

"I'm sorry, Striker," the man said, his voice low.

"It happens, Hal," Bolan replied. "Not your fault. We'll see you at ten sharp...with answers."

"With as many as I can give you," Brognola responded, and hung up.

As Bolan replaced the phone, he looked through the coffee shop archway and into the lobby proper. Two SPs were standing at the registration desk asking questions.

He moved quickly back to the table, the look on his face alerting the woman that something was wrong. She was on her feet immediately.

"What is it?" she whispered urgently.

"Maybe nothing, I—" Then Bolan saw the SPs through the window in the outer courtyard. Several of them were walking around the pool, checking the rooms that faced it. It was obvious they were searching for something—or someone.

Bolan turned 360 degrees, then realized there were no other exits from the coffee shop except through the lobby. The kitchen might have had an exit, but it was possible it would come out on the parking lot, near the Air Force vehicles.

He picked up the check for the coffee. "Come on," he said, taking Julie by the arm and moving toward the archway cashier stand. With any luck, they could slip quickly past the registration desk and wait it out in the rest rooms located in the lobby hallway. But as they neared the archway, that hope was dashed.

The SPs had left the desk and were moving quickly toward the restaurant. The cashier was smiling expectedly at them, but Bolan turned and moved back into the room.

"Still hungry," he said over his shoulder, and led his companion toward the long breakfast buffet table set up in the front of the room.

"What are you doing?" she asked, as he picked up two plates and handed her one.

"Saving our lives," Bolan said, his eyes scanning the room to see if anyone was watching them. Satisfied, he quickly crouched to the floor, pulling the woman down with him.

The long tables holding the buffet had been covered with white linen tablecloths that hung to the floor. Without a word, Bolan scurried under the table.

"Come on," he whispered urgently.

She picked up an end of the cloth and peered at him under the table. "This is your idea of saving our lives?" she asked, her face incredulous.

He grabbed her arm and jerked hard, so that the woman tumbled from her crouch and fell beside him. He pulled her under completely, letting the tablecloth fall back in place.

"What kind of maniac are you?" she rasped, scrambling away from him.

"Quiet."

"Don't you shush me," she whispered. "This is ridiculous. We're grown-up so this is no way to—"

"All right," Bolan whispered in return. He drew the Beretta from his combat harness. "Do you want us to blast our way out of here?"

Her face sagged when she saw the gun, memories of the previous night flooding back, reminding her that she was on somebody's hit list.

"All right," she said quietly, nodding. "We'll do it your way."

"Okay," he replied, holstering the weapon. "The first thing you need to do is to keep quiet. The second thing is to trust me."

"I'll try."

The table shook slightly, and voices murmured just out of their range of hearing. Then the toes of military boots were poking beneath the tablecloth. Bolan saw the woman's eyes go wide. The Air Force had decided to eat.

The feet moved slowly past their position, both of them holding their breath as the SPs stood just inches from them.

Something hit the floor with a metallic ping, a booted foot kicking it under the table. It was a ring of keys.

"Damn!" he heard from above. The man got down on hands and knees to retrieve the keys.

A slight gasp escaped Julie's lips, but she stifled it with her hands.

Bolan began edging the key ring back toward the linen that separated them from death. All at once, a hand poked under the cloth, searching.

Bolan drew the gun out again, the barrel nearly touching the tablecloth. Time stood still as the large-knuckled hand continued to fumble around the floor.

"Just lift up the damned thing," a voice said. Bolan's finger eased onto the trigger, tensed slightly.

"Yeah, I...wait!" the kneeling man said, his fingers finally brushing the keys, then closing on them. "Got it!"

The man climbed back to his feet and moved farther down the line. Julie Arnold let out a huge sigh as the SPs moved away.

"Is your friend getting us out of here?" she whispered when the men had left the table completely.

"Tomorrow," Bolan said.

Julie's face tightened. "We could be dead ten times over by tomorrow."

"Yeah," Bolan replied. "I know."

"What are we supposed to do in the meantime, steal meals from the buffet table?"

Bolan holstered the Beretta. "We'll get a room after they've gone. You got any money?"

"I didn't stop to get my purse when we were running for our lives back there," she said, the anger growing in her voice. "And what are you telling me, that we're going to spend the rest of the day and a night in a motel room together?"

"Unless you've got a better idea."

"Yes. Two rooms."

He shook his head. "I've got forty-seven dollars and twenty-three cents in my pocket. That's not going to get us two rooms."

"You did say you worked for the *United States* government, didn't you?" she asked.

"As far as I know."

"You sure we can trust this friend of yours?"

Bolan nodded. "With our lives."

"You're so sure."

"After the attack on you and your husband he doesn't know who to trust right now," Bolan admitted. "He doesn't want to put us in any more danger than we're already in."

"Look, mister," she whispered. "I'm just a citizen, you know? I pay my taxes and do my work and can't figure out why I'm having to hide under a goddamn dining-room table in a Holiday Inn. I mean, the government's just the government, right?"

Bolan had no answer for her. He shrugged. "I can't make you stick with me," he said. "You're free to do whatever you want at this point. But just remember that your husband is dead because somebody in the Justice Department is picking up a paycheck someplace else, and remember that once they commit murder, they continue to commit murder to get what they want. And what they want is for you to be dead just like your husband. Now, if I were you, I'd be thinking about the only man you can be sure of who doesn't want you dead."

"You," she said.

"Right. Can you trust *anything* else?"

"I'll start with that," she said. "We'll get the room."

"Good girl." Bolan leaned forward and lifted the tablecloth a little, peering under it to see that the coffee shop was filled with blue uniforms. "They're *all* eating."

More feet appeared at the table, and Bolan put a finger to his lips. The woman nodded, but uncertainty hung on her like fog on a marsh. She needed sleep; she needed time to grieve, time to understand what was happening to her. Most of all, she needed answers, and in that respect she was the same as Mack Bolan.

They waited under the table for another thirty minutes, military personnel coming and going at the buffet the entire time. He kept a close eye on Julie Arnold, watching for a sign that the pressure was getting to her. But she held together, if just barely.

Though she had seemed totally honest when talking to him, Bolan couldn't shake the feeling that there was more going on than she was willing to tell. It wasn't hard to come to a conclusion like that, however, given the nature of their surroundings, so he simply filed it away for future reference and wondered, instead, what could be so important about research into electrical energy.

The room finally began to clear. Bolan waited until the last of the SPs had been gone for several minutes before sliding out from under the table, his unused plate still in his hand. A busboy who was clearing the buffet stared down at him, startled.

"Lost a contact," Bolan said, lifting the tablecloth for Julie Arnold. "Come on out, darling."

He stood, helping her up, while the silent busboy stared openmouthed. Bolan and Julie Arnold handed him their plates.

"We . . . changed our minds," she said, the two of them walking past him.

They paid for the tea, then walked to the edge of the lobby. The last of the Air Force vehicles was pulling away from the portico.

"I'm going to go register," he said. "You wait in the rest room in the hall."

"Why?"

"Two reasons," he replied. "One, they're probably looking for us to be together. And two, without you I'll only have to pay for a single."

He gave her a half smile, which elicited a ghost of a response. She moved off reluctantly, not wanting to part with her protection. As soon as she had disappeared into the ladies' room, he walked to the registration counter.

A man in a green suit was busy plugging keys into the beehive behind the counter when he approached.

"Excuse me."

The man turned, an automatic smile turning up his thin lips. "What can I do for you?"

"I'd like a room," Bolan answered.

The man nodded. "Sorry, I didn't see you pull up." He slid the registration card and a pen across the desk.

"No room with all the government people out there," Bolan replied amiably. "What is it, some kind of convoy or something?" He wrote hurriedly, making up a salesman job and a phony car and license for himself.

The man leaned across the counter. "Believe it or not, they're looking for some kinda Russian spies or something."

"Here?" Bolan asked, sliding the card back.

"Swear to God," the man said, raising his right hand. He looked down at the card. "Will you be paying in cash, Mr. Basist?"

"Always," Bolan said, handing the man two twenties. "I don't believe in plastic. No, sir. I hope they find those spies soon. Those Air Force boys are liable to take up every room between here and Jackson."

"You might be right about that. They looked like they was mighty fired up about finding them two," the man said, making change for the money. "And you'll just be staying the one night?"

Bolan nodded, smiling. "Unless those spies hijack us all or something."

The man smiled with him, then handed him back two dollars and change for his forty. "Don't you worry none about them spies," he said, and opened his sport jacket. A .38 was stuck in the waistband of his pants. "I'll blow 'em straight back to hell if I see 'em."

"I'll sleep better knowing that," Bolan said, and took the room key from the man, patiently waiting as he showed him where the room was on the desk map.

Bolan waved and moved out the front doors. Then he walked around the lobby building to come in the back way. He moved quietly up the hall next to the registration desk and gently tapped on the ladies' room door. Julie Arnold poked her head out immediately.

He put a finger to his lips and took her by the arm, hurrying her out of the building and up the outside stairs to the second-floor room. It had a decent view of the parking lot, and for the first time, Bolan began to feel partly secure.

He parted the curtains and spent a minute looking out at the parking lot. When he turned around, Julie Arnold was staring at the bed that occupied the center of the room.

"Bolan..." she said, a catch in her voice.

"Look," he said gently. "You've got too much to worry about right now to waste any time worrying about my sexual intentions. We've both been through a lot and deserve some sleep. If it'll make you feel any better, I don't ever intend for both of us to sleep at the same time, anyway. Someone's going to have to keep watch. I asked you to trust me before. I meant it. All right?"

She nodded, relieved.

"Good. You can shower first."

"Oh, God," she said, putting a hand to her chest. "I really need one!"

He inclined his head toward the bathroom. "Go ahead."

She turned without a word and hurried to the bathroom. A moment later he heard the water running in the shower, and shortly after that, he could hear her crying. She had finally, mercifully, let down her guard.

JULIE ARNOLD SAT WRAPPED in a sheet she had pulled from the bed because she couldn't stand the thought of putting the same sweaty clothes back on. A white, hotel towel was wrapped around her wet hair, and she stared at the telephone while listening to the muffled sounds of Bolan showering in the next room. It was time to make the call.

She lifted the receiver, feeling foolish. After all, she'd had access to the 800 number for more than ten years and had never used it. It had probably been out of service for a long time. She dialed an outside line, then punched up the numbers she had committed to memory as part of her training.

Tension tightened up her insides when she heard the number ring on the other side, and when it was answered after one ring, she nearly came off the bed.

"Go on," the voice on the other end prodded.

"Uh..."

"Go on," the voice repeated.

"This is...Lady Madonna," she said, finally choking the ridiculous words out.

"Hold, please."

"I don't have much time, I..."

The voice had already left the phone.

Within thirty seconds, another voice was on the line. "Report, please."

"Report?" she asked. "Look. Somebody killed my husband last night and tried to kill me and the man who was protecting us."

"We have received confirmation of that," the voice replied. "Are you all right?"

"Well, yeah...considering," she said. "Where were you people?"

"We're trying to get our own reports coordinated now. Where are you?"

"I'm in a little town called Vicksburg, Mississippi," she said, feeling guilty and not knowing why. "In a motel."

"Why?"

"We're waiting for someone from the Justice Department to come and help us. Look, the Air Force is trying to find us. They're the ones who—"

"It's all in our reports," the monotone voice answered, cutting her off.

"Can't you do something?" she asked, voice strained.

"We're trying to plug the leaks now. Remain with your present situation until further notice. Trust no one, especially the man you're with. Report back in two days for more information. We're depending on you. What happened to your husband's notes?"

"His notes?" she said, angry. "God, his head was blown off last night, and all you worry about is—"

"Please," the voice said. "We share your sense of loss, but it's a matter of some urgency to know where the notes are."

"Gone," she said. "Left back in the car."

"Maintain cover," the voice said. "And good luck."

The line went dead. She hung up, confused. This had been her emergency number, her ace in the hole, and they had simply cut her adrift. She picked up the receiver again, prepared to call back and straighten everything out, but just then the water stopped in the shower and she hung up quickly.

A moment later, Bolan, wrapped in a towel, poked his head out of the bathroom. "You all right?" he asked.

She nodded. "Trust no one," the voice had said. "Especially the man you're with." She looked at him. Over the past twenty-four hours she had learned to trust no one except him.

"Why don't you try to get some sleep," he said, using another towel to dry his hair. "I'll take the first watch."

She nodded, dutifully pulling her legs up onto the mattress and covering herself with the spread. She closed her eyes, and exhaustion overtook her despite the turmoil in her mind. She drifted slowly into a slight and troubled sleep filled with visions of death and dreams of uncertainty.

Chapter Three

Bolan was surprised at his own reactions as he and Julie walked through the national park that had once been a killing ground, the quiet, rolling countryside that had seen all the horror, destruction and inhumanity that warfare can be. As they passed the monuments to the suicidal charges and desperate defensive measures that had made this particular ground worth the cost of thousands of lives, he felt saddened by the realization that there would always be war, always be irrational killing.

It had been called the Civil War, and yet there had been nothing civil about it.

For forty-seven days during the spring of 1863, this particular parcel of dirt, grass and trees had been the most important place on Earth for the armies of the Potomac and the Confederacy. This ground, which commanded a high view of the Mississippi River and the mouth of the Yazoo, was laid siege to by the Union army under Grant and Sherman, and was the last stretch of the Mississippi not under Union control. Its taking would cut the Confederacy in two and crush any hopes the South had of winning the war.

It was the turning point, and everyone involved had known it. Perhaps the more farsighted of those soldiers had realized that any clash between industrial and agrarian civilizations could have only one outcome, but for everyone else it wasn't obvious until after many thousands of lives had been claimed by thirst, hunger and disease. General Grant accepted the surrender of the remaining 37,000 Confederate troops, represented by

Lieutenant General Pemberton, on July 4, 1863. Independence Day.

The killing ground then became ordinary ground once more. Agrarian civilization died in the American South. Grant became President, and countless youths on vacation felt military passions surge within as they ran about these battlefields or stopped to read the plaques commemorating the courage and self-sacrifice of the fighters.

Bolan thought bitterly of the world's glorification of war. He had seen no glory in Nam, and doubted whether any of the soldiers fighting starvation and dysentery had seen any glory at Vicksburg. The young needed to be taught that glory was in the living, not the dying.

Perhaps there would be no more need of the skills of men like Mack Bolan. Perhaps he could thankfully outlive his usefulness.

"Why does he want to meet us here?" Julie Arnold asked as they walked the paved road leading through the battlefield.

"It would be difficult to be followed here and not know it. Besides, it's a place my contact knows."

She shook her head and took out the comb that was stuck in the waistband of her slacks. It was the only luxury they'd been able to afford and she kept using it, her lifeline to reality.

"I feel so silly," she said, vigorously combing her dark hair. "I'm sure that your friend will simply walk in here and take care of all this. But right now, it seems so damned strange and—"

"Don't get your hopes up," Bolan interrupted, as the road they walked began to slope upward. "There's a lot more going on here than we know about."

She took his arm, turning him to face her. Bolan read the vulnerability in her eyes. "Please don't tell me that," she said.

He shrugged and continued walking. "Have it your way."

"Bolan, I'm scared," she said to his back.

He turned and looked at her. "You should be. Stay that way."

They crested a hill. An entire field of small white crosses stretched before them, set in even rows side by side, up and down the rolling hills, facing a panoramic view of the Mississippi River, the great artery of America. To the right, at the bottom of the long hillside, was anchored a partially reconstructed "ironside" fighting vessel, which had been sunk during the siege and was raised more than a century later as a historical exhibit.

Bolan scanned the mammoth field of crosses, spotting a lone man a hundred yards distant. "There he is," Bolan said, taking Julie by the arm and moving her in that direction.

Brognola spotted them at fifty yards and hurried to meet them. "Glad to see you made it," he said, his rumpled suit looking as if he'd slept in it. He shook hands with Bolan, then turned to the woman, taking her hand. "Dr. Arnold, you have my sympathies and sincerest apologies for what happened. You and the country have suffered a great loss."

"You look bushed," Bolan said. "Problems?"

The man looked at him sadly. "You might say that. I haven't slept since I talked with you yesterday."

"Did you get everything straightened out?" the woman asked.

He shook his head. "Something's going on, something big. I've never come up against anything like this before."

Bolan watched Brognola, trying to put a finger on his attitude. He and Hal had been through rough times together. His demeanor seemed one of defeat, his tiredness more emotional than physical.

"What's wrong with you people?" the woman asked loudly. "You drag me around the country, playing hide-and-seek like children. I'm the wife and research assistant of one of your top scientists and I want some answers, not games! Just tell me what the hell is going on, and let me get back to my life. I have a husband to bury."

Bolan and the big Fed shared a look. "His body's missing," Brognola said. "It may never be recovered."

"This is insane!"

"Please, Dr. Arnold," Brognola urged, looking around. "Please keep your voice down."

"Why?" she demanded, gesturing around the cemetery. "All these people are dead."

Bolan moved to put a comforting arm around her shoulders, but she jerked away, staring daggers at him. He turned to Brognola. "Just tell us what you know," he said.

"You're not going to like it," he replied. "The same day that the space shuttle blew in 1986, a man named Jerry Butler was shot dead. He—"

"Jerry...?" the woman interjected, her eyes widening.

"You knew him?" Bolan asked.

"Of course I knew him," she answered. "Theoretical electrical research scientists come few and far between. We hadn't corresponded for a long time, but all of us in the business tend to share information. It's a small field."

"A lot smaller than you realize," Brognola said quietly.

She just stared, all out of quick answers.

He continued. "A newspaperman named McMasters was killed with Butler. The only leads in the case come from neighbors, who said that Air Force personnel were spotted in the vicinity."

"Air Force?" Bolan repeated.

Brognola nodded. "It gets worse. Since then, a total of ten scientists working in the same field have been killed worldwide."

"My God," Arnold said, a hand going to her mouth.

Brognola turned to stare out beyond the graves to the river, which snaked its way through the lowlands far below. "Four in the United States have died," he said. "One in Russia and two others in Soviet satellite countries—East Germany and Poland. One in Japan. One in Canada. One in Great Britain."

"That's everybody," the woman said softly, her face drained of all color. "Dobinski . . . Fujiyaki . . . God, Martha Green. This is incredible."

"You and your husband were the last," Brognola said, turning away from the river. "Now it's just you."

"Why weren't we told?" she asked.

Brognola looked at the ground, unwilling to meet her eyes. "That wasn't my decision," he said. "The conventional wisdom allowed that we could protect you and that you needed your heads clear to work up your projects."

"Why wasn't *I* told?" Bolan asked.

"The Pentagon—" Brognola began.

"The Pentagon trusted me enough to put me in the line of fire, but figured me too big a security risk to know why," Bolan suggested. "Right?"

"Something like that," Brognola admitted. "I told you you wouldn't like it."

"Why?" Julie Arnold asked, finally coming down to the obvious. "Why did this happen?"

"Everything becomes conjecture at this point," Brognola said. "Everyone killed was working on projects dealing with liquid electricity."

"*Liquid* electricity," Bolan repeated. "What exactly is that?"

"The problem with electricity," Arnold said, "is that storage for anything that requires a great deal of it is a near impossibility . . . unless you find a way to carry a substation around with you. Theoretically the electric charge can be reduced to a series of tightly packed, bonded electrons that can be stored in a medium, say water, to be siphoned as needed. In the laboratory, we've managed to put upward to a billion volts in a single drop of water. Unfortunately we've never quite devised a method that holds that charge. It dissipates quickly."

Bolan was fascinated. "Are you saying that if you could find a way for the water to hold the charge, you could, on one drop of water, run an electric car for . . ."

"Forever," she finished. "Your car would wear out long before your drop of water."

"Amazing."

"I have to ask you what happened to your husband's notes."

"Lost," she told the big Fed hesitantly. "Lost with the car."

Brognola exhaled a long breath. "How familiar are you with the research?"

"Very," she claimed, then pointed to her head. "I have a photographic memory. It's all up here."

Both men stared at her. "If this was perfected," Bolan said, "cities could be run on it, rocket engines..."

"Weapons," Brognola said. "Dr. Arnold, with what you carry inside your head, you are one of the most important people in the world right now."

"The ultimate endangered species, you mean," she returned, her voice hard.

"Any idea of who's doing this?" Bolan asked.

Brognola shook his head. "This was never a priority project, Striker," he said. "We funded some research, mostly through colleges. The Russians funded some...hell, most of them were dead before we realized there was a conspiracy going on. Who'd have thought that this..."

He put his hands in the air, letting the sentence drift off. "We still don't know why, but we tightened up our security on the Arnolds. We pulled all our lines in, tried to keep out any leaks. That's why we used you. You were unconnected in any respect. You didn't know, so there was no one you could tell. We figured it was the same with everyone involved in setting up the safehouse. I handled this one myself, and I swear that no one except Pentagon brass, top Company people and my own staff were in on it."

Bolan finally realized the reason for Brognola's mood.

"This is a major, high-level coup we're talking about," the Fed confided. "Someone highly placed is destroying all research into liquid electricity. And we don't even know why. Look. They're working on a whole different track, and judging from their worldwide connections it's a huge operation."

"Could this tie up in any way with the *Challenger* disaster?" Bolan asked.

"I brought a whole data file with me on that subject," he replied. "The results were negative all the way around, but you might want to go through the files yourself."

"Just hold it a minute," the woman said. "Before you people start pointing your fingers, I want to know what the government intends to do to protect *me*."

Brognola looked at her hard. "I'm sorry, but I owe you the truth. You've got three choices at this point: one is to go back to Washington and publicly come to the Justice Department and ask for help; second, you can take off on your own and try to hide; third, you can try an idea I've been setting up on my own."

"The first idea is what got me here to begin with," Julie Arnold said.

Brognola nodded. "And if you take the second, everybody, including the government, will be out looking for you, since you apparently have information worth killing for locked up in your head."

"What's the third idea?" the woman asked.

"Let's go to my car," Brognola suggested, walking away slowly. "In every instance, the researcher was killed and his research destroyed. The knowledge, not the man, was the important thing. You have the means, not only of your destruction but of your salvation, at your fingertips."

"I don't understand," the woman said.

"Transcribe your knowledge. Get it into print where it's public knowledge. Once the information is out there, you lose your importance. There's no reason to kill you."

"You're not speaking for the government," Julie Arnold stated flatly.

They reached a small drive that circled through the outskirts of the huge cemetery. A Jeep Cherokee was parked on the drive, other cars occasionally moving past, wideeyed occupants getting a quick lesson on the value of life.

Brognola climbed into the driver's seat, Bolan taking the passenger side. Dr. Arnold climbed into the back seat.

"I'm speaking for myself," Brognola admitted, turning to face Bolan and the woman. "The government would want you under wraps, giving the information to no one but them. I can't trust anyone right now, and you shouldn't, either."

The woman narrowed her eyes, confusion on her face. "But the government—"

"The government is like any other bureaucracy," Brognola interrupted. "It's the largest employer in the United States, and not all of its employees are going to be good or even honest." He pointed out the window toward the cemetery. "Before you become just another unmarked headstone like your husband or these soldiers, you'd better do some serious thinking. You're just a pawn right now; you need to actively get into the game."

"Why should you help me?" she asked him.

"Two reasons," he said without hesitation. "First off, your husband died because something in my department went wrong. I owe you as a human being. Secondly, I sincerely believe that this information needs to be made public. If everyone has it, it loses its strategic importance."

"The truth shall make you free," Bolan said.

"Perhaps it will make us all free," the Fed replied.

Julie Arnold looked out the window for a moment, her eyes scanning the rolling fields of death. "What's your plan?" she asked at last.

"I spent the night at the computer and by the telephone," Brognola said. "I put something together that might help us all the way around, and the beauty of it is that no one except the three of us knows anything about it. When Jerry Butler was killed, he was working at a government think tank in Florida called the Grolier Foundation. From what I've heard, his research was further developed than everyone else's, yet no records of any kind were found. His death started all this, and it may have resulted from a leak at Grolier.'' He looked at Bolan. ''Striker, I've set you up to take Butler's place at Grolier.''

''I'm no scientist.''

''You don't have to be. I can get you a small project to work on that will pass muster. All you've got to do is playact. Your cover name is David Sparks. And you, Dr. Arnold, will be his wife.''

Julie started. ''Now, wait a minute....''

''Hear me out.'' The ghost of a smile touched Brognola's lips. ''You two pose as husband and wife and move to Florida. While Mack is poking around Grolier, coming at this thing from one end, you can be transcribing your notes and getting protection from one of the best in the business. No one will know but the three of us. And to start you out...''

He reached across the dash, opened the glove compartment and pulled out a large manila envelope that contained the Jeep's registration, identity papers and a large amount of cash.

''The Jeep and money are yours. You have new identities. They won't hold up forever, but maybe they'll help keep you safe until you're either ready to present your findings to the world or Mack uncovers something on his end. So what do you think?''

She looked at the money, then at Bolan, her eyes finally settling on Hal Brognola. ''I think I want to get very, very drunk,'' she said, and as far as Bolan was concerned, he couldn't blame her a bit.

Chapter Four

The small motel bar had been decorated with a Polynesian theme, with huge, grotesque masks on the walls above crossed spears. Dried grass hung from the canopy above the bar, and all the drinks had Polynesian names and came served in coconuts or hollowed-out pineapples. The lights were dimmed, highlighting the dancing, globed candles in the center of each small table. Eddie Rabbitt and Ronnie Milsap blared through the jukebox, though, reminding anyone who was likely to forget exactly where they were.

Bolan wasn't likely to forget.

The motel was cheap, just like its club. Besides Bolan and Arnold, a few Spanish merchant seamen put to port at the Mobile, Alabama, harbor leaned against the bar, while playing quarters to see who would dance with the dime-store hooker in the miniskirt. The bartender never smiled, the cocktail waitress, dressed in a shiny blue evening gown, didn't do anything but. Bolan cared nothing about the details; he'd come in here because of the dim lights.

"You ever been married before?" Julie Arnold asked, her voice slurring as she sucked the straw of her fifth drink.

Bolan frowned, shaking his head.

"Of course you haven't," she said, taking the tiny umbrella garnish out of her pineapple and tossing it onto the table, where it joined a growing stack.

"What do you mean by that?" he asked, watching as the hooker took to the small parquet dance floor with a dark Castilian with a huge black mustache. The man's buddies clapped in time with the country and western song.

"A man like you," she said, shrugging. "A killer. What would you do if dinner was late or your old lady had a fender bender?" She pointed her finger like a gun. "Pow!"

He stared at her. "You don't know anything about me."

"No?" She stared at him over her pineapple, trying hard to focus her eyes. "I was there with you that night, remember? How many men did you kill out there in the woods—six, seven?"

He returned her gaze. "I didn't count."

"Of course you didn't," she replied, and her attitude was beginning to wear on him. "How many have you killed in your life? How many lives have been snuffed out because someone paid you to—"

"Stow it!" he hissed. "You're in no position to pass judgment. I saw plenty that night, too. I saw a young woman riding on the coattails of an old man so some of his talent and fame would rub off on her."

"Stop it!" she said loudly, pulling her hands out of his grasp.

There was some loud talk at the bar, and one of the Spaniards broke away from the group and moved toward the table.

"Great," Bolan muttered, sitting back resignedly.

The man reached them, his buddies urging him on. He swayed slightly and stared down at the woman. "Does this man bother you?" he said in heavily accented English.

"Yes," she replied, glaring at Bolan.

"Maybe you come and join up with us," he said, and put a hand to his chest. "I, Miguel Corona, will protect you."

"Maybe I will," she said, smiling triumphantly.

Corona looked at Bolan, his black eyes flashing. "You will stay out of this, *señor.*"

"I wouldn't think of interfering," Bolan said.

The man grinned, his teeth a picket fence. He wrapped a callused hand around Julie's arm, then turned to his friends. *"¡Esta cobarde!"* he called, all the men laughing.

He tugged at her arm and the woman was pulled to her feet. She laughed at Bolan as she was led to the bar.

He felt himself getting tired, another full day on the road wearing him down. They had left Mississippi right after their meeting with Brognola, dropping him off at Van de Graaff Field in Tuscaloosa.

The whole deal was rotten from top to bottom as far as Bolan was concerned, but he was going along with it because he felt a sense of responsibility toward the woman because he had accepted the mission and her husband had been killed. He watched her at the bar, drinking and joking with the seamen, not realizing she'd have to pay the freight after the place closed. She wouldn't last a week without him.

What motivated Julie Arnold, he couldn't imagine. She was no drinker, that was certain, and no femme fatale; yet there was something just beneath the naive surface that he couldn't quite put his finger on. Whatever it was, it nagged at him and kept him from being completely at ease with her. He was usually a good judge of people, and it bothered him that she messed up his emotional radar enough to keep him off balance. The fact that he disliked her more every minute didn't help matters.

The song on the jukebox ended, and the hooker took her partner by the hand to pick some more. Bolan watched the situation at the bar carefully, though it would serve the woman right if he left her there with the Spaniards.

A slow song came on, a steel guitar crying in its background. The hooker moved back onto the floor, and Julie Arnold was led by her protector to join them.

The waitress showed up with the second drink Bolan had ordered. "Looks like your girlfriend likes to live dangerously," she said, smiling.

"Looks like," he replied, taking the Scotch from her and paying the tab, rather than letting it build. An old habit for someone always on the run.

"I'd keep an eye on it, if you know what I mean," she said.

Bolan nodded. "Thanks."

The woman wiped the table. "What do you want me to do with all these damned little umbrellas?"

"Get rid of them before she gets back," he replied.

The waitress wandered off, and Bolan returned his attention to the dance floor. Julie Arnold and the Spaniard were dancing close, cheek to cheek. The hooker and her friend had already stopped pretending and were standing in the middle of the floor, kissing.

The first thing Bolan and Julie Arnold had done after leaving Vicksburg was to stop and buy new clothes, and Julie was looking great in a double knit dress in greens and browns.

Apparently Miguel Corona thought so, too. He couldn't keep his hands off her. Bolan watched, his gaze narrowing as the man's large hands returned again and again to Julie's buttocks, only to have her pull them forcefully above her hips. With every attempted intimacy, the remaining sailors at the bar laughed louder, and Bolan could see Corona beginning to get angry. It was almost time to stop the game.

"¡Querida!" Corona said loudly, grabbing Julie roughly and pulling her tightly against him.

"I said, no!" Her eyes darted frantically to Bolan, her mouth forming a silent call for help.

Bolan sighed and took a sip of his Scotch. He moved out onto the dance floor, reaching into his pocket for a little help.

Corona had Julie doubled over, his mouth clamped on her neck.

"Do something," she said through clenched teeth.

"Want me to shoot him?" he asked dryly.

"Bolan!"

He placed a hand on the man's shoulder. "That's enough, pal," he said.

The man ignored him, and began running his free hand over Julie's body. Bolan reached out and grabbed him, pulling hard.

Corona let go of Julie, and she fell to the floor. His face was twisted with alcohol-induced rage, and without a word, he cocked a big fist and tried to take out Bolan with one punch.

The warrior was ready, sidestepping easily and catching the fist in the palm of his hand. The sailor's expression became puzzled when he felt the paper Bolan held.

Corona pulled back, gazing at the hundred-dollar bill jammed between his fingers. His eyebrows shot up, and he looked at Bolan in perplexity.

"That's for you." Bolan ignored the hand that Julie Arnold was waving around as she looked for help up. "Go have your fun somewhere else."

The man's friends had formed a semicircle around him, ready to offer assistance.

"Let's call it a night," Bolan suggested.

"Sabas mucho dinero," Corona said, his face settling into a menacing scowl. "Maybe you could share some more with my friends and me."

Instead of answering, Bolan unbuttoned the sport jacket he was wearing and eased it open, giving them a glimpse of the combat harness and the holstered automatic pistol.

The men backed away, their faces going slack, then the hooker said, "Looks like you boys got some extra cash. Let's party!"

The atmosphere turned jovial again, the Spaniards celebrating their windfall as Bolan reached out to help Julie Arnold, who was on all fours, drunkenly trying to get to her feet.

"Go to hell," she said, batting his hand away. She wobbled to her feet and tried to straighten her disarrayed hair with her hands. "I need another drink."

"Not tonight, Mrs. Sparks," Bolan replied. "I think we've had enough excitement for one trip."

They reached the table. Bolan picked up the woman's purse and hooked it on her arm.

"I said I wanted a drink!" she demanded loudly, the sailors laughing in response.

Bolan picked up his glass and drank what remained of his Scotch. "I'm going to the room. You stay down here with your friends. I'm sure they'll be able to entertain you for the rest of the night."

She thrust out her lower lip and stared at the crowd at the bar. "I was getting kind of tired anyway," she mumbled. "Come on, Dr. Sparks. Let's go to bed."

They walked out the exit and into the Alabama night, heavy with humid air pushed up from the Gulf. Julie sagged against him as he walked them toward their room.

"I just went from one husband to the next," she said into his jacket, her voice tired. "That's me, little Julie Jacobs Arnold. Just cart a dead one out and bring on the next one."

"Easy," he said, his arm casually around her.

"Easy's easy for you to say," she replied, words slurred, as he led her up the flight of wooden stairs that led to the second-floor rooms. "I feel like the last of the Mohegans."

When they reached the door, Bolan leaned her up against the frame while he fished the key out of his pocket.

"My whole world is gone," she said. "Everybody I've known and worked with over the past ten years...gone."

Bolan got the door open, and Julie all but fell into the room, landing heavily on the nearest of the double beds. He entered the room, locking and chaining the door behind him.

"You should sleep now," he said, taking off his sport jacket and draping it on the back of a chair.

She sat up, staring hard at him. "I don't want to sleep—ever," she said. "I want to be dead...like Harry and Martha and..." Her voice caught in her throat, lips trembling as the words stammered out. "At a conference in

Denver once I—I had a...what do you call it...fling...with Jerry Butler. The only time I'd ever...ever..."

She began to cry in earnest. Bolan went to sit beside her on the bed. "It's natural for a survivor to feel guilt," he said. "It's natural, but not justified."

She moved to him, sobbing, their arms went around each other, but her hand touched the Beretta holster and she drew back quickly, in aversion.

"Don't psychoanalyze me." She turned away from him, sniffling. "If I want advice, I'll go to a shrink, not a hired gun."

"Suit yourself." Bolan stood and shrugged out of his harness. "Just trying to help."

He walked into the bathroom, pulling his sweater over his head and off. He turned on the hot water in the sink and splashed his face.

Julie leaned against the doorframe. "*Who* are you trying to help?" she asked harshly.

Bolan pulled a white, threadbare towel off the rack and began to dry his face. "What do you mean by that?" He brushed past her and into the room. She swiveled with his movements, one hand held stiffly behind her.

She was behind him, talking to his back. "I mean, how do I know whose side you're on?" she asked loudly. "You think that I haven't noticed that people only care about Harry's notes? Maybe you're here to—"

"What do you mean, people?" he asked, turning to face her.

She had one of his guns, the Beretta, in her hand and was pointing it at him. "Bang, bang," she said. "You're dead."

Anger washed over him as he walked up quickly to snatch the gun from her, his right hand instinctively balled into a fist. "Don't you ever do that again," he said through clenched teeth.

"You gonna kill me, killer?" she taunted. "Why has the Justice Department left a killer to guard me? Why do we have to live together while I do the transcriptions? I think maybe my knowledge is the only thing keeping me alive right now."

He tossed the gun on the bed, then reached out and took her by the shoulder. "Why did you say 'people' only care about the notes? Who did you tell besides Hal?"

"You're hurting me!" she said, trying to break from his grasp.

"Tell me!" he demanded.

"Nobody!" she shot back. "It was just a figure of speech."

"Who did you call yesterday?"

Her face went slack. "Wh-what?"

"When I checked out of the Holiday Inn they made me pay fifty cents for a phone call. Who was it?"

"Time," she said, lips sputtering. "I called time."

He let her go, and the woman fell, sobbing, onto her bed. Bolan stood over her helplessly, his mind torn between anger and compassion.

"Look," he said softly, "I'm sorry. I'm not sure what I..."

She suddenly jerked up from the bed, glaring at him, red-eyed, her wet cheeks streaked with mascara. "Has it ever occurred to you that your friend in Justice might have set us *both* up as bait on this thing?"

"No," Bolan replied. "The man's—"

"No?" she repeated. "Well, it sure looks like he'd already done a pretty good job the night Harry got shot. Maybe Hal is using us as tethered lambs to draw out the man-eaters. Or maybe he just wants to control our actions so he can take care of us quietly."

"The guy's sticking his neck out a mile for you on this," Bolan replied. "You're a fool to suspect him."

"And you're a fool not to," she said, then bent down to take off her shoes.

"I want to make sure the car's locked up," he said, slipping the sweater over his head.

Julie Arnold had her back to him and was undoing the belt that cinched her waist. Her back muscles moved fluidly beneath the form-fitting dress, and Bolan had a sudden stab of longing for circumstances beyond the ones they were trapped in. Without a word, he picked up the room key from the desk and walked out the door.

The hot air was rife with fishy harbor smells and sweaty music as he walked along the veranda and down the stairs to the parking lot. Julie's warning about Brognola had really gotten to him, not so much because she had raised the question, but because he had already thought of it himself. He had been set up once, why not again? But could he trust the woman, either? Her story about calling time made absolutely no sense—both of them had watches. But why would she lie?

Bolan walked through the parking lot and around the side of the building where he'd left the Jeep. He had taken several long strides toward it before he saw the other car. It was parked on the drive with its headlights on, no more than five feet from the Jeep. A back door was open, a man halfway out.

He tried to stop and slide back into the shadows, but it was too late. The driver of the car had spotted him.

The car door slammed shut, the vehicle roaring off immediately. Bolan ran toward it, trying for a license tag, but the car had already screeched around the corner of the building.

Bolan watched after the car for several minutes, but it was gone. Probably kids looking for something to rip off. Bolan walked over to the Jeep, giving it a quick but thorough going-over for signs of forced entry before locking it and walking back to his room.

When he went back up the stairs the room was in darkness. As quietly as possible, he made his way to his bed. He could hear the woman's even breathing from the other bed. He stripped down and slid between the cool sheets. He thought about keeping watch, but no one, not even Brognola, was supposed to know where he was. The incident in the parking lot notwithstanding, he felt they were probably safe for the moment.

He closed his eyes, welcoming the rest.

In the other bed, Julie Arnold feigned sleep and listened patiently for the sounds of Bolan settling in for the night. She lay wide awake, her emotions strung up like an overwound mainspring, bottled up inside, unable to find any release. She was scared, mad and despondent, and the son of a bitch lying beside her only made matters worse. If only they had told her what to expect. If only she hadn't followed orders by marrying Harry...

Chapter Five

From the outside, through the binoculars, the Grolier Foundation looked just like any other place of business, albeit one that was a bit heavy on security. It was a five-story structure, plain and unornamented, the windows done in reflective glass in keeping with current trends in minimalist architecture. A tall, chain link fence topped with rolled barbed wire surrounded the entire place a good fifty floodlit yards from the building. As the parking was underground, this fifty-yard, asphalt no-man's-land was the domain of the security people and their dogs, who seemed to prowl twenty-four hours a day.

"I feel conspicuous standing out here," Julie said from beside Bolan.

"We're not breaking any laws that I know about," Bolan returned, swinging the binoculars to take in the large billboard beside the main gate. It was just readable in the deepening twilight.

"There," he said, handing the binoculars to her. "Look at that sign by the front gate and put that photographic memory to use."

Puzzled, she took the field glasses from him and put them to her eyes, moving them in a wide circle, looking for the building.

They were sitting atop an overpass on Interstate 4, in Orlando, Florida, looking to the east and Orlando Avenue as the late rush-hour traffic sped beneath them.

"I don't see..." Julie was saying. "Oh, there it is. What do you want from me? The damned sign is only a listing of parent companies and subsidiaries of subsidiaries."

"Fix it in your head," he told her, as a car moved rapidly past them. "The government subsidizes this place, but I know that most think-tank funding comes from major corporations or individuals who might have a commercial use for the ideas generated there."

"Kind of like mine and Harry's work with the university," she said.

"Right. There are very few pies in this country that have only one set of fingers in them."

She handed him back the binoculars. "For what it's worth, I've got it."

He nodded, glancing around again. "Okay. Let's get out of here."

They drove off the overpass, heading west on Aloma Avenue. The small house that Brognola had provided was barely a ten-minute drive from there. It was so convenient to work that he couldn't help but wonder if Jerry Butler had lived there.

He glanced at his companion. She was busily absorbed in the reports Brognola had given them concerning the deaths of the other scientists. She had done little else but read them since they had left Alabama that morning. It was as if the killings, so lacking in reason and meaning, needed some kind of resolution in her mind before she could learn to live with them. She was hanging on emotionally by her fingernails, and it bothered him that he had done very little to understand that.

"Since we've decided to take this thing on," he said, "maybe we should try to put aside our differences for a while. Life's going to be tough enough as it is."

She looked up, her eyes barely touching him before fleeing to the relative safety of the view out the front windshield. "We're like oil and water, Bolan, but for once I agree with you. I still don't trust you, but I did accept this whole deal and the responsibilities that go along with it. If we can't be friends, we can at least be civil."

"Right. I'm getting hungry. Want to stop and get groceries before we go home?"

"I'll just do that later," she said, a little too quickly. "I suppose you'll want me to cook for you."

"Your choice," he answered, turning down Avondale Drive and entering the lower-middle class neighborhood that would be their home. "I've been making my own dinner for a long time now. If you want to keep it separate, that's fine with me."

"Separate but equal. We'll divide everything up like roommates."

"Fine."

Avondale was narrow but palm lined. It seemed to be the refuge of older people retired on small, fixed incomes and young families just starting out. The cottages were packed in tightly, twenty feet back from the road. They were either weathered frame or stucco and were invariably painted aqua or pale yellow. The Sparkses' was pale yellow stucco.

As they pulled into the driveway, a youngster from next door rode past on a ten-speed bike much too large for him. He waved happily, nearly falling off. Julie smiled as the Jeep was backed into the carport.

"Have you read any of the reports Mr. Brognola left with us?" Julie asked as they climbed out of the Jeep.

"Haven't had much of a chance," he returned. "I've been driving, remember?"

"The reports relating to Jerry's death are very strange."

"In what way?"

They walked to the door off the carport, and Bolan unlocked it, letting them into the kitchen.

"It seems that several days before the shooting," she related, following him through the sparsely furnished house, "Jerry called a newspaper, the *Titusville Banner*, and told them that he had proof that contraband was being sent up on the space shuttle flights."

"Titusville has grown from a nowhere burg to a major city because of its proximity to the Cape. I'll bet that went over well." Bolan had moved into the small living room. When he sat on the edge of a foam rubber daybed, a cloud of dust rose. "What sort of contraband?"

Julie shook her head and took a chair across from him, the documentation on her lap. She frowned at the room's obviously inexpensive furnishings. "If my friends at Brandeis could see me now," she said quietly, then shrugged, her eyes fixing Bolan with deep blue. "It never came out. The *Banner* was totally unwilling to even talk to him about it. As you said, too much of the city's economy depended on NASA and the Cape to stir up any trouble."

When she had a calm and placid look on her face, as she did now, Bolan found Julie Arnold to be one of the most beautiful women he had ever seen. Their eyes locked for just a second, then he looked away. "Wasn't there a reporter killed with him?" he asked.

"I was getting to that," she said absently, shuffling through the stack of papers until she came up with the one she had been searching for. "The day after he called the Titusville paper, he called the *Miami Herald* and set up a meeting with a Mr.... McMasters, telling him the same thing he'd told the *Banner*."

"Namely that contraband was being flown by the shuttles, but not offering any proof," Bolan put in.

"Basically," she replied, and turned to the next page. "He told McMasters that he would offer proof upon their meeting. The man was intrigued, but not convinced, especially since Jerry sounded distraught on the phone. McMasters got in touch with NASA on the spot, and they put him in touch with a General—" she consulted the paper "—Cronin, who was and is in charge of passenger and matériel manifests on the shuttle flights. The general said he'd never heard of anyone named Butler, but that matériel manifests had been declassified and were available to anyone who wanted to look at them. Further, he stated that equipment going on the shuttle was examined by any number of inspectors before being uploaded. He then offered to send McMasters a copy of the manifest on the spot."

"And?"

She shrugged, her face a blank. "And nothing. Mc-Masters kept the appointment with Jerry, but confided to another reporter that it looked like he was just another crackpot. Jerry had moved to a bungalow in Titusville. The morning of the *Challenger* flight, both he and Mc-Masters were killed and Jerry's house ransacked."

Bolan pushed back on the bed and leaned against the wall. "I remember Hal telling us that angle had been checked."

"The manifest was checked back to each company that had paid for space on the shuttle," she said, running a finger along the arm of her chair and then staring in distaste at the dirt her finger had picked up. "Now payloads are all military, but remember, at that time, commercial ventures from the private sector were being encouraged to pay for shuttle space. Everything checked out clean... except this damned house. How do they expect us to live here?"

"They probably think we'll clean it," he replied.

"My mama didn't raise me to be a maid," Julie retorted.

"What did she raise you to be?" he asked.

"You may have figured out that I'm not much of a trouper."

"You haven't done so badly," he replied, and meant it.

"What's this?" she asked, eyebrows raised. "A compliment from the original hard case?"

"Is that how you see me?"

She brought a finger to her lips, but pulled it back when she remembered how dirty things were. "I guess you're just doing your job."

"What kind of a man was Butler?"

"Brilliant, kind, gentle." She pulled her feet up into the chair, wrapping her arms around her legs. Her eyes were moist. "He couldn't have hurt a fly. He was guilelessly outspoken, especially on the topic of the military."

"What do you mean?"

"He hated and feared the military," she replied. "You have to understand that Jerry was the ultimate pacifist. Once, years before, he had apparently worked on a government grant developing electrical conductors that eventually found their way into DOD and the ballistic missile program. He felt dirty for having worked on weapons of destruction and eventually paid the government back every cent they'd put into the project. From then on he scrupulously checked out every government project he worked on, making absolutely sure his work would be used to help mankind, not destroy it."

"He sounds like a man of high principles."

"I'm surprised to hear you say that," she replied.

They stared at each other, the silence deafening.

The doorbell rang, loudly, startling them both.

"Who could that be?" she asked, her voice strung tight.

He shook his head, getting quietly to his feet. "Move into the back of the house." He pulled the Beretta from its holster, checking the load before moving to the door.

"Bolan . . . ?"

"Do it," he whispered harshly, glad they hadn't turned on the lights yet.

As Julie disappeared into the hallway, he moved toward the front door, stealing a glance through the blinds on the picture window. An air express truck was parked in the driveway.

He held the Beretta behind the door and opened it a crack to see a man dressed in what looked like a pilot's uniform standing on the porch with a clipboard in his hands. A large package was at his feet.

"Yeah?" Bolan said through the crack.

"Mr. Sparks?" the man asked.

"That's me."

The man smiled automatically. "I've got a package for you." He held out the clipboard. "Just sign on line fourteen."

Bolan reached through the space with his free hand and signed the form.

"Thank you, sir," the man said and left, the box resting forlornly on the porch.

The man had backed out and was driving down the street before Bolan opened the door wide enough to drag the package inside. The postmark was Washington, but the return name and address were unfamiliar. He figured it to be Brognola using an assumed name.

"Bolan!" came a voice from the back of the house. "Mack?"

"Come on in!" he called, and reached down to tear open the package.

She hurried back into the room. "What is it?" she asked as he ripped through the tape that held the box closed.

"I think it's from Hal," he replied, pulling hard on the cardboard. "Something to get me started on a project at Grolier."

The box came open, spilling an avalanche of Styrofoam packing noodles. Beyond those, he found a number of notebooks and chemistry handbooks. There were several tightly sealed metallic containers that had the single word, DANGER, printed on the outside. These Bolan left alone until he knew what he was dealing with. He took out a fistful of the notebooks and sat on the floor.

"The thing that gets me about your friend Butler, is that I just can't see how he could possibly connect up with the space shuttle. If he was an independent researcher working at Grolier, it would seem his work would be theoretical. We'll check past manifests, but I've never heard talk of any work done in the field of liquid electricity being done aboard the shuttle. But that's not something I'd keep up on if it was happening."

"Well, I *do* keep up with those things." Julie returned to her chair. She reached out and flicked on a lamp on a rickety wooden end table. "Believe me, there's never been any connection between what Jerry and I do...did, and the shuttle. It's totally incongruous."

"Incongruous, but the chain of evidence is difficult to ignore or put off to chance. Look at the connections.

We've got a researcher in the employ of the same government that launches the shuttle, who calls the press to ostensibly blow the whistle on wrongdoing in connection with the shuttle. On the same day, he's dead, the reporter he wanted to talk to is dead, and the shuttle blows up seventy-three seconds into a perfect flight. That's too many coincidences for me.''

"But it was all checked out and cleared," she said, holding up the papers.

"Cleared by the same government he was going to blow the whistle on," Bolan replied. "It was the government Butler feared, or he would have gone to them or the police over this thing."

A look of perplexity settled on her face and she dropped the stack of papers to the floor. "I just don't know what to think."

He thumbed through the handwritten notebooks full of chemical symbols and laboratory animal test results. "I'm not sure what to think, either," Bolan said, "but I know where to start. Disregarding the theory that Butler simply went off the deep end, that the deaths are simply coincidental robberies or whatever, it seems to me that he somehow made the jump from the theoretical to the applicable, a turn that could be accomplished right at the Grolier Foundation."

"Think there may be answers there?" she asked, standing up to stretch.

"It's a place to start."

Julie walked over to stand above him. "How about the car keys? I'm going to run to the grocery."

He reached into his pocket and fished out the keys.

She appeared to be edgy. Bolan had discovered that she wore her emotions on her sleeve and was relatively easy to read. He simply didn't know how to interpret what he saw. This time he was suspicious of her.

"Goodbye... David," she said, moving to the door.

"Bye, Bernice," he answered, and she was gone.

He got up and watched her through the blind. As soon as he saw the Jeep pull out of the drive and move down Avondale, he hurried out the front door.

She was already a block away, at the stop sign at the end of the street. He looked around quickly, spotting the neighbor boy's ten-speed leaning on its kickstand in the driveway next door.

He ran to it, hoping he could get out and back before the boy missed it. Climbing on, he put up the stand and followed the Jeep, which had already turned onto Aloma.

Darkness had come down hard, turning the hot Florida day into hot Florida night. The traffic was thick on Aloma, and the ten-speed had no light, making the going treacherous. Luckily an A&P was barely two blocks distant, and he saw Julie pull into the parking lot.

He rode quickly on the narrow shoulder and made the parking lot a minute behind her. The bike geared down easily, and he coasted through the lot, staying close to the edge in the shadows.

He felt bad following her, but her attitude had been all wrong. If something was up, he had to know.

He didn't have to wait long.

A bank of telephones stood just outside the entrance. Julie was in one of the booths, talking animatedly on the phone.

Bolan pulled up fifty feet from her and sat on the bike, watching, sadness and concern vying with the anger he felt building within him. They had a working phone at the house; there was no logical reason for her to be using this one.

His first impulse was to go over and rip the phone right out of her hand. But instead, he turned the bike around and headed for home.

He was going to have to keep a closer eye on her. Something about Julie Arnold was desperately out of sync. In Bolan's line of work, such desperation could lead very quickly to problems of a terminal nature.

Chapter Six

Mark Reilly stopped to check his appearance in the mirrored top of the vending machine in the corridor before moving through the swinging doors of the half-full White House press room. He wasn't disappointed in the boyish face that smiled back at him. With clear green eyes, a face puffed nowhere by even an ounce of fat and blond hair trimmed to military precision, he was the youngest-looking forty-year-old in Washington. With his strict regimen of exercise and diet control, he intended to stay that way.

He winked at his reflection and hurried into the room, buttoning a single button of his dark blue suit while walking up the small aisle between the rows of TV cameras and seated journalists. The President was already speaking, so very few people turned to watch Reilly's progress toward the VIP section roped off at the front of the hall.

The President stood leaning against the podium, Colonel Kit Givan, in dress blues, standing at parade rest beside him. "You know," the President was saying, "in this day and age, all we hear is militarism this and militarism that, and it makes us forget that the American military is here to protect all of our citizens all the time. That's why it gives me particular pleasure today to honor our military through one of its great examples—an example not of heroism in battle, but of the highest heroism in peacetime...."

Reilly reached the front of the room and ducked beneath the range of the cameras to reach General Leland's section, the general smiling and moving one of his aides so that Reilly could sit beside him.

On the podium, the President had moved to stand beside Givan, putting his arm around the man's shoulders. "For those of you who haven't heard, Colonel Maurice 'Kit' Givan was moving a convoy through Bienville National Forest in Mississippi a few nights ago. He and a small company of men came upon a fire raging out of control that threatened not only the forest itself, a national treasure, but also the lives of everyone who lived nearby. Colonel Givan then made a valiant decision, as valiant as any made in battle. Knowing he was undermanned and unequipped, he nevertheless sent a representative to get help, while doing what he could to stem the threat.

"At great personal risk, he and his men worked on a firebreak while awaiting assistance. Several men were killed in the line of duty, all of them heroes, all of them honored losses of the republic."

"Hello, Mark," General Leland whispered as Reilly sat down. He smiled in his fatherly way and shook hands.

Reilly found a smile coming easily to his own lips. "Good morning, sir. Colonel Givan looks great up there."

"Yes, he does," the general agreed, nodding, his dress uniform heavy with the outward manifestations of heroism and devotion to duty. "Like a cat landing on its feet, Colonel Givan is snatching victory from the jaws of defeat."

"Yes, sir," Reilly replied, waiting, as usual, for the general to carry the conversation in the proper directions.

The President was holding up a small stack of papers. "I have in my hand reports from emergency personnel who arrived on the scene later, all of them in praise of the job Kit Givan did in saving this historic forest. The colonel's firebreak saved literally hundreds of lives and hundreds of thousands of acres of preserved forest."

"Were you briefed on the Arnold situation?" General Leland asked.

"Yes, sir," Reilly said. "I think things are going smoothly in that direction. We had a phone meeting with the woman last night. She and her Justice Department contact are cohabiting in Orlando, Florida.''

The general raised an eyebrow. "Why is that?"

"They want her transcripts," Reilly said, as always amazed at the alertness and intelligence flowing through the general's eyes. "They want her to write down all she knows about Arnold's research."

"Was he near anything?"

Reilly shook his head. "Not anything close to the breakthroughs that Butler had made."

Leland looked at his watch, then back at Reilly. "Why Orlando? Isn't Grolier located there?"

"That's the other part," Reilly said. "Her contact has been set up at the institute to see if he can trace Butler's movements through there."

A spark of humor crackled from Leland's eyes. "Enterprising. It will be interesting to see how far he gets."

"One problem." Reilly straightened the crease in his trousers. "The woman is asking for backup assistance and more information than we're able to give her."

"How long has she been on the payroll?"

"Nearly ten years."

The general turned his attention from Reilly and watched the stage, tapping an index finger on his chin the entire time. Then he looked back at Reilly, pointing the finger. "Give her a raise," he said, "and try to maintain regular contact. Fill her in on *anything* but what's important, just to give her the illusion that we're answering her questions. Tell her that her contact is under suspicion." He leaned closer, his words a rasp in Reilly's ear. "Whatever you do, don't let her get far from contact. Don't lose her. She's the key here. Women are undependable at best. Don't give her the chance to blindside us. We're too close to success to get bogged down with these people. Whatever happens, don't risk the success of the mission under any circumstances."

"Yes, sir."

"And what about that clown from Justice...what's his name...Brognola?"

"He won't be a problem," Reilly responded confidently. "You can depend on me."

Leland nodded solemnly. "I know I can, boy. You're a credit to your country and to the Company."

"Thank you, General."

Leland shook his hand again. "It's me, thanking you, boy. Keep up the good work."

"This project means more to me than my life, sir."

"Good," Leland said, nodding. "Good."

"And so," the President concluded, smiling wide, "it is with the greatest pleasure that I honor the military services of this country by honoring one of its bravest and most loyal servants. Colonel Givan, step up to the podium and receive your presidential citation."

Applause swelled through the room as flash units exploded like a flock of electronic fireflies. Kit Givan grinned sheepishly, holding his plaque up for the cameras.

The President moved up closer to the bank of microphones set on the podium. "And that's not all. We have with us today one of the most distinguished and highly decorated airmen ever to wear the uniform to make a special presentation. He also happens to be Kit Givan's commanding officer—General Mordechai Leland."

The general leaned toward Reilly, patting his leg. "Take care of it," he said, then stood, waving to the appreciative crowd.

Mark Reilly watched as Leland walked proudly onto the stage, a stage most often filled by bickering civilians who knew nothing of this great country and its needs, a stage glowing brightly under the glare of the rack of medals that filled Leland's chest. To Reilly the man was a giant in a land of gnomes, a prophet in a wasteland of useless words. He was a man of action and commitment in a world that worshiped entropy.

General Leland walked to the microphones, even the President stepping aside. "I suppose you're all wondering why I called you here today," he said smiling, the reporters and visitors laughing in response, some of them applauding. "But seriously, it's not often that we get to honor our servicemen, the uniformed military that every day of our lives protect us from aggression both here and abroad. The fact that I am so honoring one of my own command causes a deeply felt pang of emotion in my heart.

"These are the dark days of the republic as our own political and economic systems are being tested by hard times and desperate people worldwide. The fact that we have gathered to honor the men who protect our liberty, then, is a sign both hopeful and profound to my way of thinking. It is a sign that we haven't lost the faith of our founding fathers in democracy and the basic values of civilization. And so it is with a great deal of pleasure that I not only give my congratulations to Kit Givan on his presidential citation, but I also inform him that effective this day, he is being promoted to the rank of Lieutenant Colonel, United States Air Force!"

"Whoooo!" Givan yelled loudly, and moved to the general to enthusiastically shake his hand.

Applause was loud in the room, Reilly pounding his own hands together, tears forming in his eyes.

As more flashbulbs popped, the President, Leland and Givan joined hands, raising them high in the air in victory.

HAL BROGNOLA TYPED Givan's name into the computer and waited patiently as it linked with the Pentagon computer and requested his authorization code. When the cursor began flashing on the screen, however, he realized that he didn't remember the code.

Feeling foolish, he stood quickly and moved to the door of his small office so he could get the code from Marie, his secretary.

He opened the door and looked out into the large open work area. It was completely empty. Brognola looked at his watch. It was 12:00, and everyone in the department had gone to lunch.

Marie's desk was just a few feet from his door. As he ambled toward it, he removed the ring of keys from his pocket and took off the small desk key. He opened the middle drawer and withdrew the black code book.

He found the code quickly and moved back into the office, shutting the door behind him. He entered the code and watched as the records came up on the screen.

What he saw was only surprising in the immensity of its utter incongruity. As he scrolled slowly through Givan's record, he found the portrait of a tirelessly dedicated man: high-school honor student and athlete; graduated first in his class at the Air Force Academy; Rhodes scholar; combat experience in Nam flying more than one hundred missions out of Korat, Thailand, in F-4 fighters as B-52 support. He had turned down promotions that would have left him desk bound. His list of citations included both the Silver and Bronze stars, plus two Purple Hearts. The record even included an incredible story of his escape and ultimate rescue from North Vietnamese captors when he had been shot down over Hanoi in 1970. The man had done everything but emerge in full uniform and wrapped in an American flag from his mother's womb when he was born.

Brognola leaned his chair back and covered his face with his hands. This was the same man Bolan had accused of shooting down a famous research scientist in cold blood and attempting to kill others.

He sighed and sat up straight in the chair, staring once more at the screen. If it was Bolan's word against Givan's, there was no doubt as to who the Pentagon would believe. Without any proof, accusations would just be so much hot air. There could possibly be a distant chance of digging up the bodies of the airmen supposedly burned to death fighting the fire to see if 9 mm parabellums could be recovered from them. But they were being buried with full honors in Arlington National Cemetery, and it would take overwhelming evidence to convince the government to ruin such a publicity coup with a nasty exhumation. Brognola would need much more to go on than Bolan's word to accomplish anything.

He moved back to the machine and scrolled down to the record of Givan's last assignment. There had to be a reason for the man to have been in that forest at that time of night.

Sounds of movement could be heard from the big room outside—people returning from lunch.

He read the glowing letters on the screen. In 1980, Givan had requested, and received, a transfer to Pentagon security and was put in charge of training security forces at the Pentagon, the White House and both houses of Congress. Three years after that, General Mordechai Leland had the man placed on his personal staff, involved in a project called GOG that was classified in the file under the heading of National Security.

"Damn!" he muttered, and heard more movement outside. He looked toward the door and noticed a moving shadow through the crack at the bottom.

"Marie!" he called. "Could you bring me that book of passwords? I need the list of security authorizations."

He sat there for several seconds, then tried one of the codes he could remember to get into the GOG file. The words ACCESS DENIED flashed angrily on the screen.

"Marie!" he called again to no response.

He pushed back from the desk and moved to the door, throwing it open. Marie's desk was empty. She wasn't back from lunch. He looked up quickly and saw a door on the far side of the room just closing.

"Wait!" he shouted, hurrying through the maze of desks and computer terminals to get to the door. He jerked it open and stuck his head out, but the halls were full of people. There was no way he could determine who had been in there.

It seemed harmless enough, yet his senses were tingling, telling him something was terribly wrong. If he had learned one thing, it was to always trust your instincts.

As he made his way back to his office Brognola's attention was drawn by the glowing characters of the only operating computer in the large room—and was startled to see a duplication of the denial of access to the GOG program that was flashing on the terminal in his office. Someone had been eavesdropping on his computer conversation.

With a flick of the finger, he shut down the machine in front of him, then walked deliberately to his office. This time he locked the door.

The big Fed sat behind his desk, pulled open the bottom drawer and took out the chamois-covered item within. He unwrapped the long-barreled .38 and snapped open the cylinder to check the load.

Satisfied, Brognola shut the cylinder and stood, unbuttoning his suit coat. Mind adjusting into combat mode, he stuck the gun in the waistband of his pants, then rebuttoned the coat. He picked up the telephone and called home, his wife answering on the third ring.

"Helen," he said. "Don't argue, just do as I say. Phone the kids and tell them we'll be out of town for a while. Then pack a bag and go visit your mother for a couple of weeks."

"Hal, I—"

"No argument. Just do it quickly. I'll call you tonight and explain."

With that, he hung up, his hand shaking slightly on the receiver.

Chapter Seven

Floyd Bacon spoke slowly, as if weighing the meaning of each word he said before saying it, and his rather glazed brown eyes had never once found Bolan's in the ten minutes they had been together in his overappointed, spotless office.

"As director of the Grolier Institute, Dr. Sparks," he said, "I want you to know that I am here in case you need any help in preparing your work for publication or presentation."

"I appreciate—" Bolan began, but Bacon simply kept on talking.

"But beyond that, your area of endeavor is your own. I know nothing about the fields of research engaged herein, nor do I care a great deal beyond the natural publicity that ensures the survival of an institution such as ours. I have even less interest in the constant bickering, overactive egos and childish behavior of the *respected* scientists who toil here. Do I make myself clear?"

"Quite clear," Bolan replied.

Floyd Bacon was old. He was bone lean, like a praying mantis, his spindly wrists practically lost in the cuffs of his shirt and jacket. His skin was smooth and pampered-looking, his blue-veined hand soft and its clasp weak.

The old man fell silent for a long moment, then spoke again. "I see that your field is poison gases." He coughed deeply, a handkerchief coming up to his mouth. "This is no doubt militarily applicable and will enrage some of the more dovish members of our fifth-floor staff."

"I'm sure I can—"

"No matter how bad it gets, Dr. Sparks, you are on your own. It is not my job to act as referee. I administer this facility—period. So, don't come to me with your social problems. Your paycheck comes from the government. Go through the governmental grievance procedure if someone insults your parentage, your intelligence, your religion or your ethnic origin. I'm not your confessor, and I'm not a complaints department."

"I can take care of myself," Bolan said.

For the first time, Bacon looked up and met his gaze. He held it, inexplicably, for nearly half a minute before once again returning to the papers on his desktop.

"I would take you up to Five and introduce you around," Bacon said, "but I haven't been up there in two years and I don't see any reason to start now. Look for Robbie Hampton. He'll get you straightened away. Did you fill out a W-4?"

"Yes," Bolan answered.

The man nodded slowly, then gestured to the door. "Welcome aboard. I hope you don't have any strong antisocial tendencies."

"Thank you," Bolan said, standing.

Bacon ignored him then, as if he had left already. The old hands reached out, took a stack of papers from his In basket and put them in the Out. Then he sat back and sighed deeply, closing his eyes.

Bolan left quietly, briefcase full of chemical information dangling from his right hand, his photo ID badge attached to the lapel of his sport jacket. He passed Bacon's secretary—who also ignored his presence—and moved out into the hall, nearly bumping into a five-foot-tall mechanical man wearing a Groucho Marx nose with attached glasses and mustache.

The robot bent and studied his badge. "You're new here, aren't you?"

"That's right," Bolan said.

"Well, this is a gala day...and a gala day should be enough for any man."

"Could you direct me to the elevator?" Bolan asked.

"Sure . . . walk this way," the robot said, ambling along the fake marble halls with an exaggerated swivel in the hip area.

"My name is Arthur," the machine said.

"Sparks," Bolan answered. "Are you self-directed?"

"Alas, no. I am being driven by remote control from Dr. Smyth's laboratory on Floor 2. Dr. Smyth also most ably provides my melodious voice. Here's the elevator."

Bolan walked up to the sliding doors and pushed the "up" arrow. He searched Arthur's face and saw that his "eyes" were actually miniature TV cameras.

The elevator opened, both Arthur and Bolan stepping inside. "Would you push 2 for me?" the robot asked.

"Sure." Bolan pushed both 2 and 5, and the doors closed. "What exactly are you being developed for?"

"We are studying the feasibility of the computer-operated, self-generated engine that can recognize, by analog, different terrains so that it can move itself to destinations by discerning roadways and signs and sticking to them."

"Quite a program," Bolan said as the elevator jerked to a stop. "Good luck."

The robot lifted an arm in parting and left the elevator, happily singing the refrain from "Lydia, the Tattooed Lady."

The doors closed again, and Bolan resumed his journey to the fifth floor, wondering how the brutal murders of Jerry Butler and Dr. Arnold could have anything to do with this nuthouse. He found that he was nervous, too. The warrior who could walk alone and confident into any situation was entering an arena where his well-honed battle skills would be of little use to him. And yet, this arena could be as dangerous as any he had fought in. Were Jerry Butler alive, he could testify to that fact. He would have to be extremely careful. The wars here would be fought with words, but backed up with something far deadlier.

When the doors slid open on the fifth floor, Bolan was confronted with a large waiting room furnished expensively. At its far end, a uniformed security guard sat reading a comic book in a closed-in booth with a barred cutout. Hallways branched out on two sides from the waiting room. A noise echoed through the whole floor, a high-pitched screeching that sounded frightened, faraway and nearly human.

He walked to the guard station, the man still intent on his reading, his lips moving silently as he took it all in.

"Excuse me," Bolan said, the security man starting and nearly falling out of his tilted-back chair. "My name's Sparks," Bolan said. "I'm supposed to start working here today."

"Oh...oh yeah!" The guard picked up a clipboard. His eyes scanned slowly, lips silently moving as he read. "Here you are, all neat and tidy." He looked at his watch. "Arrival: 10:32. You're a little late."

"Sorry," Bolan apologized.

"Want me to show you your office?"

"Right now I think I'd like to meet Dr. Hampton."

"You bet, Dr. Sparks." The young man stood, fumbling with a ring of keys attached to his belt. "Just call me Chuck. If you need anything, I'm your boy." He got one of the keys into the lock on his station door and let himself out.

"What the hell is that noise?" Bolan asked, as Chuck moved to the elevator and locked it so no one could come up to the floor.

"Dolphins. That's Howard's project."

"How does anyone get any work done around here with all the racket?"

Chuck's face fell, perhaps in anticipation of trouble. "You get used to it," he said, leading Bolan down the west hallway. "Pretty soon it'll fade away in your mind, just like Muzak."

"I don't like Muzak, either."

Chuck took a long breath. "I think that Robbie is in the break room."

They moved along the hallway, past storerooms and other unoccupied cubicles, Bolan still lugging his briefcase. The walls on either side were paneled maple and would have been extremely pleasant had they not been covered with spray-painted graffiti pictures of Kilroy and cartoon women with mammoth breasts.

"What . . . ?" Bolan began, Chuck looking at him with raised eyebrows.

"Howard again, I'm afraid," he said. "He's real smart, so they indulge him."

"I see."

"Here we are."

Chuck led him into a large, homey-looking combination break room and lounge. Half the room was brightly lighted and contained a large bank of vending machines, as well as several long tables. The other half was dimly lighted and had the look of a comfortable living room, furnished with sofas and easy chairs, and shag carpet on the floor. Several people occupied this part of the place.

"Over here," Chuck directed, leading him across the room.

All conversation stopped as they approached the group, Chuck stopping in front of an older man who wore a red plaid flannel shirt and who had an unlit pipe clenched firmly between his teeth. The man smiled up at them.

"Dr. Hampton," Chuck said, "this is Dr. Sparks, our new loony."

Hampton stood, extending a hand. He was extremely tall and lanky, with salt-and-pepper hair and eyes as deep as a well. "Call me Robbie. Welcome aboard."

"I'm David," Bolan replied, shaking his hand. "Strange place you've got here."

"It gets stranger. Let me introduce you around."

"I'd better be getting back," Chuck said, moving off.

"Thanks," Bolan called after him.

The boy waved. "Remember Doc, anything you need."

"Nice kid."

Hampton chuckled softly. "He's our housemother. Come on, let's talk to the inmates."

A gray-haired man with long muttonchops and dancing eyes sat on a red leather easy chair, drinking coffee. He wore a string tie and seemed to have a permanent smile fixed on his face, as if he found the world perpetually amusing. He stood as Hampton led Bolan toward him.

"Isaac Silver," the man introduced himself, "citizen of the world. Most people call me Ike. My field's extraterrestrial communication. What's yours?"

"Gas," Bolan replied.

"As in petroleum?"

"As in nerve and mustard."

The man's smile widened. "Fascinating. You and I will have a great deal to discuss."

Bolan and Hampton moved away, then, and approached a sour-faced, middle-aged woman wearing a white lab coat. From her place on a flower-printed sofa, she looked at Bolan disdainfully.

"This is Margaret Ackerman," Hampton said. "We call her Peg, or Peggy if we really want to get her goat. Peg is our resident biochemist."

The woman ignored Bolan's proffered hand. "I try to undo the damage that your kind does," she said.

"Nice to meet you, too," Bolan replied dryly, which infuriated the woman, who puckered her lips angrily.

Next to Peg on the couch was a large black man. He stood and was eye to eye with Bolan.

"Fred Haines," Hampton said. "Solar energy." Bolan shook hands with the man, noticing arm tattoos poking out from under the sleeves of the tan jumpsuit. A long, thin scar ran from Haines's ear to his jawbone.

"You stay in shape," Haines observed, in his low, melodious voice. "That's good for your mind. You keep your vices under control, also good. You, unfortunately, don't eat right, your skin tone is ruddy, your—"

"And you've been to prison," Bolan interrupted, "where you had a lot of lousy dental work."

The man smiled widely and said, "I like you already."

Hampton patted Bolan on the shoulder. "I'll introduce you to the rest of the family as we run into them. We're just sitting around figuring out why the world is so screwed up. Care to join us?"

Bolan held up the briefcase. "As you can see, I haven't even settled in yet. I really need to see my office, if that's okay for now."

"Perfect," Hampton agreed, turning to the others. "We'll pick up on this later."

The others responded halfheartedly, and Hampton led Bolan out of the comfortable living room and across the break area to the door.

"I hope I'm not taking you away from anything important."

The man took the pipe out of his mouth and stuck it in his shirt pocket. "Just the usual. You'll get used to it. First time in a crazy house?"

"I've always worked alone before," Bolan replied.

As they neared the open doorway, they were almost run down by a man hurrying in. He was short, with curly brown hair. A cigarette dangled from a corner of his mouth. He wore a three-piece suit, with a wide tie loosened at the neck.

"Oh...Robbie," he said with a thick accent, cigarette bobbing. "I need to talk to you about harvesting machines and capabilities."

"Let's schedule it for tomorrow morning." Hampton turned to Bolan. "I'd like you to meet—"

"Can't we do it sometime today?" the man asked, agitated. He seemed to be in a tremendous hurry in everything he did—walking, talking, smoking. "This problem is holding me up."

"Okay," Hampton replied, shrugging. "I'd like you to meet David Sparks, the newest member of the team. David, this is Yuri Bonner, our resident geneticist."

"Pleased to meet you," the man said, quickly shaking Bolan's hand. "Pardon my, er...rudeness, but I'm in a hurry. Thank you very much."

"I'm glad..." Bolan began, but the man had already hurried off in the direction of the vending machines, quickly waving off greetings from the others in the living room.

"Russian?" Bolan asked, as they moved through the doorway into the hall.

"Refusenik," Hampton revealed. "Soviet dissident. Came over in the great migration when détente was at its peak during the Carter administration."

"Is he always in such a hurry?"

"Always. I think he feels the need to prove himself among us. I've never seen anyone push himself the way Yuri does."

"How about you?" Bolan asked. "What's your specialty?"

Hampton put the pipe back in his mouth. "Don't have one. I guess I'm kind of a...thinker. My 'job,' as it were, is to talk abstractly to the others about what they're doing and try to extrapolate some of their ideas into the future to see where they might be taking us. Guess I'm kind of a father figure around here, a sort of comfortable chair."

"I noticed some blankets and pillows. What were they for?"

The man removed his pipe and laughed. "Sometimes the work doesn't go by the clock."

They reached the waiting room, Chuck again immersed in his comic book. As they walked by, the elevator door slid open and Arthur the robot rolled out.

"Hello, Arthur," Hampton greeted, stopping close to the machine. "And hello to you, too, Charlie," speaking to the operator.

"Come away with me," Arthur mimicked in his best Groucho, "and we can be married and divorced before you know it."

"What have you got there, Arthur?" Hampton asked.

The robot raised its powerful metal arms. He was carrying a compact but heavy-looking electrical transformer. "A present from Dr. Smyth to Dr. Silver, to help with his radio transmissions."

"Didn't Charlie and Ike fight over this piece of equipment just last week?"

"We are giving it to Dr. Silver," the robot said. "Trying to share it was like being married to two people at the same time."

"Bigamy," Hampton put in.

Arthur's head swiveled to Bolan for the punch line. "Of course it was big of me. It was big of all of us!"

"Well, he's down in the break room," Hampton said.

"Hale thee and farewell," the robot replied, wheeling down the hall. Hampton and Bolan took the opposite corridor.

"Smyth is a bit eccentric with the robot," Hampton said as they walked, "but he's the greatest computer brain in the field of applied research alive today. He'll have a breakthrough with Arthur before the year is out."

"That transformer looked heavy," Bolan noted.

Hampton nodded. "Once he can program the machine to travel and operate on its own, he intends to assign it tasks that will show its versatility and usefulness. It's an extremely powerful piece of engineering."

As they moved down the hall, Bolan noticed and recognized the names on the doors. "Our offices?"

"Offices and labs," Hampton replied. "You should be quite pleased with yours. It's the best that money can buy."

Just then a door ten feet farther on slammed open, and a small computer flew through the space to crash against the wall. Seconds later, a straggly teenager with long curly hair came charging out of the room, turning in their direction.

"Ah, Howard," Hampton began, "I'd like—"

"Go to hell," the boy shouted, shoving his way past them to hurry down the hall.

"Don't tell me," Bolan said. "That was the dolphin boy."

"Howard Davis. He's not so bad once you get to know him."

They continued walking, skirting the demolished machine, the dolphin sounds loud as they walked past the open doorway.

Hampton stopped at the next entry. "Here we are," he announced, "and before you ask, your lab is sound-proofed, so Howard's experiments won't bother you."

A key was stuck in the lock. Hampton opened the door, pulled the key out and handed it to Bolan. "The only one," he said. "The door's always locked when it's shut. Nobody will come snooping."

Bolan pocketed the key and they walked into the lab. "Wow," he whispered. The room was as big as a barn, and jammed full of lab tables and equipment—a chemist's dream.

"The powers that be had this place stocked for you," Hampton said, closing the door behind them. "Anything else you need, you can requisition it quickly enough."

"Fine." Bolan let Hampton lead him through the maze to the walled off corner of the room.

"Your office is down here," the man said, walking with his hands behind his back.

Bolan followed him to the office, which wasn't large or impressive. It was totally unornamented concrete, painted the same yellow as Bolan's bungalow. There were two filing cabinets and a government-issue gunmetal-gray desk with a computer terminal and telephone on top. A chair had been pushed into the well. Windows with venetian blinds looked out onto the lab.

"Same story here," Hampton said. "Nice it up any way you want to. Bring your own stuff or requisition. There are some request forms in the top drawer."

"You seem to know everything."

The man smiled, removing his pipe from his mouth and looking at it. "Guess I'm the welcome wagon."

"Where's the guy who had this place before me?" Bolan asked, pulling out the chair and sitting.

Hampton's face became sullen. "That was Jerry Butler. A brilliant but troubled man. He had, I think, some sort of emotional breakdown and left the institute. Shortly after, he was killed, murdered." The pipe went back in his mouth. "Jerry was always looking for conspiracies. God knows, maybe he found one."

"You liked him a great deal?"

The man nodded. "Like a son. He had ethics, values. You don't often see that in a place like this. Brilliant minds tend ofttimes to be selfish minds—not Jerry's."

Hampton took a breath and smiled. "I'm going on like an old lady. Maybe I take my job here too seriously."

"Don't worry about it," Bolan replied. "I'm the one who asked."

"Sure," the man returned. "I know you're probably anxious to get settled in, so if there's anything you need, the list of extensions is there by the phone. Any more questions before I go?"

Bolan leaned back in his chair. "Just one," he said, pointing to the pipe. "Do you ever light that thing?"

Hampton took it out and looked at it as if surprised it was there. "Nope. A nasty habit. I just chew on it, satisfies the primitive sucking instinct."

Bolan grinned. He stood to shake Hampton's hand. "Good to know you, Robbie."

"I think we'll get along just fine," the man said, then turned and walked out of the office.

Through a partially open blind, Bolan watched as the man crossed the lab and closed the door behind him. As soon as he was gone, Bolan picked up the phone and dialed Julie.

"It's me," Bolan said. He balanced the receiver between chin and neck and knelt on the floor, running his fingers under the desk. "This phone hasn't been secured."

"I understand," Julie replied.

"You okay...no problems?"

His fingers moved from the desk bottom to the inside of the well.

"I've been busy," she answered. "Everything's fine."

"Good. I'm settling into my new office."

"How is it?"

"You wouldn't believe it if I told you," he said, and thought about his drive with Julie and her husband. "Then, again, maybe you would."

His fingers found a hard knot stuck to the underside of the well. At first he thought it was old gum, but it came off too easily. His hand came out with a miniature transmitter—a bug. He'd have to go over the room an inch at a time.

"When will you be home?" she asked.

He dropped the bug on the floor and ground it under his heel. "Don't really know. Later. Will you be there?"

"You've got the car. Where would I go?"

There was a solid tension, like a wall, between them. "Okay. Guess I'd better get on with it."

"Fine," she said coldly. "See you tonight."

"Yeah."

He hung up, feeling a tightness in his chest, then sat back and stared around the room. He was alone and naked in a strange and dark world. Even his guns had been left at home because of gate security. He looked at the floor, at the crushed piece of electronic gadgetry. Did "they"—whoever "they" were—spy on everyone, or just him? Was he close to something, or simply hearing the echo of a long-dead memory?

A shadow crossed his mind and he jerked his head toward the distant lab door. It was partway open, the swirl of a white lab coat just visible through the opening. He stood and the swatch of cloth disappeared. He was sure that Robbie had closed the door.

He was also sure that Robbie had told him that only the single key now residing in his pocket could open that lock.

Chapter Eight

There had been a four-car pileup at the intersection of Aloma and Edgewater Drive minutes before Bolan's arrival there. A restored 1962 Thunderbird lay upside down on a bed of broken glass directly in the center of the intersection, effectively blocking the roadway. Three other cars were scattered like dented Tinkertoys in various strategic locations, preventing traffic from easing around the obstruction. The rapidly growing mob of angry commuters honked and sought egress from their plight by driving over sidewalks and meticulously kept front lawns.

To make matters worse, a score of emergency vehicles blocked off all other avenues of escape. Three police cars, two ambulances, three tow trucks and a hook-and-ladder fire engine defined the periphery of the madhouse, their lights flashing wildly, turning the whole thing into a colorful, noisy Florida carnival on a hot spring night. Drivers of the various vehicles argued among themselves, police running from group to group. The driver of the Thunderbird, blood streaming from a cut on his forehead, scuffled with the attendants who tried to put him in an ambulance, all the while screaming that if he was late for dinner again, his wife would kill him.

Bolan leaned back in his seat, his cellular phone between shoulder and cheek.

"I don't know who put it there, Hal. It could have been for Butler, or it could have been for me. It could stay there all the time. I can't even come up with a guess as to who'd be on the other end of the thing. All I know is that it was definitely a listening device of relatively new design and it seemed operational.''

"Striker," Brognola said, his voice tiny, sounding as if it were coming down a tunnel, "I want you to know that I'm the only one who knows you're down there. I've set this up carefully."

"You and Julie Arnold."

"What does that mean?"

"It means that Julie Arnold knows I'm here, too."

There were several beats of silence. "There's something you're not telling me."

Bolan watched as one of the less damaged cars was driven out of the intersection, clearing a small lane for northbound drivers. "I'm not sure that I completely trust her."

"What's happened?"

"Nothing serious," Bolan replied. "She's made a couple of unauthorized phone calls, one from Vicksburg, one from a supermarket when she could have used the phone at home. One of the reasons I had the phone put in the car was so that I could keep an eye on it."

"Striker, this whole thing could be harmless," Brognola advised. "A secret boyfriend, maybe... Nothing else really makes sense."

"I understand that," Bolan returned. "Neither does it make sense to find a bug in my office first day I'm there. If you think I'm being overcautious..."

"No," Hal said bluntly. "Don't take any chances. We can't rule anything out at this point. Whatever is happening, I have a feeling we're just touching the tip of it. Like reclaiming pyramids from the desert, we're going to have to dig down to the bottom to find the entrance to the burial vaults."

As another wrecked car was dragged out of the intersection, Bolan looked in his rearview mirror to watch a line of headlights extending back into the gathering night as far as he could see. "Now, I got a feeling you're holding out on me," he said. "What's going on up there?"

"A couple of things," Brognola replied. "First of all, they gave your buddy from the other night a presidential citation."

"Givan? You've got to be joking."

"The man's a national hero, pal."

"Wonderful."

"He's got a record that General Patton would have been proud of," Brognola informed him.

"You couldn't prove it by me," Bolan said. "What else?"

"I tried to get all the way into his files and find out why he was supposed to be in the woods that night, but ran into a dead end. He's somehow connected up on some secret project involving the Pentagon that I, so far, haven't been able to come up with the authorization to see. It's called Project GOG."

"GOG," Bolan repeated, no bells tinkling in his memory. "What else?" An ambulance, siren screaming, left the scene with the Thunderbird driver aboard, bumping up a curb and traveling across several lawns until it passed the obstructed intersection and the worst of the traffic jam.

"I think—no, I'm sure—that I'm being followed," Brognola said. "I don't know who yet, but I know they're after me."

"What about Helen...?"

"I sent her away for a couple of weeks. The kids are off at college. I think they're okay where they are."

"Good." A big city truck had joined the other emergency vehicles, and a group of chain gang convicts jumped out of the back with brooms in hand. They began sweeping the intersection, as two of the tow truck operators stood close together in collaboration, trying to figure out how to get the upside-down T-Bird out of the way.

"You're exposed up there, Hal," Bolan said, "vulnerable. Don't stick your neck out too far."

"Don't worry. I leave the heroics to you clowns."

"I mean it, Hal."

"Noted, big guy."

A cheer went up from the crowd at the intersection. Bolan stood on his seat to get a better look. The tow trucks, joining together in a rare show of solidarity, had hooked chains side by side on the door of the T-Bird and were pulling in concert, the car creaking, then rocking back and forth, then finally rolling back over onto its wheels. The cheer grew in intensity, and the convicts strutted around the intersection, thrusting their fists into the air in victory.

Bolan sat down and started the Jeep. "I want you to check on a couple of people for me," he told Brognola. "First a man named Fred Haines. He's been to prison, so you might start with the federal records before even going to the security clearance file. The next guy's probably not even a citizen. He's a Russian by the name of Yuri Bonner. He came over in the late seventies."

The cars ahead began to move slowly through the mess as the Thunderbird was dragged, finally, out of the intersection and one of the cops began to direct traffic. Bolan geared up and moved with the flow.

"You got suspicions?" Brognola asked.

"Not really. Just going through the preliminaries. At this stage, I'm not taking any chances."

Bolan proceeded through the intersection and continued along Aloma at the speed limit.

"I'll have this intel for you as quick as I can. Meantime, you watch your butt," Brognola said gruffly.

"Business as usual for me," Bolan replied, "but I want you to take your own advice."

"Sure, Striker. Check in same time tomorrow."

"Got it." Bolan hung up, moving into the right lane in preparation for the turn onto Avondale. His first day at the institute had been a strange one. It didn't take him long to discover that beneath the veneer of friendliness that seemed to pervade everything there, the scientists were motivated by competition and ego gratification. They were intelligent people, intelligent enough to know that the government gravy train they were riding was only as stable as the results they could produce. It made them protective of their work and competitive with the others on the project, which, predictably, led to barely cloaked resentments and jealousies.

He'd made some headway in setting up his own project. Actually the project belonged to another researcher connected with DOD, who, judging from the letter that accompanied his files, was none too happy about having someone else horn in on his glory. Though chemical warfare was officially banned, research continued. And this research was especially interesting. It was shooting for a gas that, like nerve gas, wouldn't have to be breathed to be effective, but that could pass directly through the skin. The gas, however, wouldn't kill or cause permanent injury. Called K-14, it was a derivative of ketamine, an anesthetic mostly used by veterinarians, and would render its victim helpless for up to two hours, by causing a blockage in the command center of the brain and leaving the victim unable to perform simple motor functions. Its sensation was euphoric. War without suffering, without pain? It raised a great many philosophical questions.

He turned onto Avondale, hot wind and palmetto bugs hitting him in the face as he drove home—to Julie. Her place in the scheme of things he couldn't even imagine. What had started out as a simple relationship had gotten increasingly complex and difficult to understand, all in the space of a few days. A week ago he hadn't even known her. Today, their fates were inextricably linked, and it seemed as if it had always been that way.

He reached the house, turned in the driveway and under the carport. There was another problem with Julie, too, something that was getting in the way of everything else. He was attracted to her. The more he tried to deny it to himself, the stronger the attraction became. It was something he'd have to overcome. And soon.

He unlocked the side door of the house and stood in the kitchen for a moment, listening to the sound of a tinny and mechanical voice.

"Julie," he called.

The television was switched off abruptly, and Julie Arnold, dressed in jeans and halter, sauntered into the kitchen. "You're pretty late," she said.

"Hung up in traffic." Bolan moved to the refrigerator to take out one of the beers she had brought home from the store. Absolutely nothing had been done to the house. Everything was where it had been last night. The dust was as thick, the furniture in as much disarray. They would have to take some time to straighten up.

"Did you get the phone in the car?" she asked.

"Yeah," he replied, popping the beer top and moving into the living room. "One of the security people from work took the Jeep and had it done for me. Apparently they're used to acting like messenger boys for the brains in the institute. What are you doing?"

She followed him into the living room and sat on the floor amid a small pile of reports and a tape recorder. "Did some transcribing into the tape recorder. I've also been listening to the tape that your friend, Hal, gave us."

Bolan sat on the edge of the daybed and leaned toward Julie. "You mean the tape McMasters did with General Cronin?"

"Right. NASA Matériel Disbursement. Want to hear some?"

He sat back. "Sure."

She spent a moment rewinding the tape to the right place, then turned it on. The first voice Bolan heard was obviously McMasters's. It was clear and close, not something picked up through a telephone.

"...sorry to bother you. I imagine you're quite busy with the launch date so close."

The responding voice was staticky and sounded far away. "Actually the contrary is true," Cronin answered. "We're all loaded up and ready to go. Our part of the flight is finished."

"Then you've got a few minutes to answer some questions?"

"Sure. Always anxious to accommodate the press."

"Good. Does the name Jerry Butler mean anything to you?"

"Butler...Butler. I knew a Jane Butler once, quite a woman, she..."

"No. This would be more recent. I believe he's a scientist of some sort."

"Of some sort..." A long pause. "It seems, Mr. McMasters, that you don't know the gentleman very well yourself."

"He contacted our office last evening, General. He's made some claims about the *Challenger* flight."

"What sort of claims?"

"He says that, 'certain dangerous contraband items are being sent into space on the shuttles.' That's an exact quote."

"What sort of contraband?"

"I'm supposed to meet with him tomorrow morning to find out. I wanted to talk with you first, since you are directly responsible for the loading of matériel, to see if you know Butler, or know what he's talking about."

"It seems to me I've heard something similar to this from someone on the Titusville paper...."

"Yes, sir. I believe he went to them, also."

"They had enough sense to know bullshit when they heard it, Mr. McMasters...if you'll pardon my French."

"Your point is made, General Cronin. Now, if you—"

"Let me get this out, Mr. McMasters. The United States space program is, and always has been, beyond reproach. We have no secret agendas, no hidden cargo. It has always been important to the government as a whole that it be obvious to the country and to the world at large that our exploratory missions into outer space are of peaceful intent. With that in mind, NASA in general and Matériel Disbursement in particular has always been careful to make our payloads and our intentions a matter of public record. That is to say that we'll gladly make a manifest of matériel available to anyone who wants a look—for this flight and for all preceding flights. Would you like a copy of the manifest?''

''Well . . . certainly, sir, I didn't mean to imply—''

''Quite all right. I just want you to realize that the world is full of nuts like your Mr. Butler, who are willing to say anything about anything to gain publicity, or kicks, or whatever sick pleasure they derive from disrupting the normal flow of life and government.''

''I understand that, sir. I also understand that a lot of people probably called Werner Von Braun and everyone else who pioneered the space program nuts, too. My job as a newsman is to separate the nuts from the sweetmeat, if you know what I mean.''

''I do indeed. You're only doing your job.''

''Yes, sir. And believe me, nothing untrue or slanderous in any way will come out of this office. I always double-check my facts.''

''Then none of us have anything to worry about. I'll send a copy of the manifest around to your office. Good day, Mr. McMasters.''

''And good luck, General Cronin, on the upcoming flight.''

''Don't need luck. Just a favorable tail wind.''

Julie shut off the tape recorder and looked expectantly up at Bolan. ''What do you make of that?''

Bolan shrugged and took a sip of beer. ''Don't know. It's interesting that General Cronin spoke with the newsman himself. NASA has an extremely good public affairs office that would normally handle this sort of request.''

''What are you saying?''

''Nothing,'' Bolan replied. ''It's simply interesting that General Cronin takes such a personal interest in disbursement publicity.''

''Maybe he's just protective of his department.''

''Maybe. Something else struck me as even more interesting. Butler thought contraband had gone up on previous flights, as well.''

She rose to her knees and pointed. "I get it. We can go back through previous manifests and find out what companies have repeated over a period of time."

"Right," he agreed. "It will narrow, at least, the companies we need to look at. That is, of course, if there's anything to this at all, and if the stuff was listed on the manifest."

Julie leaned over and began to arrange the pile of papers on the floor. "Jerry Butler was a great many things," she said. "But he wasn't crazy."

"How long since you last saw him?"

She looked up at Bolan. "A couple of years, I guess I..."

"A lot can happen to a man in a couple of years."

Anger flashed across her face, her lips tightening. "Then why has everybody else been killed? Why is my husband's body rotting...somewhere...I..."

She turned her head, a hand going to her mouth as she choked back the tears.

"I'm sorry," Bolan said, feeling awkward again. "I didn't mean—"

"Let's just drop it, okay?"

"Sure."

There seemed to be no in-between with Julie Arnold. She was either rock hard or butter soft, and she always caught him off guard with whatever the mood was.

"How was your day?" she asked, trying hard to be matter-of-fact.

"I feel like a baby-sitter."

She half smiled. "Head people are a different breed. They live and act like children. It's really part of the package. It takes a special kind of person to be able to think that abstractly for a long period of time. If you want to survive there, you'd better start acting like a baby, too, or you'll give yourself away."

"Maybe I already have," he replied, not sure of how much to tell her. "I found a listening device attached to the underside of my desk today."

She stood, picking up the papers and tape recorder and setting them on the coffee table. "There's stew in the refrigerator if you want any," she said, moving to stare out the front window.

"I thought you weren't going to cook for me," he said, and saw her shoulders stiffen.

She turned slowly, her eyes unreadable as she looked at him. "It's hard to make stew just for one." She then held his eyes, something indescribably sad oozing from her and crossing the distance between them.

He felt the jolt of their unspoken contact, felt the sadness and retreated to the kitchen.

"I appreciate it."

Bolan removed the pot of stew from the refrigerator and set it on the burner of the gas stove. "Will you join me?" he called, turning on the burner.

"No," she called back. "I've already eaten."

"Suit yourself." He felt bad about having walked out on her as he'd done. He stood watching the stew bubble in the pan. After stirring it for a moment he let it boil again, then took it off the stove.

Julie moved to the kitchen doorway and leaned against it, staring as Bolan took down a plate and ladled some food onto it.

Aware of her eyes on him, he walked to the table and sat facing her. He smiled uneasily, then took a bite of the food. "It's good," he said, unable to keep the surprise out of his voice. Then, with more admiration, "You're a good cook."

"Have you ever considered the possibility that your friend, Hal, could have planted that device in your desk?" she asked softly.

He put the fork down and stared at her. "No, I haven't. And if I had, our conversation today would have dispelled any doubts."

"You talked to him today?"

Bolan nodded and picked up his fork again.

"Why didn't you tell me?" she demanded.

"I hadn't gotten around to it yet."

She sat beside him at the table. "Well, did he have anything interesting to say?"

"A little. It seems that Colonel Kit Givan has received a presidential citation for fighting a certain Mississippi forest fire...."

"Where does that leave us?"

"In pretty bad shape in comparison. Also, Hal thinks he's being followed, but doesn't know by whom."

"Did he try to do anything with Givan's file?" she asked.

Bolan nodded. "He tried. Got into his file, but has so far been unable to update beyond two years ago."

"Why?"

"Givan's been put into a top-secret project for the Pentagon. Hal hasn't yet been able to obtain the authorization to crack it."

"How convenient. Is that all?"

Bolan frowned. "Yeah. So far. I don't suppose you've ever heard of Project GOG."

She laughed. "Gog? You mean as in the biblical Gog?"

"I'm not sure I follow you."

She relaxed, sitting back. "Here's where a Jewish education and a photographic memory can help you out. The legend of Gog appears twice in the Bible, once in the Old Testament, in Ezekiel, and once in the New, in Revelation."

"And what's it about?"

"War, basically," she replied. "And the coming of a Messiah."

"War," he repeated.

"Ezekiel foretells a great war, where Gog will come from the north, from the land of Magog, and fight a war with Israel that will decimate it. But after the conflagration, a Messiah will come and destroy Gog and bring about a new age of peace and prosperity to all of Israel."

"Fascinating."

"In the New Testament, I think the concept was re-worked into a showdown between God and the Devil...."

"You mean the Second Coming?"

She nodded. "Let me quote a little Ezekiel for you," she said, closing her eyes for a second and nodding. When she spoke her voice was low and forceful. "'I will punish him with pestilence and with bloodshed; and I will pour torrential rain, hailstones and sulfurous fire upon him and his hordes and the many people with him.'"

Bolan stared hard at her. "Pretty strong stuff."

She nodded. "Many fundamentalist Christian sects interpret the threat from the north to mean Russia."

Bolan pushed the bowl away from himself. He wasn't hungry anymore.

Chapter Nine

Mack Bolan stared intently at the squirming white mouse he held by the tail, its little body twitching madly as it squeaked in terror.

"Come on, Hershel," he said. "Be a man about this. It's not even going to hurt. And I promise it won't kill you."

The mouse seemed to squeak even louder, its voice like oil-hungry door hinges.

Bolan thinned his lips in exasperation. "You'll probably enjoy it."

While holding the mouse in a rubber-gloved hand, he picked up the small atomizer that lay on the long lab table and sprayed a fine mist onto the animal's haunches, being careful not to let it breathe any of the ketamine mixture.

There was a knock on the lab door.

"Coming!" Bolan called, and set Hershel into the mouse cage along with his other cronies. The little guy hurried to his exercise wheel to run out his frustrations.

Bolan watched him for a second, identifying with the frustration. It was his fourth day at the institute, as everyone called it, and he was beginning to think that he could stay there forever without discovering anything useful on the Butler killing.

The man's name came up very seldom in casual conversation on the fifth floor, and there were few avenues Bolan could take to bring up the name without arousing suspicion. The "head people," as Julie called them, were too smart to be taken in by any trickery he could devise to draw them out. It became clear that it could take months for them to accept him enough to talk candidly. Then, it was probable that they'd have nothing to open up about. The institute could be a total dead end or it could provide all the answers. Only time, a great deal of time, would tell; and it was quite possible that he didn't have a lot of time to play with. What he needed was a way to juice things and hurry them along. He just didn't know how to do that. He'd spent the past three days going over the office and the lab, hoping that Butler had left something, some clue, behind. The search had been fruitless.

He needed, in the jargon of his research field, a catalyst to speed up the process.

He moved across the large room and opened the door to Robbie Hampton's smiling face. The man carried a mug of coffee and wore his usual flannel shirt buttoned to the neck.

"Hope I'm not bothering you," Robbie said.

Bolan smiled, moving aside so Hampton could enter. "You're my guru, Robbie. You could never be a bother."

"Guru, my ass." Hampton walked in and headed directly to the mouse cage. "It looks like you're doing just fine without my advice."

"Fine, you say?" Bolan replied, and pointed to Hershel on the wheel. "By now he should be zonked out on the cage floor in a state of total incapacitation. Does this look like a mouse with a disassociation problem?"

"Just moderately," Robbie said, leaning down close to the cage. "Look at his right leg."

Bolan looked. Hershel's right leg twitched slightly and kept slipping off the wheel. The drug had had some localized effect on the area sprayed, but apparently hadn't made it into the bloodstream.

"Close," Bolan said, "but no cigar."

Robbie straightened. "The problem with trying to make ketamine into a nerve gas is obviously going to be a problem of the delivery system, not of the drug itself."

Bolan thought hard, trying to bring the real researcher's notebook to mind. "The nerve gases are derivatives of phosphoric acid and destroy the nervous system by inhibiting certain enzymes," he said, trying to sound as if he knew what he was talking about. "Ketamine, on the other hand, stimulates the nervous system while at the same time causing a dissociation in the relay center to the cerebral cortex."

"But ketamine doesn't reach the bloodstream through osmosis like nerve gas," Robbie put in. "So you're trying to compound the two."

"I want something that can't be shut out with a respirator, but not something that will kill or harm a human being."

"The peace bomb," Hampton said dryly, smiling. "Even if you can bind the molecules to get the desired effect, how will you minimize the danger of the phosphoric acid?"

Bolan was in deep water already. How the hell did Robbie know so much about everything? The mixture used in the atomizer was one of the previous failures of the real researcher. A word popped into his head that he remembered from the notes, and he decided to use it, hoping for the best. "I'm cutting the whole thing with atropine."

"Of course!" Robbie said, and Bolan figured he must have found the right word. "The atropine will counteract the nerve gas before it damages the system irreparably."

Bolan fell into it then, realizing on his own why this particular experiment had failed. "The problem becomes one of keeping the nerve gas active long enough to get the whole mess into the body."

Hampton stared at the mice again, quietly rubbing his chin. "I'll think some about this," he said after a moment. "Maybe I can help."

Bolan pulled off one of his rubber gloves and dropped it on the table. "You amaze me, Robbie."

"How so?" the man asked as he took his pipe out of his breast pocket and stuck it in his mouth.

"Everybody else here has an area of study that they've devoted their lives to," Bolan said, removing the other glove. "But you seem to be fluent in everyone's language."

"I appreciate the compliment," the man answered, "but it's really no mystery. I don't know so much about anything except the thinking process. You see, when researchers get heavily involved in a problem, they tend to develop a sort of tunnel vision that renders them incapable of looking at the broader implications of their research. I was a writer in my younger days, and writers have to be able to extrapolate and look at the consequences and possibilities in all directions. It's an acquired habit, really. No big deal. I usually supply continuing data and possibilities to people who are experts in a given topic. They listen, then take it from there. It's all very symbiotic."

He took hold of the pipe as if he were taking it out of his mouth, but instead, he simply lapsed for a moment, his brows knitted in thought.

"At least that's how it usually works," he said finally. "With Jerry Butler, it worked just the opposite. The more advanced his research became, the less he'd open up to me."

"I wonder why?"

Robbie slapped his forehead, coffee sloshing in his cup. "God, silly me. I forgot why I came down here. Yuri wants everyone to come to his lab. I think he's made some sort of a breakthrough."

"Anything interesting?"

Robbie smiled. "I never steal my collaborators' thunder. I'll let Yuri tell you himself. Can you drop what you're doing?"

Bolan looked at the mouse cage and frowned. "It doesn't look as if Hershel is going to cooperate." He took off his lab coat. "Why not?"

"Good." Robbie led Bolan toward the door and when they reached the hall he turned, his face serious. "It was odd about Jerry. He knew me, I mean, he knew me well. But he seemed to slowly cut everyone off from his life.

We'd been having dialogues about the possibilities of his research—''

"Which was?"

The man smiled. "Of course," he said. "You have no idea what I'm talking about. Sorry. Jerry was involved with liquid electricity, and his problem was in some ways similar to yours...he needed a vehicle, something that would hold a charge indefinitely—a delivery system. Anyway, I think he was approaching a breakthrough, which is usually when the researchers want me the most so I can give them possibilities. But Jerry just cut me, and everyone else, off. He even began working hours when no one else was here."

"You think he found the breakthrough, then simply guarded it?"

They were moving along the hall, closing in on Bonner's door.

"I think that's possible, yes," Robbie replied. "For all the good it did him. He left on the sly. After his death, government people spent weeks in his lab, trying to piece together notes or ideas or anything."

"But they found nothing," Bolan concluded.

This time Robbie did take the pipe out of his mouth. "How did you know?"

Bolan smiled. "I extrapolated."

The man chuckled gently. "You've almost got too good a sense of humor to be in this business," he said, then stopped walking. They were in front of Bonner's door. He raised a fist to knock. "Shall we?"

"A question first. If you are involved in everyone's project, how do they know that you won't give their secrets away?"

"Everyone wonders about that eventually," Robbie replied. "The answer is simple—give secrets away to whom? Everyone here is ultimately responsible to the government, in our case the Department of the Air Force, so nothing *belongs* to any of us individually. The other thing is, I don't know how things work, just what you can do with them when they do work. It would be tough to sell my fiction writer's mind to...say, the Russians.''

That made sense to Bolan. Robbie knocked on the door.

Ike Silver responded. ''Well, the latecomers,'' he said, opening the door wide. ''Yuri has just solved the greatest problem facing man on Earth today.''

Robbie held up his cup. ''And I brought my own coffee.''

''Well, aren't you the clever one,'' Silver declared. ''Always on top of things.''

They entered the room, a lab and office set up just like Bolan's—with an incredible exception. Plants filled the entire lab, huge plants with mammoth leaves and fruit, genetic hybrids developed by the Soviet scientist. The ceiling had been reconstructed as a skylight, bright sunshine pouring in. Bolan saw wheat that rose in thick stalks to the ceiling and a row of corn with ears almost as big as footballs, which had been cut back to keep them from growing through the ceiling.

A lab table was cleared in the center of the room, overhanging branches shading it like an outdoor picnic table. Everyone from the fifth floor was there, as well as Dr. Smyth in the guise of his robot, Arthur, and Floyd Bacon, who hadn't been to Five in two years. They were all sitting around the table drinking coffee and eating what appeared to be chocolate cake. Arthur was wheeling around the lab, looking at all the plants and trees. Yuri was on his feet, nervously pacing and chain-smoking.

Bolan and Dr. Hampton approached the table, Ike Silver ambling at his own pace just behind. Lab stools were lined around the table, and Bolan took a seat across from Fred Haines and Margaret Ackerman, who seemed to spend a great deal of time listening to any conversation Bolan was involved in. Howard Davis sat several stools away from everyone else, lost in his own world, eating cake with his fingers. His mouth and chin were covered with chocolate. The director occupied the head of the table. He sat stoically, staring down at a tiny sliver of cake set on his plate. Even Chuck was there, serving coffee to anyone who wanted it.

Robbie took the seat next to Bolan and reached to cut a slice from the cake in the center of the table. He handed it to him.

"No, thanks," Bolan said. "It's a little too early for me to—"

"You must," Robbie interrupted. "It's important."

"Important," Bolan repeated, and let the man put the plate before him. He looked up to see everyone staring at him. Even Yuri had stopped pacing and was standing behind Haines.

Bolan was beginning to suspect that something was wrong with the cake.

"Eat, my friend," Yuri urged. "We don't have all day."

"All day for what?" Bolan asked.

Robbie handed him a plastic fork. "Go ahead."

Bolan put the fork to the cake and cut into it. It felt like real cake. He brought it to his lips, hesitating slightly.

"Would you please eat, Dr. Sparks," Floyd Bacon ordered, his voice brittle like old paper. "We're on a tight schedule."

Bolan bit into the cake tentatively, letting the piece sit for a moment in his mouth until the proper signals had registered in his brain and he tasted it. "Good," he said, chewing. "Excellent!"

The entire room burst into spontaneous applause, Ike Silver walking over to pat Yuri Bonner on the back as everyone talked excitedly.

"What's going on?" Bolan asked, puzzled. Haines smiled at him through a mouthful of prison dental work.

"That cake you're eating is made from a genetic hybrid of the cocoa bean," he announced.

"Improved chocolate?" Bolan asked.

"I'll say," Peg Ackerman answered. "No calories."

Bolan was amazed. "None?"

The woman circled thumb and index finger. "Zero."

Bolan held up his plate. "Then I'll have another piece!"

Everyone laughed, except for Peg, who simply scowled, as usual, in Bolan's direction.

Yuri waved them all to silence. "I want you to know," he said, "that this is simply...an offshoot—is that how you say?—of main work. Mr. Bacon says we need to...to..."

"Justify our existence," the director said slowly. "And this should do quite nicely. The government and the public likes to know that their money is being well spent, and to the millions of overweight people out there, this will be the most well-spent money in history. It's even good PR for the Air Force, who'll let Yuri keep the patent."

"You'll be rich," Haines put in.

Bonner frowned deeply. "Money," he said, and spit on the floor. "In America, we have ninety percent of the world's resources and money, yet millions starve. What's the good?"

"Yuri is trying to save the world through food," Ike Silver said, and it sounded like an insult. "For what reason I couldn't imagine. I see nothing about the world worth saving."

The robot wheeled up to face Silver. "You're an elitist, Ike," it said. "If we're not here to help our fellow man, what *are* we here for?"

"You're a good one to talk about human values," Silver told the robot, "after the way you screwed me with that transformer."

"Gentlemen..." Floyd Bacon said, his already pale face losing what little color it possessed.

"What do you mean by that?" the robot countered, rolling up until it was nose to nose with Silver. "I gave you that transformer out of the goodness of my heart."

"Yeah," Silver responded, "then turned around and put in a requisition for an even more powerful one by saying that I commandeered yours, which effectively cuts me out of next year's budget."

"I don't want to hear this," the old man muttered, pushing slowly away from the table.

The robot reached a metal hand to tug on Silver's string tie. "Elitist."

"And why not?" Silver queried. "There's no intelligent life on this planet. Why should I be dragged down by the ignorance of its inhabitants?"

"Hear, hear," Howard Davis said through a mouthful of cake.

"I really must go," Floyd Bacon said, standing slowly, just as he did everything slowly. "My office will take care of the publicity on this thing, Yuri. Congratulations."

Yuri hurried over to help the old man across the floor. "My appropriations for next year..."

"Should be helped considerably by this project," the director said, moving toward the lab door. Chuck abandoned the coffee machine to walk the old man out and unlock the elevator doors.

Yuri walked back to the table, reaching beneath its top where the director had been sitting. "Excuse a minute... please," he said, then laterally slid the table's granite top back a foot to expose a small amount of storage space beneath. Manuals and charts filled the space.

The man removed a picture and slid it toward Bolan. "This is my real work."

Peg Ackerman was staring at the storage drawer. "I didn't know the tables could do that."

"Sure," Yuri said. "Is handy, huh?"

Bolan returned his gaze to the picture. It was an artist's rendering of a field full of what looked like cacti without the prickles.

"What is it?" Bolan asked.

"Is... food," Yuri said, shrugging. "Cross tobacco genes with animal genes, breed out need for much water and grow in any soil." The man smiled. "Is good for you, easy to raise and tastes good, too. I will feed many hungry with this."

"You can fatten 'em up," Ackerman jeered, "while Sparks mows 'em down."

"You're not being fair, Peg," Robbie admonished, taking a sip of his coffee. "You have no idea what David's research entails."

"What are you talking about?" Peg said, her eyes never leaving Bolan. "He's here shilling for DOD in chemical warfare. Hell, his field of experimentation isn't even legal!"

"Manufacturing isn't legal," Robbie said, "and field use isn't legal. Experimentation is open. Besides, David isn't working on those kinds of weapons."

Yuri slid the top closed. "What kind is he working on?"

"Peaceful weapons," Bolan said.

"An oxymoron," Howard observed. "Contradiction in terms."

"Is it?" Bolan said choosing his words carefully. "When I was in Nam, we field-tested a gas that made enemy troops nauseated. They simply threw down their guns and got sick and surrendered. No one was hurt. No one was killed. An international outcry was raised against our use of chemical weapons and we were forced to stop. We went back to more 'humane' methods: M-16s, bouncy bettys, napalm, search-and-destroy. Even if my research is never applied, at least I know it can't be used to hurt people. The rest of you can't say the same thing."

Howard Davis stood, his young face contorted in anger. "I resent that. I'd never let my research be used wrongly."

"You all live in a dreamworld," Bolan growled. "We're all working for the same government, and they can use our findings to do anything they want."

"Not mine," Howard vowed. "Never."

"I saw something else when I was in Nam," Bolan said. "A squad of dolphins with bombs strapped to them. They were used to mine Hanoi harbor."

"No!" Howard said loudly, and swept his arm across the table, knocking his plate and coffee onto the floor. "I don't believe you!"

The boy stomped out of the room, slamming the door behind him.

"I think I can understand the morality of banning the nausea gas," Robbie said, sitting back and chewing on his pipe. "If we must have wars, they *should* be ugly, horrible things. If we can't be repulsed by them, we'll never understand their uselessness."

"You're thinking in a vacuum," Bolan said. "People have never gotten along during the course of the entire history of the world. Maybe if we can fight our wars painlessly, we'll start doing other things painlessly and stop the cycles of violence and revenge that lead to war."

Ike Silver laughed. "You're all idiots. The stupid creatures who run this world will never be happy until they've destroyed it and sent us back to the oblivion we deserve."

"That's your answer to everything, isn't it?" Bolan suggested. "I feel sorry for you and all the simple joys in life you must have missed." He was getting carried away and knew it, but he didn't care at this point. While good people scratched like animals in the dirt just so their families could have a meal, Ike Silver sat above it all, passing judgment in his ivory tower, all of his wants taken care of.

"Save it for church, pal." Silver's smile had disappeared from his face.

"How long were you in Vietnam?" Fred Haines asked, his eyes boring into Bolan.

"What difference does it make?"

"Well, it's just unusual," Peg Ackerman noted, a look of relaxed superiority now lining her face. "It's unusual for people with our... backgrounds, to have spent time in the service."

"Especially in a war zone," Haines added, and smiled to show Bolan he wasn't just stabbing in the dark. "Although, I guess to think of it, you're not like us in a number of ways."

Bolan looked over at Robbie. The man had leaned back, deep in thought, his teeth clenched hard on the pipe.

"What's that supposed to mean?" Bolan asked.

The woman slid forward in her chair. "It means you're a square peg in a round hole, Dr. Sparks, an incongruity."

Bolan's battle senses began tingling. Like bloodhounds on the hunt, they were with each step losing the false trail and closing in on him. But did it mean anything?

"Sometimes I wonder," Haines said, "if Dr. Sparks is really what he says he is."

Bolan returned the man's unwavering gaze. He was looking into the eyes of a hard man, something they both shared and understood. "Suppose you tell me what I am," he invited.

Haines shrugged. "Maybe an investigator sent to check up on us to see if we're doing a good job."

"Maybe someone checking into the death of Jerry Butler," Ackerman suggested, smiling when Bolan's eyes jerked in her direction.

"I think you're all being extremely inhospitable," Robbie admonished. "I'm surprised at every one of you. Dr. Sparks and I worked on his project just this morning, and I assure you, it's quite interesting and viable."

"Sure it is," Ackerman said. "Perhaps, then, David, you and I can have a little discussion about the chemistry involved."

Bolan, almost caught earlier by Robbie's layman's knowledge of what he was doing, knew he could never pass Ackerman's scrutiny.

"I don't need to pass your little test, *Peggy*," he said, standing abruptly. "You're not my boss, and I'll be damned if I'm going to give you access to my project so you can steal it."

Haines laughed. "Maybe he *is* one of us!"

Bolan looked at Yuri. "Thanks for the cake. Good luck with your project."

With that, he walked away from the table and out the door, turning immediately in the direction of his lab. Actually the argument was a godsend. He'd been trying to think of a way to get out of Yuri's quarters and back to his own lab. He wanted to check the storage drawers in his own tables.

He moved quickly, passing Howard's door, which was partly open. Hearing something besides dolphin noises within, he stopped and peered through the crack.

The entire center of the lab was filled with a tank five feet high with stairs leading up to it. Howard sat at the top of the stairs, leaning his arms against the edge of the tank. He was crying, sobbing. Beside him, two dolphins had poked their upper torsos out of the water and were chirping softly, nudging the boy. It looked for all the world as if they were comforting him.

Bolan backed away from the door and used the key to get inside his lab. Even away from the confrontation, his nerves were still on edge.

He was suspected. His cover, if not blown, was rapidly deflating.

Earlier he'd been looking for a catalyst. Well, he'd found it the easy way. He'd become the sacrificial goat. It was time to start looking over his shoulder. He liked meeting trouble head-on, on his own terms. Watching his rear was something that never appealed. But this was one game he didn't get to play on his own terms.

He shut the door, listening to the reassuring click of the lock. He hadn't found any bugs since that first day, and he performed a routine sweep daily. He didn't trust his co-workers any more than they trusted him.

There were six granite-topped tables in the lab, six chances of success and failure. He picked one at random and walked to it, searching beneath the overhang of the top for the same latch that Yuri had sprung. His fingers found a small flange, no larger than a screw head. He pushed it, immediately feeling the release of tension in the tabletop.

The top slid back easily, exposing the drawer. It was empty.

He slid the top closed again, moving to the next table, where he repeated the process to the same result. Table number three opened to several spiderwebs, the hulk of a dead cockroach trapped in one of the webs.

But table four, the one closest to the lab office, was a different story. A white box meant to hold typing paper lay within. He stared at it for a moment, wondering if this was the buildup to a great letdown. Finally he reached in and took it out, its weight reassuring him that something was, indeed, inside.

He set it up on the table and slid the tabletop closed. The box was dusty, only Bolan's fingerprints marring its coated surface. It had obviously stayed within the drawer for a long time.

He reached out and took the top off the box, revealing a strange assortment of odds and ends. He took them out one at a time. There was a notebook filled with equations. He thumbed through it quickly, understanding none of it. There was a road map of the state of Arizona, an equipment manifest for the fateful *Challenger* flight and, finally, a sheet of paper filled with numbers arranged in groups like words—a code?

He stood there staring at the tangible evidence of Jerry Butler's fears and suspicions. It was all real now, every bit of it, and still it made no sense.

What did make sense was that Jerry Butler had suspected something nasty was going on, enough so that he began to research in private and to hide his results, even couching them in code. The man had then apparently found answers to his suspicions, and had, just as apparently, been killed for them.

Those answers were now in the hands of Mack Bolan— and Mack Bolan was in enemy territory. He didn't know anything about chemistry, but he knew a killzone when he saw one.

Chapter Ten

The intensity of Julie's face stood out sharply in the yellow-orange glow of the flame of the disposable lighter she held over the page.

"Good God, Mack," she said, her voice low and reverential. "I had no idea he'd progressed this far."

"She can make sense out of the equations," Bolan said into the receiver. "She thinks he came up with something."

"Keep her on it, Striker," Hal Brognola said on the other end, his voice heavy with concern. "I think we're on to something big here. Are you still secure there at the institute?"

"Ouch!" the woman said, the flame winking out as she dropped the lighter. "That thing gets hot!"

They were sitting in the Jeep in the carport, the pink-veined sky darkening by degrees all around them.

"Not really." Bolan shushed the woman with a finger to his lips. "They suspect me already. It's liable to come unraveled at any point. Did you get that intel I asked you for?"

"Yeah, finally," the Fed replied. "Though I had to move heaven and earth to get the authorization. Somebody tied the security up there so tight, I practically needed a crowbar to get into the files. You ready?"

"Shoot."

Julie had thumbed the lighter again, the flame casting a glow on the inside of the cab. "Good God... good God." She was flying through the pages, her eyes quickly scanning the lines of numbers. "Oh Mack."

"On one Fred Haines," Brognola said. "Quite an interesting history. Slow student as a child, diagnosed as learning disabled, recommended special schooling but not funded. Only went to fourth grade. Lived on the streets . . . tough kid . . . hell of a rap sheet. Joined Black Panther organization in 1966 . . . imprisoned for armed robbery and conspiracy in 1970. IQ tested as genius while in prison, 1972, and transferred to federal minimum security facility where he received educational and vocational training. Became fascinated by the politics of energy and turned his attention to clean energy sources, focusing on solar. Developed 'orbiting island' theory of solar to electric transfer in 1978. Paroled in 1979 and offered research position at Grolier Foundation, which he has kept until present. Nice friends you've got."

The light flickered out again. Julie reached over to grab Bolan's arm with shaking hands. "I think he did it, Mack. My God, I think he did it. He suspended the liquid in a negative ion shell. The charge had nowhere to dissipate to!"

"She says he broke through," Bolan told Brognola.

"That's what I was afraid of. If he did, indeed, find the key to this thing, whoever is using it has killed off the other researchers so no one else will have the knowledge. This is important, Striker. That notebook is our only link to a whole branch of knowledge. Guard it, whatever you do. Have Julie stop transcribing her own stuff and start transcribing that notebook into readable English."

"If they've read me over at Grolier," Bolan said, "we're liable to have a whole army down on us."

"So far, nobody knows you have the book. I think you might be safe as long as that information stays underground."

"Got it. How about Yuri Bonner?"

"Short and sweet," Brognola replied. "Soviet geneticist . . . and Jewish. Continually denied emigration visa on security grounds. Sentenced to ten years in the gulag for dissident activities connected with the monitoring of the

Helsinki Accord. Released in 1979, emigrated to Israel where he lived on a kibbutz. Came to U.S. in 1984 and was swept immediately into Grolier. Considered the world expert on hybrid plant and animal life.''

"Good," Bolan said. "Thanks, my friend."

"What about the code you found? Want me to run it through the computers up here?"

"I'd have to get it to you, wouldn't I?" Bolan answered. He watched out the windshield as the kid next door played Frisbee with his father. "It looks like a simple position code to me. I haven't had too much time with it yet, but if I can't crack it in a couple of days, we'll figure out some way to get it up there."

"Okay. What do you need me to do?"

"I think you need to tear through the manifest," Bolan answered. "Track down every company. Look back through the past manifests and see if any commercial enterprise repeats a number of times and check those first."

"What do you mean, check them?"

"How do I know? I have no idea what we're even looking for... just anything that doesn't seem to be on the up-and-up. At least see what everybody sent on the flights. Any more on the GOG project?"

"No," Brognola answered. "And it may be difficult to find much."

"What do you mean?"

"I've tracked it through the system. It's connected up somehow with DOD and their unearmarked funds." A deep weariness ran through Brognola's voice.

"What are unearmarked funds?" Bolan asked, glancing at Julie, who was totally absorbed in the notebook.

"Taxpayer money is always accountable...almost. But there is a certain amount of money, up in the billions each year, that slips into the Department of Defense budget to go toward secret projects and developments and is protected under the umbrella of national security."

"There's no accountability of the funds?" Bolan asked.

"Well, one must assume that there is somewhere," Brognola answered. "Some chain of command understands and authorizes the spending, linking to the President through the NSC."

"But the potential for abuse..."

"I know. Anyway, as near as I can figure, this GOG thing is a 'special project' in the research and development area, under the control of General Leland of the Pentagon."

"Kit Givan's boss," Bolan said. "Great. There's no way you can crack it?"

"I'm trying, Striker. That's the best I can do. Do you have any ideas concerning that Arizona map you found with the other stuff?"

Bolan looked into the rearview mirror. A late-model Chevy van with tinted black windows had pulled up across the street, but no one had emerged from it.

"None," he replied. "Maybe it means nothing. I keep looking for the key that ties all this together, but I haven't come up with anything. Can I get you to check on some of the others at the institute?"

"I can do you better than that. I've got the authorization code that will let you into the personnel records there. You can just use your office terminal to find anything you want. Ready for the number?"

"Just a minute." Bolan turned to Julie. "Can you memorize something for me?"

She stopped reading, reluctantly stifling the lighter, and turned to him, nodding. "Go ahead."

"Let's have it," Bolan said into the receiver.

"Okay," Hal said. "It's 2Q2-1719."

Bolan repeated the number to Julie.

"Got it," she said, going back to her reading.

Bolan checked the rearview again. The van was still there.

"There's something I don't quite understand," he said to the Fed. "If GOG is a government-sanctioned project and Givan was acting under orders when he attacked us in the woods, then isn't it possible that we're lining up against the government on this thing?''

"No. The government would never sanction the killing of innocents like this."

"We're talking degrees, Hal. Governments sanction all sorts of unsavory—"

"No! If I believed for one minute that the government I've devoted my life to was behind these killings, I'd commit suicide."

"Hal—"

"I mean it, Striker. Sure, strange things go on. Running a country and conducting worldwide foreign policy leads us down a lot of pretty unbelievable avenues, but this is nothing more than cold-blooded murder for selfish gain. Someone in the government may be behind it, but not as a policy-implementing arm of our republic. We're bedrock in a world of quicksand, my friend. Believe that, and trust me."

"Then, what the hell's going on?"

"I've got a theory," Brognola replied. "But it's too...frightening to say out loud yet."

"I feel like we're playing chicken with a steamroller."

The head Fed chuckled softly. "Just as usual, Striker. Getting soft in your old age?"

"No. Maybe just worrying about someone besides myself for a change. What are you doing with the weekend?"

"I'll be in here every day, trying to work this thing out."

"I'll keep in touch," Bolan said. "Take care, Hal."

"You too, big guy. Believe what I told you."

"Sure."

When Brognola clicked off, Bolan turned full in his seat to watch the van across the street. It had yet to disgorge any passengers. Suspicious under any circumstances, it was downright incriminating given the present state of affairs.

"Can we go in now?" Julie asked, looking at him across a span of darkness. "I've burned all my fingers."

"I think we're being watched," he said.

She turned to look at the van. "By whom?"

"That's the question, isn't it?" Bolan returned, noting the fear in her eyes. "Come on, let's go in the house."

They got out of the car and entered the house through the side door. Not being absolutely convinced of Julie's loyalty, he'd been reluctant to give her the notebook. But it was a chance he had to take. There was no one else around who could interpret it for him.

They walked into the living room, all the lights still off. They could see out to the street, but couldn't be seen from it. The blinds were open. The van was still there, ominously quiet.

"What are we going to do?"

Bolan tightened his lips. "I'm tired of sitting around and waiting for things to happen. I think it's time to stir up the mix a little bit."

He walked to the switch and turned on the bright overhead light, making them highly visible from the outside. "Come here," he said, taking her by the arm and drawing her close to him in the center of the room. "Kiss me like you mean it."

"Wha..."

He pulled her tightly against him. At first she stood stiff, rigid in his arms. He tilted her head up and he found her lips with his, kissing her deeply.

There was a second's hesitation, a fear almost, then she suddenly relaxed, giving herself fully to the kiss, molding her body to his as he felt himself grow hard against her. She was all softness and gentle perfume.

He forced himself away from her, their eyes still locked tight, and for just a second all the doubts and suspicions vanished. They were two lovers giving and taking equally, sharing as one. He wished with all his being that they were anywhere in this world than where they were right then.

"Take my shirt off," he whispered, surprised at the hoarseness in his voice. "I want them to think we're going to be occupied."

"Mack..." She slowly unbuttoned the shirt as he let his hands roam freely over her body. "I need... I need..."

He kissed her again, his resolve nearly evaporating as she ran her palms gently across his muscled chest, then moved up to his shoulders to slide his shirt off.

He gathered her in his arms and held tightly. "Let's move back to the bedroom," he whispered in her ear.

"Oh, yes," she agreed, her breath coming in short gasps.

They broke the embrace and walked, arm in arm, out of the living room to her bedroom, which faced the front. He took a deep breath and forced himself to reality.

"Okay," he said, pulling away from her, "turn on the light. I think I can sneak up on them now."

"You mean..." she began, her face lost in perplexity. "That we're... we're not..."

"Turn on the light," he repeated, then went to his room to get the combat harness that hung on a chair.

He slipped on the harness, then covered it with a light jacket. He hurried back to Julie's room and poked his head in the door. She was sitting on the bed with her arms folded across her chest, face angry.

"I'm going out the back window. Hide in the closet in case they try for the room."

"I'm not hiding in any closet," she said, face set hard.

"All right."

He withdrew the .44 from its holster and tossed it onto the bed. "Then at least hold on to this."

She stared at the gun as if it were a dead cat, and he felt a sadness well up inside of him.

"Julie, I..."

"Go on," she said, her eyes still fixed on the automatic.

He walked quickly to his bedroom window and climbed out, hurrying through the backyard to the yard next door.

Bolan stopped at the front corner of the house next door, peered cautiously around and saw that the van was still parked in front of his house.

This was no place for gunplay, a residential neighborhood full of children, but Bolan wasn't about to let this opportunity slip away without making some points.

Staying in the deepening shadows of a tall hedge, he quickly traversed the lawn, then crossed the street. He turned in the direction of the van and approached it rapidly from behind. The van bore South Carolina tags.

The warrior slid the Beretta out of its holster, leaving the safety on. He reached out and wrapped a fist around the back door handle, his thumb gently depressing the catch release. It was unlocked. With a hand still on the latch, he put his right foot on the back bumper, prepared to throw open the door and follow it in.

He was a half second from springing into action, when Julie suddenly turned on the front porch light and threw open the screen door, which banged against the house.

The driver responded by throwing the van into gear and jamming his foot on the gas. The van leaped forward, and Bolan fell backward onto the street, landing awkwardly because he hadn't been prepared for the fall.

The van disappeared quickly, taillights winking as it squealed around a corner.

Julie ran across the street. "Mack..."

"Why did you do that?" he demanded, rising painfully to his feet. "You could have gotten me killed!"

"I was...worried about you," she stammered, staring at the ground. "I'm sorry. I—I guess I wasn't thinking."

He reholstered the Beretta. "I only hope it's because you weren't thinking," he said darkly, unable to keep the anger out of his voice.

"I said I was sorry!" she yelled, and, turning, stomped off.

Bolan watched her retreating back. What a fool he was to have trusted her.

HAL BROGNOLA HUNG UP the phone and leaned back in his desk chair. He took Bolan's nightly phone calls with a sense of relief that he and Julie Arnold had survived another day. This business was a lot stickier than it should have been, mainly due to the fact that this time their quarry was also hunting them—and they had absolutely no idea of who it was. But one thing he was sure of: whoever was behind the killings was camouflaging himself with the trappings of the United States government. The real problem was going to be isolating that camouflage and cutting it out without hurting the government as a whole.

He reached into the pocket of his sport jacket and pulled out a cigar, slowly unwrapping it from crinkling cellophane as he thought about the *Challenger* flight, of the seven people who died a horrible, screaming death, as their cabin plummeted to its fatal rendezvous with the sea. He stuck the cigar in his mouth and thought about lighting it. Surely even Helen wouldn't begrudge him a smoke at a time like this. But he left the lighter in his pocket, instead honoring his commitment to give it up.

No, he could never believe that the government could be capable of that cold-blooded murdering of its own citizens. There had to be another explanation. Unfortunately the other explanation had to be just as bad. His research on Project GOG had led to a number of dead ends, all pointing to the notion that a secret organization existed within the command structure of the United States that was making its own sort of policy decisions running contrary to the stated policies of the government and the country as a whole.

Why? Toward what end did this mechanism operate?

Brognola took the cigar out of his mouth, rolling it between thumb and index finger. It wouldn't do to speculate this soon on the possibilities; he had to keep his head clear and his options open right now, lest he jump to the wrong conclusions. He was going to have to build a solid groundwork of evidence before he could justify any action.

He looked at his watch. It was late, already dark outside. Everybody but the lawyers down the hall had already gone home. Lawyers never went home. It was part of their makeup. He thought about it, then considered how empty his home was going to be without Helen. Instead, he juiced his computer terminal and phone modem, then started working his way into the vendor files to start getting addresses and information on the private companies who paid the government to carry their materials into space.

Access to these files was relatively easy, well within the security authorization codes on his list. He phoned the proper computer net, and accessed his way into the records. Then he reached into the long drawer in front of his desk for the manifest. It wasn't there.

He sat staring at the open drawer for a minute, then remembered giving the manifest to Marie to make a photocopy. Leaving the connection to records open, he got up and walked out of his office.

The large outer room was in darkness, some light spilling from his office across Marie's niche just outside his door. A light glowed solid on the push-button unit at the bottom of her phone, denoting the open connection he had left with the records computer in his office.

He tried the drawer; it was locked. He took the keys from his pocket and used the smallest one on the desk lock, which sprung with an audible click.

He pulled open the drawer, finding the manifest right on top. He removed it, then began to shut the drawer, stopping only when it was almost completely closed. A light, a faint red glow, seemed to emanate from within the drawer. He barely noticed it, and wouldn't have if the lights in the room had been on.

Brognola slid the drawer open again, kneeling to get at eye level. There was an unmistakable haze coming from the drawer.

Cautiously he reached inside, feeling around in the back behind the paper clips and the staple machines until his hand came upon something square and metallic, no bigger than a package of cigarettes.

He pulled it out, a small red running light glowing on top. It was a tape recorder, and it was recording on a cassette no larger than a postage stamp.

He stared at it dumbly for nearly a half minute, not wanting to make the connection that was begging to be made. Marie had been his secretary for nearly five years. She not only kept his appointments straight, talked him down when he was angry and got his reports filed on time whether he was finished with them or not, but she also helped him choose anniversary presents and provided an incredible array of friendly services that went far beyond ordinary secretarial work. To make the connection that the tape recorder forced him to make was to admit that someone close to him was a deadly enemy and that his trust and friendship had been completely misplaced.

The small machine sat glowing in his hand. He looked at it, then at the light on her telephone. He set the tape recorder on her desk and walked back into his own office, hung up the phone and broke his modem connection. Then he walked back into the larger room. The light was out on the tape deck. The damned thing was attuned to his phone line. Every call was recorded. A secured line was useless when its extension was bugged.

He took the cigar out of his mouth and spit out a piece of leaf. He opened the tape recorder and ejected the small tape into his hand, replacing the unit in Marie's desk.

This at least explained a part of the problem. There was a leak in his office, all right, maybe more than one. But this one hurt bad. Marie had an eight-year-old son with spina bifida, a real weight for a divorced woman to carry. He'd always wondered how she was able to afford the proper medical care the boy needed. Now he knew.

He had a friend in Enforcement named Greggson, whom he trusted implicitly. Now that he had someplace to start, it was time to bring a select group into the scenario. They could begin with a search warrant on Marie Price. Greg would have gone home for the weekend by now. He'd have to get him there, and he'd rather not do it by telephone at this point.

He went back into his office and gathered some paperwork to take home with him. Given the passwords, he could do the legwork on the matériel manifest from his computer at the house, though it was time to get a technician out from Greg's office to check the integrity of his lines at home, too. At this point nothing could be taken for granted.

Cigar planted firmly between his teeth, he walked out of his office and through the nearly deserted corridors of Justice to take the elevator to the underground parking garage. He'd go home and grab a bite to eat before finding his way to Greggson's house. Once they sat down together, he figured it would be many hours before they stood up again. Greg would take a lot of convincing.

He got off the elevator at the third level underground. The parking garage was dark, cold concrete, cut by the fuzzy glow of irregularly spaced fluorescent lights. He moved across the quiet landscape rapidly, his senses honed keen on the whetstone of the current trouble.

The big Buick was waiting for him in its assigned place. He unlocked the door and climbed in, putting the key in the ignition. But something stopped him from turning it.

He sat for a moment, wondering what was wrong. The car looked the same, felt the same, but something was off base. He berated himself for his foolishness, his hand going to the key again, stopping again.

Something was— He stared out through the windshield. Something about the hood...

That was it! Last year when Eileen had been home from college, she had been involved in a small fender bender that had bent the frame just enough so that the hood wouldn't close all the way unless it was pushed in just right.

The hood wasn't sitting level now, even though he never drove it that way for fear of its popping open at high speed.

Rigid with tension, he pulled the hood release and stepped out of the car. He moved to the front, eyes scanning the still-deserted garage.

The second latch slid easily, the hood wobbling to the open position, the small light within coming on. He peered inside. It wasn't difficult to find. A small blob of C-4 plastique explosive was stuck on the block, just next to the starter, the detonation caps poking out of the gray mass, trailing wires to the starter.

Hands shaking, Brognola backed away from the car. This was the first bomb, the obvious one. There would probably be another, either in the tail pipe or hooked into the brake system. This was a job for the bomb squad.

He moved slowly away from the car, watching it. Things were beginning to unravel faster than he could have imagined. To make this obvious attempt on his life meant that his adversaries were either in a tremendous hurry or immune to retribution.

Both observations chilled him to the bone. He turned and ran from the garage.

Chapter Eleven

Bolan walked back into the living room with his fifth cup of coffee. He'd been up all night, to no avail, and now was having to keep himself awake with caffeine.

He moved to the low coffee table, its surface covered with papers, and folded himself up painfully to sit on the floor in front of it. His knee still hurt from where he'd fallen out of the back of the van the night before, a constant, nagging reminder of Julie Arnold's vacillating loyalties.

The woman wasn't here now. After the previous evening's experience, he'd taken her to a motel for the night, then he stayed at the house, a target, waiting for the return of the men in the van.

It was a wasted night. Neither the van, nor anything else for that matter, came down Avondale Drive all night long. It was the quietest neighborhood he'd ever seen. The closest thing to excitement was the newsboy throwing papers around five in the morning.

And now he sat before the clues he'd found in his office at Grolier, trying to stay awake long enough to make head or tail out of them.

He took another sip of coffee and rearranged the papers in front of him. The house seemed strangely empty without Julie in it, which was odd since they didn't get along together.

He had replayed the events of last night a hundred times in his head, trying to get a handle on her actions. But just like everything else that had happened in the previous week, the truth of the matter simply eluded him. He was a cat chasing his own tail, satisfaction always just out of reach.

He picked up the paper in front of him, which contained the code Jerry Butler had used. It seemed to be a position code that used abstract symbols from a recurring pattern of symbols to represent letters of the alphabet. He had tried and discarded several different positioning possibilities, but it still seemed to him that he'd be able to get it without too much trouble. And that was the part that made no sense. If Butler was going to use a code, why one that could be easily cracked?

He heard an engine roar in the driveway, and glanced out the open window to see the Jeep rolling to a stop. Julie climbed out, arms loaded with packages.

Bolan grimaced in pain as he stood once again on the sore knee and limped over to the door.

"Well, I see you're still in one piece," Julie said, breezing past him.

"And I see you've been busy."

She turned, smiling at him. "I've been shopping. I woke up this morning asking myself why we shouldn't spend a little of that cash your friend, Hal, gave us, since we're risking our lives and all."

"Why not?"

"Go out to the car and make yourself useful," she said. "There are other things to bring in."

Bolan moved outside and saw little Mel from next door riding up and down Avondale on his too-big bike.

"Hi, Dr. Sparks," he called, waving and almost losing his balance.

Bolan waved back. "Hiya, Mel."

He looked into the rear of the Jeep. A television set, still in the packing crate was there, as well as a boxed-up computer. He opened the door and took out the TV, carried it into the house, then went back for the other box.

Julie was standing in the living room when he returned with the computer. She was wearing a new sundress, with the tags still on.

"How do you like it?" she asked, turning in a circle.

He smiled, unable to stay angry with her. "It suits you," he said, and meant it. The dress molded her gentle curves nicely, yet gave the impression of comfort and ease of movement. She had also fixed her hair in a French braid, and he could imagine what she must have looked like as a college student ten years before when Harry Arnold had asked her to marry him.

"Where do you want this?" he asked, holding the box out in front of him.

"Anywhere for now," she replied with a casual wave of the hand. "We'll decide later. I figure to transcribe on the computer, using the TV as a monitor."

"I don't think it's wise for us to stay here," he said.

She stared at him quizzically. "Why? Did something else happen last night?"

"No." He put the computer on the floor next to the television. "But we're hardly living here in secret anymore."

"You don't know who that was last night," she said. "It could have been the killers, or your people, or the institute, or two lovers looking for a quiet street, or drug dealers making a buy, or—"

"All right," he interrupted, putting up a hand. "You sure you'll feel safe here while I'm at the institute?"

"I'll be fine," she assured him, then stared down at the tags on her dress. "Could you pull these off? That's the trouble with setting up housekeeping...we don't have scissors yet."

She moved up right beside him, and he bent to the first tag. It was on the side panel of the low-cut dress, along her rib cage. With a hand on her side he jerked the tag off with his other hand, the contact with her body electric.

She slapped his hand hard and glared at him. "Not after last night, Dr. Sparks," she nearly hissed, then moved away from him.

He straightened abruptly, but before he could say anything, she turned to the package-laden chair and pulled out a small white paper bag.

"I'll bet you haven't eaten anything today," she said.

"Well...no," he admitted, off guard.

She held the bag out to him. "Here. Got one of those breakfast things at a fast-food restaurant. It'll make that coffee a little tamer if you eat something with it."

He took the bag and sat on the sofa. "Thanks." He was totally confused, unable to figure out what was going on in this woman's mind. She was the most frustrating person he'd ever known, jumping from one feeling to the next like a bee flitting from flower to flower, always changing, always keeping him off balance.

He opened the bag, removing the Styrofoam package that held the English muffin and poached egg. She'd meant well with the breakfast. At least he thought she meant well.

"Where's Jerry's notebook?" she asked.

He leaned over the coffee table and shuffled the papers until he found it.

"You going to start transcribing today?" he asked as he handed it to her.

She shook her head. "I'm going to spend the rest of today committing this to memory so I can transcribe tomorrow from my own head. It'll be easier. I don't know why you didn't give this to me last night. I could have been studying it at the motel."

"Whoever has this book is in danger. I didn't want you to have the responsibility unless I was nearby."

They shared a look, both of them knowing he was lying. The simple fact of the matter was that Bolan wasn't about to let the notebook out of his sight, in case something happened to it.

"You know," she said, "with all this information inside my head, I'm in danger, too."

"You're in danger anyway," he replied, taking a bite of the egg sandwich. "If you can transcribe this information fast enough, though, maybe it will be over soon."

"One way or the other," she said, frowning, and wandered out of the room with the book.

He watched the empty doorway for a moment, feeling at a loss because she always was able to so easily tie him up in knots.

Taking a breath, he slid painfully back to the floor and pulled the coffee table up close. He picked up the paper he'd found in Butler's lab table and looked at it again. From the grave, Jerry Butler was speaking to him through a series of predictable symbols. He stared at the writing, then sorted through the various unsuccessful attempts he had made at cracking the code, all using variations of geometric designs in which to fit letters in some sort of coherent, recurring style.

Bolan was sure of the type of code, and it was simply a matter of rote work, running through the possibilities until he hit on the right one.

As he idly drew on the paper, Bolan tried to understand the mind of the man who had made the code. Intelligent and motivated, Jerry Butler had perceived trouble, undoubtedly of a military nature, while working at the institute. He then began trying to ferret out the trouble, meanwhile hiding his research and his detective work from what he felt were prying eyes. Apparently discovering something, Butler left the institute in a hurry, not even stopping to take his discoveries with him. Or perhaps he left copies behind intentionally, hoping someone like Bolan would come looking. One thing that made sense was the thought that Butler had already lost his discovery or he would never have left the notebook behind. Given the chance, he was sure the scientist would have destroyed the notebook rather than let it fall into what he considered to be the wrong hands. That fact was important when tied to the space shuttle. Something had apparently been shipped on the *Challenger* that was tied to Butler's research—and both Butler and the shuttle were destroyed to protect that secret. But what?

Bolan drew two parallel lines on the paper, then connected them with a line drawn at right angles to the parallel. He drew another line, parallel to the connecting line. What he was left with was a design of nine spaces that looked like a ticktacktoe board. That could handle nine of twenty-six letters of the alphabet. If he put dots within the framework, he could get nine more letters.

He picked up the scratch paper and studied it for a moment, the entire code falling into place. Then he drew variations on his piece of paper.

He worked furiously then, noting the symbols and translating them on the key he had made. Within two minutes he had come up with three separate groups of words as spelled out in the coded message:

twisted lizard
waterfront legend sea specs
seasonal gift of god

He read the words, read them again as he got back up on the couch. No wonder Butler had used such an easy code to hide his findings—it had simply been an access code to another code, a far more intricate and difficult one. And Bolan had absolutely no idea of how to crack this one.

And so the mystery deepened, leaving Bolan right back where he had started, which was exactly nowhere.

THE RAIN MATCHED Brognola's mood. He sat parked in front of the Georgetown condo watching a gray sky that came almost all the way down to the wet gray pavement. The condos were Victorian in style, large and ostentatious; red brick and oversize eaves were reflected in the puddles that slicked the roads and sidewalks of the fashionable neighborhood that Marie Price could never afford on a government salary.

Brognola chewed nervously on his cigar and checked his watch again, just as he'd been doing every minute for the past half hour.

It was nearly eleven in the morning. Greg should have been there an hour ago.

The house had been quiet since he'd shown up, as quiet as a dormant volcano. He was angry at the woman he'd placed so much trust in, and was angrier still that the result of that trust had so nearly been fatal. Whatever the source of the disease that seemed to be infecting the government, its symptoms went deep, even showing up in the halls of the Justice Department. He felt like a surgeon getting ready to operate on a cancer, hoping all the while that the ultimate prognosis would be favorable.

He heard sounds on the street, checking the rearview to find a gray Mercedes drawing to a stop behind him. Another car, a red Trans Am, pulled up on the other side of the street, right in front of the condo.

He got out of the car; Gunnar Greggson, smiling wide, stepped out of his car dragging a big, black umbrella with him.

The men shook hands. "Sorry I took so long," Greggson said. "You can't imagine what it's like hunting down a judge on a Saturday morning for a search warrant. Care to share my dry space?"

"You're here," Brognola said, waving off the umbrella. "That's all that matters."

The Trans Am opened up, disgorging two men dressed in blue jeans and light rain jackets. The men looked at the house, then drifted across the street to where Greggson and Brognola waited. Both men were young, and both still looked half-asleep. "That the place?" the blond agent asked, indicating the condo with a nod of his head.

"Yeah."

"Quite a spread on a secretary's pay." Greggson gestured to the men. "These are our agents, Ted Healy and Oscar Largent. Both of them were nice enough to give up part of their day off for us."

"I appreciate it," Brognola said, shaking hands. "This shouldn't take too long."

Oscar Largent started to walk down the street. "I'll take the back door."

"You won't have any backup," Ted Healy called to him. "Don't take any chances."

Largent gave him the thumbs-up gesture and kept walking, disappearing around the corner within a minute.

"We'll give him another minute to get positioned," Healy decided, and looked at his watch.

"Did you get the bombs from my car all right?" Brognola asked.

"Yeah," Greggson said. "They were delivered to my house last night." He laughed. "My wife made me keep them in the garage."

"I don't blame her," Brognola replied, then shook his head. "I hope you know you're sticking your neck right out with me now."

"That's my job, isn't it?" Greggson said, his eyes meeting and holding Brognola's. "Don't congratulate me for doing the right thing."

"That's why I came to you, Greg."

"Let's move in," Healy said. He dug into an inner pocket and pulled out the warrant, plus his identification. "Are you sure she's in there?"

"I can't be sure of anything," Brognola growled. "I drove past her parking space in the back alley, and a car with a Justice Department parking sticker was in her slot."

"Close enough." Healy walked across the street and along the bricked pathway leading to Price's front door, Brognola and Greggson right behind.

They reached the door, a large, heavy-looking piece of maple, and Healy rang the bell without hesitation. There was no answer. He rang again, then turned to stare at Greggson when no one answered.

Greggson nodded. Healy turned to bang on the door with his fist. "Open up!" he called loudly. "Federal agents!"

Still no one answered. "Open up!" Healy called again. "We have a warrant and will facilitate entry on our own!"

When nothing stirred within the house, Greggson looked at Brognola. "It's your show, buddy. What do we do now?"

"We get inside any way we can. Do we have the authorization for that?"

Greggson smiled slowly, his lawyer's face settling into the kind of satisfied expression usually reserved for winning a case. He shrugged. "We have the authorization for anything you want to do. Or we can get it later."

"We'll never get through that door," Healy said.

"Then let's try a window," Brognola suggested. "At worst, we'll replace a little glass."

A large, potted geranium sat on the porch near the door. Healy bent and picked it up, then walked through the housefront shrubs to the den window.

"Here we go." He threw the plant against the window. The sounds of shattering glass drew the neighbors to their front doors.

Healy followed the plant through the window, his service revolver drawn and in his hand. Within seconds, he had unlocked and opened the door for Greggson and Brognola.

They walked into the place, Brognola finding himself faced with a life-style he wasn't sure *he* would be able to afford. They were standing in an entrance foyer, living area to the left, dining to the right, a long staircase in front of him. Healy ran to the back of the house to let his partner in.

"This feels bad," Greggson said. "I'm afraid—"

"You, too?" Brognola cupped his hands to his mouth. "Marie! Dammit, it's Hal. Where are you?" He turned to Greggson. "I'm going upstairs."

When he walked into the master bedroom, his mind was inexplicably struck by the study in contrasts the place presented. The room was all frilly pinks and stuffed animals, the kind of place a teenaged girl might live in. Travel posters filled the walls, and a sheer pink scarf hanging over the nightstand light cast a melancholy haze over the room. There was no place in this room for the image of stark reds and blacks that defined the heap that lay in the center of the bed.

He walked over to the woman, anger dissipating to pity as he gazed at her. Her naked body had been stabbed and slashed repeatedly, mutilated almost beyond recognition—the price of detection high in Project GOG.

Greggson had approached the bed, and Brognola could see that the man could only look at the remains of Marie Price out of the corner of his eye. "They play hardball, your friends," Greggson said, and Brognola could hear the shakiness in the man's voice.

The Fed retrieved a robe and carried it back to the bed. He could hear Largent and Healy moving through the rest of the house. "Still think you don't need to be thanked for doing the right thing?" he asked, as he covered the body with the robe.

"I think we'd better be extremely careful." A moan escaped the man's throat, and he ran from the room, a hand to his mouth. Brognola almost wished that he could throw up. Unfortunately, for him, the pain was far deeper than what could be brought easily out of his stomach.

The two agents entered the room, Largent walking to the body and peering silently under the robe. He dropped it back in place and glanced at Brognola. "There's a dead kid in the next room," he announced, and another emotional blow slapped Brognola.

"I think the house has been rifled," Healy said, "but they tried to make it look like it hadn't been."

"Yeah." Brognola looked around the room. "I think all this was staged for our benefit so the police will investigate it as a rape, murder and robbery. I want you guys to poke around...."

"Should we call the D.C. cops?"

"Later," Brognola said. "You look around first. I want bankbooks, ledgers, photographs, diaries...anything that might be useful. I'll bet that she had a boyfriend with DOD. Find what you can find and do it fast."

As they hurried from the room, Greggson appeared at the doorway, his face as pale as milk. He leaned against the frame, unable to look at the body. "I think I'd better send my wife away for a while."

Brognola nodded. "We're up to our armpits in this. Whoever did this is covering tracks in a massive way, and they won't stop at either of us. Can we get anything useful out of all this?"

"Bank records will help," Greggson said. "At least we'll know where she's getting her money. There may be useful prints...a lot depends on what we're actually looking for."

Brognola grunted and started out of the room, but Greggson grabbed his arm. "What exactly are we looking for? What the hell's going on here?"

Brognola shrugged the man's hand off his arm. "It's too early to say, I—"

"Tell me!" Greggson demanded, his eyes locking with Brognola's.

"I think that someone is getting ready to try to take control of the government."

Chapter Twelve

Bolan ran the electric razor over his face, its whine the sound of hornets as he watched the employment and life-style records of Margaret Ackerman scroll leisurely across the CRT screen in tiny green letters. He'd been studying her, just as he'd been studying everyone at the institute, since six that morning, and of all the interesting tidbits that he had picked up on his co-workers, the file on Ackerman was the most interesting.

He shut off the razor and put it back in his desk drawer. There was something about Margaret Ackerman that didn't add up.

On the others, there had been enlightening material. Howard Davis, for example, had been a tortured genius from childhood. At first judged as retarded, he was put into a state institution until a curious social worker discovered quite by accident the status of his mind when he picked up her guitar at age eight and played it beautifully without ever having touched one before. At that point he was thrust, unprepared, into the mainstream. Skipping most of grade school, he was advanced to high school, from which he graduated with honors at age twelve. He had graduated college at fifteen and had somehow managed a doctorate in marine biology by age seventeen, at which time he went to work at Grolier. No wonder the kid was difficult: He'd never been socialized in any respect.

Robbie Hampton, on the other hand, had followed a predictable and steady route his whole life. Among his honors were included almost every imaginable grade school, high school and college award. He hadn't been just a writer after that, but the author of three bestselling novels in the 1950s. He'd also done diplomatic duty in South Africa during the Kennedy and Johnson administrations. He'd been at the institute for nearly twenty years, far longer than any of its other denizens.

As a young man Ike Silver had joined the Communist party briefly in the 1940s, rejecting it within months. But it wasn't enough to save him during the McCarthy-era witch hunts in the early fifties. He lost an important physics chair at MIT and found himself blacklisted for several, hungry years. Perhaps that experience had something to do with the man's hatred for things human and his longing for the peace of the stars.

As Bolan studied his co-workers, the thing that struck him the most was that they defied easy definition. The surface wasn't enough to see the man. They were complex human beings with priorities that would probably never be known outside of their own minds. It made his job of ferreting out a traitor, if any, that much more difficult.

Ackerman's file, however, would raise the suspicions of anyone looking through it with barely more than a casual eye. Her track record in biochemical research had been less than stellar. She graduated from USC with a B.S. in chemistry in the early sixties and had been 304th in her class. She went from there to a variety of jobs well outside of her field, taking another ten years on and off to acquire her Ph.D. Then she struggled through assistant professorships at various small colleges, finally landing a full professor's job at Bowling Green University in 1978. The record showed her teaching at Bowling Green for two years, at which time she quite suddenly was offered the position of head of the biochemistry department at prestigious Boston College, which she held until she came to Grolier mere weeks after the disappearance of Jerry Butler.

He wondered how she got the offer from Boston College with her small experience and slender record, and he wondered why someone wielding such a key administrative job would chuck it to return to pure research. It wasn't the way the careers had gone for the other researchers, each of whom had exhibited a total addiction and devotion to his field of study to the exclusion of everything else.

It was all confusing, just like Jerry Butler's second set of code words. Bolan had spent the rest of Saturday and all of Sunday trying to make a dent in that code without success. Meanwhile, in Washington, Brognola had been in danger as he searched for the truth. One thing the Fed had said in their Saturday conversation that made sense to Bolan was the notion that something was going to happen soon. With the attempts on Brognola's life and the killing of Marie Price, it seemed obvious that the enemy was drawing in bold strokes, bold enough that the reasons behind the attacks could be uncovered before very long. Apparently the opposition wasn't worried about anyone drawing conclusions and tracking them down. Something, in other words, was almost ready to happen. But what? And when?

He looked at the screen again, knowing that he was going to have to move faster and push harder if he was to learn anything. That thought in mind, he picked up the telephone and dialed Robbie's extension. He didn't trust any of his co-workers completely, but he trusted Robbie more than most and decided to use the man to provide some vital data.

The man answered after the third ring. "It's your dime," he said, voice light.

"Robbie...David Sparks."

"Good morning, David. You're at work bright and early this morning."

"You ought to know. Your car was here when I got in today."

"Never made it home last night is why. Yuri had me up half the night working on harvesting techniques for his new food."

"You doing anything special right now?" Bolan asked.

"Yeah," the man answered. "Trying to put enough coffee in myself to stay awake through the day."

Bolan laughed. "Why don't you bring that coffeepot in here for a few minutes and I'll see if I can help you stay awake. I left the door ajar."

"Sounds good. I've got a couple of books to put away, then I'll be right there."

"See you," Bolan said, holding the receiver in his hand and cutting off the connection with an index finger. He hated to depend on Julie for anything, but he needed her feedback on Ackerman's record. He raised his finger and dialed an outside line, then home.

The phone rang seven times before Julie answered. "What's wrong?" he said, when she finally picked up the receiver.

"I was busy. I knew it was either you or a wrong number, so I got it when I could. What's up?"

He calmed himself for a moment, angry that she'd keep him on the hook when she knew how precarious and volatile their situation was.

"Any problems?"

"Of course not. Everything's fine. I've been transcribing Jerry's notes."

"How's it going?"

"Are you kidding? This is the real McCoy, Dr. Sparks. When this gets out it will change the way we live. Just imagine an airplane that doesn't need to carry thousands of gallons of flammable fuel, or a rocket whose engines run off a pint of water with absolutely no danger of explosions or complications."

"Yeah," Bolan said. "But think about all the gas stations it will put out of business."

"Gas stations don't make money on their gas anyway," she returned. "You'll still need tires and tune-ups."

"You've researched all this."

"For years."

"Let me ask you something that has nothing to do with what you're working on," he said, reaching out a hand to scroll to the information he needed. "Listen to this...."

Bolan proceeded to read Ackerman's employment record, Julie squealing slightly when he read the part about Boston College. "What do you think?" he asked when he had finished. "Pretty odd?"

"It's worse than odd, roommate," she said. "It's a downright lie. I was involved with the university community for over ten years through my association with Penn State and got to know a great many people. Donovan Phelps was a great friend of Harry's and he's headed BC's bi-chem department for at least fifteen years. Maybe more. He's an institution up there. Has been. Still is."

"Then Peg Ackerman couldn't have worked there?"

"She could have worked there," Julie amended, "that's possible. But she never headed the department—ever."

"Ho!" Bolan heard a call from across the lab, and he looked up to see Robbie coming in, coffeepot and cup in hand.

"Well, thanks, Bernice," he said, waving Robbie over to the office. "This is all very interesting."

"You're welcome. Get the bad guys, okay?"

"Soon as I can tell them from the good guys," Bolan said. "Bye."

He hung up just as Robbie came into the room. He had stopped at one of the lab tables and had brought a stool with him because Bolan's office had only one chair.

"Well, neighbor," Robbie said, "how are our mice today?"

"Still associated." Bolan reached out and dimmed his computer screen. "I've found, though, that if I subject my compound to heat before spraying it, more of the reactant material gets into the bloodstream. Unfortunately, that counteracts some of the effect of the atropine."

Robbie nodded, as he situated his stool and poured Bolan a cup of coffee. "I thought I noticed one less mouse when I came in."

"Yeah. Brunhilde was my first casualty."

Robbie handed Bolan his coffee. "She gave her life in the cause of science," he said, smiling. "Better the mouse than a human subject. You know, I've been thinking about your peace bomb, and it seems to me that a better use for it than in a war would simply be as a domestic crowd-control device. Say, you've got a riot on your hands—racial, students, whatever—how much better to simply put the little darlings into, what's your word...disassociation, than to beat them up or teargas them or arrest them. You simply blanket the area with gas, put them out of commission for an hour or so, then let them pick themselves up and go home on shaky legs, sadder but wiser. No Geneva Convention to worry about, no wrongful death suits or police brutality. Just polite, passive restraint. In other words, maybe this needs to be taken out of the hands of the military completely."

Bolan opened his arms wide. "You've got me convinced. Now just convince the Air Force of that."

"Not impossible. Stranger things have happened."

"On that subject," Bolan said, taking his opening, "I've never worked for the government before. How, exactly, do they go about checking our research? Do they trust us to fill them in, or what?"

"What brings this up?" Robbie asked, narrowing his gaze.

"I've been thinking about your friend, Jerry Butler," Bolan said, and took a sip of the coffee. "You said that he made a breakthrough, but perhaps wanted to keep it away from the Air Force. Could he really do that?"

"A touchy subject," Robbie said, his jovial face straining to a less dignified expression. "We all like to believe that our experiments will lead to world improvement and not add to the fund of destructive possibilities. Jerry, for example, accepted this post because he believed the Air Force was developing a new jet engine to run on liquid electricity, and that it would benefit the whole world to the tune of hundreds if not thousands of lives a year."

"He believed?"

Robbie put up a hand. "Let me finish the thought. Jerry never confided in me, but I had to think, given his dovishness, that he found something that changed his mind about their intentions. How else to explain his actions? But anyway, back to the point. We all like to believe that we're doing good, yet, ultimately, where's the good of any discovery? Einstein thought about the humanitarian possibilities of unlimited energy when he came up with the theory of relativity at age twenty-six; yet it was Einstein himself who urged Roosevelt to mobilize the U.S. to produce the atomic bomb. The yin and the yang. Everything has a good and a bad side. It's unfortunate that Jerry didn't understand that fact."

"You still haven't answered my question."

"In a sense I have," Robbie replied, getting off the stool to look through the plate-glass window into the lab. "I think all of us need to understand the fact that change has no morality, that change is *beyond* morality. Jerry would probably still be alive if he had understood that fact."

"Are you saying that the Air Force killed him?"

Robbie turned then, and fixed Bolan with sad eyes. "They don't trust us to fill out the proper reports and keep them current. They feel we're too independent to be trusted. I found a listening device in my office one time. I examined it, then put it back. It's still there. They may use spies, or hidden cameras. Hell, David, they *own* us—our brains *and* our morality. And how our discoveries are used is a lot more important to them than it is to us. They take the games seriously."

"Then how did Butler find out about them?"

Robbie shrugged, then turned back to stare out the window. "Maybe he found a listening device, or caught someone going through his stuff. Maybe he just became paranoid for no reason at all. It's all flexible, David. All plastic. Nothing's real. Everything is open to speculation."

The phone rang, startling both men. Bolan picked it up. "Sparks."

He was greeted by Howard Davis's hysterical voice. "Get in here, quick! Please hurry!"

"What . . ." Bolan began, but the boy had already hung up.

Bolan jumped to his feet and moved to the door.

"What is it?"

"Some kind of trouble in Howard's lab," Bolan explained, and hurried out, Robbie on his heels.

Howard's door banged open as the boy charged out of his lab and hall. "Thank God," he said, and grabbed Bolan by the arm, hurrying him inside.

"What's wrong?"

"Quickly . . . the tank," the boy said, his eyes wide in terror. "It's Morty."

They rushed to the tank, Bolan peering over the side as Howard climbed the stairs. One of the dolphins was dormant in the water, its body stiffened into a painful-looking S-shape, its head underwater.

"I think he's caught a virus," Howard said quickly. "If we don't get his head above water, he'll drown."

Bolan was already kicking off his shoes, his hands working at the buttons of his shirt. "Is there something you can do?" he asked, watching two other dolphins swimming languidly at the far end of the pool.

"While you hold him up, I'm going to try a massive injection of antibodies."

Bolan, stripped to his pants, hurried up the steps and jumped into the forty-foot-diameter pool, the water coral-reef warm.

"Talk to him," Howard urged as he prepared a large hypodermic needle. "He's a reasonable creature. Tell him what you're going to do."

Bolan looked at the beautiful grayish-blue mammal, its skin tone turning to a sickly off-white. He moved in close and saw the pitiful eyes of a creature desperately crying out for help. And he responded.

"Come on, Morty," he said gently, soothingly. "I don't want to hurt you. I only want to help."

The dolphin was the size of a small man and far more powerful looking. It chirped sadly as it strained unsuccessfully to get and keep its head above water.

"I just want to help you," Bolan repeated, and slid his arms under its belly, lifting gently, Morty allowing him free rein.

The dolphin was heavy, but the water's buoyancy helped, as Bolan twisted back slightly to get Morty's head up. He held the heavy animal close as it cried out softly to him.

"You got some muscles, Nam boy," Fred Haines said from behind him. He turned slightly to see Haines and Peg Ackerman standing side by side at the water's edge, the wall of the pool almost level with their heads.

"And some scars," Ackerman observed. "A couple even look like healed bullet wounds."

Ike Silver joined them. "It looks like our poison-gasser has got some feelings after all."

There was a splash as Howard jumped in. He carried the large syringe above his head as he waded over to Bolan.

"Good, Dr. Sparks," he said low. "Morty likes you . . . you're doing fine . . . fine."

Tears welled up in the boy's eyes as he stroked the suffering dolphin. "Oh baby," he cried, "I'm so sorry. This will hurt a little bit, but maybe we can help you."

He injected the dolphin near its dorsal fin, the creature crying loudly as the needle went in. The other dolphins in the tank became agitated, swimming faster.

The boy sobbed as he injected Morty, and Bolan saw an empathy in him that he would scarcely have thought possible from the sullen youth who had spray-painted the institute walls.

Howard removed the syringe and wrapped his arms around Morty's head, the dolphin chirping to him in its fear and its pain. The boy responded in equal measure with clicks and whistles of his own, and Bolan's own feelings about the closeness of a researcher to his work strengthened.

"Quite a take-charge guy," Haines said. "Maybe we should give him a medal."

"I didn't see you jumping in."

"Why should I when we've got a bona fide hero working here?" the man replied, smiling widely.

"Leave him alone." Howard looked up at Bolan with childlike trust in his eyes. "Do you think he'll be okay?" he added, referring to Morty.

"You're the expert, Howard, but he seems to have relaxed a bit already."

Howard smiled wanly and went back to stroking Morty and soothing him in dolphin language. Bolan could have sworn that the dolphin was listening and responding.

All at once, one of the other dolphins charged at them, dipping underwater to come up below Morty's tail, just scraping it with his dorsal fin. Morty jerked from reflex, nearly knocking Bolan down. He had barely regained his balance and got Morty back in his arms when the other dolphin charged them, doing the same thing.

Morty twitched wildly in Bolan's arms, and this time he did lose his balance, splashing backward and losing the dolphin.

He crested water and tried to retrieve Morty.

"Leave him!" Howard ordered, holding out his arms. "I think they're helping."

Bolan stood spellbound as the dolphins repeated their seeming attack on Morty. Each time they brushed the base of his tail with their dorsal fins, he jerked from reflex, bringing his head out of the water for breath. It was an amazing act of kindness and lifesaving prowess.

Howard had already climbed out of the water and rolled a large tripod with a video camera over to the water's edge, where he began to photograph the phenomenon.

Bolan hefted himself onto the lip of the pool, wondering whether, if three people found themselves in the same situation as the dolphins, two of them would be willing to spend all of their time trying to save the drowning one.

Life could be so simple if people would just allow it to be.

He eased over the side of the tank and stepped onto the floor, dripping water. Howard ran and grabbed a towel, which the soldier took gratefully, wrapping it around his shoulders to hide, too late, his warrior's body.

"I'll never forget this," Howard vowed.

"I just hope Morty's okay," Bolan replied, drying his hair with the towel.

"It's out of our hands now."

Bolan smiled at him. "You know, kid, you're all right." He held out his right hand. Howard, beaming, shook it; and if there was, indeed a list of suspects in Jerry Butler's demise, Bolan had just crossed the boy's name off the list. Great. That only left everybody else.

Bolan was beginning to get cold from the rush of the air-conditioning on his wet body. He needed to change pants and dry off completely.

He turned to Robbie, who was busy looking through the viewfinder of the camera. "Know where I can get some dry clothes?" he asked.

Robbie turned, smiling at him. "I've got clothes here if you think you can get into them."

"I'll give it a try. I'm going down to my office to dry off."

Robbie nodded, moving away from the tripod. "I'll see what I can scare up and bring it down to you."

"Great."

Bolan walked to the door, wondering what they would have done if the other dolphins hadn't helped. He might have stood in the pool all day. He walked into the hall and noticed that someone else must have thought the same thing.

Peg Ackerman was just leaving his office, closing the door behind her. Her mouth dropped open when she saw Bolan looking at her, then hardened to a tight slash. She set her face and walked resolutely up to him, trying to simply pass him.

He grabbed her arm. "Give me the key," he demanded.

"I don't know what you're—"

"Give me the key, Peg," he repeated, "or I'll search you right here."

Her eyes flashed hatred as she dug a key out of the pocket of her lab coat and thrust it into his hand.

"Now let me—" she began, trying to jerk her arm away, but Bolan tightened his grip.

"What were you doing in there?"

"Nothing."

"Tell me now, Peggy. Or you're not going to be very happy."

"I just wanted to see what you were doing," she said through clenched teeth. "I wanted to see...who you were."

"Where did you get the key?"

Her eyes met his, and if looks could kill, he would have been hanging on a meat hook somewhere. "They gave it to me when I started to work here. I never gave it back."

He stuck the key in his pocket and let her go. "Just focus on your own work and stay out of my lab."

"Just who the hell are you?" she rasped.

"Just who the hell are *you*?" he returned.

She turned on her heel and stomped away, never giving him a backward glance.

MARK REILLY DROVE the borrowed utility truck slowly past the house where Julie Arnold was living with the operative from Justice. The driveway was empty; Bolan was at the Grolier Foundation. Good. He drove another block and parked under an aging palm tree, taking a minute to check out the neighborhood before stepping from the truck.

General Leland had told him to take charge of the woman personally, and that's just what he intended to do. Opportunities to stand out didn't come along that often, and this was the perfect chance to show the general his ability and loyalty. The general had given him a chance despite his past record, and he intended to reward the man's trust. Historic changes were in the works, and Mark Reilly fully intended to be at the forefront and a part of those changes.

He zipped the red Florida Power and Light coveralls up to his neck, then strapped on the worn leather utility belt that officially made him a meter reader for the city of Orlando. He then moved off the street, angling up the closest driveway and into the backyard of an aqua-colored wood frame house. The meters were set at the back of the lots, and when he found one, he took a pad out of his utility belt and pretended to write on it.

His surveillance team had been nearly caught on their first night of stakeout, so he knew he'd have to take care of this himself. He had taken sick leave from the Company to make this trip for General Leland. Agency brass weren't especially happy with his abrupt departure, but in the course of a few days, their feelings wouldn't matter anyway.

He proceeded to the next house, coming ever closer to Julie Arnold's place. The woman had been waffling a bit on the phone, and he was just worried enough that he thought he'd speak with her in person. There wasn't a doubt in his mind that, once he contacted her, she would do what he wanted. He'd always had a way with women, but more important, he had faith in his ability to sell himself and his program. The keys were enthusiasm and positive thinking. Anything could be accomplished if one put his mind to it, which was precisely why he was so excited about what was going to happen in the days to come.

The deal with Julie Arnold was touchy, especially given her connection to Brognola at Justice. Even though time was short, it wouldn't be wise to take out too many people. And from studying the information in Bolan's file, Reilly knew the man wouldn't go down easily. If at all possible, they wanted Bolan out of the action, spinning his wheels at the institute. He was kept under constant surveillance there, and it was doubtful the man was going to discover anything. His boss, Brognola, was another matter again. He was pushing too hard and was going to have to be taken out, the consequences be damned.

Even so, Reilly had to keep Arnold in check and on his team. She was his ace in the hole, the stopper if Bolan should get out of control.

JULIE ARNOLD SAT at the computer keyboard, eyes closed, pulling information directly from her mentally visualized page of Jerry Butler's notebook and translating the equations into language a layman could understand. She saw it all, just like the page of a book, and simply scanned the detailed mental image, picking out the info she wanted to use.

It would only take her three or four days of concentrated effort to get the notes in a readable form. What would happen then, she couldn't imagine. Nothing made sense, nothing seemed...concrete anymore. Ever since Harry's death, she'd lived in a strange nightmare of conflicting beliefs and emotions, not knowing who to trust, or even what was real. At times Bolan seemed like her protector, at other times her adversary. But if he was her adversary, what could he possibly want from her?

The fact that she was attracted to him made things far worse. Other than her brief fling with Jerry Butler, she'd withered away for ten years in a loveless marriage that had been more like a business relationship, and she desperately needed emotional release. She feared that her emotional needs were clouding her reasoning processes—a mistake that could be deadly under the circumstances.

If only she knew what Bolan wanted...

There was a knock on the kitchen door, and she felt the cold hand of fear on her. She jumped up, her heart stuttering in her chest, and hurried to the front window. There were no cars in the drive, none on the street that didn't belong there. Maybe it was just a neighbor wanting to borrow something.

She walked cautiously toward the kitchen, the knock coming again. The kitchen door had a small, lace curtain covering its window. She tried not to make any noise as she moved aside the curtain to peer around its edge.

The meter reader was standing there in the carport, looking impatiently at his watch. If he was there to ask her where the meter was, she would look really foolish not having an answer for him.

She took a breath. The quicker she dealt with this man, the quicker he would be gone. He was lifting his hand to knock again when she pulled the door open.

"Can I help you?" she asked.

He smiled at her through even white teeth. "I'm looking for Lady Madonna," he said, and, ignoring her startled expression brushed past her and into the house.

She followed him through the kitchen and into the living room, where he stood gazing around, a look of distaste on his face. "What a dump," he muttered, unzipping his coveralls to expose the three-piece suit beneath.

"Do I know you?" she asked tentatively.

He gave her an easy smile. "We've spoken on the phone many times. My name is Reilly. I'm your Company contact."

"I don't mean to be rude, but do you have some kind of identification?"

"Sure," he said, and stepped out of the coveralls, folding them neatly and laying them on the coffee table. Straightening, he pulled a wallet out of his inside breast pocket and opened it up to the Agency ID. "Any idea of where our boy is right now?"

She nodded as she checked the photo identification. "He's at the institute. I just talked to him a few minutes ago."

"Good." Reilly turned as if to sit on the couch, then changed his mind. He picked up the coveralls and set them on the couch seat, then sat on the coveralls. "Sit down. We'll talk. I'll answer all your questions."

She threw herself gratefully in the chair. "You have no idea how badly I need some answers. I feel like I'm going crazy with this thing."

"I'm sorry that we've had to keep you in the dark as much as we have," Reilly apologized, looking her in the eyes and holding the look. "We don't like to send out our field agents without proper information, but truth is, we've been in the dark ourselves and are just putting a few things together."

"I'm all ears. Let's hear it."

"Let me start by telling you that we're proud of the way you've served your country over the past ten years, and doubly proud of the work you're doing now. You're a hell of a woman, Julie...do you mind if I call you Julie?"

She smiled, flattered. "No, not at all."

"Good. Call me Mark."

"Well, Mark," she said, "I don't know that I've done that awfully much. Keeping track of my husband's research..."

"You've served deep cover successfully for ten years, Julie," he replied. "Very few agents could claim a record like that. The backbone of the United States intelligence services are composed of people just like you. You've sacrificed a great deal for your country, and your country won't forget that."

She brightened. "God, I'm glad to be finally talking to someone who makes some sense. Now, tell me what's going on here."

"Okay." He leaned forward, resting his elbows on his knees. "Now, I have to stress that we're still putting this together, but here's how it looks right now. As you know, the Department of the Air Force has been subsidizing liquid electricity research for a long time. A couple of years ago, one of our researchers, Jerry Butler, had a breakthrough in the field...."

"I know," she said, pointing to the computer that was set up on a folding chair. "I've got his notes right there. I've been transcribing them."

He nodded. "I've heard. Anyway, we think that there was a KGB spy at the Grolier Institute who managed to get wind of the research and Jerry Butler found out about the spy. He ran before they could get the information from him, but they caught up to him at Titusville. I can only imagine what they did to him before he died."

"What about the phone calls to the newspapers and the space shuttle problems?" she asked.

"Smoke screen, I think. We have no way of knowing that it was Jerry Butler who made those calls. They wanted to make him look like a crackpot who left himself open for murder and robbery. The *Challenger* disaster was simply coincidental and tended to lend undue credence to the story."

"What's this to do with Mack and Hal Brognola?"

"I'm coming to that."

The man stood, stretching, and walked to the window, checking the street. Julie watched him moving around. He was sleek, like a cat. And with everything he said, a bit of weight lifted from her.

He turned to face her. "We don't think Jerry Butler gave them everything they wanted, we think he managed to hold some of it back, or perhaps even gave them erroneous information. It is our opinion, not easily reached, that Hal Brognola and Mack Bolan are agents working with the KGB and that they killed the others working on liquid electricity before realizing they didn't have all the information. They lifted you with the intention of forcing you to finish the research."

Julie felt as if she'd been slapped in the face. "No," she said. "Mack's no foreign agent, he..."

"Before you say anything else, take a look at this," he said, walking across the room. He reached into a pocket and removed a folded computer printout and handed it to her. "This is just a small taste of Mack Bolan's record. It just covers the past few years. He's a terrorist and a mass murderer. His nickname is The Executioner." He sat on the arm of her chair.

Julie, incredulous, studied the record. It showed, full-blown, the part of Bolan's character she tried not to think about. He was wanted for various crimes in nearly every country on Earth. Every major police and intelligence operation worldwide kept files on his actions. She was horrified, then sickened.

"I—I don't understand why we'd have somebody like this working for us, he—"

"He works for Hal Brognola directly," Reilly said, "and the KGB indirectly. He's not on government payroll."

She handed the printout back. "This is so hard to believe. Mack has a rough side, but underneath there seems to be an honesty that . . ."

"He's a good actor," Reilly admitted, shrugging. "He's using you, that's all." He leaned to the side and put his arm around the woman, hugging her briefly. "I'm sorry that you're being thrust into this end of the business, but things just worked out that way."

"But on the road that night . . ."

"A tragic mistake," the man said, straightening. "Once Bolan had kidnapped you and your husband, the Air Force tried to stop him. The shots at that point were accidental. The plan has proceeded basically as it was supposed to. He's simply got you doing what he wanted your husband to do."

She looked up at him, finding comfort in his eyes. "That means that when I'm through . . ."

"He'll probably try to kill you, just like he killed all the others."

She felt light-headed, and put a hand to her face. "This is all happening so fast. Why have you left me in this situation?"

Reilly reached out and took her hands. "Because he doesn't know that you're in contact with us. For the first time we've got the upper hand on an entire clandestine network. We want as many of their contacts as we can get before this is over."

"So, you're using me like he is."

He leaned down, so that they were eye to eye. "Using you? You work for us, remember? Over the past ten years we've put more than four million dollars into Swiss bank accounts with your number on them. That's using? We're simply expanding your role. We're asking you to come to the defense of your country in its hour of need. Is that too much to ask, Julie? I don't think so."

"What do you want me to do?" she asked, her mouth dry, her mind whirling.

"Just what you're doing now," he replied, dropping her hands and walking back to sit on the couch. "If they meet with others, take note of the names and faces. When it gets tight, we'll have other orders for you."

"Oh, Mark," she said. "I don't know if I can handle something like this. What if I finish the transcribing?"

He smiled wide. "You'll do fine! I've got confidence in you. The government has confidence in you. We'll give you all the support you'll need."

"You mean like those idiots that Bolan almost caught the other night?"

"Those weren't our people," Reilly said. "I don't know what you're talking about."

"What are you doing with Jerry's research?" she asked.

"I think they're designing a new jet engine powered by electricity," he replied. "Look. This whole thing will be over in a week, ten days tops. We'll keep a close eye on you. When it's all over, we'll give you a bonus and send you away on a long vacation."

"And then I'm through with this covert crap?" she said.

He raised his right hand. "Word of honor," he said, then snapped his finger. "Oh, I almost forgot." He reached into his jacket pocket and pulled out a miniature plastic bag containing a small, white pill. He stood and carried it over to her, setting it on the arm of her chair.

"What is it?" she asked, staring.

"Now, don't get upset. This is standard operating procedure. Nothing to worry about."

"What is it?" she repeated.

"It's your salvation in case you get in trouble," he said, using a finger on her chin to turn her face away from the pill and toward him. "If things should look bad, or get tight, slip this into something . . . his food, a drink. It will dissolve almost immediately. He'll feel very little pain. Death will be close to instantaneous."

"No," she said, amazed, trying to shake her head out of his grasp. "I could never kill, I—"

"Julie," he said firmly, "this is no game. We're playing for the survival of the country, the survival of millions. You are, in essence, a soldier working for the United States. If you have to, you'll kill . . . to save your life, or if I tell you. But you'll do it, all right. At this point you have no choice. He's a vicious murderer. If you have to do it, the world will applaud you. Are you with me?"

"It's not that I don't understand . . ."

"Are you with me?" he repeated. "Are you standing firm with your country and justifying all it's done for you all these years?"

"Y-yes," she said, looking down, ashamed. "I'm with you."

"Good."

He moved back to the couch and climbed back into his coveralls. "Watch yourself," he said as he zipped up the front. "You're playing against a real pro. But remember that you have the upper hand. He doesn't know you work for us. Just play along, do as he says and keep an eye out for his contacts. It'll all be over soon. You're safe as long as you're still transcribing."

With that, the man strapped on his utility belt. "Call whenever you need to," he said. "Try to call every day."

"I will," she said in a small voice.

He nodded, smiling. "It's a wonderful thing you're doing. Your country won't forget."

With that, he disappeared into the kitchen.

Julie sat, staring at the pill. She never even heard the kitchen door open and close. Somehow, she had thought that if she only had some answers all her problems would be solved. She'd never realized what a blessed thing ignorance could be.

She sat silently for a time, listening to the sounds that floated in through the window. She got up and walked into the bedroom, hiding the pill in the side pocket of her purse. Then she threw herself on the bed and cried for nearly an hour. For the first time, she envied Harry's position. There were far worse things than being dead—such as being in love with your murderer.

Chapter Thirteen

The stairs leading down to the subbasement were one-piece aluminum and shook slightly with every step. Hal Brognola took them slowly—the stairwell was darkened—keeping one hand on the rail and the other clutched tightly around the stack of computer printouts that he had spent all day acquiring. Ted Healy and Oscar Largent kept pace behind him, speaking occasionally to each other in short, clipped sentences, their dialogue confined exclusively to security matters. They were Greggson's present to Brognola, twenty-four-hour-a-day bodyguards.

They cleared the bottom of the stairs and stood, staring into the maw of a world that existed within a world. If a large building could be compared to a body, then its vital systems—heat, cooling, water and waste disposal—were the veins, arteries and muscles of that body. And as Hal Brognola stared into the dark, shadowy maze of creaking pipes and valves that filled and confused the stadium-sized room he realized just exactly how much his discovery had changed the tenor of his life. He had entered the dark and alien world of twisted subterfuge and found that even his surroundings reflected that alienness.

"It's down here," Oscar said, taking the lead as they walked into the beating heart of the Justice Department.

Brognola walked quietly between the two men, his nose twitching with the musty odor, his brown cordovans wet from the small puddles that stagnated on the smooth concrete floor. A dirty business. From somewhere in the conduit jungle a motor kicked in, the sound of whooshing air competing with it.

"I think the boiler room is off that lighted corridor to the right," Ted Healy called from the rear. Largent waved in acknowledgment, then dutifully turned down a narrow, Sheetrock corridor that was lit by a single, naked bulb in the ceiling.

A doorway was situated at the end of the corridor. Largent signaled Brognola to keep a distance as he opened the door and peered within. Smiling, he motioned for the two men to follow him in.

Brognola entered; Greggson and his bodyguards were already there, sitting on wooden folding chairs beside the huge round boiler that provided hot water and steam heating to some of the older parts of the building. Other chairs had been brought in so that everyone could sit.

"The maintenance people?" Brognola asked as he walked in.

Greggson smiled. "All up in my office working on an 'emergency' with the air-conditioning. If I broke it as well as I think I did, they'll be up there for quite some time."

"Good." The head Fed sat, printouts piled on his lap. "Oscar, why don't you position yourself at the end of that hallway and let us know if anyone comes. We'll brief you later."

Largent gave a casual salute and hurried out of the room, closing the door behind him.

"Well," Brognola said, looking at Greggson, "how are you holding up?"

"I'm scared shitless," Greggson admitted, everyone laughing to ease the tension.

"How are things going with the Marie Price investigation?"

Greggson cleared his throat and opened a file folder onto his lap. He frowned at the contents for a moment. "First off," he said finally, "I think we've managed to keep the government out of this completely. The D.C. police have been cooperative, and are representing the matter to the press as a straightforward rape-murder, while working with my office on the government angles."

"How long can that hold up?"

"How long does it need to?"

Brognola smiled. "I wish I knew. I suppose all we can do is take this a day at a time and hope for the best."

"And meanwhile," Greggson continued, "we've managed to glean a few interesting facts from our investigation of the house and the Price woman's bank accounts."

"Just a second." Brognola pulled a small spiral notebook and pen out of his sport jacket pocket. "Okay. Let me have it."

Greggson pulled a pair of black-framed glasses out of his own jacket and put them on to ride halfway down his nose. He pursed his lips, then spoke, his eyes fixed on his reports. "Whoever killed her and the boy did a pretty good job rifling the house. They must have done it in the middle of the night, because none of the neighbors saw anything at all. There were a great many pieces of charred paper and photographs in her fireplace, however. So maybe they burned everything. But we did manage to find a key to a safety-deposit box and called around until we found the place. I got them to open up the bank yesterday—using government authorization but no paperwork—and got into her box. It was a big one, and it was full of cash...several hundred thousand dollars in cash. There were also uncashed checks totaling over fifty thousand dollars drawn on the account of a firm in Florida called the Baylor Goggle and Optical Company."

Brognola looked up from his notebook. "That name," he said, putting the notebook on the floor, "is incredibly familiar."

He began to go through the preliminary printouts of the information Bolan had asked him to glean from the matériel manifest of the *Challenger* flight. He found what he wanted almost immediately and read it off to Greggson. "A subsidiary of the Baylor Goggle and Optical Company called GeoScan had cargo on the fatal *Challenger* flight and on the previous three flights."

"What sort of cargo?" Greggson asked, staring over the rim of his glasses.

Brognola flipped through several more pages. "Apparently GeoScan sent up several satellites from which they can take infrared pictures of the planet and somehow find the absolute best places to drill for oil. It's simply a service industry to the oil business."

"Why did they give Marie Price so much money?" Ted Healy asked.

"I don't know," Brognola replied, "but from the way she set it up, it looks like she wasn't declaring it on her income tax. We'll check that." He made a note on his printout and looked up at Greggson. "Did you find out when she opened the safety-deposit box?"

"Yeah." Greg referred to his own notes. "She took the thing out in April 1983."

"Jesus," the head Fed whispered, and pulled the woman's personnel file out of his stack. He held it up, pointed to the first page. "That was just two months after she came to work for Justice."

"I think that maybe it's time to concentrate on Geo-Scan and Baylor."

"I'll take care of that." Brognola made another note. "Did you find anything else?"

"Yeah, a little," Greg replied. "She didn't have any really close friends, but there's a woman in the office she used to take lunch with named Lydia Green, who told us that Marie had been dating an officer connected to the Pentagon, named Michaels. We checked that out and found that General Leland has an adjutant named Captain Norman Michaels. We showed the Green woman a photo and she said it was the same man she saw Marie Price leaving the building with once."

"Leland again," Brognola said wearily. "Everything keeps coming back to him, doesn't it?"

"Do you realize," Greggson said, "what would happen to us if we tried to pin something on Leland?"

"He's only the most beloved man in the Administration," Brognola returned. "Why should there be a problem?"

"All we've got is extremely circumstantial," Greggson said. "I would never walk into court with a case like this."

"I went to Marie's funeral today. There was nobody there but family."

The door burst open, and Oscar Largent stuck his head in. "Someone's coming."

"Get in and close the door," Brognola ordered. "Ted, hit the lights."

Healy flipped the light switch, and the windowless room was plunged into total darkness. Largent opened the door a crack to peek through, a shaft of light from without slicing through the room.

They sat there in utter silence, listening to the sound of approaching footsteps echoing hollowly on the concrete floor. The sound peaked, then subsided.

"He's passed," Largent said. "Looks like one of the maintenance men."

"We'll give him a minute," Brognola whispered.

"I feel like an idiot," one of Greggson's bodyguards said dully.

"You wouldn't," the head Fed replied, "if you'd found a bomb under the hood of *your* car."

"Where do we go from here?" Greggson said low.

"I'm afraid we're going to have to bring more people into it," Brognola replied, his mind just barely a step ahead of the developments. "I think we should start putting tails on these guys—Leland, Michaels and Givan for now, others as they become known. The fact that they had a relatively unimportant secretary under such an incredible payroll says a great deal. Such as, where are they getting so much money and exactly how many people are in on this damned thing, whatever it is."

"He's coming back," Largent said, and everyone quieted again, listening to the footsteps.

Brognola sat there, relating to his new world and its new protocols. How much easier, he thought, to simply take a leave of absence and get the hell out of Dodge for a while, just leave this problem for someone else. There was, of course, no one else, and if what he thought about Leland and his bunch was, indeed, true, then he could be the only person standing in the way of a military takeover of the United States government.

"He's passed," Largent informed them, opening the door wide.

"Get the lights," Brognola commanded, Healy hurrying to comply.

"Gentlemen," Brognola said, "I feel that we are engaged in a war here, a war whose consequences could be just as devastating as any war has ever been. Our enemy comes from within and moves with the trappings of right and justice. He will be a tough and a shrewd adversary who, potentially, already has taken many of those closest to us. I'm sorry that we must meet in places like this, sorrier still that we are dealing from the hand of weakness, not of strength. But I mean to see this through, even if I have to *live* in a place like this. I hope you all feel the same."

There were mumbled affirmations from the five other people in the room. "I think I speak for everyone here," Greggson said, "when I say that we are in this with you one hundred percent. We are, all of us, committed to action."

"Good." Brognola continued. "What we have is simple: the *Challenger* disaster, a cry for help from a top scientist who is then killed, the killing of the rest of the researchers, ultimately tying into Givan's killing of Harry Arnold on a Mississippi back road. We have the bugging of my office, the attempted murder of me and the successful murder of my secretary, all ultimately circling back again to the *Challenger* disaster. Project GOG is a highly classified reality under the control of General Leland, who ties to everything else that's happened. There is a military connection, though we don't know of what strength. It is now time for us to recruit our own small army to help us in the investigation. I want all of you to think hard and pick out several names you truly believe are clear of this stigma and would be willing to help us. Will you do that?"

The voices were loud this time. "Yes."

Brognola nodded. "I can't guarantee anyone's safety, just as no one can guarantee that in wartime. We're going to start putting tails on the people we suspect most strongly and see where they lead us. Meanwhile, from my end, I'm going to dig out everything I can on Baylor Goggle..."

"Maybe that's your GOG," Greggson said. "Goggle...GOG, a connection?"

"Maybe," Brognola said.

"What about your man in Florida?" Greggson asked.

"He's had pretty fair success. He's protecting our last researcher, has uncovered the secret of liquid electricity and is working on a code that might shed some light on this whole business."

"Yeah," Largent said, "living the high life in Florida, not a care in the world, nothing but success."

"Nothing but success," Brognola repeated, and wondered why he didn't believe it.

Chapter Fourteen

On hands and knees, Bolan looked under the chassis of the Jeep, his morning ritual before going to work. It looked clear, so he stood, his knee still sore from Saturday night, and unlocked the hood latches.

The kitchen door opened, and Julie walked onto the stoop dressed in a bathrobe, a paper bag in her hand. "Good morning," she said sweetly, and walked down the three steps to the drive.

"Good morning," he returned, opening the hood and peering within. "You're up early this morning."

"Thought I'd see how the other half lives," she said cheerily, and Bolan was immediately suspicious of her saccharine sweetness.

"We live half-asleep," he replied, and slammed the hood back into place. He pointed to the paper bag. "What have you got there?"

She held up the brown bag. "It's a meatloaf sandwich left over from last night's dinner. I thought you might be getting tired of all that machine food."

He took the bag, wishing he could see through the happy mask that was her face. "Thanks a lot." He walked around to the driver's side door to check the hair that he had wet and plastered across the doorframe last night. It was still in place. "And I want to thank you again for making dinner last night."

"It was a pleasure. What would you like tonight?"

"Come on, Julie," he said. "What is this sudden turn-around?"

She shrugged. "Guess maybe I've decided to call that truce after all. If we've got to live here together, at least we can be friendly about it. Besides, this place is bringing out my nesting instinct."

"Right." Bolan climbed into the Jeep. Something was going on; he just couldn't put his finger on it.

He started the car, the woman climbing the steps to the kitchen and turning around to wave pleasantly at him. He returned the wave with a pasted-on smile and backed out of the driveway, heading the vehicle down Avondale in the direction of the institute.

Julie had been acting oddly ever since his return from work last night. Where he thought she would razz him about the too-tight flannel shirt and cords he wore, courtesy of Robbie, she instead was agreeable and sympathetic, greeting him not only with a hot meal, but with cold martinis, as well.

This was not the same woman whom he'd been living with the past week. Something had happened to change her. He just wished he could figure out what it was.

The traffic was thick on Aloma, the morning sun, still low in the eastern sky, already heating things up. Bolan drove mechanically, with only half an eye on the road, his mind eaten up with the riddles that seemed to confront him on all sides.

Of the riddle of Jerry Butler's code, he knew of no solutions. He had spent several fruitless days trying to crack the code within a code, but no amount of substitution of letters, numbers or symbols seemed to have the least effect on the nonsense words of the code. He was thinking very seriously of transmitting the whole mess to Hal and forgetting about it. Yet Hal had already made it clear he didn't want to trust Washington's cryptographers.... Bolan sighed heavily.

Of the riddle of the spy at the institute, he was a little more sure. Peg Ackerman's employment record was obviously bogus, and though she came to the institute after Jerry Butler's demise, there seemed to be a great deal more than coincidence connecting the two. If that was, indeed, the case, he'd find out today. It was time to run Peg Ackerman up the flagpole and see who saluted. He was tired of waiting for things to come to him. He was tired of the passive approach. It was time to stir things up, time to shake the nest—and he was just the guy to do it.

He drove through the gates at Grolier feeling better than he had for a while. He had been playing the game under everyone else's rules, but that was about to come to an end.

He drove into the garage under the building, parking on the second level. He climbed out of the Jeep, jerking a hair out of his head and wetting it across the crack between the door and doorpost.

He carried his briefcase containing Butler's code and his map of Arizona into the elevator. The map was another riddle that hadn't been solved.

The car made it all the way to five without stopping. Chuck waved to him as he stepped out. "Morning, Dr. Sparks."

"Morning," Bolan returned. "Where is everybody right now?"

"Most of them are down in the break room."

"Thanks." Bolan had already started toward the offices. He turned abruptly and headed back toward the break room.

Most of his colleagues were in there, sitting in the living room drinking coffee and smoking. Robbie wasn't there. Neither was Howard Davis. Yuri Bonner sat close to an end table light, furiously writing on a notepad while chain-smoking endlessly.

"Good morning everyone." Bolan sat in one of the easy chairs, his briefcase on his lap.

"Our hero," Ike Silver said derisively, shaking his head. "The patient lived, by the way, Doctor."

"Morty?" Bolan asked. "Good."

"Yeah," Fred Haines confirmed. "Muscle-bound Namboy researcher saves talking fish. Pretty good headline, huh?"

"What have you got against me, Fred?" Bolan growled.

"Nothing, Nam boy," he returned. "I like you. I just don't know who you really are, that's all."

"And why you're really here," Ike Silver added.

Bolan sat up straight. "What difference does it make?"

"We don't need nobody in here spying on us," Haines said, his smile fading. "So, why don't you stop screwing around and tell us what you want."

"I wonder who's kept the suspicion high about me," Bolan said, looking around the room. "Could it be...you, Peg? You're certainly being quiet now."

The woman glared at him over her coffee cup.

"It don't matter who said what about what," Haines retorted, angry. "Fact is, you ain't who you said you were."

"Who am I then?"

"Maybe an Air Force snitch," Peg put in.

"And who might you be, Peg?" he asked. "I mean, really, who are you?"

"I don't have to answer—" she began, but Bolan interrupted.

"You don't have to answer, but I do." He laughed shortly. "Is that it?"

"Now, don't go changing the subject," Silver chided.

"I'm not." Bolan turned to Peg. "Okay. Where did you work before you came here?"

She sat staring at him.

"Listen, Sparks—" Haines began.

"No, you listen," Bolan said. "I'm sick of the third degree I get around here. Your background isn't so great, either, but right now I'm asking the lady a simple question. It shouldn't be too difficult to answer, an easy, declarative sentence." He turned to Peg again. "I'm asking you where you worked before you came here."

"I don't have to answer your questions." She stood as if to leave.

"Yes, this time you do have to answer," he said. "Just like you wanted to make me answer your chemistry questions the other day like a schoolchild."

"And I recall you didn't answer," she returned, and moved across the room. Bolan moved to block her escape.

"But you're going to," he insisted. "Come on, this is easy. Neatness doesn't even count. Just tell me where you worked."

Everyone was staring at her; she raised her hand to nervously rearrange her already perfect hair. "This is...silly."

"Just answer," Haines urged her. "That's all."

"Where?" Bolan persisted.

She looked around again, licking dry lips. "Well, I used to teach chemistry at Bowling Green, I—"

"No," Bolan interrupted her. "I mean right before you came here. What job did you give up to take this one?"

She cleared her throat and looked down at the floor. "I, ah, was in the biochemistry department at Boston College."

"Don't be modest, Peg," Bolan said. "You *ran* that department, didn't you?"

She looked at him, her eyes hard and unforgiving. "Yes," she said quietly. "I did."

"Well," Bolan said, "that's quite a trick considering that Donovan Phelps has run that department for many years. What did you do, shove him aside and use his office?"

"I don't have to answer your questions."

"Especially if I'm looking for the truth," Bolan replied. "You've wanted to say it about me. I'll say it about you: you're a fraud, Peg. You've lied about your previous employment and maybe you lie about everything else. Just who are you?"

The woman looked around for support, finding nothing but hard, lined faces peering back at her. Even Yuri had stopped writing and was staring at her with the kind of look probably reserved for Russian KGB informants.

"Don't listen to him," she pleaded. "He's just trying to throw blame onto me to keep it from himself."

"I suppose a phone call to Boston College can clear you," Bolan said, walking over to the blue phone that sat on the coffee table and picking up the receiver. "What *is* the area code there, Peg?"

She just looked at him, her lips moving soundlessly. Then she bolted, running through the room, the table area and out the door. Bolan watched her go, his suspicions confirmed. Now what to do?

He wanted to follow it up with her, but the kind of interrogation he had in mind would be frowned upon at the institute. His next step would be to pull her address from the computer records and pay her a friendly little visit later tonight. Peg Ackerman's days as a mystery woman would be coming to an end. He'd pushed her in a direction, now it was time to see just what direction it was.

"What gives between you two lovebirds?" Ike Silver asked. "You're like two scorpions stinging each other to death."

Bolan turned to him. "Even here reality intrudes, doesn't it, Ike?"

The man ran a hand through thinning gray hair. "Reality's what I make it to be. You, then, are only as real as I choose you to be."

"There are billions of us running around out there, Doctor," Bolan replied. "You may ignore us, but you can't wish us away. We have hopes and dreams and wants and needs, just like you with your superiority and ease of judgment."

Bolan walked up to where the man sat and poked an index finger in his chest. "Well, you don't have the power to define me. While you hide and feel superior, me and my kind are out there living life, feeling happiness, sadness and joy. You talk about the grandeur of the universe, but my kind is experiencing it firsthand, while you can only hide and condemn through your petty fears. You contribute nothing useful to the world around you. All you do is take up space and breathe air. The sleaziest bum on Skid Row is better than you because he's at least trying to live some sort of a life. No, Ike. You're the one who's not real.''

He turned to Haines. ''Where's Robbie?''

''I saw him in his office,'' the man said, his brown eyes scanning Bolan's face as if he were looking for something.

Bolan nodded, then turned and walked out. He had intended to stir the pot, and it hadn't taken long. Now that he had flushed the quail, it was time to track it.

''What happened to Dr. Ackerman?'' Chuck asked as Bolan passed his checkpoint.

''What do you mean?''

''She just came charging up here and took the elevator. I don't think I've ever seen her move so fast.''

''Guess she's got an appointment,'' Bolan replied and walked to Robbie's office, knocking lightly. The woman was on the run, but he didn't figure her to get too far just yet.

The man answered almost immediately, smiling when he saw Bolan. ''Well, David,'' he said, swinging the door wide. ''Come in.''

Bolan followed him into the lab. He liked Robbie's lab better than any of the others. It was like a small library, with reference books lining floor-to-ceiling bookcases all the way around and tables containing every sort of scientific investigative device. Microscopes, centrifuges and scales were jammed together and filled the place like a general store for eggheads.

''I just made some coffee,'' Robbie said as he led Bolan into the place. ''Want some?''

''Not today.'' Bolan followed him back into his office. ''It's my thirst for knowledge I want to satisfy.''

They sat in the office, Robbie's seniority apparently good enough to get him two chairs. Robbie crossed his legs and stuck the pipe into his mouth. ''What can I do for you?''

"I want to ask you about Peg Ackerman's project."

Robbie looked quizzical. "What about it?"

"You told me once she was working on immortality," Bolan said. "What did you mean by that?"

The man reached into his desk and pulled out a white bag. He opened it and removed a glazed doughnut. "Want half?" he asked, shrugging when Bolan shook his head. He set his pipe on the desk, then dunked the doughnut into his cup of coffee and took a soggy bite. "Peg was working on fibroblast cells, the ones that turn out collagen, the packaging material of the human body. The original supposition was that cells could divide and continue to divide forever, but Peg found that cells only divide for fifty generations before dying. Even if a cell was frozen midway through the generation process and kept for a long time, when it was thawed out, it continued its reproduction, only to die again after the fiftieth generation. All this shows limitations of life for humans. Peg's actual work here has been experimentation with enzymes that slow down damage to the DNA during cell regeneration to somehow expand this fifty-cell limit."

"Has she had any luck?"

"Not really," he said, taking another bite. "At risk of insulting one of my esteemed colleagues, Peg's not much of a researcher. I never was sure how she got the job here. Her work has been pedestrian at best."

"Do you know much about her background?"

Robbie shook his head. "Very little. She's always been closemouthed about her personal life and never talks about anything but business. Although I've always felt she's an unhappy person."

"Was Jerry Butler an unhappy person?"

Robbie took a sip of his coffee. "Sure got a lot of questions today."

"I'm a curious boy."

The man stared into his coffee cup. "So, do I drink all the crumbs down at the bottom of the cup or dump the whole mess?"

"Drink it."

Robbie got up and dumped the rest of the coffee into a small sink in a lab table just out the door. "That's a sign of accepting responsibility, by the way," he said. "You've made the crumbs, now you must accept the responsibility of their future."

He came back in and sat again. "Jerry was a motivated man and protective of his work and its usage. His work was his life. I think he may have been happy at one time, but ultimately made himself unhappy by taking it all too seriously. Did you know that the last year here he wrote in nothing but code?"

"Code? What kind of code?"

"He had this theory that a code could be devised that could ultimately be understood only by someone with a similar background and upbringing. In other words, a code that didn't depend on knowledge of positioning or replacement to break, but rather a similar understanding of symbols and abstracts. The basic idea was a code that could never be understood by a foreign power, for they could never understand American idioms or share in the lifetime of culture that goes into an American's life."

"Fascinating," Bolan said. "So his code was meant to be looked at symbolically, rather than literally. With the words actually standing for other words and ideas."

Robbie nodded. "That's what he had sunk to. He coded and hid things and walked around in a complete stage of paranoia most all the time. I tried to get him to slow down, but he'd have none of it. It was another unhappy case in the final analysis."

Bolan stood, his mind whirling with the revelation about the code. "I appreciate the info. Now I must . . ."

"You're on to something," Robbie said, "and it doesn't have anything to do with poison gas."

Bolan pointed at him. "Now don't *you* go getting paranoid," he said, and waved, walking out of the room. He wanted to get on Peg Ackerman's trail, but after talking with Robbie he had to invest a little more time with the code.

Now that things were happening, they were happening quickly.

GENERAL MORDECHAI LELAND always spoke to civilian visitors from behind his huge, polished ebony desk in order to let them know that there was, and always would be, a boundary between him and the outside world, a buffer that separated him from the petty and confusing priorities of the civilian population.

The three-man congressional fact-finding team from the Armed Services Committee was no exception as far as the general could tell. Civilians all, they exhibited the usual civilian simpleminded egalitarian approach to life that, carried to its extreme, could make the necessary defense of a country nearly impossible. Civilians liked to believe that people are people no matter what, and that they could be depended upon to act rationally if presented with rational behavior. It was what Leland called the myth of rationality. For the truth of the matter was simple: the world is a jungle whose rule is destined for the strongest.

"But General," the representative from Maine said, "if we continue to blindly fund SDI research and still try to keep up our standing Army plus attritional missile replacement, we'll never have enough money to keep the country itself running smoothly."

"Your statement seems incomplete, Mr. O'Connor," Leland said as he stared across the long desk, its small American flag reflected in the sleek top. "It doesn't seem to include your feelings about our enemies' development of the same tactical weapons."

"They can't afford it any more than we can," O'Connor replied, looking at the other committeemen seated beside him in the stiff, hardbacked chairs the general preferred for his guests. "If we don't develop SDI, then neither will they."

"Are you prepared to speak for the Russians, Mr. O'Connor?" Leland sat up straight and folded his hands on the desktop. "Are you prepared to tell me with any certainty that if we stop development of the Strategic Defense Initiative the Russians will halt their own, highly advanced particle beam program?"

"Representative O'Connor is not on trial here," the representative from Missouri said.

"No one is on trial here," Leland replied, smiling. He had them going now. Bleeding hearts were always idiots when it came to the harsh realities. "Except for, perhaps, the people of this country who don't know yet that you gentlemen are sitting here trying to destroy the freedom and security of the United States of America."

"Come on, Lee," George Hallis coaxed. "You and I have known each other for a good number of years, and we both know how the game works. Now the point here is, we've got to start trimming defense somewhere. Elections are coming up, and everybody's more worried now about domestic policy... it's just business, you know."

"Just because we've known each other, George, doesn't mean I've ever agreed with you. My point is simple: without a strong defense, it won't matter how much we spend on domestic programs, because we won't have a country to run anymore. I don't care if half the population is starving to death. If we don't keep up defense, *all* of us will be starving to death."

"This is no time for rhetoric," Hallis said, his pudgy face reddening around his tight collar. "You know that economics run the world...."

"Exactly!" Leland said loudly, slamming a hand down on the desk to emphasize the point. "This world will be run by whoever spends the most money on defense. It's all economics."

Bootan, the freshman representative from Missouri spoke up. "We've come over here in friendship to see if we could find a way to work together in trimming this budget. If you insist on antagonizing us, we'll just start cutting where we want without your help."

Leland looked at the man. He couldn't have been more than thirty. The general spoke gently. "You ever been in a war, son?"

"N-no, I haven't, but I don't see—"

Leland put up a hand to silence the man. "I've been watching men die in combat in defense of this country for over forty years. I've written so many letters to grieving widows and mothers that I'd be a rich man today if I had a dollar for every one of them. I work every day for the defense of this country. Do you think I'd ask for financing for unnecessary programs at the expense of the citizens I protect? I swear to you, sir, on the graves of my soldiers, my countrymen, that there is not any expense in this country as important as our defense spending, and not one penny is being wasted in that department. Part of the reason, Mr. Bootan, that you're sitting here today is that you've managed to rise to prominence in the greatest country on this planet because people like me have been on the job protecting your freedom. How many men died in Vietnam so that you could sit here today? No, sir, I'm not going to blithely put this country in danger to satisfy your silly partisan budgetary considerations."

The three representatives exploded at once, all of them talking, the boy from Missouri nearly livid with anger. Leland sat calmly, his hands still folded on the desk, and let them talk. After all, never let it be said that Lee Leland was not open and available to the people of the country. He, of course, paid no attention to them. Like all civilians they simply took their freedom for granted and pretended that it was the result of parchments containing laws and rules or churches containing goodwill and brotherhood for all. As far as Leland could see, the only thing keeping the country free from within was the fact that everyone, not just the rebellious few who promote revolutions, had access to weapons, and all that was keeping it free from without was the best, most advanced fighting

force in the world. Nothing else mattered. It was all piss-
ing into the wind.

"You've got to understand," Hallis was saying, "that
the country is in bad economic straits right now, that
compromise—"

"I don't care about that, George. I can't care about it.
Raising the money is your job, not mine. My job is protecting this nation. I think, that if you straightened out
your priorities, *you'd* spend your time defending this
budget above all else and trying to increase it if you
could."

"General Leland . . ." Bootan began, but the ringing of
the private line interrupted him.

Leland looked down at the red phone. It was the priority line that could ring him out of any meeting. "Gentlemen," he said, putting a hand to the receiver, "you'll have
to excuse me for a moment."

He picked up the receiver, clearing his throat before answering. "Leland."

"General, this is Norm Michaels . . ."

"Yes, Captain?" Leland slid a machine-tooled box in
the shape of a B-1 bomber across the desk to the representatives.

"News on Project GOG," Michaels said. "Can we
talk?"

"Only generally." Leland watched as George Hallis removed the top of the airplane to find the stash of cigars
within. He covered the mouthpiece. "Dominican Republic. Try one."

"The news is from our mole in Orlando."

"Go on," Leland said, as he smiled and acknowledged
the thanks of the congressional delegation for the cigars.

"The man from Justice seems to be hot on the trail of
something," Michaels informed him. "He's pushing his
cover wide open at the institute trying to force everyone's
hand."

"But you don't know the extent of his knowledge?"

"No, sir. I just didn't know if we'd want any leaks at this—"

"No, no. You were absolutely right to call me."

He sat back for a moment, watching as the lazy civilians sated themselves on his generosity. Dark, gray smoke filled the room as the out-of-shape and pampered men laughed, smoked and sold America right down the river. They wouldn't be happy until the country was dead, ground under the heel of expediency as more and more was given over to the forces of revolutionary thought. Not by a bang would the country die, but rather it would experience the slow, agonizing death by compromise that would chip away the freedoms one at a time, all presided over by fatted governmental cattle whose only real claim to fame was the fact that they could smile, shake hands and make empty promises.

"General?" Michaels interrupted his reverie. "Did you hear . . . ?"

"Yes, I've just been thinking."

"Sorry, sir."

He looked once again at the men before him. Not one of them would be fit to polish the boots of the lowliest airman on the cushiest air base in the safest part of the world, yet here they sat, ready on a whim to dismantle the necessary protection the country was due. They wouldn't—not if he had anything to say about it. He had thought about and planned for this moment for many years, knowing he'd recognize the moment when he saw it. The only funny thing was, he had never figured that some overactive snoop sitting in a think tank in Florida would be the one to push him over the edge.

"It's time to put a stop to all this," he spoke calmly into the phone. "I want you to mop up operations down south and put the full project on the clock."

There were several seconds of quiet on the line before Michaels said with a quavering voice, "I am required by regulations to inquire if you are authorizing the immediate implementation of Project GOG, full realization to follow in five calendar days from this date?''

"Yes, Captain," Leland replied, a surge of excitement bolting through him. "You may start the ball."

"My God," the man said, laughing nervously. "We're really going to do it."

"You have your orders, Captain. Good luck and godspeed to you."

"Thank you, sir," the man said, and Leland hung up feeling a peace he hadn't known since V-J Day.

He took a long breath, somehow able to look a little more tolerantly at the civilians now. "All right, gentlemen," he said, opening his hands expansively. "Where were we?"

Chapter Fifteen

Bolan moved silently through the lab, turning off lights, still devoting half his mind to the code that refused to reveal itself to him. Unlike most codes, knowing how it worked did nothing to translate the thing. He was stuck with trying to interpret the mind of the electrical genius who invented it. The words on Jerry Butler's paper had, no doubt, been meaningful to him—unfortunately he was dead.

He walked past the cage containing the white mice. Another had died that afternoon, and he had spent enough time with the whole project to know that even though his experiments in looking for the perfect vehicle to carry the ketamine were failing miserably, eventually, through trial and error, the problem would undoubtedly be solved and the "peace bomb" completed. Then, as Robbie had told him, would come the real debate about bloodless war.

Bolan wasn't sure how he stood on that particular issue, since it seemed to him that warfare was simply a symptom of a far greater problem—greed and the human heart. Everyone seemed to study, experiment and discuss in areas that dealt with the symptom as if it were the problem, when what they all really needed to be doing was trying to figure out why it is that every man wants what every other man has. If this problem could be addressed successfully, all the others would go away.

It was time to go home. His momentary excitement after talking to Robbie about the code had cooled over the long hours of unsuccessful trial and error. He put his briefcase on the desk and prepared to load his failures into it for transmission to Brognola along with Robbie's thoughts on the subject.

He picked up the piece of paper containing Peg Ackerman's address, which he had gotten from the computer. Maybe hers was the ticket he should have punched from the first. He'd have a private confrontation and get the intel that he needed.

He put the address in his briefcase, then picked up the map of Arizona. He started to drop it in the bag, then stopped. He had always thought of the map as a clue separate from the code, but perhaps it wasn't, perhaps the map was meant to tie into the code in some way. It wouldn't hurt to look at it for a moment.

The desk chair creaked beneath his weight as he sat and slid the briefcase aside, opening the Arizona map in front of him. He brought out the page that listed the code words and tried to figure out how the phrases could possibly connect to anything on the map.

If everything was, indeed, symbolic, then so was the map. On a very simple level, the map suggested travel to Arizona. The next logical question would be, then, travel *where* in Arizona? He stared at the map for a moment, then realized that, perhaps, the name of an Arizona town could be hidden in the code.

Hands shaking in anticipation, he turned the map over and slowly began to read through the long alphabetical list of cities and towns, saying each name aloud and thinking about any implied relationship to his code list.

He stopped at the Gs, at Gila Bend, a tiny place in southwest Arizona on state highway 85, just off Interstate 8. The Gila monster is a lizard indigenous to that region; the words "twist" and "bend" could be synonymous. Twisted Lizard—Gila Bend. It fit. But what in the world could it mean?

There was a knock on his door. Bolan quickly stuffed everything into his briefcase, mind reeling, and hurried to open the door. Ike Silver stood there, weaving slightly.

"I'm drunk," the man said and walked past Bolan to stand in the darkened lab area. He drank deeply from a halfful quart of Scotch and looked around. "It's dark in here."

Bolan pointed toward the glowing office in the rear. "Come on back, Ike, and you can tell me all about it."

"Delighted," Silver said, following Bolan through the darkness. As they walked, Bolan as a matter of course picked up a lab stool and carried it back with him.

They reached the office and sat, Bolan making sure none of his intelligence work was in view. "Okay, Ike, what's the problem?"

"You're a son of a bitch, you know that?" the man said, pointing his finger as if it were a gun.

"I've been called worse."

Silver waved him off. "I somehow go for weeks without knowing how wasted my life is," he said, words slurring heavily. "But you find it n-necessary to remind me when you get the chance. You think I don't know what I am? You think I'm so stupid that the . . . uselessness of all this doesn't pound on me?"

"Ike, I—"

"No!" the man yelled, setting his bottle on the government-issue desk. "Let me finish what I got drunk enough to say. I'm weak and I'm a coward. I stood up for myself once a long time ago and paid for it for years after that. I was crushed, my spirit broken when my university chair was taken away from me because of past political mistakes. I even tried to commit suicide."

The man rolled up his sleeves, exposing jagged scars that ran across both wrists. "I'm so smart, but I cut myself across the arteries instead of along them. So, I failed...and lived."

"Your problems are behind you," Bolan said. "You can get yourself together."

Silver stood. "My cowardice isn't behind me!" he exclaimed loudly, a hand to his chest. "That's my real problem, isn't it?" He dropped back onto the stool, tears just touching the corners of his eyes. "I fought the system and it broke me. I've been hiding here ever since. I could hide it from the others... but not from you, Sparks. You refuse to play our games."

"Is that why everyone feels I don't belong here?"

The man nodded. "You don't take us as seriously as we take ourselves. You insist on putting our bullshit on human terms."

"You know, Ike," Bolan said, reaching out to pat the man's arm, "if you can face up to your problems, you can lick them. You're a coward merely because you think of yourself as one."

Ike stood again, wearily this time, and walked to the desk, picking up his bottle and looking at it. "Anyway," he concluded, taking a small drink and moving to the door, "I just wanted to tell you that you were right about me... and that I'm sorry."

The man walked slowly away. "We all have fears," Bolan called to Silver's retreating back. "Cowards are the ones who pretend they don't."

The man stopped walking and turned to smile warmly at Bolan. "Thank you for that."

All at once, there was a pounding on the door. "Mack Bolan!" a voice called loudly. "This is the United States Air Force. You will open the door and surrender to us immediately!"

"Who am I speaking to?" Bolan asked, his hand going to the telephone, his mind racing. There were no outside windows in the lab, no other exits.

"This is the Air Force! You will open this door and surrender yourself!"

The phone was dead in Bolan's hand. He tore the heavy receiver out of the unit and stuck it into his waistband.

Silver was moving back toward him. "Who are those people?"

"Bolan!"

"There's a civilian in here with me!" Bolan called, then looked at Silver. "They want to kill me. It's not your fight."

"They can't come in here like this," Silver said. "What can I do to help?"

"You got a gun on you?"

"Heavens, no!"

"Surrender now!" came the voice from the hallway. "We only want you. The civilian will not be harmed!"

"All right!" Bolan called. He should have expected this after the way he had drawn out Peg Ackerman. "I'm coming to the door."

He started for the door, Silver trailing behind him. "You said they wanted to kill you! Why are you giving up to them?"

Bolan just looked at him.

"It's because of me, isn't it?"

"It's not your fight," Bolan said quietly.

Silver pulled on Bolan's arm to stop him. "You're wrong, Sparks, or...Bolan or whatever your name is. This time it is my fight. Those people can't come in here and push our researchers around."

Bolan frowned at him. "This is real, Ike."

"Open this door immediately!"

"No, sir!" Ike called loudly. "He will not open the door! This is a private research facility, and you cannot come in here. My name is Isaac Silver and I—"

The clatter of an automatic weapon drowned out Ike as the door shivered, the knob blowing off.

"Come on!" Bolan yelled. He grabbed Ike by the arm and propelled him back toward the office.

The door burst open, and several men in uniform charged into the darkness of the lab.

"Fire at will!" the squad leader called. Bolan threw Ike to the floor in front of him as the SPs opened up with M-16s on full-auto, bright flashes of light strobing the room.

They crawled through the office door as the whole lab came apart around them in a deafening chain-saw rattle of glass and plaster. Blinds danced madly on the office windows as gas-powered slugs whistled through them to smash into the opposite walls. One round exploded the ceiling light, the rooms thrown into inky blackness.

Outside, beakers were turned into glass shrapnel as the bullets tore up the equipment on the lab tables. Someone's M-16 tore into the mouse cage, the square metal box dancing and sparking on the table before crashing to the floor, the few still living mice scurrying wildly away.

"Give me a lighter!" Bolan yelled to Ike above the din. "Quickly!"

He poured the rest of the Scotch into the paper-filled trash can while Silver dug into his pockets for a lighter.

"H-here," the man stuttered, his hand shaking uncontrollably.

Bolan grabbed the lighter and pulled his briefcase onto the floor.

The autofire stopped.

"Here they come," Bolan said, thumbing up the flame on the lighter.

"Move in," the squad leader ordered. "Spread out. He might be armed."

Bolan pulled a wad of paper from the trash and set it alight, the whole room glowing with hazy light. He dropped the flame into the can, and the alcohol went up with a loud whump. A bright plume of blue-white fire burst from the can, followed by thick gray smoke.

By the light of the fire, Bolan reached into the briefcase and took out two of the experimental atomizers of ketamine compound, one for each hand. They'd caught him without his weapons, but he wouldn't go down easily.

"Take the empty bottle," he ordered Silver.

"But what...?"

"On three I want you to throw it through that window by the door, then be ready to follow me out this side window. Ready?"

"God . . . I'm scared."

"Me too," Bolan replied. "And Ike, I want to thank you for what you did back there."

Bolan watched him smile in the flickering light of the trash fire.

"I'm ready," Silver said.

"One!" Bolan called, and suddenly water was pouring on him from above—the sprinkler system. Fine, it would generate more smoke. "Two. . ." Ike was coughing from the smoke, and Bolan's eyes were burning furiously. "Three!"

Ike stood and threw the Scotch bottle through the remains of the window with a loud crash; automatics were up and tracking, 5.56 mm hornets whipping across the room.

Bolan, screaming, stood and charged the window opposite, the chair out in front of him like a battering ram. "Come on!" he called, and smashed into the window space, diving through behind the chair.

He rolled, coming up in a crouch to see Ike, silhouetted against the backlight of the fire, trying to climb through the window.

He was too slow.

The guns swung his way, chopping him in two just as he got a foot on the lab side of the office.

There was no time to mourn. Bolan reached forward, grabbed the chair and charged directly at the nearest muzzle-flash.

Before the Security Policeman could get off a shot, the chair connected with flesh that gave, and the man was driven back against a table. He fell to the floor with a groan. As the SP struggled to his feet, Bolan sprayed him in the mouth with one of the atomizers. His flailing stopped in seconds.

"Someone's down!"

Bolan heard feet pounding toward his position and had just enough time to grab the man's M-16 and roll away.

Fred Haines's voice boomed from the doorway. "What the hell's goin' on in here?" Then the lights came on.

Bolan jumped to his feet, the room a smoke-filled nightmare around him. "Run, Fred!" he yelled, and saw a blue uniform exposed through the shifting smoke.

He fired a short burst, which emptied the gun. A scream pierced the lab, followed by the thud as a body fell to the floor. Two down.

The warrior hit the floor again, drawing fire as he crawled past the body of the man he'd paralyzed to take cover behind one of the tables. He was completely surrounded, and had no idea of how many Air Force men were actually in the room. Water continued to pour from the ceiling sprinklers and was now an inch deep on the floor. He wished he'd had time to stop and search the body for more ammo, but the body had been too much out in the open.

"I think he's out of ammo, Sarge!" an SP called from the haze.

The smoke was beginning to dissipate, and its cover wouldn't last much longer. He had to somehow gain that door.

"Okay," the squad leader called. "Hendricks, Jenks, Webber...take him!"

Three of them.

Bolan jerked to his feet, throwing the M-16 at the wraiths he saw splashing toward him through the smoke and water. He grabbed the telephone receiver from his waistband and jumped to the tabletop, launching himself at his assailants.

Bolan came down on two of them, all three losing their footing on the slippery floor and landing in a heap. He drove the heavy receiver repeatedly into the face of the SP on his right, the guy groaning as the cartilage of his nose broke.

The other SP on the floor with Bolan took a second to get leverage, then threw the warrior beneath him; the third man, still standing, tried to get a clear shot.

"We've got him!"

Bolan had seconds to act before he would be immobilized. The man on top of him bared his teeth, reaching back to pound Bolan with a big fist. Hand free, Bolan came up with the atomizer, hitting his assailant full in the face.

The man gagged then screamed, lurching off Bolan to grab at his throat. As Bolan pushed to his feet, he shoved the stricken SP into the airman with the M-16, both of them tripping over the injured man on the floor. Something snapped, was pulled off the E-3's neck as he fell. Bolan looked down to see the man's dog tags in his hand.

Through the dissipating smoke he saw that airmen were on all sides. He dived between the tables, coming up with a dripping automatic.

The SPs had given no thought to a coherent plan. Thinking Bolan an easy target, they had neglected to post men at the door, which was the only escape route. Bolan vaulted over the top of the lab table, M-16 blazing, autofire raking the room and pinning down his attackers.

As the Executioner splashed toward the doorway, an airman leveled a carbine at him. Not even breaking stride Bolan swung around the M-16 and diced the SP from sternum to pelvis, the guy's uniform exploding red as he jerked spastically, falling forward onto the table.

Bolan leaped over the table, coming down hard on the floor and rolling through standing water as screaming death tore up the room around him. Staying low and using the tables for cover, he rushed through the door and into the hallway.

Breathing hard, he leaned against the doorframe, the paneled wall opposite splintering to pieces under the withering, directed fire. Bolan pushed off the doorframe and sent a short burst back into the room, driving the airmen back. Now *they* were the ones who were trapped. The only way out was through that door.

He stood, switching the M-16 to single shot in order to conserve the last of his ammo. He whirled to the sound of the next office door opening, only to see Howard Davis poking his head out.

"What's happening, David?" he asked. "It sounds—"

"Get back inside!" Bolan ordered. The boy jerked quickly into his office and slammed the door.

Bolan pivoted and fired twice into the lab, hitting an airman in the thigh. The man dived behind a lab table, crying out in anger and pain. There had to be six or seven more, and the warrior didn't have the firepower to take them all.

He turned back and glanced down the hall. Could he make it to the elevators and stay alive? He'd have to try.

Then he saw Chuck, moving cautiously down the hall with his gun drawn.

"Dr. Sparks?" he called tentatively. "Is there something—"

"Behind you!" Bolan yelled, and the boy turned to see Arthur, Smyth's robot, rolling up behind him.

Chuck looked back at Bolan. "It's just Arthur, I . . ."

The robot slammed into him, driving him against the wall.

"No!" Chuck screamed in pain. "No-o-o!"

Bolan watched in openmouthed horror as the robot's powerful arms reached out and crushed the guard's head. The skull broke with a loud crunching sound.

The robot then turned to Bolan, the photocells that were its eyes glowing manically. It began rolling slowly, creaking, toward Bolan.

Autofire from the lab snapped Bolan's attention back to his assailants. They were laying down a heavy pattern, preparing to charge at the door.

Bolan pivoted again, blind, and fired once more into the lab, keeping them back. Even if he stayed on single shot, they could force him out of ammo quickly.

He turned to face the robot, which was twenty feet away and closing. Bolan brought around the M-16, firing once, twice, the bullets pinging harmlessly off Arthur's heavy armor. And still it came.

The warrior was trapped—the robot a mere ten feet away, the killzone of the doorway inches behind him. He popped two shots into the lab, then tried to shoot out the robot's remote-controlled eyes, but missed.

Suddenly a screaming figure came barreling down the hallway, Fred Haines charging full tilt onto the back of the robot. His face was strained with rage as he rose, pulling at the robot's head with powerful hands.

Bolan turned back to the doorway, surprising a water-slick face no more than two feet in front of him. He got off one shot, blowing out the airman's left eye. The body, slipping on the sprinkler-slick floor, tumbled forward, sliding through the doorway. Bolan grabbed the gun from the man's lifeless hands.

He brought the weapon up and fired a hard burst this time, driving everyone to cover. Then he turned in time to see Howard Davis come out of his office with the long pike he used when guiding the dolphins through their paces.

The robot was turning in circles, trying to dislodge Haines, who had covered the photocells with his hands, blinding the machine. Howard poked hard at the rolling legs of the robot, trying to unbalance it.

"The wall!" Bolan yelled. "Try for some leverage!"

Howard moved in front of the thrashing machine, jamming his pike hard into the panel-and-Sheetrock wall, anchoring it. When the robot creaked forward and met the pike, Howard threw his weight on his side of the pole and the robot tottered with the unequal weight distribution. Finally it fell forward with the screaming Fred Haines riding it to the floor.

Bolan pulled away from the doorframe, turning to the others. "Are there stairs down?"

"Off the break room!" Haines shouted above the din of the weapons fire.

"We'll need a diversion!"

"Trust me!" Haines ran down the hall.

"How did I do?" Howard asked.

"Great! Now get the hell out of here! Don't take the elevator. Someone was down on Two manipulating Arthur. Now get!"

Howard was up and running, putting a hand to his mouth as he passed Chuck's body. Within seconds, Haines was beside Bolan again, a wine bottle in each hand, a piece of torn cloth dangling from the necks.

"Molotov cocktail?"

Haines grinned. "I guess my checkered past has come in handy after all."

Bolan reached into his pocket and pulled out Ike's lighter. He hitched the M-16 onto his shoulder and took one of the gasoline cocktails from his companion.

"Ready?" he said, thumbing the lighter.

"You bet," Haines replied, eyes dancing.

Bolan lit the fuses, and he and Fred lobbed the bombs through the doorway. The bottles smashed against a table. Orange fire bloomed through the opening, and men screamed in agony.

"Let's go!" Bolan yelled as the gas spread across the water, turning half the room into an inferno.

They charged down the hall toward the waiting area, Haines scooping up Chuck's gun as they passed the dead guard. Firing continued behind them. Someone, probably Howard, had used a lobby chair to block the elevator doors, blocking that avenue. Chuck's guard station phone rang incessantly.

They could hear a commotion behind them, but kept running and didn't turn to look. They hit the swing doors of the canteen on a dead run, pounding into the break area.

"There!" Haines yelled, pointing to the red exit light in the far corner.

They never slowed in their race to the door, bursting through it to the stairs just as the uniformed killers broke into the break area, firing on the run.

"Phew!" Haines said, winded, as they pounded the stairs. "I ain't had this much fun in fifteen years."

"Not bad for an old-timer!"

Five flights passed in a blur and they came out on the first level of the parking garage to find Howard, bent over, gasping for air.

"More...exercise than I'm...used to," the boy gasped, as Bolan patted him on the back.

"You did great, kid," he said.

"Now what?" Haines asked.

"We've probably got less than ten seconds to get the hell out of here," Bolan returned, eyes already scanning the darkness of the parking garage. "Fred, you take Howard in your car. It's me they want, not you."

Haines stared at him for several seconds, his urban terrorist's mind immediately grasping the logic of Bolan's words. "Got it. You gonna be okay?"

"Yeah. Thanks to you."

Haines handed Bolan Chuck's gun, then grabbed Howard by the arm, pulling him across the lot. "What the hell!" he called over his shoulder. "It was fun!"

Bolan stood his ground until he heard the roar of the hard guy's engine and the squeal of tires. Then he hurried to the stairs again, moving down to level two.

He jogged out into the nearly deserted parking area, shouts erupting from near the building entrance. He ran to his Jeep and cranked the engine to life.

He geared into reverse, watching shadows charging his position from the distance. Backing quickly, he jammed the brakes and threw it into first, the vehicle jumping forward with a squeal as the first bullets tore into the plastic back window.

He distanced them quickly, racing across the parking lot at sixty miles an hour, not a security guard in sight.

The outside gate was closed. Bolan didn't give a thought as to whether the vehicle could survive the impact. He merely tromped on the gas, set the wheel and ducked.

He hit the gate hard, metal grinding against metal as the barrier slammed open. A twisted pole grazed his shoulder as it hurtled through the windshield.

Bolan slumped down, the pole gouging a huge hole through his seat, preventing him from sitting upright. Without slowing, he twisted the metal junk hard, finally jerking it loose and pushing it back out through the windshield and onto the pavement. He was free.

Ike was dead, and Chuck, maybe even Smyth. He had drawn Peg Ackerman into the open, but had been lulled by the leisurely pace of the institute. He'd known that the GOG people played for keeps, but had let himself slide enough out of the combat mode that he hadn't expected the severity or swiftness of the repercussion. He'd been lulled by civility. He felt the deaths of his co-workers were partly his fault, but he wasn't enough of a martyr to not place the real blame exactly where it lay—squarely on Peg Ackerman's shoulders.

The gloves were off now. He'd opened the hostilities and Peg's people had responded in kind—and now he owed them.

He became aware, finally, of something in his hand, looking down to see that the dead airman's dog tags were still wound around his fingers. He pulled the chain off and stuck it and the tags in his pocket. This time he had evidence.

He drove quickly, but had slowed down to within the speed limit, his mind slotting back to combat mode, settling into patterns of surveillance and awareness. As he drove Orlando Drive toward Colonial, he used a free hand to reach over and pick up Chuck's gun from the passenger seat.

The weapon was a short-barreled .38 revolver, the kind that was called the Police Special. Using one hand to drive, he clicked open the cylinder to a full load, then snapped it closed, taking off the safety. The .38 would do in a pinch, but he itched for the feel of Big Thunder in his right hand.

Two blocks before reaching the intersection of Orlando and Colonial he heard sirens, checking the rearview mirror to see two fire trucks speeding up behind him. He pulled out of the lane and slowed to a stop, watching as the trucks hurried past.

Bolan felt the short hairs at his nape prickle as the fire trucks turned onto Colonial, in the same direction as he was headed.

When he turned in, he could see the flames licking at the sky just above rooftop level several blocks ahead and just off Colonial to the south. The flames served as a beacon, drawing him, and within two minutes he found himself looking at the raging inferno that had been the home of Peg Ackerman.

Smoke filled the night air, the light cast by the cherries of police cars and fire engines barely slicing through it. The smell of charred wood permeated everything. Bolan pulled up as close as he could and walked toward the fire, a small crowd being kept at a distance by several police officers.

He checked street addresses just to be sure, as neighbors rushed around their houses with hoses, trying to protect their roofs from errant cinders. But the fire hoses were taking most of the water, leaving pitiful little pressure for everyone else.

Bolan moved up and merged with the crowd, watching as the two-story frame house was consumed. The heavily suited firemen were hosing mammoth jets of water onto the structure to no avail. It was a raging, uncontrollable inferno.

He tried to go closer, but a policeman stepped in front of him. "Back behind the line."

"I know the woman who lives there. Can't I..."

"Better use the past tense, buddy," the cop said, and pointed to a group of coughing firemen who carried a stretcher to a waiting ambulance.

Bolan pulled back, skirting the crowd to come up on the ambulance just as they were loading the covered body into its back.

"Please," he said, reaching for the cover. "I need—"

"Who are you?" a burly fireman asked, grabbing Bolan's hand; the man's face was smeared with soot beneath the heavy metal hat that he wore.

"I—I'm her husband," he said, reaching again for the blanket.

He wasn't stopped this time as he peeled back the woolen cover to gaze at Peg Ackerman, who had died from smoke inhalation, her eyes wide in horror, her mouth opened in a silent scream.

Bolan dropped the covering and stumbled away from the dead woman.

"Hey!" the fireman called. "Come back here!"

But Bolan had already turned and was running, tripping over hoses in the street as smoke choked up everything, twisting the landscape into a surreal nightmare.

He'd had no idea of what he was setting in motion this morning when he'd rattled her cage. They'd gone for him and, apparently, were cleaning house completely, killing their informant, clearing the boards. As he reached the Jeep and jerked open the door, there was but one thought on his mind: were they going for Julie, too?

Chapter Sixteen

Bolan tore through the streets, his thoughts as dark as the moonless night that presided over the chaos that seemed to be spreading through Orlando.

He fought for control, his feelings for Julie clouding his rational mind, only to find himself pushing the Jeep too hard, his foot locked on the gas as visions of Peg Ackerman's death mask pushed unrelentingly to the forefront of his brain.

Why didn't he take to the mattresses after he'd discovered they were under surveillance? He didn't because Julie didn't want to and he gave in to her. Why did he let the woman cloud his judgment? He'd been a fool to let her stay there, worse than a fool—stupid. And now they'd have to pay for that, perhaps with their lives.

He took the corner of Aloma and Avondale on two wheels, nearly rolling the vehicle, the revolver sliding off the seat.

"Damn!"

Bolan regained control and gunned the engine, speeding down the dark residential streets, keeping his eyes on the road and alert for any pedestrian who might stray into his path.

He screeched to a stop in front of his house and saw the van that he had fallen from Saturday night parked two houses away.

He jumped out of the Jeep and ran around to the passenger side. As he tore open the door, the sound of gunshots cracked obscenely from within the house.

The warrior knelt on the floor, reaching beneath the seat, feeling around wildly for the .38. As his fingers closed on cold steel an explosion rocked the house, shattering the front window, which spewed a huge ball of flame.

He stood and charged toward the house, autofire punctuating each step. Another gasoline bomb exploded in the house, flames eating away at the interior. He remembered how quickly Peg's place had burned.

The warrior reached the kitchen stoop and jumped the steps to stand beside the door. Within himself he found that place of calm, and took several deep breaths to keep himself under some measure of control.

He reached out and tried the knob. Locked. He brought up the .38 and smashed the butt against the kitchen window, reaching a hand through to open the lock from the inside.

Quietly he opened the door and crept into the dark kitchen, which was rapidly filling with smoke. He could feel the heat through the walls.

Several single shots boomed, and he recognized the sound of Big Thunder. He hurried through the kitchen, chancing a quick look around the doorframe into the hallway.

The entire living room was engulfed, tongues of fire licking into the hallway. At the end of the hall, a lone figure crouched before Julie's doorway fifteen feet distant, reloading a shotgun.

Bolan stepped into the burning hall, an intense machine of destructive energy geared for the kill.

"Looking for someone?" he asked.

A startled face looked up from the shotgun. Bolan didn't give the man a second to realize what was going to happen to him; he raised the .38 and squeezed the trigger. The small gun coughed in his hand, its messenger tearing a third eye in the forehead of the killer, who slid, wide-eyed, into a sitting position on the floor. Five shots left.

Another gunner poked his head out of the bedroom doorway, and Bolan let go a shot, driving him back into the room. The Executioner eased past the flames and against the wall the door was on, pressing his back against the hot Sheetrock.

A shotgun blast tore into the wall near Bolan's previous position, the gunner coming halfway through the door.

Bolan fired twice, both shots taking the man chest high. He stumbled through the doorway, still alive, and disappeared into the darkness of Bolan's room.

There were more shots from Julie's room. Bolan slid along the wall, turning back once to see that the entire hallway behind him was engulfed in flames.

The air was getting thin, the smoke choking.

He heard glass breaking in his room as he came around Julie's doorframe to find a third shooter hiding behind a dresser, firing a shotgun at Julie, who was inside a closet on the other side of the room.

Bolan drilled two shots into the man just as his weapon discharged for the last time. He whirled, startled, as Julie staggered out of the closet, wild-eyed, her hands locked around Big Thunder. She fired a shot from the huge handgun before dropping it to the floor.

"God, Julie!" Bolan yelled, running to her.

"Oh, Mack!" she cried, collapsing into his arms and clinging to him desperately. "They came . . . came and—"

Part of the ceiling fell in, and where walls had once stood, sheets of flame now roared.

"The window, quick!" Bolan yelled, picking up a vanity chair and throwing it through the only exit.

"Wait!" Julie quickly retrieved Bolan's combat harness from the closet.

The big man, combat harness slung over his shoulder, climbed through the window, then reached back in, helping her through just as the rest of the ceiling fell.

Julie staggered away from the inferno, wanting to throw herself on the ground to rest.

"No!" Bolan took her by the arm to keep her on her feet. "There's still one of them out here. We'll rest later."

They moved around the front of the house, the very air hot with fire, sweat pouring from Bolan's face. He discarded the .38 and pulled the Beretta from its sling in the combat harness.

Jack Durbin, his next-door neighbor, was out hosing down his roof, his son, Mel, standing beside him. Suddenly a shadow staggered out of the bushes.

Bolan tracked with the Beretta, but the shadow darted to Durbin's side, putting him in the line of fire. The hood grabbed up Mel, wrapping the youngster in his arms, a gun to his head. Durbin had dropped his hose, he and his wife pursuing their child's abductor.

"Back!" the punk yelled.

"Stay away from him!" Bolan ordered, bringing up the Beretta in a two-handed Weaver's grip.

"No!" the mother shouted, horrified. "No shooting! Please!"

The man dragged the petrified boy to his van, Bolan tracking him with the Beretta.

"What do you think?" the goon asked, dark eyes flashing as he passed barely ten feet in front of Bolan. "Want to watch the boy die?"

"Let him go," Bolan said, and he gauged his shot, convinced that the man would kill the boy as soon as he reached the van. Mel was hoisted high, head-to-head with the killer. Only a small portion of the man's face was visible, a risky shot at best.

"Go to hell," the punk said, squeezing Mel tighter and jamming the barrel of his automatic pistol into the boy's ear.

"For God's sake!" Jack Durbin screamed. "Don't argue with him!"

Bolan could see half a smirk peeking out from behind the boy's head and walked slowly abreast of the kidnapper as the man got closer to his van.

"Let it go." Julie's voice came from behind.

"You just keep the parents off me."

"Mack—"

"Do it!"

The man kept moving. A few more feet and he'd be back into the shadows, no shot possible. Sirens were closing in from Aloma.

Bolan took several deep breaths and tried to detach himself totally from his surroundings. He had made this shot, difficult as it was, several times in the hellgrounds. But nobody died if you missed.

"Drop the gun!" the goon ordered, and Bolan had run completely out of options.

He had reached a place beyond thinking, almost as if he had become the barrel of the gun. An extension of his finger, he pointed it at the place where the laws of physics told him he couldn't miss. His fingers pulsed with his heartbeat on the trigger...

"Drop it now!"

...and when he was between heartbeats, he let his mind float and become a gun sight, and he squeezed the trigger gently and lovingly.

The sound of the gunshot brought him immediately back to reality. The goon was down, and little Mel was crying loudly, charging past Bolan to the waiting arms of his parents.

Bolan turned to see the flashing lights of the fire engines and police cars at the end of the block. "Let's get the hell out of here."

BROGNOLA STOOD in his living room, a glass of Scotch in his hand. His sleeves were rolled up past his elbows, and his tie unknotted, collar unbuttoned.

He was glad that Helen wasn't there to see what they'd done to her house. The living-room furniture had been either pushed against the walls or removed to the garage, replaced by the plain wooden table full of telephones in the center of the room. The walls were covered with maps. Brognola's house had become the command center for counterinsurgence on Project GOG.

The room was full of people, trusted allies willing to put themselves on the line for the preservation of the union and the constitution. They manned the phones or worked the computer terminals tied into the phone modems. There was an air of urgency surrounding the entire operation, and Brognola was proud that so many good people were willing to give so much just on his word and the word of Gunnar Greggson.

Hendry, a skinny young man with glasses, had one of the phones turned over on its back, alligator clips attached to phone leads running back to a counter of some sort. Small headphones were resting on his neck as he applied a screwdriver to the bottom of the phone. Brognola stopped beside him.

"How's it going?"

"Your phone lines are clear," Hendry said. "No sweat. If anyone tampers with them at this point in any way, this will happen..."

Hendry stuck the screwdriver onto one of the leads, causing a red light set in a black box on the table to light up.

"Thanks." Brognola looked at his watch, worry lining his face. It was after nine, and Bolan hadn't made his nightly call. The Fed took a sip from his tumbler, set it on the table and cleared his throat.

"Okay, people." He spoke loudly to be heard above the buzz of conversation. "As you know, we've been making some progress with Baylor Goggle. Let's see where we're standing right now with everything."

Greggson was sitting in the corner on a fold-up metal chair with one of his computer people. He raised a hand and spoke. "I think we should address the problems and possibilities of cracking into the GOG computer network."

"Go for it."

The computer man, a Japanese-American named Bob Ito, stood and smiled shyly. "The question has been raised of the possibility of particulars about Project GOG being filed directly in the government computer network. In my opinion, that's not just possible, it's probable.''

"That wouldn't be very smart," said a woman near the phone bank. "I mean, why would anyone put their plans for a takeover of the government in the government computers where anyone could see them?''

"Several good reasons." Ito pushed back a shock of black hair that had fallen on his forehead. "First of all, if you're dealing with the military, you would be putting information into a system that everyone uses already, the quickest and easiest way of disseminating information. Secondly, not just 'anyone' could see them. The file would be coded, so only people who knew the proper password could access the file. Theoretically the idea is beautifully simple. You could pull a complicated coup d'état right under the noses of those you wish to depose, simply by using their own systems against them.''

"If that's the case," Brognola interrupted, "then couldn't we access the same files by working to find the password with experts like you, Bob?''

"Perhaps," the man conceded. "You must keep in mind that computer hacking is a great deal like espionage, working through layers upon layers. For instance, whoever thought up this program, if it exists, would have to consider the possibility that someone, either deliberately or by calculation, would try to crack the file. So, safeguards would be set up.''

"What sort of safeguards?" Brognola asked as he walked to the window, peering through the brocaded curtains and into the moonless Silver Springs, Maryland, night. He pulled the cigar he'd been chewing on all day out of his breast pocket and stuck it between his lips, fighting the urge to light it.

"Perhaps a person would put a worm on the program," Ito said, "that would crash the whole file should someone try to enter by using passwords at random, or try to bypass the password completely with fancy footwork.

With a worm, you not only would deny access but destroy the evidence completely.''

"Are there any ways around that?" Greggson asked.

Ito smiled broadly. "The catch with any 'foolproof' system is that if the human mind can conceive of the puzzle, the human mind can crack it. It simply becomes a matter of time and eliminating all the existing possibilities."

"Time is something we don't have much of," Brognola reminded him, still looking outside—was that a shadow flitting across his front lawn? "What are your suggestions?"

"There are two choices. You can either go at the file directly—the quick way—and face the possibility of a major error, or you can go at it the slow, safe way and depend on ultimate success . . . perhaps too late. My suggestion to you at this point, is that we go at it slowly, working down through the passwords and security clearances that we know, then proceeding with caution. That way, we can always switch to the quick approach if things get tight."

Oscar Largent spoke up. "What we need to do is nab one of these guys and force him to give us the password."

"Walk carefully," Ito told him. "It would be simplicity itself to change a password if they felt their security had been breached."

"On that subject," Brognola said, moving to another window to scan the perimeters of his yard, "how is our surveillance going?"

"Right now," said Ann Beckman, an agent from Enforcement Division, "we've got Leland and most of his staff under observation twenty-four hours a day. They seem to be involved with routine, except for Captain Norman Michaels, who is moving around a great deal, engaged in a large number of nonroutine activities."

"We'll concentrate on him." Brognola squinted into the night gloom and saw the shadow again—or was it another shadow? "If he jumps, we'll get him."

"If he jumps where?" Greggson asked.

"I wish to God I knew. We need evidence right now, hard evidence. If we can dig up something substantial on this we won't need to depend so much on the computer—" He stopped cold.

There it was again. The shadow seemed to be moving closer to the house...and another...and a third.

"Kill the lights and hit the deck," Brognola ordered, reaching for the .38 in his waistband. "Someone's out there."

He hit the overhead switch himself, others reaching for freestanding lamps that had been taken from tables and set on the floor.

Then all hell broke loose.

Automatic-weapons fire exploded the stillness of the night like rolling thunder, the darkened house crying loudly with the breaking of glass, porcelain and splintering wood. A barrage of fire tore mercilessly through the living room, the people on the floor pelted with a shower of glass, plaster and wood fragments as windows and frames imploded in a continuous devastating rampage of destruction.

"They're going to try to take the house!" Brognola shouted. "We've got to defend the perimeters. Those with weapons spread out down here. Everyone else...follow me upstairs!"

People began to crawl on hands and knees to defendable positions, Brognola moving toward the front hall on his stomach. He made the hallway, followed by several of his Justice colleagues. His house had become a shooting gallery, an unrecognizable noisy horror in the moonless dark. He finally pulled the cigar out of his mouth and threw it onto the floor—two-thirds had been blown away.

The carpeted stairs were just off the dining room, protected by an inner wall. Ann Beckman was right behind him. Brognola turned and patted her on the back. "Go!" he ordered. "Wait at the top of the stairs!"

She started up, followed by the others. Distracted by the sounds of gunfire and shattering glass, Brognola stole a quick look into the dining room. A line of withering fire was tearing Helen's grandmother's breakfront and dining table to shreds, Noritake china exploding in porcelain shards. Hot rage was consuming him. Damn them! Damn them to hell!

He started up the stairs, glancing back once to see a black-clad figure diving through the remnants of the dining-room window. He raised his gun, firing three times in quick succession. At least one of the slugs struck home as the man fell backward out of the house.

"Somebody take the dining room!" he screamed, and fired again as another shadow approached the window.

Largent and Healy ran at a crouch to join him at the stairs, Healy's left arm hanging limp, dripping blood.

"They're coming through here!" the head Fed told them, the two men dropping to the glass-filled floor.

Brognola turned and raced up the stairs. Four people waited for him at the top, Greggson among them. "You should start packin' fire, Counselor," he advised. "Come on!"

Brognola led them through the dark upstairs, running into the room that had been the fourth bedroom when he'd bought the house, but was now an office. Complete with filing cabinets and a large desk, the room also contained a weapons case where the Fed stored his hunting rifles and handguns.

He rushed to the desk, fumbling in the dark for the key to the gun case; he couldn't find it. In desperation he hefted a moonrock paperweight and hurled it at the front of the case, shattering the glass.

He ran to the case and pulled out two rifles he kept for deer season, digging down in the bottom of the case for boxes of shells. He felt his heart racing and forced himself to calm.

"On the roof!" Greggson called, and the head Fed ran to the window to see a man in black climbing onto the small balcony that defined the second story of the old frame house.

Brognola fired twice, driving the man back. Greggson took up a position at the window with a rifle, Brognola moving back to the weapons case to reload the .38.

He handed the .38 to a woman beside him. "Know how to use this?"

"No."

"Just hold it up and look down your finger and squeeze the trigger," he instructed. "Shoot at anything that moves."

She took the gun and he grabbed a Remington 12-gauge pump shotgun for himself, hurriedly shoving shells into the chamber from a box he had spilled on the floor.

"Spread out!" the Fed yelled. "Keep them out of here!"

He charged out of the room and ran into the master bedroom. Sheer-curtained French doors opened onto the balcony. As he entered the room, he could see a man easing himself over the balcony rails. Angered, he pumped once, this time putting the shotgun to his shoulder and taking the time to sight.

When he pulled the trigger the glass doors exploded, the man screaming and falling off the balcony. Brognola charged out onto the balcony, where he had a commanding view of his large lot.

He could see fifteen attackers, already in disarray and falling back with their wounded. The element of surprise gone, they were proving more vulnerable than the defenders in the house. Brognola's warning had turned the trick.

He fired, missed, pumped and fired again, hitting a retreating man in the leg. As he sprawled on the lawn two men rushed forward to help him away.

Brognola pumped his weapon again, but they were taking to the shadows and were beginning to distance him. He moved to the edge of the balcony and, putting a leg over the low rail, began to climb down the rose trellis.

He jumped the last ten feet to the ground, his own people already filtering out of the house to chase the interlopers.

His head light from the anger and the excitement, Brognola tore across his well-manicured lawn, adrenaline pumping.

They'd done it. The sons of bitches had come to his house and tried to take him on his own ground. He charged into the street, just as three cars screeched away. He raised his shotgun and drew a bead on retreating tail-lights, but stopped himself at the last second, remembering this was a residential neighborhood.

He stood there fuming. How dared they violate him in this way! His wife could have been killed, his children. Leland's goons hadn't known who was going to be there, nor did they care. They had come to kill whomever they could find. "You won't get away with it, Leland, you bastard," he said with deep intensity. "I swear you won't get away with this. This is my home, *my home*, and by God, you'll pay!"

Oscar Largent ran from the house to flag him down as he walked slowly back, calming himself. "Your man, Bolan, is on the line."

"Good," Brognola said, easing his mind, at least, in that direction. "Did we get any of them?"

"They didn't leave anyone behind."

"Just like a military operation," Brognola growled. "Check the grounds carefully. See if they left anything or anybody behind."

"Yes, sir."

"What about our people?"

"Cuts and bruises," Largent reported. "Ted took one in the forearm, but it went through clean."

"Thank God for that."

"Yes, sir."

Brognola crossed the last few feet of the front lawn and entered the house. The place was a shambles, everything that was still standing covered with glass, wood and plaster. The furniture on the ground floor would have to be replaced, as deep gouges had been dug into everything. He looked at the hundreds of bullet holes in the walls. Some carpenter was going to earn his vacation just puttying up the holes.

Greggson was coming down the stairs as the Fed walked into the dining room for a quick look—and was sorry that he had.

"What do we do now?" the lawyer asked. "Find a new place?"

Brognola stared hard at him. "We board up the windows and post guards. Leland isn't going to run me out of my home, not now, not ever. If he wants me, he can come on. We'll give him all he can handle."

Greg smiled. "Down, boy."

"Sorry," Brognola said sheepishly. "It's just that they've hit me where it hurts most, this time. And it cuts so deep I'll never forget it. I'm going to be a bulldog on Leland. I'm going to get my teeth into his leg and never let go."

"Trying to say you're mad?"

"They've destroyed more than furniture here, Greg," he said. His friend nodded solemnly. "Check all the phone lines, would you?"

Brognola stepped through the mess of the living room, smiling briefly as he picked up the phone. "I'd about given you up for dead," he said into the receiver.

"You wouldn't have been far wrong," Bolan replied. "It all came down here—at the institute, at my house, at Peg Ackerman's."

"Isn't she the woman we're running the security check on?"

"Yeah," Bolan replied, "but there isn't much we can do with her now. She's dead."

"Are you all right?"

"So far," Bolan said. "I'm calling from the Jeep. It's all we've got left. It's possible we've got a tail. What about you? I hear you had troubles."

"You got that right." Brognola briefly explained the situation.

When he'd finished, Bolan said, "Sorry about all this. Maybe I'm responsible. I got tired of waiting and flushed the woman out this morning."

"We'll keep checking on her, but I'm afraid..."

"Of what?"

"I can't say just yet," Brognola replied. "We'll check."

"I've translated part of the code," Bolan said. "It's a place, Gila Bend, Arizona."

"What the hell?"

"Yeah. What the hell. I think my days undercover at the institute are over. What now?"

"I want you to check on something for me. One of the *Challenger* vendors was a company called GeoScan. It's a subsidiary of Baylor Goggle and Optical based in Sanford, Florida."

"Just north of here," Bolan informed him, the line staticky. "Where do they fit in?"

Brognola took a breath, lifting up the base of the phone so one of the Enforcement people could sweep the glass shards off the table. "My secretary had been receiving large weekly payments from Baylor since she came to Justice. It was money she never declared, and we can find no reason for her receiving it. Baylor Goggle and Optical, among other things, manufactures rubies for industrial lasers. Our purchase orders here show a great many purchases by DOD from Baylor, but never delivery. Money's gone out to them in the millions just from us, yet we checked their income tax records today and found that they list a gross income of about a million five a year."

"Have you called them on it?"

"No," Brognola said, putting the phone back on the table. "That's what I want you to do. I don't trust anyone but you to handle it. The place has been in existence since 1937, but was purchased several years ago by an investment firm called Centurion Investments. We're checking them back now."

"In other words, you just want me to poke around."

"Yeah, that's it," the head Fed replied. "Something's obviously not on the up-and-up. I just want you to nose around a little and see what they're doing out there. Meanwhile we'll be finding out what we can from our end."

"Right," Bolan said. "Are we getting close to anything?"

"The circle's widening," Brognola replied, tiring as his adrenaline rush wore down. "Both sides have drawn blood. Beyond that, I know nothing."

"Nothing," Bolan repeated. "I'd hate to tell that to all the folks who've died so far."

BOLAN TOOK A QUICK LEFT at the last second and without warning, burrowing through a darkened residential neighborhood. He clamped the telephone receiver between his neck and shoulder to keep from losing it.

Julie knelt on the passenger seat, looking back through the shredded remnants of the plastic rear window. "He turned, too," she said, then a second later, "Oh my God, another one."

"We're being pursued, Hal," Bolan spoke calmly into the phone. "I'm taking evasive action."

He jerked the wheel hard right, then right again at the next corner, heading back to the main road. He stiffened in the seat, reaching down into his pocket.

"Striker, I'm hanging up!"

"Wait!" Bolan shouted, pulling the dog tags out of his pants. "I want you to run down someone for me. I jerked the tags off an SP at the institute."

"Go."

"Johnson, LaMar," Bolan read, then recited the SSN. "He looked like the real thing to me, Hal, Air Force two-striper."

"I'll get on it."

"They're still coming," Julie said from beside him.

"They're pros," Bolan told his friend. "I've got to give it my attention."

"Caution, big guy," Brognola said. "I want you intact for the rest of this thing."

"You know me."

"Yeah, that's why I'm warning you."

Bolan hung up and checked the rearview mirror. Two sets of headlights were closing from a distance of a hundred yards. He looked at Julie. "Get into your seat belt," he ordered, reaching back with one hand to pull his own around.

He hooked his belt, watched Julie do the same. "Look," he said. "We're slow and not very maneuverable. The only thing going for us is the ruggedness of the Jeep. Our best shot is to get off the road and go overland with the four-wheel drive. Just hang on. I can get us out of this."

"You've got the wheel," she said tensely. She sat half turned in the seat, watching him and the road behind.

They came quickly up on Colonial Drive, Bolan slamming on the brakes to avoid traffic on both sides. He watched the rearview, the chase vehicles gaining rapidly. Traffic was thick, but he had no choice. Taking a slim shot, he goosed the vehicle into the traffic, hanging hard left and fishtailing into the right lane, bleating horns following him as he gunned it, moving toward Orange Avenue. Their hope lay to the south, in the orange groves off Oak Ridge.

Horns blared a block behind them, and they knew the chase was still on.

"Both of them," Julie said. "They're still there."

Bolan grunted. They were good.

For ten minutes they played cat and mouse, Bolan moving in and out of traffic, his adversaries always right behind, chopping his lead a car length at a time. He just couldn't get up the speed he needed on the straightaways to distance them. They turned south onto Orange, traffic thinning, then west again on Oak Ridge. Suddenly the city was gone, and they were plunging into dark, reclaimed swampland, their headlights the only guide as they ate black asphalt at seventy miles an hour.

The warrior checked the rearview. Two sets of headlights were taking up both sides of the two-lane road, and they were closing fast. He hoped his strategy had been right. Once again, he had to question his own motivation. He wanted this settled out of town and away from innocent people, but had he been alone, he would have stopped here and held his ground in a firefight. But he hated to risk it with Julie in the car.

They heard the first shot at the same moment the side-view mirror shattered, which was blown right off the Jeep.

"Get down!" he yelled, and Julie hit the floorboards as acres of orange groves blurred past on both sides.

The shooting intensified, Bolan ducking as low as he could, while looking for an advantageous place to pull off the road. Automatic fire raked the car, and the windshield shattered, Bolan smashing out the remnants with the butt of Big Thunder as bullets thudded into the body of the Jeep.

Suddenly the Jeep veered sharply as a shot took out one of the rear tires. Bolan tried to ride it down as the vehicle swerved off the road, knocking over a barbed-wire fence and barely getting between the rows of bushy trees without crashing into them.

Branches slashed through the open windshield as they barreled over the terrain. Bolan regained control and killed the lights, slowing to twenty. Julie climbed back up on the seat, eyes wide, and looked behind.

"They're still coming. They're leaving the road."

"Right."

He switched to four-wheel drive and picked up speed, moving through the truck lanes of the grove, bouncing wildly through chuckholes. He cut across the rows, moving through the endless lines of trees that were set in neat rows.

"I can't see them," she said.

In response, Bolan slowed slightly, but continued the dangerous route between the lanes. The grove looked large, perhaps a thousand acres or more, but he couldn't go far on three wheels.

"Still no sign?" he asked, as they careened wildly, lifting off the seats with each change of row.

"No...nothing."

Julie continued scanning behind and around them, and Bolan slowed even more, listening to the grinding of an impaired axle that was on the verge of collapse.

He stopped the vehicle in a truck lane, making sure there were no lights on anywhere in the vehicle.

"Okay," he said quietly. "Let's check it out."

They got out of the Jeep, the machine leaning seriously to the passenger side.

"Bolan, I—"

"Shh," he whispered, finger to his lips. "Don't slam your door."

They stood in the orange grove, nothing but rows of dark trees as far as they could see in any direction.

The night was still, the aromatic, pungent odor of oranges a physical presence all around them. Bolan listened intently. Far in the distance he could hear the revving engine of a car trying to get out of a ditch. They were safe. For the first time in hours he relaxed.

Julie sagged against the Jeep, burying her face in her hands. "Life with you is just one carnival after another, isn't it?"

He moved up close to her. "Are you okay?"

"Of course I'm not okay!" she snapped. "Do you think normal people live this way?"

The soldier reached out a comforting hand, but she turned from him, jerking away. "Oh, just leave me alone."

He shrugged. "Fine."

The first thing he needed to do was to check the damage to the wheel. Moving behind the Jeep he walked to the closest orange tree and found the five-foot gas jet pole that the orange growers use to keep the trees warm during

Florida's cold spring evenings when the temperature got below freezing.

He reached into his pocket and pulled out the disposable lighter that had belonged to Ike Silver and had already saved his life twice that night. When the chips had been down, Ike had been there. Bolan wondered if he'd be able to say the same for Julie Arnold.

The debacle at the institute had left an emptiness in the pit of his stomach. He hadn't known any of the dead very well, but all of them deserved better than being chewed up and spit out simply because they'd been in the way when the GOG boys had come for him.

Bolan thumbed the lighter and held it to the top of the jet, turning on the gas. It lit with a thump, the blue-white flame lighting the immediate area like a campfire.

He walked back to the Jeep and squatted by the back wheel to take a look. The tire was nowhere to be seen, the shreds of rubber lost somewhere on the trip through the grove. The rim was bent, but if he could devise a decent lever, it could be straightened. He'd be able to get the spare on and drive them out of there. But not tonight. Tonight he wasn't going anywhere.

He felt Julie's eyes on him as he walked back to the trees and picked an orange off the branch. He returned to the Jeep and sat on the ground, leaning against the broken wheel while he peeled the fruit.

"Look," she said from several feet away. "I didn't mean to jump all over you. I—I killed a man tonight, I—"

"You shot him," Bolan corrected, pulling apart the orange, "but he was already dead. I don't miss. So, you didn't do what you thought you did. Here, keep up your strength."

She walked over to him and accepted the proffered segment. "I would have killed him. I *wanted* to kill him."

Bolan shoved a segment into his mouth. "The alternative would have been to let him kill you."

She slid down to sit beside him. "It was horrible. I was in the bedroom, thinking about taking a shower. They...

they just tore right through the front door. I...I didn't think, I just ran for your guns, and they were there, shooting, and I...I..."

"You shot back," Bolan said gently. "Even civilized people have to do it sometimes."

She looked up at him, the gaslight alive in her eyes. "I guess so," she said softly.

He handed her another segment. "The thing I don't get," he said, "is the fact that they seem to know every step we're going to take before we take it. We've reduced this operation to the most basic level, cut out all links in the chain, and they *still* seem to know."

A look of pain crossed her face that he couldn't quite understand, then she looked down at the ground without responding.

They sat eating for a moment, Bolan feeling the aches and pains in a body that had taken a lot of punishment over the years. Then Julie said, "What do we do now?"

"You mean besides trying to stay alive?" he asked, not expecting an answer. "Well, there's a place that Hal wants us to check out just north of here called Baylor Goggle and Optical Company. He seems to think—"

"What?" she interrupted. "Did you say Baylor Goggle and Optical?"

He turned to stare at her. "Ring a bell?"

She nodded. "Remember when you asked me to commit the billboard outside Grolier to memory?"

"Sure."

"Well, one of the companies that helped pay the salaries of the institute's employees was a subsidiary of Baylor Goggle. Isn't that weird?"

"Wait a minute," he said waving her off. "I think, I..."

"What?"

"The second series of words in the code," he said.

"Waterfront legend sea specs?"

"Yeah. Think about it. A port city, a waterfront city, is usually located on a bay."

"And 'legend' is synonymous with 'lore,'" she said, picking up on it. "Bay-lore...Baylor. But what about specs...specifications?"

"No," he said. "Specs is a slang term for glasses."

"Glasses...goggles, right?" she said excitedly. "Then sea is simply the homonym for see."

"Right. See...optic. Baylor Goggle and Optical. But Baylor is here in Florida, not in Gila Bend."

"I'm still hungry," she groused.

He gestured around. "Help yourself. It's your turn to cook."

"You plan to stay out here all night, don't you?"

He nodded. "It's going to take me several hours to fix the tire. I'm not up to it tonight. We'll sleep in the Jeep, fix it in the morning, then be bright-eyed for our meeting at Baylor Goggle tomorrow."

"Where I come from," she complained, "camping out means staying in a hotel without a makeup case."

"Well, right now no makeup case is the least of our problems. I'm worried about gas and about us eating something tomorrow besides oranges."

Julie smiled and stood up. "Living with you teaches a person self-reliance," she said, removing a wad of cash—the rest of Brognola's money—from her pocket. "I never travel light, Dr. Sparks."

"Bolan," he said, staring at the money. "The name is Bolan."

Chapter Seventeen

Hal Brognola knelt on a mat in the soft earth of the begonia bed beneath the dining-room window and tried to repair the damage to the garden as best he could. Working in the garden was a pleasure that he and Helen shared, something simple that could take their minds off the pressure and phoniness of Washington life and remind them of the common bonds and values that guide people's lives. All that was ruined now, the garden destroyed in a matter of minutes during the firefight of the night before.

He turned the trowel in the rich, dark earth, exposing a worm that inched away quickly to get into the shade.

"Someone's coming," Ted Healy called from the porch, where he stood guard with a riot gun.

"Thanks," Brognola said, standing and taking off his leather gardening gloves. He turned to the street, half a football field away. One of his people was waving an arm from behind the barricade of cars that blocked the entire front of the property.

Brognola waved back, walking to the porch to pick up his suit coat from the wooden swing. As he put it on he saw Greggson approaching, flanked by his bodyguards.

"Good morning," the man said when he'd reached the porch. It looked to Brognola as if he hadn't slept in days.

"There's coffee inside," the Fed said in response, reaching out to shake Greggson's hand and lead him into the house.

"This place is beginning to look like a bunker," Greggson said as he observed the guards on the upstairs balcony. Brognola's people had finished the job on the windows that the intruders had started the night before, knocking out the rest of the glass and filling up the spaces with sandbags with cutouts for weapons. "Are we operational again?"

"Completely," the Fed replied, pointing to the activities in the living room. Five people sat at the phones on the table, while three others sat before CRT screens, working the computers. "I can do anything here that I can do at the office, plus have the benefits of my own security system. We were up most of the night with this, but it was worth it."

"Have the operatives I sent over arrived yet?"

"Yeah," Brognola said. "Come on back to the den, we're ready to have a briefing."

The men walked through the dining room, white sheets covering the scarred furniture, then through the kitchen, a mess of paper plates, cups and fast-food wrappers, and into the sunken den.

A dozen casually dressed men and women milled around the large, airy room. Here, too, the windows were sandbagged. Two women dressed in jeans did warm-up t'ai chi in the corner, while a man who was stripped to the waist vigorously pedaled the exercise bike that Brognola used as a dust collector. A pool table, which had been moved to one side, held a slide projector pointing toward wall space that was covered by a hastily tacked-up sheet.

"Is it ready?" Brognola called to Hendry, who fiddled with the projector.

The man smiled and nodded.

"Let's get a seat."

"Not until I've had some of that coffee you promised," Greggson said wearily, then walked to the wet bar to pour a cup from a steaming carafe. As he stirred sugar into the coffee, he called across the room, "What's gotten into Leland? I stopped by Justice before coming out here today and they said he'd been calling all morning, hopping mad." He held up his coffee. "Can I bring you one?"

"Sure," Brognola replied. "So, our boy's mad. I hope he chokes on it."

Greggson returned to the sofa and handed Brognola one of the cups. "Chokes on what?"

The man from Justice took a sip, found it too hot and set the cup on the gold-carpeted floor. "I pulled a DDS-113 on him this morning."

Greggson looked at him quizzically. "Maybe I'm not up on my regs the way I should be, but doesn't a DDS-113 have something to do with gambling?"

Brognola nodded. "Evidence has come to my attention of a massive bookmaking operation being run on government property, the Pentagon in particular."

"Bookmaking," his companion said suspiciously. "You don't mean..."

"That's right. Terry Richards's football pool."

"But you bet in that one all the time!"

"Just gathering evidence."

"God, and that's right under Leland's nose."

"That it is." Brognola reached down to try the coffee again. "I typed up the authorization last night, and hit those offices bright and early this morning with a team of investigators. They tried to stop me, but regulations are clear about the Justice Department handling such things. The attorney general had signed it himself."

"You, of course, didn't go there for any other reason."

"Well," Brognola said expansively, drawing out the syllable, "if one of my electronics people just happened to be there with the investigators, and if he just happened to install listening devices in key places, I'd be a fool not to listen, you know?"

"Who'd you get?"

"We'll start with Leland's personal secretary."

Greggson shook his head. "I didn't hear any of this."

"I understand," the Fed replied, then set down the coffee again and clapped his hands. "People! Let's have your attention!"

Everyone drew closer, Brognola motioning them to seats on the floor or on chairs, facing the makeshift screen on the wall.

He waited until everyone had gotten settled and quiet before continuing. "You all know basically why we're here, and I'd like to welcome you newcomers. I won't thank you because you are performing the work and the duty of any good American in helping preserve the greatest system ever devised for self-rule, but I will tell you all how proud I am of you.

"Our operation is divided into two parts: research and observation. You, ladies and gentlemen, are part of the observation team. Your job is to conduct surveillance on certain suspect individuals and report back on behavior patterns. If somebody will get the lights, I'll show you some of our targets."

As soon as the room was plunged into darkness, Hendry hit the projector switch, a bright white light coming on, spotlighting the center of the sheet.

"General Mordechai Leland," he said when the general's face appeared on the sheet, the picture taken by telephoto lens as the man was getting into a car. "Primary target. In the top six or seven at the Pentagon, distinguished record, loved by the President, connected at NSC. Also, the operations manager of Project GOG, whatever that is. We want everything on him—his contacts, his women, his eating habits, his phone conversations if we can get them. Next."

Another picture came up. "Captain Norman Michaels. Leland's adjunct and right-hand man."

"He looks like Oscar!" someone shouted.

"We're watching Michaels carefully," Brognola said. "He's been running around, going to the cleaners, the bank. It's almost as if he's putting his affairs in order. He seems, at the very least, to be preparing for something. We're staying on him."

The next picture came up. "Lieutenant Colonel Kit Givan. Assigned to Project GOG and, according to our evidence, a cold-blooded killer. We're also watching him carefully.

"A new face," the Fed announced when the crew-cut blonde came onto the screen. "His name's Mark Reilly. He's a Company man, under-assistant to the head of Covert Operations. We photographed him three times yesterday meeting clandestinely with Leland or members of his staff. He is officially on leave of absence from the CIA.

"Some of you will draw his assignment. For those who do, watch out. He's a strange one. He's got a history of suffering from manic depression, something he feels has kept him from promotion. When he was in Vietnam, a squad he led was implicated in a village massacre in which all the civilians had been tortured and killed with Ka-bar knives. No formal charges were ever filed. Watch him."

A small parade of others came and went on the screen, members of Leland's staff or outsiders with whom he'd had contact. Brognola flagged them all by importance, assigning surveillance details by a point system from most to least important in order to conserve manpower.

When the slide show was finished, he said, "We feel that Leland has a network that extends beyond, perhaps far beyond, the pictures we've shown today. We are only able to pick up on conspirators as they become available to us through contact with known conspirators. I must stress to you, then, that absolute security is a must. Trust no one. Send your families away if you can for reasons that become quite obvious when you look around our command post. Are there any questions?"

"When do we take this higher up?" an agent from Greggson's division asked. "It seems that the legality of what we're doing could be put into question immediately."

"Which is our problem," Greggson answered. "We feel that time is short, so short that to go through regular channels would totally defeat our purpose. We're doing what we feel we must, but to take this through the system right now would be disastrous. When we feel we have acquired a preponderance of evidence, even illegally obtained evidence, we'll go on to the next step. Our only purpose at this moment in time is in stopping what we suspect could be an attempted military takeover of the government. We'll worry about legalities later. But until then, we're on our own... and yes, I agree that we are operating totally outside of the law. We haven't performed so much as one legal act since this whole thing began. So, at least give us high marks for consistency."

Everyone laughed, somebody turning the lights back on. Bob Ito entered the room, his face slack and puffy, his eyes tired. He wore faded jeans and a T-shirt that read Nuke the Whales. "We've had some movement from the bug at the Pentagon," he said.

Brognola stood, picking up his coffee. "What's happened?"

"We just picked up Leland's secretary making an airline reservation for Captain Michaels, for tomorrow morning."

"He's not flying military airlift command?" Greggson asked.

Ito shook his head. "Commercial," he said. "They probably didn't want to log it."

"Where's he going?" Brognola asked.

"Miami International," Bob Ito replied.

"All roads lead to Florida," Greggson muttered.

The Justice chief turned to Hendry, who was still fiddling with the slide projector. "Put Michaels back up on the screen."

The man started the projector, quickly running through the pictures until reaching Norm Michaels. It was a shot of the man leaving the Pentagon, dark glasses covering his eyes, a briefcase dangling at his side.

"Oscar," Brognola said. "Go up and stand by the screen."

Hoots and applause followed the agent as he walked to the screen and turned around, squinting into the bright light.

"Somebody give him some sunglasses," the Fed ordered, and the task was quickly accomplished.

He stared at the two heads side by side. The men were somewhat alike in build and facial structure, but were hardly twins. But, then again, for what he was thinking he really didn't need a twin.

JULIE ARNOLD SAT behind the wheel of the used Cadillac, trying to stiffen her back against the pain she'd inflicted by sleeping in the Jeep, and watched white, watery soap running down the windows, totally blocking her view out. Then came the huge rotating brushes that descended upon her from all sides, cleaning the soap-loosened dirt from the car.

Once, when she was in high school, she'd made love with the captain of the swim team as his car was being pulled through an automated wash like this, the two of them just barely straightening their clothes as the red-and-white buffer brushes were finishing up. It had been so many years ago—a lifetime, maybe more than one.

Buying the Caddy had been mandatory. The Jeep had been so pocked with bullet holes and abuse that they'd drawn attention everywhere they went.

The rinse cycle came up, compressed water sheeting down the windows, making it seem as if she were driving underwater. She was still confused about last night, still wondering who the hell the men were who'd come to the house. According to Mark, they couldn't have been Bolan's people because he needed her alive to translate the notes. So, if they weren't Bolan's people, and they weren't Mark Reilly's people, then who were they? A third party that even Mark Reilly didn't know about? Perhaps he'd been wrong about Bolan. It was all so confusing.

She was in new clothes again, the beginnings of another new wardrobe to replace what had been lost in the previous night's fire. She would never have thought that she could get bored with shopping, but that's just what was happening.

The car was dragged through the buffers, and she smiled, thinking about how she'd put her shorts on backward in her mad scramble to dress after her car-wash liaison, and how her mother had never believed her story about absentmindedness. That had been four years p.a.— pre-Arnold, four years before her life had gotten totally out of her control and started her on a course that had ultimately led here, wherever here was.

As the vehicle emerged from the buffers and into the bright morning daylight of the thriving metropolis of Sanford, Florida, Bolan was waiting for her, dressed in an apple-green three-piece suit with an off-white tie and white shoes. He'd changed in the service station rest room.

She pulled off to the side, several teenage boys in coveralls running to the car to wipe it down. Bolan came over and climbed in the passenger side.

"Howdy," he said in a loud nasal voice while reaching out to pump her hand vigorously. "Name's Harvey Susskind, regional sales rep for NuVue Photocopiers, biggest little company east of the Mississippi. Here's my card."

He pulled a card out of his pocket that reiterated the information he'd just given her.

"You just might fool them."

"I'd better," he replied. "The suit was too tight for the combat harness, though. I've got it in the briefcase."

"You don't expect trouble, do you?" she asked, feeling a tightness in the pit of her stomach.

"I always expect trouble," he said. "You hungry?"

"I should be."

"Okay. Why don't you drive around until you find a good place to eat? I'll drop you there and you can get some lunch while you're waiting for me to come back."

"Why can't I go with you?" She waved away the boys with the rags and started the car.

"How many traveling salesmen visit clients with their wives?" he replied.

That made sense to her. She pulled out of the combination gas station and car wash, heading down St. John's

Avenue, the main road in the tiny, miniresort city just off
Lake Monroe and St. Johns River.

The city was a conglomeration of fast-food restaurants
and malls containing nationally recognizable stores and
shops, lending credence to her theory that all of America
had homogenized into one, huge predictable city. She
pulled in by a seafood restaurant with a view of the lake,
the tires of the Cadillac crunching loudly on the gravel
parking lot.

She stopped the car and looked at him. "I don't want to
have to spend the rest of my life here," she said.

"If you're telling me to be careful," he replied, "I appreciate the thought."

They both got out of the car, Bolan walking around to
take the driver's side.

"I mean it," she said. "You can find out what you want
without sticking your neck out."

He climbed into the black car and started it. "Don't
worry," he said, and waved casually. Without another
word, he geared up and drove off, leaving her standing
alone in the lot.

She turned and walked to the entrance, feeling empty on
her own. Mark had asked her to call in every day, and this
would be the perfect opportunity. But, somehow, she
didn't think she'd do it. Bolan had saved her life last night
for whatever reason. She couldn't just forget about that.
If she were to call Mark Reilly and get the terminate message on Bolan, she didn't know what she'd do. Better to
leave things well enough alone. She couldn't be expected
to perform a task she hadn't been told about.

Mack Bolan was the enemy. It had been proved to her
through his record and through her contacts. But in her
heart it didn't line out that simply. Whatever his motives
and his allegiances, she couldn't help but feel that the man
had been forthright and honest with her. She and Bolan
had shared more honest emotion in a week and a half than
she and Harry had in ten years. It was difficult, perhaps
impossible, to forget that despite the facts.

The restaurant was decorated like a galleon, with rope rigging strung around and heavy plastic tables made to look like crumbling, weathered wood. She ordered a fisherman's platter, which she didn't eat, and several cups of coffee, which she drank too fast. Every once in a while she'd look up and see the view of Lake Monroe through the large window next to the table. Two weeks ago her worries had been simple—what to have for dinner; was it going to rain today; would she be wide enough awake to put in a full day's work. But that had been two weeks ago.

Now she wondered if Bolan was still alive.

BOLAN DROVE NORTH along Highway 17, the road just skirting the edge of Lake Monroe, late-morning sunshine glinting on the wind-choppy water in brilliant flashing tendrils of diamond-brightness. His ugly suit was too tight. He felt confined in mind and body.

Though officially listed as being in Sanford, Baylor Goggle was actually halfway between Sanford and a small township called DeBary. The traffic was sparse on 17, with most of it going the other way, toward the water sports.

Strange, that something so large as Project GOG would reach a matrix here in small-town northern Florida. But that looked like what was happening. Baylor had been tagged and confirmed from three separate sources, its importance increasing with each new revelation, and yet he had no idea of what to expect there. The salesman's disguise was, perhaps, extreme, but given the mysterious nature of what went on at Baylor, he felt the full treatment was necessary, even down to the NuVue business card and literature he had picked up at a dealership that morning.

Had he not seen the building, nestled in a grove of trees several hundred yards off the highway, he would have missed the unmarked turnoff completely. He hit the brakes hard, skidding loudly on the two-lane blacktop, then turned down the gravel road leading to Baylor.

Baylor Goggle and Optical seemed to be an anomaly, a factory that thrived on anonymity. Not only was its highway exit unmarked, but when he had checked in town earlier that day for directions, no one had known what he was talking about, much less where it could be found.

He drove the gravel road slowly, a rising cloud of dust following like a ship's wake. As he drove, he pictured Julie's face as he left her in the parking lot. She'd looked lost and alone and, as usual when there was trouble, he felt guilty leaving her behind. But he couldn't bring her with him. He'd already found himself hampered by trying to protect her while still doing the job, and such divided loyalties would ultimately lead him only to ruin. By binding himself to her through compassion, he was, quite simply, making them both easier kills.

The gravel road ended at a small paved lane that went right up to the building, which was unornamented concrete a couple of hundred yards square, undistinguished in all respects. Next to it was a parking lot, which was surrounded by a chain link fence. The whole site covered about four acres. A guard shack sat at the end of the fence, right before the drive went past the building's front entrance, but it was unoccupied. Beside the shack was a small billboard that read:

BAYLOR GOGGLE AND OPTICAL COMPANY
AUTHORIZED PERSONNEL ONLY
NO SOLICITING

The guard wasn't there to tell him he wasn't authorized, so he drove right in. There was a late-model Lincoln parked on the circle drive that ran past the main entrance, and Bolan parked behind it. Interesting. The only sign marking the building so far had been the one by the guard shack.

He got out of the Cadillac, and, carrying his new briefcase, walked along the twenty-foot sidewalk leading to the double glass entry door.

When he pulled the door open, he could hear a buzzer going off somewhere farther back in the building. As soon as he walked in, he felt that something wasn't right. He was facing a receptionist's station, complete with PBX and appointment books, but nobody occupied the desk. From the reception area a hallway led to more offices and then, farther on, was the factory itself. Muzak was playing gently in the background, but there were no other noises—no talking, laughing or shifting feet—nothing.

The reception area seemed somewhat sterile, but that might have been designed to put on a nice appearance for visitors. The company logo was set up on the wall: the letters BGO written on the three sides of an equilateral triangle with an eye in the center.

"Can I help you?" came a man's voice from down the hall. He appeared seconds later, still slipping into a sport jacket.

Bolan put a friendly grin on his face. "Harvey Susskind," he said, reaching out to pump the man's hand. "I'm your new regional representative for NuVue Photocopiers. Just thought I'd stop by, drop off our new catalog and see how I could be of service."

The man stared at him for a few seconds, looking unnatural in his suit. He was a big, ugly man who would have seemed far more at home swinging through the trees in the real jungle than fighting it out in the corporate variety. "Didn't you see the sign?" he asked finally.

Bolan looked puzzled. "Can't say that I did."

"Well, we do a lot of government contract work here, Mr. Sussman..."

"Susskind."

"Whatever. Anyway, all of our employees have security clearances, and we're not allowed to let anyone in who doesn't."

"Whoo," Bolan said loudly. "Sounds important. But now that I *am* in, maybe if I can just talk to someone in your purchasing department—"

"Sorry," the man interrupted. "Everyone's gone to a funeral today. Our... office manager passed away."

"Everybody but you."

The man smiled through crooked teeth. "Somebody has to watch the store," he said. "Now, Mr...."

"Susskind. Let me just show you our brochure. You'll be amazed at . . ."

"Why don't you just leave it with me," the man said, "and someone will call your office if we're interested."

"What kind of work do you do here, Mr. . . . I don't believe I caught your name."

"Not important," the man replied, "and our work here is classified, which is why we have the sign out there. Now, leave your brochure and your card, and we'll phone if interested. Don't call again, Mr. Susskind. This place is off-limits to you. Thank you."

The man walked around the receptionist's station and put a firm arm around Bolan's back, exerting pressure in the direction of the glass doors. Bolan let himself be led away. The man smelled somewhat of alcohol and had a two-day growth of beard. He didn't fit into a business environment.

Bolan was ushered out into the sunshine, the day already heating up to humid nightmare.

"Goodbye," the man said firmly, turning immediately to walk back into the factory.

Bolan stood for a moment, but decided that leaving now would be his best bet. He got in the car, backed up to get around the Lincoln, then drove off.

As he made his way back down the gravel road, he kept looking in his rearview mirror, watching the building through a haze of rising dust. He had only been there a few minutes but in that time he'd only seen one person at the plant. Judging from the fifty or sixty cars in the employee parking lot, that simply didn't make sense.

Perhaps today was unusual and everyone *had* gone to a funeral, but somehow, he didn't think so. The man he'd talked to was a goon in civilized clothes, not the kind of man to work white collar and get left in charge when everyone else was gone. He was as phony as Bolan's Harvey Susskind and as subtle as garlic.

He reached the highway and headed back toward Sanford. Now that he'd seen the place in the daylight, it was time to check it out at night. Something odd was happening at Baylor Goggle and Optical, and Bolan was determined to find out what.

"WHAT DO YOU EXPECT tó do?" Julie asked him. "Walk right in and pretend you belong there?"

"I'll cross that bridge when I come to it," Bolan replied, slowing down on the nearly deserted highway so he wouldn't miss the turnoff. "All I have to do is get a look at the operation. That shouldn't be too difficult."

"You make trespassing and breaking and entering sound like a stroll in the park," she said. "This is illegal! They could shoot you!"

He turned, a smile tugging at a corner of his mouth. "And you, too."

"Great! Thanks for reminding me."

"It's going to be all right," he said, pulling onto the shoulder. He killed the lights. "I don't plan on getting caught. This is a recon. I can handle it, okay?"

She nodded. "Nothing like last night, please."

"It'll be all right," he repeated, and reached out to pat her on the arm.

She took his hand, squeezing tightly, trembling. "What can I do to help?"

He started the car and turned onto the one destination road, leaving the headlights off. "Get the car turned around, and keep the engine running. Be ready to run like hell if you need to. If things get tough, don't wait for me."

"Mack..."

"Promise," he ordered. "Part of my job is protecting you, and I intend to do it."

"But, dammit..."

"Promise."

She looked away and nodded slightly. "I promise," she said in a small voice.

Bolan drove slowly, inching along to keep down the noise and dust. He stopped the car before reaching the paved roadway at a place out of view of the building. He was togged completely in black, the three-piece suit already consigned to a trash can back in Sanford. He got quietly out of the vehicle and slipped into the combat harness, then donned a light, black jacket.

Using a cork he'd picked up at a bait and tackle shot, he lit the end on a disposable lighter, then blew it out, using the charred remains to quickly blacken his face.

Julie slid across the seat to sit behind the wheel, using the automatic button to move it closer to the pedals.

"Remember," he said, leaning down to speak through the window, "turn it around, keep the engine running, keep the lights out. If anybody but me comes for the car, get out without a second thought. I can take care of myself, you can't. If something happens to me, drive until you think you're safe, then call Hal."

"Be careful," she said, then impulsively pulled his face to hers and kissed him quickly, almost in embarrassment.

He smiled. "Now you've got black smudges on your face."

She pulled down the rearview and slid in front of it, wiping at the burned cork that had been transferred to her face.

"Remember," he said again, "engine running."

The warrior then trotted away from the car and down the road, keeping to the edge of the forest. Twenty yards from the car, the road veered toward the factory and away from the Cadillac. He could hear its engine purring in the background, but just barely.

He left the road completely when it wound around to the front gate, and picked his way carefully through the dark forest, exiting on the fringe of the parking, as far from the guard shack as it was possible to get.

Just as during the afternoon, the lot was full of cars—the night shift? The area was well lit, but the cars themselves could provide a measure of protection. And he saw no employees.

He moved up to the fence, taking off his jacket and throwing it against the links to check for electrification.

Considering the lack of security he'd encountered so far, he wasn't surprised to find the fence dead cold.

Retrieving the wire cutters that stuck out of his back pocket, Bolan went to work on the fence, cutting a hole for himself a link at a time. Something that the goon had said earlier made absolutely no sense. The man had informed him that people were kept out for governmental security reasons. If, indeed, the work going on in the factory required top-secret clearance, then the place would have been crawling with government-checked security, much as Grolier had been. And yet, Brognola had told him that Baylor did, indeed, do some government work. Why, then, the discrepancy?

He worked quickly on the fence, clearing a crawl hole for himself within two minutes. He got in, and, running in a crouch, planted himself between two parked cars.

Rising cautiously, he peered over the hood of an old Escort wagon. There was a light on in the distant guard shack, but no sign of movement or life.

Strange. There was a large spiderweb between the side-view mirror on the Escort and its body, as if the car had sat there for a while. Crouching again, he moved to the next cars in the line, slowly making his way toward the employee entry gate to the plant.

On the next row of cars, the Chevy Nova he hid behind had a front flat tire. He stood up straight and checked the car beside him. It also had a flat tire, and the cobwebs on this one were *inside*.

He moved to the next row of vehicles. Something major was wrong here. The next car he came to, an Olds Cutlass, had busted headlights, the windshield shattered. He tried to open the car door, but it was jammed tight. He pulled a penlight out of his harness and shone it through the window. As he expected, a key was stuck in the ignition.

This was no parking lot, it was a junkyard. The whole lot was filled with junkers to give the appearance of a work force. Why?

He walked quickly through the lot, heedless of any security, and came to the employee gate in the fence. Through the gate was a delivery alley, then a series of doors on the other side leading directly into the factory end of the building.

A chain locked the gate. Bolan got out his clippers again and cut through the chain. But the gate had rusted shut, and still did not want to open. He forced open a space large enough to squeeze through, then hurried across the alley to the doors on the other side. The entryway was couched in shadows, the light bulb in the fixture above broken.

The three metal doors, side by side, were locked. The building, like many factories, had no windows, no other means of entrance or exit except the doors. Bolan took a burglar's pick from the harness and went to work, pushing open the door seconds later.

He found himself in a darkened locker room, using the penlight to cut through the gloom. Here, too, cobwebs attested to disuse, and thick layers of dust covered everything.

Bolan made his way into the factory, by this time not surprised to see an empty building. Baylor Goggle and Optical, at least here in Sanford, Florida, was a sham. He shone the light all around, revealing nothing but bare concrete floor and bare walls as far as his light would carry. This place might have housed a thriving business at one time, but not now and not for quite some time. The United States government had been doing business with a nonexistent company, one that still issued clandestine checks to key government personnel, one that apparently employed someone to stay there and put on a phony front for any casual visitors. Curious.

He turned away from the empty factory and headed toward the administrative offices. Perhaps this place only took care of the paperwork for the company, the factory space no longer needed. It didn't seem likely, but it was possible.

He walked darkened hallways, filthy from disuse, and finally moved through double swing doors to administration. The difference was like night and day. This part of the structure was clean and well kept, but the few offices he peered into were empty.

A sound made its way to his ears, a distant and tiny noise that seemed muffled by the walls and doors of several rooms. He followed the sound, moving through a doorway marked Executive Director.

He was standing in what could only be described as a dining room. It was a large office. But instead of a desk, a wooden table with one chair sat in the center. There was also a pantry, a small refrigerator and a hot plate.

The sound was louder here, and he could nearly make out voices. A door that led out the other side of the room was marked, Conference A. He approached it cautiously, holding the penlight in his mouth and withdrawing Big Thunder with his right hand.

When he turned the knob, the door opened into a den with sofa and recliner and tables containing books, magazines, food wrappers and empty beer cans. The noise he'd heard had been a television, a nighttime soap opera filling its nineteen-inch screen. The man he'd seen earlier lived here, apparently a watchman at night and a fake employee during the day. That had been the buzzer he'd heard on entering this afternoon. It alerted the caretaker to interlopers.

But where was he now?

He caught just the barest glint of movement reflected in the TV screen and dived over the top of the couch, smashing into a coffee table as 9 mm parabellums spitting from the muzzle of a MAC-10 lit the place like daylight and tore into the couch, white down filling the room like snowflakes.

Bolan rolled, his mind whirling, and came up firing the AutoMag. A small corner of his brain wanted to try to take his assailant alive, but it wasn't possible in the confined space. It was kill or be killed, and the Executioner wasn't ready to trade in life for the unknown just yet.

He fired off a line of slugs—chest level—across the room, which connected with groaning flesh halfway through its arc. The man fell heavily, dead before his body even hit the floor.

Bolan came out of his crouch, stuffing from the couch falling around him, Big Thunder held two-handed in front of him. Navigating by the light of the TV, he moved to the body, kicking the MAC-10 away from it before relaxing his own defenses. He turned on the overhead lights to examine the man who'd greeted him earlier in the day.

He searched the body, then, quickly, the offices themselves, coming away with nothing more than he had learned in his first minute in the building—namely, that it was an empty warehouse designed to look as if it weren't. Perhaps a serious investigating team could find more, but to Bolan's eye, the place had been kept conspicuously clean, a street meant to lead nowhere but to a dead end.

He checked the dead man's pocket, coming out with a set of car keys. The man's wallet contained nearly a thousand dollars in cash and a check for two thousand more from the Baylor Goggle account. There was no other identification in the wallet—no driver's license, no social security card, nothing.

A time check showed Bolan that he had been in the building less than thirty minutes. Not much time, but probably an eternity for Julie in the Cadillac. He turned off the television, then used the dead man's keys to let himself out of the building.

The Lincoln was newer and appeared to be in better shape than the Cadillac. Since it wasn't of any more use to the nameless dead man, he unlocked the door, climbed in, then drove it to the bend in the road where Julie was parked.

Afraid to take it around the corner, in case he scared her away, he got out of the car, walked to the Cadillac and opened the passenger side door.

"God, I'm glad to see you," she said quickly. "I was scared silly waiting out here. What happened? Did anything—"

"I didn't have any trouble," he said. "The building is empty."

"Empty!"

He shrugged. "I did get us another car, though," he said. "Just back around that bend and we'll take it."

"But doesn't it belong to someone?" she asked.

"Don't worry about it," he said. "It's ours now."

She looked at him quizzically, but didn't question further. Putting the car in reverse, she backed up slowly and pulled up next to the Lincoln.

"Now what?" she said.

"We find the nearest airport."

"Airport." She laughed. "For the love of Mike, where are we going?"

"Arizona," he replied succinctly, and left the car.

Chapter Eighteen

Hal Brognola and Gunnar Greggson sat side by side on vinyl chairs in the waiting area, holding up copies of the *Washington Post* in front of their faces, occasionally lowering the tops of the opened papers to sneak a look at the American Airlines ticket counters.

Washington's National Airport was early-morning busy, the airlines' rush hour, as men in business suits and carrying hand luggage hurried for shuttle flights to New York and Philadelphia. Behind them, through the plate-glass windows, cabs, buses, hotel shuttles and private cars continuously disgorged passengers, all apparently late and looking in disgust at their watches, just as Brognola and Greggson were doing.

"The damned flight is supposed to leave in twenty minutes," Greggson growled, turning to glance quickly at Brognola. "No way are we going to have time to pull this off now."

"I'm thinking," Brognola replied calmly. "He'll be here. All we can do is take this thing a step at a time."

"Yeah, but we've gotta have someplace to step *to*, my friend."

"What time are our people set to go at Baylor Goggle?"

"Ten hundred hours," Greggson said, turning to the sports section, "if the police aren't there. If the police *are* there, we scrub. After talking to your boy last night, I think we might be tying people up for nothing anyway. Has Bolan gotten away yet?"

Brognola cocked his wrist and looked at his watch. "He should be in the air now. They've got a rental car waiting for them on the Phoenix end, and they'll drive down to Gila Bend early this afternoon."

"You think there's anything to it?"

The big Fed took a breath. "I'd have to check it out either way."

"Yeah. You think it's a mistake for him to take the Arnold woman with him?"

Brognola turned to the comics section, settling in for probably the only laugh he'd get all day. "I hate to say it this way, Greg," he replied, "but he's got no choice but to take her with him. Her brain carries our only connection to a completely new technology that our enemies have apparently already accessed. If she dies, theoretical research in liquid electricity goes backward twenty years. I want her in his sight every minute of every day until we get those mental notes transcribed."

Greggson quieted for a moment, then said, "How about them Mets, huh?"

Brognola turned partway in his seat to look at the man, when out of the corner of his eye, he caught a flash of Air Force blue. He turned quickly, then covered his face with the paper. "Don't turn around," he said, pulling his paper closer to his face, "but our boy just now climbed out of an SP jeep and is making his way inside."

Both men angled themselves away from the door, burying their faces until Captain Norm Michaels had passed. He carried a blue zip-up bag under his arm and an extra uniform in a garment bag was slung over his shoulder. A briefcase was swinging at his side. His right wrist was handcuffed to it. He wore dark sunglasses.

"Would you look at the time?" Greggson said. "There's no way we can—"

"I'm still thinking," Brognola interrupted. "Shh."

Brognola watched the man strut to the counter like a rooster in the henhouse. He was having a difficult time not thinking of Michaels as the man who attacked his home, even though, logically, he probably had nothing to do with it. The head Fed hated this man without reserve, hated everything he stood for. And probably all because of a sense of violation over what had happened at the house.

He watched the man pick up his ticket and spend an extra minute joking with the woman behind the counter, also in a blue uniform, at the expense of the people waiting behind him. It was going to give Brognola the greatest pleasure to flatten one of Leland's boys and start the momentum in the other direction.

Michaels walked away from the counter, directly toward the boarding area. He had barely ten minutes to spare before the scheduled departure, and Greggson was right. There wasn't enough time to do what they had to. But there were ways and there were ways.

Brognola folded his paper. "Let's go," he said, standing quickly and starting after the man, Greggson jogging to catch up.

Michaels moved through the concourse, then spoked toward the American Airlines terminal, the two Feds twenty paces behind him.

The captain checked his watch as he walked, Brognola wondering how he could read the face through the dark glasses. He recognized two more of his men on either side of Michaels, angling slowly in, boxing the man loosely.

Then all at once, Ted Healy, walking the other way, bumped right into Michaels, who stopped dead, everyone else closing in immediately.

"I'm so sorry," Healy was saying, his hands on the man.

"That's quite all..."

The man beside Michaels had pulled up the overcoat he'd been carrying, jamming the barrel of a hidden .45 hard into the man's ribs, then pushing sideways.

"Hey, wait. What are you..."

Brognola and Greggson had reached the scene by this time, five men grabbing quickly and pushing sideways, hustling the man through the rest room door that had the Closed sign hanging on it that they had planted earlier.

The rest room was large, with gleaming white tile and aluminum fixtures and smelling of ammonia. Michaels, showing absolutely no sign of fear, struggled against the five of them.

"Who the hell do you think you are?" he grated through clenched teeth as he pulled against them.

"Down on your knees," the man with the .45 ordered, sticking the barrel of the weapon against Michaels's forehead. His name was Wortham and he had done hard time with the Company.

"Fuck you!" Michaels said.

Wortham smiled and cocked the weapon, easing the safety off. "I'd *love* to blow you away, soldier boy."

Michaels went down slowly, the anger never leaving his face. Then he saw Brognola. "I know you," he said. "You sorry bastard."

"Get to work," Brognola said, his eyes never leaving Michaels's.

Ted Healy got behind the man, jerking downward on the collar of his dress uniform jacket, pulling it right off and tossing it over one of the stall dividers. Wortham dug through the man's pockets, coming out with the handcuff key. He tossed it to Morales, who was holding on to Michaels's right arm.

Morales bent to the handcuff.

"Don't touch that," Michaels warned, his voice icy. "That briefcase contains highly sensitive and classified documents, whose exposure opens you to a charge of treason and espionage against the United States of America. Do I make myself clear?"

Morales hesitated, while Wortham rolled up Michaels's left shirt-sleeve. Morales looked up at Brognola.

"Do it," the Fed said intensely. "What he's got in that case hasn't been issued by *my* government."

"Ow!" Michaels said as Wortham jabbed him with a syringe, pumping clear fluid into his arm. "What's that?"

Morales bent to the handcuff again, his hand shaking slightly as he put the key in the lock.

"I'm warning you again," Michaels said. "You remove the briefcase and you will be buying yourself into criminal liability on a massive scale."

Morales looked up again. "Mr. Brognola, are you sure..."

"Give me the key," Brognola demanded, holding out his hand, impatient fingers twitching.

Morales gave him the key, and the big Fed bent to the handcuffs.

Just then the airline speaker in the rest room ceiling crackled. "This is the last call for American Airlines flight 501, nonstop service to Miami, Florida, now leaving at Gate 17. All aboard please."

"What do we do?" Greggson asked, bending to take Brognola by the shoulder.

"Go out to the pay phone," he said.

"Yeah?"

"Call the airline and tell them there's a bomb in the luggage compartment of flight 501."

"*That's* what you've been thinking about all this time?" Greggson asked, exasperated.

"It'll work. Do it."

Greggson stood, walking to the door. "I hope we have a good lawyer," he said, and moved quickly out of the rest room.

Brognola turned the key in the handcuffs, the lock springing, the unit dropping from Michaels's wrist. The man was leaning backward, threatening to topple over.

"I'm warning you," he said sleepily, his eyes heavy-lidded, his sunglasses riding down on the end of his nose.

"Get the chair," Brognola said, picking up the briefcase, which was far heavier than he had expected, and moving away from the others for space to get into the case.

Wortham hurriedly retrieved the wheelchair they had pushed into the john when they'd hung the Closed sign.

Morales and Healy began pulling the man to his feet, as he drifted into unconsciousness.

"Come on, Admiral," Healy coaxed. "We'll put you in a nice chair."

"Thash good," Michaels said sluggishly, his eyes completely closed. "Thash real good."

Brognola used the key to open the cuff on the briefcase, which in turn snapped the catch, the case springing open. Inside was a fully loaded MAC-10, plus government authorization to carry it on an aircraft. Next to it was a stack of banded money, a thick stack of fifties, and finally a bar of gold that must have weighed twenty pounds, which accounted for all the weight.

He pulled those things out of the case and set them on the tile floor. "Oscar!" he called loudly, and the man came out of the stall dressed in a captain's uniform, complete with Norm Michaels's dress jacket.

Greggson reentered the rest room shaking his head. "I did it, God forgive me. I committed another major felony."

"Get over here with the camera," Brognola called to Largent, who had stopped at the wheelchair to take Michaels's watch and rings. As an afterthought, he pulled the man's sunglasses off his face and put them on.

The big Fed pointed at the stuff on the floor. "Get pictures." Then he turned to Morales, Healy and Wortham. "Get our buddy Norm ready to travel."

Brognola set the case on a sink with a mirror. The rest of the briefcase was full of papers. On the top was a manila envelope addressed to: General Albert Richter Cronin—Eyes Only.

He pulled it out and handed it to Oscar. "Get pictures of every page and put them back in the same order that you removed them."

He turned back to the case, Greggson already into the papers beneath the orders. "These are copies of Michaels's orders, too," the man said. "And whatever Project GOG is, it's scheduled to go at 0900 on Saturday, the 27th.''

"Day after tomorrow," Brognola said. "Good God."

Greggson was scanning the paperwork, tearing through it. "He's supposed to return to Washington sometime before Saturday, and at 0800 that morning is to take command of the Marine honor guard at the White House."

"But he's in the Air Force," Brognola argued. "How do they expect him to command Marines?"

"You're forgetting who trained those Marines," Greggson said, and looked up at Brognola.

"Kit Givan." Realization sank in. "They may be Marines who're guarding the President right now, but they all belong to Leland. The enemy already controls the White House."

"And something else," Greggson said. "From the looks of these orders, I can't help but think that something of a major cataclysm is expected Saturday morning."

"What makes you say that?"

"Listen to this." Greggson cleared his throat, then read, "'Though all normal channels of communication will have broken down or no longer exist, elements of command will keep in contact through the GOG satellite system.' Or how about this? 'Panic will settle down on its own after a time. Disaster management is not our responsibility.'"

The two men stared at each other. Brognola had trouble finding his voice to speak. "Does it...say what sort of disaster they're expecting?" he finally managed, his voice low, his stomach feeling as if it were full of powdered glass.

Greggson looked grim, his face drained of all color. "Not that I've seen yet."

"Done," Oscar said, handing the manila envelope back to Brognola.

The big Fed handed him Michaels's orders. "Do these, too," he said. "I want you to study this stuff carefully on the plane. You've got a lot of serious bluffing to do once you reach Florida."

Oscar, looking for all the world like Michaels, smiled wanly. "Only if none of them know him already," he said, then took the material and set it atop a trash can to photograph.

As Brognola turned to watch the job they were doing on Michaels, he heard the flight delay announcement for flight 501 to Miami. The three agents had lashed Michaels to the chair and had covered him from neck to feet with a large blanket. At that moment, Ted Healy was fitting a long-haired blond wig on the sleeping man's head, as Wortham hastily applied lipstick and rouge to his face. Enter Norman Michaels; exit Norma Michaels.

Brognola turned back to Greggson. "We can't go this alone anymore," he said.

Greggson nodded. "We've got to choose carefully, though," he said. "Get out of our own circles and I don't know who to trust."

"I've got someone in mind," Brognola replied.

"The last time you had something in mind," Greggson said, "I committed a felony."

"Think of it as research. You're simply getting a chance to view the criminal mind from the inside."

"Why am I not reassured?"

"Ready," Oscar said, as he handed the stack of papers back to Brognola. The head Fed began putting everything back in the case just as it had been before.

"Ready over here," Ted Healy said, wheeling Michaels up closer to the exit.

Brognola snapped the briefcase shut, closed the hand-cuff on the handle, then gave the key to Oscar. He then reached out and snapped the other cuff onto the man's wrist. Greggson had recovered the blue zipper case and the garment bag and gave them to Oscar, completing the disguise.

"I won't pull any punches," Brognola said to Largent. "I have no idea what your chances are on this thing. To be frank, at this point we're buying time with you—maybe hours, maybe minutes. I can't make you do this."

"I knew all that when I accepted the assignment," the man replied. "And I didn't accept it lightly."

"You have the beeper?"

Largent took a fountain pen out of his shirt pocket and clicked the top. "It's activated," he said, and replaced it.

"You know we can't pick you up any closer than a fifty-mile range," the head Fed told him, "so this might not do you any good for a while. I have no idea what you're walking into down there."

"I'll make contact as soon as I can."

Greggson moved over to take the man by the shoulders. "Good luck, Oscar," he said. "The survival of the country may depend on what you do in the next few hours."

"Good luck to you, too," the man replied, then looked at his wrist. "I'd better go."

"Yeah," Greggson said, stepping away from him. The other men in the room quietly wished Largent well.

Oscar Largent nodded once, then turned and strode out the door into the flow, his stomach churning. Behind, he heard the door open again and turned slightly to watch, out of the corner of his eye, as the wheelchair bearing the limp body of Captain Michaels was hurried out the door by Healy and Wortham, who turned and took it in the opposite direction.

He felt odd as he moved toward the gate, as if he were expecting someone to recognize that he wasn't the man he pretended to be. That bothered him the most, the uncertain feeling of inhabiting someone else's life.

The other part, the dangerous part, wasn't nearly as difficult to him as playing the role of someone else. Largent had been raised to believe in the ultimate goodness and justice of the U.S. Constitution. His father had been a preacher and a man of high principles, who believed that happiness and security could only come from grounding oneself in the bedrock of an ethical system. He had taught that belief to his five children. The thought that someone could want to overthrow the system that justly governed the country in exchange for a private brand of situation ethics, was simply more than Oscar Largent could bear. Being in a position to do something about it excited and energized him.

But pretending to be someone he wasn't—that was scary.

He made it through baggage check, opening the briefcase with the key and showing the man there the paperwork for the SMG without incident.

Then he moved toward Gate 17, all the passengers who had been deplaned because of the bomb threat now being let back on the aircraft.

He got in line with them, feeling as if every eye in the airport was on him. He looked around nervously, continually shifting his feet. Then, suddenly, he was face-to-face with the boarding stewardess. Mouth dry, he handed her Michaels's ticket.

She looked at it for a second, then looked at him, tearing off the boarding pass and giving it back to him. "Nice to see you, Captain Michaels," she said, smiling at him. "Welcome aboard."

He returned the smile. "Thanks," he said, and walked down the boarding bay toward the plane. Now, officially, he had become Norman Michaels, traitor.

"YOU MEAN PEOPLE actually *live* out here?" Julie Arnold said, squinting through the blinding sunlight on Arizona Road 85. The sun caused the white sand stretching on both sides of the road to glow like fire and made driving a torturous adventure.

"People live in all sorts of places," Bolan said, reaching out to turn up the air-conditioning on the rented Cougar. "Here is as good as any."

"If you're a piece of cactus," she returned, pulling down her sun visor a little more and trying to scoot up in the seat.

They had arrived at Phoenix Sky Harbor International two hours before and had rented the car immediately, making the trip south on the nearly deserted state road that cut right through an area known as Centennial Wash—which was a polite way of saying there was desolation for hundreds of miles all around.

Southwestern Arizona was a land of extremes. Known as the Basin and Range region, it consisted of long, open-ended basins and valleys separated by individual mountain ranges. Add to this the extensions of the Mexican Sonoran Desert that jutted into the region from the south and you were left with a flat, arid land of cactus and rugged undergrowth punctuated by mountains that jutted abruptly from the flatlands in night-and-day contrast. It was a surreal landscape, made stranger by the intense heat that rose in shimmering waves from the basin floors to roast the life from anything not protected with shade and water.

"What time is it?" Julie asked, her arm thrown over her face, covering her eyes.

Bolan looked at his watch. "Nearly one o'clock," he said, smiling at the woman's Western-cut jeans and checked shirt. They had bought what they'd considered suitable clothes back in Phoenix. Bolan hoped that the folks in Gila Bend considered them suitable, too.

Bolan had noticed that Julie had relaxed considerably since they'd left Florida that morning, probably thinking that moving this far from the action effectively took them out of it. He didn't share that feeling at all, but hated to break her mood by telling her that. Over the course of the past few days, he had come to ascribe a great deal of importance to Jerry Butler's coded messages, and Butler wouldn't have bothered with all the trouble over Gila Bend unless there was something to it. What, he couldn't imagine.

"I still don't know what you expect to find out here in the middle of goddamned nowhere," she said, turning to stare at him under the protection of her arm. "And you look ridiculous in that stupid hat."

He pulled his new cowboy hat a little farther down on his forehead. "I'm not having trouble with the sun like you are." He tapped his finger against the brim of the head-gear in a jaunty salute. "And to answer your first question, I don't know what I expect to find, though I think there's a connection between Baylor Optical and Gila Bend."

"So, what do we do, march into town and ask if anything unusual's been happening?"

"Why not?" he said. "I'll tell you that the first thing I'm looking for is a manufacturing business of some kind, one that's been started in the past few years. My supposition is that, whatever Baylor Goggle was supposed to be used for, it's really taking place at Gila Bend."

"A pretty flimsy connection," she said.

He frowned at her. "You got any better ideas?"

Julie sat up straight, kneeling on the seat to look at him. "Yes," she said. "We forget about all this and go hide out somewhere until it's all over with."

"You know I can't do that," he replied.

She pouted out her lower lip. "Spoilsport," she said, turning back around to sit properly. "Is this place going to be like a real city?"

"Not much of one," Bolan admitted. "It's got about two thousand people living there. They might even have indoor plumbing."

"Not funny," she said, folding her arms across her chest.

He laughed, then pointed ahead. "I think we'll get to see for ourselves in just a minute."

Julie squinted out the windshield. Less than a mile in the distance a small town rose impossibly out of the desert heat. On both sides of the road small horse ranches broke up the monotonous landscape. The shoulder of the road-way was littered with paper trash and broken beer bottles, sure signs of encroaching civilization.

They passed a Welcome to Gila Bend sign, then moved into the city proper, which consisted of a great many one-story structures, most of them geared toward eating and filling cars with gas. Bolan smiled, seeing many of the same restaurants he'd seen in Sanford the day before.

They slowed down, noticing the other signs of civilization: churches, a schoolhouse, police and fire stations, a movie theater, a bank and an inordinate number of motels. He'd seen it all before.

The types of businesses Bolan noticed made him feel a little better. This was a tourist town, a city that existed simply because people needed a place to stop for the night on their way into or out of California and the large stretch of Mojave Desert that cut it off. He saw no signs of industry apart from small, local businesses; anything unusual would stand out prominently, like those mountain ranges jutting cleanly out of the flatland.

He drove into what looked like the center of town, the place where the two main drags intersected. A stone courthouse there seemed to be busy, plus a supermarket, auto-repair shop and gun shop. He pulled up at an angle to the sidewalk, between the yellow lines, and got out of the car, Julie dutifully climbing out the other side.

It was hot, as hot as Bolan had ever imagined, and the air was thick with dust. He stretched, loosening his muscles, and looked around. It was time to have a talk with Julie.

He walked around to her side of the car, decidedly uncomfortable in the cowboy boots that pinched his feet. Julie looked miserable and was fanning herself with the road map they had picked up in Phoenix.

She looked up at him and frowned. "You're going to be serious now," she said. "I can tell."

"Look," he said, glancing around. "There's a reason for most everything I do."

"So I've noticed," she said.

"Every step we've made so far has been observed," he went on. "We've nearly died because of it several times. If, indeed, Project GOG is entrenched here, it means we've walked into the viper's den. We have no idea how many locals could be on their payroll. Regardless of what you think about all this, we've *got* to maintain our cover while we poke around. We can't arouse any suspicion. It could be deadly for both of us. Do you understand what I'm trying to tell you?''

She nodded, the relaxation draining from her face to be replaced by tension. ''You're telling me to get with the program,'' she said.

''Play the part as if your life depended on it. We're husband and wife. We're here looking to get away from the city slickers and big city life. If I'm wrong about this place, we'll have a good laugh about it later. But if I'm correct, our ability to handle this right may be the only thing that will keep us alive. Got it?''

She nodded, her eyes fearful. ''You're really worried about this, aren't you?''

''You bet I am.''

She searched his face with her eyes. ''I won't let you down,'' she said at last.

He hugged her quickly, then reluctantly let her go. ''Thanks,'' he said.

She looked around with wide eyes. ''Okay, Tex,'' she said. ''Where do we start?''

''I noticed a bar across the street. Not a bad place to go for gossip. And the name is Sparks, not Tex.''

''Does that mean I have to be Bernice again?''

''We've still got the IDs,'' he said. ''We might as well use them.''

He turned toward the blacktop street, waiting until a rusted pickup coughed past before crossing. Not a great deal was going on. It was the hottest part of the day, and only fools and people with necessary business to conduct were outside. Bolan wondered which category he fit into.

They crossed the street slowly, their clothes not much different than those he saw around them. There was the modern equivalent of the general store off to their left, where a bearded old man covered with dust was supervising the loading of supplies onto an ancient flatbed truck by a pair of teenaged boys.

They made it across the street, passing a parked car that had a saddled horse tethered to the door handle, then up to the entrance of a hole-in-the-wall with the unlikely name of Zanzi-bar. An Olympia Beer sign in neon filled the only unpainted part of the picture window, and the push-open door was windowless and painted red.

"Ready?" he asked softly.

She made a clucking noise. "Anytime you are, Mr. Sparks."

Bolan pushed open the door and walked into absolute darkness, his eyes traumatized by the switch from bright sunshine. The place smelled like all small bars—like beer, cheap soap and sweat, the music serious country-and-western, heavy on the twang.

Julie followed right behind, bumping into him in the darkness. They stood there for a moment, letting their pupils dilate enough to see the dim outline of a bar and tables. Then they walked to the bar and took a seat. Customers, all men, were scattered around the place in small groups, a washed-out aging blonde waiting on them and laughing in a high nasal whine that might have been cute when she was seventeen years old. The bartender was younger. He wore a T-shirt harping a Hank Williams, Jr. tour and had sandy brown hair and a mustache.

The man walked up to them and seemed to be studying their faces. "What can I git you?" he asked.

"A couple of draws," Bolan requested.

"Sure," the man said, moving away.

"What's a *draw*?" Julie whispered in his ear.

"Beer," he said.

"I *hate* beer," she rasped. "You know that."

"I don't care if you drink it," he said. "That's not what we're here for."

She sat back on the swivel stool, pouting.

The bartender returned, dropping two coasters on the bartop and setting two pilsner glasses of beer on the coasters.

"Two bucks," he said, taking a five from Bolan, then going to the register to make change. He came back and left the money on the bar. "You folks new around here? Don't believe I've ever seen you in here before."

"Just got in," Bolan admitted.

"Passing through, then?"

"In a way," Bolan said, taking a sip of the beer, then setting the glass back down. "We've finally had enough of so-called middle-class American life and decided to get away, just leave it all behind and start fresh someplace simpler, you know?"

The man nodded. "You folks down from Phoenix?"

"Yeah," Bolan replied.

The man cocked his head. "I tried livin' there myself," he said. "I'd just got back from the war and thought I'd settle around a lot of people and get back in the swing...but it didn't work out that way."

"You in Nam?" Bolan asked.

The man nodded. "Hundred and First Airborne, air cav."

"Huey-boy," Bolan said. "You fellas sure helped me outta some jams back then."

The man looked at the bartop. "I took some shrap trying to rescue a Marine recondo team set up on a hill to watch troop movements. Damned NVAs were coming at 'em with German police dogs, can you imagine that?" He stared for another minute, reliving a private hell, then said, "God, they blew the living shit outta us that day." The man cleared his throat. "I been on disability ever since."

Bolan stuck out his hand. "Name's Dave Sparks. This is my wife, Bernice."

The man smiled, forcing himself out of his past. "Mike Reardon," he said, shaking hands with both of them. "Glad to make your acquaintance. So, you thinkin' about movin' down to these parts?"

"Maybe," Bolan said. "If it feels right."

"What line you in, Dave?" Reardon asked.

"Auto mechanic."

"Always use another one of those." The man smiled. "And if you want a slower pace, this is the spot for it. We ain't had no excitement since the preacher's wife run off with the Bible salesman back in '79. Is that quiet enough for you?"

Bolan glanced over at Julie. Contrary to her statement about beer, she had just finished hers and was pushing the glass back toward Reardon. "How about a couple more?" she said.

"I haven't finished mine yet," Bolan said.

"Hell, they're for me!"

Reardon laughed and drew two more beers from the Coors tap.

"Seems to me a lot of little towns are getting ruined because those factory people are moving in to get nonunion help," Bolan said when Reardon returned.

"Not around here. The closest thing we got to a factory here is the pottery works on the Indian reservation north of town, and they been there about as long as the town has."

"Nothing much new coming in, then?"

Reardon laughed and went over to draw a beer for himself. "You're the newest thing since *I* moved here."

Just then the door slammed open and a small figure strode in. "Whiskey!" the man yelled loudly. Everyone in the bar laughed and called out to him.

"I'm here!" the little man yelled again. "And I'm thirsty!"

Reardon pulled a dusty bottle out from under the bar and held it up. "Here you go, Tater!" he said.

The man stumbled to the bar, trying to see his way in the dark, the same as Bolan and Julie had. "Drinks on me as long as I'm standing!" he yelled, and everyone applauded.

The old man moved right up beside Bolan and took the bottle. He smelled of sweat, and a cloud of dust seemed to follow him around. He grabbed the bottle without bothering with a glass and made his way to one of the tables where the locals were calling out to him.

"Well, this is your lucky day," Reardon said to Bolan. "Tater's monthly trip to town."

"Who is he?" Bolan asked, watching the man make his way across the room.

"Strangest story you've ever heard. God only knows what his real name is. As long as I've been around they just called him 'Tater.' He's a prospector, has been all his life. Looked for gold, silver...he even spent time looking for uranium back when that was the big thing. Always poor as a churchmouse, you know, the town joke. But he seemed content enough, and I've learned that being content is really something."

"Touché," Julie said, holding up her beer.

"Anyway," Reardon continued, "a couple of years ago, ol' Tater come up with something new. It seems he had talked a bunch of fellas into going in with him to look for Pancho Villa's treasure."

"The Mexican bandit?" Bolan said.

"None other," Reardon replied. "Supposedly Villa buried a bunch of treasure back before Mexican independence. Lots of folks look for it, but always down in the Superstition Mountains in Mexico. Tater decided that wasn't right, and that he was going to look for it right here in Arizona, just south of here in the Sauceda range."

"Sounds like he's been out in the sun too long," Julie said dryly.

"I'm just getting started," Reardon said, keeping his voice low so the man wouldn't hear him.

"Round of beers down here!" the waitress called from the far end of the bar, Reardon hurrying to take care of it.

"Well," Julie decided, taking a long drink, "your bright idea has certainly provided some marvelous insight."

Bolan shook his head. "I don't understand it. Why would Jerry Butler code this place if it didn't mean anything?"

"Maybe to throw his enemies off the mark," she replied. "Or maybe you just interpreted the code wrong."

Bolan took a long breath. "Maybe so."

"Let's get out of here," Julie said. "We can make it up to Phoenix tonight and maybe eat at a decent restaurant and take in a movie."

Reardon moved back to stand before them, wiping his hands on the apron tied around his waist. "Anyway," he continued, "everybody thought ol' Tater had finally gone nuts, 'cause not only is the Sauceda range the wrong place to look, but it's smack dab in the middle of an Air Force testing range."

"What?" Bolan said, he and Julie turning to stare at each other.

"Yeah." Reardon shook his head. "The Luke Air Force range is just south of here. Sometimes at night you can hear 'em screaming in, bombing mock targets. It's as close to war as I ever want to get again."

"So, he's prospecting on a firing range," Bolan said. "He doesn't seem to be doing badly, either."

"That's not found money he's throwing around," Reardon said, then laughed. "On the other hand, maybe it is, because while we were all sitting here laughing at ol' Tater, he went and found him a bunch of good ol' boys who were willing to stake him to high grub and go out there with him. They been out there a couple of years now with no sign of a letup."

"That doesn't make sense," Julie said.

The man shrugged at her. "All I know's that every month Tater comes into town and spends like a sailor on leave. He buys a whole shitload of supplies, then wanders from bar to bar until he shuts down the last one at two in the morning, then he disappears for another month, back looking for that treasure."

"Have you ever seen any of his partners?" Bolan asked.

Reardon shook his head. "You'd think they'd'a gone stir-crazy by now ... at least female crazy." He turned and looked at Julie. "Pardon me, ma'am."

Julie took a sip of her third beer. "No skin off my nose."

"That sure is an odd story," Bolan said. "Nobody ever try to follow him out there or anything?"

"Not really." Reardon took Bolan's empty and got him another. "Folks in Gila Bend mind their own business. Somebody followed him partway once, just to see if he was really going down that way, and sure enough, he headed down south on 85, then left the road at Sauceda and headed due south overland. I guess you don't have to go to the big city to find crazy folk."

"Guess not," Bolan agreed. "And you say his routine's always the same?"

"Always," the man replied.

"Whiskey all around!" Tater yelled, holding his bottle in the air.

"I'd better go and do some business," Reardon said, clearing empties off the bar.

"Good to meet you," Bolan said. "If me and Bernice decide to move down here, we'll look you up."

"Good with me, Sarge," he called, and went back to work.

"Come on," Bolan said, taking Julie by the arm. "Let's get out of here." He led her off the stool, out of the bar and into the bright sunshine.

"O-o-oh," she said, putting a hand to her face. "Reality."

"Come on," her companion said, and took her across the street to the car.

They got inside, Bolan keying the engine to get the air-conditioning going. He turned and looked at her. "What do you think?"

"I think that everybody who lives here is crazy."

"All right."

She narrowed her eyes. "What do *you* think?"

"I think that Tater is the front man here for Project GOG."

She shook her head. "God, you're crazy, too."

He pointed across the street to the flatbed truck. It was piled high with cases of dry and canned goods. "If he comes to town every month and buys that much, then he's probably got thirty or forty people out there with him. I can imagine a couple of crazies, or three or four, but not thirty."

"Maybe there's just a few really fat ones," she suggested.

"Nobody here questions it because he throws enough money around that it's great for business."

"Maybe he's an alien and has a UFO base out there," Julie said, suppressing a giggle.

"Well, we're going to find out tonight," he said, putting the Cougar into reverse and backing out of the parking spot.

"But your buddy back there said that he closes down the bars when he's in town."

"Right."

"So, do we check into a motel and wait for him, or what?"

"Or what," Bolan answered, and turned a wide arc in the middle of the street. "My original fears stand. There's no way I'm checking into a motel in this town. We're nonpersons right now. I want to keep it that way."

He pulled into the Jackson General Merchandise slot right next to Tater's truck.

"So what are we doing here?"

"Ever been camping before?" he asked, turning off the engine.

"No," she replied, "and I don't intend to start now."

"We'll get our supplies here."

"No," she repeated.

He smiled at her. "You'll love it. Nothing but the earth and the sky and the United States Air Force to keep us company."

She slouched in the seat. "My mother warned me there'd be days like this."

Chapter Nineteen

Oscar Largent stared out the passenger-side window of the Air Force pickup truck, wondering how anyone could find his way through the maze they were traveling to arrive at a preplanned destination. He had heard about the Florida Everglades, but until he'd actually entered its impenetrable mass, half land, half water and the size of Delaware, he had no way of truly appreciating the task that confronted him.

To begin with, the transmitter in his pocket was absolutely useless here in this land of hundreds of unmarked dirt crossroads that wound and twisted and led nowhere but deeper into the inscrutable heart of the largest subtropical wilderness in North America. The road they traveled was barely wide enough for the truck and was entirely closed in on both sides by a sea of sedges, ten-foot-tall stands of saw grass with barbed blades and needle-sharp edges.

He felt as if he were driving through a primeval forest, wild orchids blooming everywhere, the cries of bobcats tearing at the night. It made him realize how alone he really was, how vulnerable.

How close to death.

He turned to the tech sergeant, named Murray, who'd picked him up at the airport. "How in God's name do you find your way around down here?" he asked.

The man laughed. "You don't, unless you got it in your blood. I probably drove this route a hundred times with a Seminole guide before trying it on my own."

"You could hide an army down here."

"Yeah," the man replied. "And some do. We've pin-pointed fifteen other camps down here, either survival-ists, or drug runners or Cuban nationals training to oust Castro."

Murray made a sharp right, bumping them over a rail-less pontoon bridge. The back end of an old Ford stuck out of the water, an alligator resting atop the trunk of the vehicle, watching their passage with unreadable eyes.

"How much farther?" Largent asked.

"Almost there."

Largent had been surprised when only Murray had shown up to greet him, the man explaining that a great deal of activity at the camp had precluded the presence of Colonel Bartello, the second-in-command, and that General Cronin, the CO, wouldn't be in until tomorrow.

"Let me ask you something, Captain," Murray asked.

"Sure, Sergeant."

"I don't mean no disrespect," the man said, "but from the looks of that briefcase handcuffed to your arm and the amount of work going on at the camp...well, it looks like something big's about to happen. I was just wondering if you'd, you know, give me a hint."

Largent turned to him and smiled. "If you ever plan on making master sergeant, Sergeant," he said, "you'll learn to keep your curiosity under wraps."

"Yes, sir. Have you ever visited our camp before, Captain?"

Largent smiled. Until he'd been picked up at the air-port, he hadn't even known there was a camp. "No, I haven't. I've been looking forward to it for quite some time."

The road tangled as they picked their way through a large grove of dwarf cypress trees and cabbage palm, their branches hanging low, shifting against the windshield as they pushed slowly through the jumble. A long green snake fell out of one of the branches onto the windshield, Murray clearing the reptile off the car by turning on the wipers.

"Now you see why I asked you to keep your window up," the man said, beeping at a raccoon frozen in his headlights on the road before them.

"How long you been out here?"

"Couple of years," Murray said, jerking the wheel hard to avoid a huge limb that was partially blocking the dirt road, which had turned to mud in this section. "I'd pulled some Pentagon security detail under Colonel Givan, and he worked me into the project."

"Any family?"

The man turned, looking at him quizzically. "Of course not."

Largent nodded knowingly. "Just checking," he said, wondering what had been wrong with the question.

They suddenly found themselves on a concrete paved road, well kept on the fringes. They passed a sign: Military Security Post—Keep Out—This Means You.

"The hardest thing about the camp," Murray was saying, "was finding the spot to put it. We've just bumped up on what may be the only bedrock in the Everglades."

They approached a six-foot chain link gate, the fence extending off into the brush on either side—an outer perimeter. As they slowed, an SP moved out of a small shack to open the gate for them, then wave them through on visual recognition, snapping a salute when he saw the captain's uniform.

They drove through, Largent returning the salute and wondering why it could possibly be important if the camp was located on bedrock or not.

They drove another quarter mile before reaching the main gate of the compound. Here they moved through another checkpoint, the overhead sign arrogantly stating: Project GOG—Operational Headquarters.

The sign made Largent as angry as he'd been since seeing the mutilated bodies of Marie Price and her son. These sons of bitches were so confident that they advertised. Sitting out here in the middle of nowhere, they could spew their vile poison publicly, out in the sunshine, as if they were real and honest men.

"Here it is," Murray said. "Home sweet home."

Once inside the compound, Largent was surprised at how little there was to it. Cleared, paved ground, sporting several Quonset huts and small, enclosed concrete buildings that looked like bunkers of some kind. He saw no barracks, no motor pool or even mess buildings. The place resembled no military facility that he had ever seen.

"I suspect that the colonel will want to see you right off," Murray said. "I think he'll be over in Charlie building, supervising the tearing down of the aboveground headquarters."

The aboveground headquarters? "Fine with me, Sergeant," he said.

The man drove him across an open space of fifty yards, pulling up in front of one of the Quonset huts, a large *C* painted on white board above the doorway. By the door, uniformed men were loading storage filing cabinets atop the blades of a gas-driven forklift, the driver tilting back the blades to hold the cardboard boxes snug.

The two men got out of the truck, Murray leading Largent through the door. The place looked like a large operations office in total disarray, boxes stacked everywhere, desks piled atop one another near the door. A severe-looking colonel, square jawed and frowning, was supervising the dismantling of a water cooler.

"Colonel Bartello," Murray called and the man turned, smiling when he saw Largent. He climbed over several typewriters, walking quickly to where the Fed was standing.

The men saluted, then Bartello stuck out his hand. "You must be Captain Michaels," he said. "I've heard a lot about you."

Largent shook the man's hand, wanting to use his fist instead. "And you, too," he said. "How's the operation going?"

"Very quickly," Bartello said, his gray eyes showing no hints of suspicion toward Largent. "We should be finished tonight."

"Excellent," Largent responded. "And General Cronin...?"

"Will be here by 1000 hours tomorrow," the man replied.

"Good." Largent knew from the orders he had studied on the plane that whatever Project GOG was on this end, General Cronin was to head it and assume command of this facility, and that the project would go off the following morning after the facility had been "sealed," for whatever reason.

"Am I correct to assume that you haven't visited our facility before?" Bartello asked.

"Quite correct."

The man smiled coyly, almost smugly. "Then I would imagine that you'd want to see the command center before you do anything else."

Largent went with the flow. "You're certainly right about that, Colonel."

"Call me Dick," the man said. "We don't need the formalities between us."

Largent nodded. "I'm Norm."

The man looked at Murray. "Any problems coming in?"

"No, sir."

Bartello nodded. "I'll drive the captain over to the bunker," he said. "You go check with the quartermaster and see how the transfer's doing."

"Yes, sir."

Murray turned and walked out quickly, Bartello leading Largent out to the truck at a more leisurely pace.

"How's the general?" Bartello asked as they climbed into the truck.

"Alive and kicking," Largent said.

Bartello looked at him as if he expected something more. "Is he excited about the future?" the man asked, firing the engine and starting off across the pavement.

"You know the general," Largent returned.

The man sighed, started to say something else but clammed up instead. Within thirty seconds they pulled up in front of one of the blockhouses Largent had noticed coming in. They climbed out of the truck, Michaels's briefcase still handcuffed to his arm, and walked to the bunker door.

Bartello glanced down at the briefcase, then opened the door. Before entering, he pulled a small looped metal detector out of his back pocket and went over Largent with it, stopping at the briefcase. "We maintain strict weapons control here, Captain. You'll have to turn the firearm over to me now."

Largent frowned, then turned his back and opened the briefcase, pulling out the MAC-10. "I wasn't told about this."

"Sorry, regulations." Bartello stuck the weapon in his belt. "We're proud of this facility," he said, ushering Oscar through the door. "We think it's the finest of its kind on the face of the earth."

Largent walked into a tiny room, the bunker walls so thick that very little room was left inside. A flight of stairs wound downward, leading to another door. Bartello walked down the stairs, Oscar following.

"This of course will all be sealed off," he said, gesturing around.

"Of course."

Bartello opened the next door, which led to another flight of steps down and yet another door. They passed three more flights before winding down to another small room, this one containing a large elevator with a window cutout made of extraordinarily thick glass.

"Here we are," Bartello said, pushing a black button set in the wall beside.

Largent felt a growing tightness in the pit of his stomach. His mind tried to push away the dark thoughts that were beginning to creep in, as if denial of the obvious would make it go away.

The elevator door slid open, and the two men stepped inside. Bartello pushed a button; the door slid closed with a sealing whoosh, and they started down, picking up speed as they went.

He looked at the control box. It showed four lower levels, the light glowing on the fourth, their destination. So far, they hadn't even reached level one.

Largent could see nothing but rock face through the cutout. A number flashed by, marking one hundred feet, and still they traveled downward.

"We control the satellites from down here," Bartello said. "Our transmitter dishes are also underground, on gurneys that can be raised for usage, then cranked back down. We could've used the fourth one, but we can cover it just fine with three."

They were traveling quite fast now, a two-hundred-foot marker flashing by. Largent was dying to know what Bartello was talking about with the satellites and decided to take a brief stab in the dark.

"Yeah," he said, "that goddamned egghead screwed everything up."

"Taking out the shuttle wasn't an easy decision," Bartello agreed, "but the general didn't have any choice after Butler shot off his mouth. A damned shame, if you ask me."

The Fed's head was spinning. He had it all, every bit of it opening up to him, but no way to communicate it back to Brognola and Greggson. They flew past the three-hundred-foot marker, still picking up speed. They'd never track him from the beeper, especially below ground. He'd have to find some way to communicate—and fast.

Finally, after the four-hundred-foot level, the machine began to slow its decline, until it was moving at a regular elevator rate. All at once, they were passing level one, a

wide open barracks, well lit, with a large number of men
moving around.

"Living level," Bartello informed him. "Rec rooms,
showers, a movie theater, even a miniature golf. It was
modeled after the Navy's specs for aircraft carriers and
then improved upon. If need be, the entire level can be
abandoned and sealed off if it gets too hot."

That was it. When Bartello talked about hot, he wasn't
speaking about the Florida weather. They slid past level
one, then moved to level two.

"Equipment and weapons storage," Bartello said.
"We've even got some tanks down here. If necessary, this
level can also be abandoned."

They continued downward, passing level four. "Food
and water storage. This is where it all stops. Our researchers at Grolier tell us that the surface of the base could take
a direct hit of twenty megatons and levels three and four
would still remain intact and functional. Of course, who's
going to put twenty megatons into the Everglades, right?"

Bartello laughed loudly. Largent, shaking inside with
rage and gut fear, forced himself to laugh with the son of
a bitch. God, they were anticipating a nuclear attack—and
laughing about it! He had come down here prepared to
deal with a coup of some kind, but this was monstrous
beyond understanding. Leland was apparently happily
plotting the end of civilization.

The elevator jerked to a stop, Largent barely even noticing it. He looked through the cutout and found himself
staring into the guts of a huge communications and operations center, a deep underground bunker from which to
wage a total, all-out war. But how? How? There was no
way that Leland could coordinate an attack or retaliation.
What about NORAD? What about the President, and the
Joint Chiefs and the NSC? How in God's name did they
intend to make this thing work?

"Here we are," Bartello said, and the door slid open.
But before Largent could step out, the man put a hand on
his chest and pushed the button to close the door.

"I can't stand it any longer," the man said. "You're a coy bastard, but you're going to have to tell me."

"Tell you what?"

"We've been put on red alert," Bartello stated. "We've begun sealing-off procedures, and now here you are with sealed orders."

Largent stared at the man. He seemed excited, highly agitated.

"You've got to tell me," he said. "Is GOG on or not? Is this the real thing?"

The Fed's mouth was dry, but somehow he managed to choke out, "It's go."

"All right!" The colonel laughed loudly, clenching his fists and thrusting them above his head. "Finally!"

Oscar Largent felt as if he had to throw up.

"GOD," JULIE SAID, "I never knew there were so many stars."

Bolan smiled down at her, the soft curves of her face glowing gently in the orange haze of the firelight. She lay on her back, wrapped in a sleeping bag, staring up into the Arizona night.

"Amazing what you can see away from city lights," he replied, throwing some more sagebrush on the fire, listening to the crackle as the dried twigs gave over to the blaze.

He moved to sit beside her, staring down from the sandstone ridge where they had set up camp just at the edge of the Sauceda range, twenty miles south of Gila Bend. "All things being equal," he said, "I wouldn't mind settling in a place like this sometime. The peace of it could really work to make you feel whole inside."

Julie smiled. "It's odd...hearing talk like that from you. I thought you were the original hard ass."

"You're not the first person who's ever been wrong about me," he said.

"I didn't mean that the way it sounded." She sat up to wrap her arms around herself. "It's cold."

"Nothing to stop the wind," he said. "No cloud cover to seal in the heat."

"There must be some clouds." She pointed farther south. "We've got lightning down there."

Bolan looked. Miles distant, through a maze of small mountains, he could see the sky light up. A small static rumble, barely discernible, reached them seconds later.

"Summer lightning," he said. "Static electricity."

"What time is it?" she asked, unfolding one of the blankets they'd purchased in town and wrapping it around her shoulders.

He looked at the watch. "Nearly eleven. We've still got a few hours left. If you want to sleep, I'll wake you when it's time."

"You sure he'll come this way?"

Bolan shrugged. "If he travels the direction Mike Reardon said he does, we'll be able to see his headlights from a distance. I don't think they'll be any trouble."

"I still think it's a wild-goose chase," she said.

"Humor me," he replied. "Enjoy a night of peace and solitude."

"I can't argue with that." She stared out over a magnificent vista of mountains and sandstone monuments, desert and arroyos, all calmed to stillness by the blanket of night that covered and preserved it, and watched over by a brilliant star field, a million eyes to savor the beauty.

Bolan wore his blacksuit, a jacket covering the combat harness. Chilly himself, he zipped the jacket up to his neck. "How did you come to marry Harry Arnold?" he asked, something he had been wondering ever since he'd met her.

"There's a question," she said, reaching out for a stand of the sagebrush and pulling it to herself. She began to tear it apart, a twig at a time, tossing the individual sticks into the all-consuming flame.

"I was young and hungry for knowledge...I guess maybe I was really hungry for the power that knowledge brings. Anyway, for all his pettiness, Harry was a genius in his field and a bona fide research scientist. I was attracted to that, and, I guess, Harry was attracted to me.

"I'd graduated from Brandeis, then met Harry at Penn State where I'd gone for my master's. Harry invited me to be his research assistant, a job I would have killed for. After I worked with him for a year, he told me he couldn't live without me and wanted to marry me. I turned him down at first, even then knowing it was the work that I loved, not Harry. He got . . . I don't know, sullen, I guess, and told me that if I wouldn't marry him, he couldn't continue working with me. It was an either-or situation."

"And you picked either," Bolan concluded.

"Is that so wrong?" she asked. "Over the years I've learned that people marry for a variety of reasons . . . and I haven't seen a great deal of validity to any of them."

"I wouldn't know," he said. "I've never been married."

"Any close shaves?"

"Yeah, once," he said, reluctantly dragging up old memories.

"What happened?"

"Nothing. She . . . died."

"Like Harry," she said, her voice catching in her throat.

"Yeah."

They sat there in silence for a moment, both acutely aware of the presence of the other, and of private pain. A meteor flashed across the sky, brilliantly burning through the atmosphere before winking out on the eastern horizon.

"That was beautiful," she whispered.

"It's like life, searing fast, then disappearing without a trace."

She leaned against him, his arm instinctively going around her. "Oh, Mack," she said. "What's brought us here together? What fate is screwing with our lives . . . our feelings?"

"If we met at a party," he said, "we'd have nothing to talk about."

She turned and looked up at him, her eyes filling with tears. "If we'd met at a party, I'd want you just the way I want you right now."

He had no words, only intense, burning need. He pulled her roughly to him, and she held on desperately, her ferocity a match for his own.

He released her and took her face in his large, callused hands, planting kisses all over it as her trembling hands worked the buttons of her checkered shirt.

"Oh, God, Mack," she rasped. "I'm so lonely, so goddamned lonely."

He pulled away from her, staring. "You think I don't know that? You think I don't understand *exactly* how you feel?"

And in that instant they hit upon the force that had driven them together and continued to hold them. Because though their lives were worlds, if not light-years, apart, their hearts were alike. In their loneliness, in their need, they were one.

Julie removed her shirt, black lace beneath highlighted against her pale skin in the firelight. Bolan stood and took off his jacket, then the combat harness, tossing them both to the ground. Then he knelt to her, taking her in his arms again, gently this time, as if she were as fragile as glass.

They kissed deeply, the kiss lingering, turning to caresses. He pushed her back on the sleeping bag, taking the rest of her clothes off, then his own. She held her arms out to him, and he moved into their comfort.

Julie looked into his eyes, fully and completely, and trusted the man who looked back without shame.

Then he was moving against her, her hands on his back tracing scar lines, trying to empathize the pain he had lived with for so long. Their bodies sought release and would not be denied, and after, they lay in each other's arms, under the sleeping bag for warmth, not wanting to let go for fear of breaking the spell.

"Let's forget about all this," she said, her head settled in the crook of his shoulder. "Just go somewhere and sit the rest of this out."

"Can't do it. You know we can't."

"It's a good dream, though."

"The best."

They lay together, listening to the distant thunder, drifting for once with their guard down, the scent of her hair wrapping Bolan in a sweet cocoon that held back the outside world. He watched her slowly drifting off to sleep, her eyes coming halfway open as she kissed him softly.

"I love you, Mack Bolan," she whispered, her eyes closing again, her breathing shifting into regular patterns as sleep finally overtook her.

He didn't move until he was sure she was sleeping deeply, then he slowly extricated himself from the sleeping bag, covering her warmly after he'd risen. He put his clothes on, then threw more sagebrush on the dying fire.

He bent to pick up the combat harness, but instead decided to leave it for a while. Since they were working so hard at pretending right now, he'd pretend for just a little longer that the world wasn't coming apart around them.

He walked back to where Julie lay sleeping, alternately staring at her and at the roadway far below. He reached out and pushed an errant lock of sleek black hair out of her face. She stirred in her sleep, smiling, and he knew that the smile was for him.

It was a feeling, a memory, that he knew he'd carry with him for the rest of his life.

However short that life might be.

Chapter Twenty

"Come on," Bolan said, gently shaking Julie awake. "It's time to get moving."

She rolled onto her back, smiling through sleepy eyes. "Why don't you call down for room service?"

He smiled despite himself. "We've really got to go," he said when she tried to pull him down with her.

"Party pooper," she said, then struggled to her elbows to watch him stamp out the fire. "Is he coming?"

Bolan pointed past her to the flatland below and the two headlights that were relentlessly moving closer to their position.

Bolan tossed her clothes to her. "Better put these on or we'll give ol' Tater more of a surprise than he bargained for."

She stretched, then climbed out of the bag, totally casual about her nakedness. She dressed hurriedly, though, once out in the chill air.

"Do we pack up the gear?" she asked, as she tucked her shirttail into her jeans.

He slipped into the combat harness, then the jacket. "We'll get it on the way back. Listen."

She stood still drinking in the sounds of the dark. "An engine."

"He's close," Bolan said, striding purposefully toward the car. "Let's follow."

She hurried to the Cougar, getting into the passenger side and buckling the seat belt, Bolan climbing in behind the wheel. He started the engine as quietly as possible, though he doubted that a jet engine would have been any louder than Tater's flatbed. He'd be an easy man to follow.

The sandstone ridge they occupied sloped gently downward on the side hidden from the road. Bolan made the trip quickly, without headlights, and drove around the base of the ridge, coming out no more than two hundred yards behind the flatbed's taillights.

Leaving the headlights off, they followed at that distance, Tater's dust cloud obscuring the man's view of his pursuers. After a mile, the flatbed left what little road there was and trekked overland, ducking in and out of the myriad small mountain passes that were scattered across the desert floor, the peaks rising around them hundreds of feet in the air.

"Just what do we expect to find out here?" she asked.

"If I knew that," he replied, "I wouldn't have to come."

"It's odd," she said. "He seems to be driving right toward those lightning flashes."

"I've noticed." The warrior's gaze was focused on the desert floor, trying to catch the hazards that headlights would normally pick up. "Don't you think it's strange that the lightning hasn't moved? It's been flashing on and off for hours, but always from the same place."

She looked over at him, her lips drawn tight, jaw muscles working. "I'm beginning to think you might not be so crazy after all."

"I kind of hoped you would've been right the first time."

They drove for another five miles, ducking in and out of mountains and dodging cactus, drawing closer to the occasionally flashing lights, the sound, now that they were closer, more like an electric hum, the stentorian wail of a transformer blowing.

Suddenly the old man's truck disappeared behind a stand of boulders that seemed to block the entrance to a ring of sandstone cliffs. Bolan slowed the Cougar, then stopped.

"Strange," Julie said. "He went in but didn't come out."

"Strange is right. Look at the way those peaks are placed. They're protected from view on all sides. If I was going to hide anything, this would sure as hell be the place to do it."

As if in response, light flared briefly from within the matrix of rock faces, the loud, unnatural hum that accompanied it nearly deafening.

"Stay here," Bolan ordered, "and be ready to take off."

"Not this time, partner." Julie opened her door and climbed out. "I didn't come all the way out to this godforsaken wilderness to sit in the car. I waited for you in Florida, and it nearly drove me crazy. Whatever we do now, we do together."

He tightened his lips. "I can't stop you."

"Damn right you can't," she replied, and started to walk toward the place where Tater had disappeared.

"Easy," Bolan said as they reached the boulders. "We'll take this real careful, a step at a time."

They came around the stand of boulders and saw a wide open space between two of the majestic rock formations that were scattered so thickly here.

"It looks like an entrance," Julie said softly.

"A hidden valley," Bolan replied. "Incredible."

They walked through the opening, sheer rock faces towering all around them, dwarfing them to insignificance. Within the rock walls were more rocks, the valley itself still hidden.

"Look," Julie said, pointing to the left, and Bolan turned to see a mobile home nestled between several large, round boulders fifty yards distant. The flatbed was parked in a clearing nearby. "Let's check it out."

They moved quickly and quietly, staying on the fringes beneath overhanging rock faces until they had come around the front of the large trailer. A light was on, and through the closed window they could hear strange moaning sounds punctuated by the same cackling laughter they'd heard at the Zanzi-bar.

The trailer was up on blocks, putting Julie and the warrior well below the window. Bolan turned to the rocks around the trailer. "Let's climb up and get a look."

They crept away from the window, moving quietly up the rock face opposite until they could see in. When they did, Bolan had to put his hand over Julie's mouth to keep her from laughing.

The mobile home was furnished elegantly, and kept up as if it had a live-in maid. Tater sat stark naked—except for his hat—on a black leather couch, a bottle of whiskey in his hand. He was watching a big-screen TV with a VCR hooked up to it. On the screen, a blond woman with huge breasts was having sex with a short man wearing nothing but his socks. Every time the people on the screen groaned, Tater threw back his head and laughed loudly.

"Some people have all the fun," she whispered to Bolan when he took his hand from her mouth.

They climbed back down the rocks, traveling the way they had come until they found another passage through the boulders, which seemed to have been strewn around by some careless hand. They walked along the path, then through a narrow channel between two of the sandstone monoliths to find themselves at the edge of a large valley, completely surrounded by rock.

"Mack, this is weird," Julie said, as they picked their way slowly into the valley.

"And it gets weirder, too." He pointed to a spot on the ground no more than five feet before them.

It was a perfectly round indentation in the ground with a twenty-foot circumference. The indentation was one foot deep, its walls perfectly smooth and hard. The inside of the place was charred black.

Bolan walked into the circle, bending to touch the ground, and came up with a handful of something. "It's like powdered glass," he observed, letting it slip through his fingers.

"What the hell's going on here?" she asked.

"Something someone wants to keep secret," he returned, turning in a circle.

"Here's another one," Julie said, running several feet farther on. "It's . . . smoking!"

He hurried to join her. Another circle, exactly like the first one—except with a deeper indentation—was wisping gray smoke from within. "I've never seen anything like this," he said.

"There's another one!" Julie exclaimed, pointing farther on, "and another . . . and look!"

She had turned and was facing the way they had come. Bolan turned with her, amazed to see a great number of similar circles cut right into the rock face of the surrounding cliffs. The holes seemed to be deep.

They had been working their way up a gentle slope, the remainder of the valley hidden beyond its crest. Julie ran toward the summit, wanting to see more, while Bolan puzzled over the holes in the ground and rock.

She hailed him from the summit. "Mack! You've got—"

A loud siren pierced the night, and all at once, floodlights were coming on, bathing the rocks and valley floor in harsh light. Julie had set off some sort of alarm.

"Mack!" she screamed, terrified as powerful floodlights bore down on them from all directions.

He charged up the rise, the sirens cutting through the night's stillness, their reverberating wails mind-numbing. Julie was losing it as she stood at the summit, half crouched over, her arms covering her head and ears, trying to shield them from the piercing horns.

He ran to her, his eyes darting to the valley that stretched out before him and the small industrial complex that filled it. He had no more than a few seconds to appreciate the smokestacks and manufacturing building backed up to a yard full of scrap metal, and cable bales and the huge coal oil tanker that provided power for the place. What his eyes fixed on was the military barracks and the Air Force jeeps parked in front of it.

He pulled her arms away from her ears. "We've got to get out of here!" he yelled, trying to be heard above the deafening wail.

Their quickest route out was the one they'd taken in. Bolan grabbed Julie's arm and began to run, but Tater, dressed in boxer shorts and hat, stood behind an M-60 mounted on the back end of an Air Force jeep, blocking their flight fifty yards distant.

The old man tripped the bolt and began to fire, dirt kicking up around their feet from impacts.

There was nothing to do; there was only flight. Bolan turned back up the hill, determined to put the rise between him and the old man.

Bullets zinging past their ears, they crested the summit, only to see a score of men pouring out of the barracks. They were armed, and Bolan could see them mounting M-60s on the saddles of the other jeeps.

Bolan instinctively turned, running toward the nearest rock face. If they could at least find cover, they'd have a fighting chance.

"We've got to make those rocks!" he yelled to Julie, whose urge to survive overtook her fears. She clenched her teeth and ran for all she was worth.

That electric hum rent the air again. Bolan's eyes traveled upward to the source, and then he saw it—the reason for the cloudless lightning and the rumble of man-made thunder. A large cannon, brilliantly lit by floods, sat halfway up the rock face they were running toward.

"Do you see . . . ?" Julie asked breathlessly.

"Yeah!" Bolan yelled. He could see men hurrying to fire up the big cannon, his mind spinning, wondering at its purpose. He jumped into one of the indentations, nearly tripped, then climbed out the other side. He turned to take a quick look. The security people were tearing across the sandy floor in their jeeps, swirling dirt and dust from their back wheels. Many were advancing on foot.

Suddenly the night crackled, roaring around them, as an impossibly huge beam of pink light issued from the wide mouth of the cannon mounted on the rock face. It ate the ground behind them, the sand catching fire and melting in a snaky line that drew closer on their heels.

Julie's face was dead-white, her mouth hanging open as she slowed, nearly stopping to gape up at the technological marvel that was drawing down on her.

"Come on!" he urged, running over to pull her away. The cannon shut down, then cranked up again as the jeeps sped closer.

"It's a laser cannon!" she yelled, reluctantly running with him. "We're not supposed to have—"

The cannon spit again, the ground flaming just beside them. Bolan felt the heat from the beam as he drove Julie on, charging right at the thing.

"Run right at it!" he ordered, as the beam quivered, searching for them, destroying anything it touched. "We're harder to track at a dead-line angle."

Smoke rose from the valley floor. The jeeps picked their way around the burned areas and the previous craters, gunners in the back firing at the fleeing pair.

"The rocks!" Bolan called. "The rocks!"

It was their only hope.

The laser stopped, cranked again. Bolan watched as the gunners tried to angle nearly straight down from their position as he and Julie charged beneath its range. It fired again, trying to draw in, getting no closer than twenty feet behind them. The big gun was now out of the picture. All they had to contend with was a small army charging at them.

They gained the boulders strewn around the base of the rock face, gas-powered slugs tearing large gouges out of the sandstone as they dropped to cover. Bolan withdrew the AutoMag and handed it to Julie.

"I know you know how to use this," he said, bringing out the Beretta and checking its load.

"They don't even know who we are," she said, her face scrunching up every time a shot ricocheted off the rocks.

"They don't care. Nobody gets to see this."

He came up over the rock, several jeeps no more than fifty feet away. They came on straight, not figuring on resistance. Bolan was ready to kick back.

He stood, a stiff arm coming down atop the boulder to steady his aim. He picked the lead jeep, five others trailing slightly behind. Taking a sure breath, he squeezed a short burst that shattered the windshield and took out the driver, his face disintegrating as he fell to the side.

The jeep swerved, crossing the path of the vehicle on its left, which smashed full force into it broadside. The impact launched the driver through the windshield and the gunner thirty feet into the air. The gunner from the lead vehicle flew sideways and crashed through the windshield of the jeep on the right. Its driver lost control, and the vehicle glanced off some rocks, rolling over and crushing its occupants.

The other jeeps pulled up short, swerving for cover as Bolan took out a gunner, the man falling backward and somersaulting out of his vehicle.

"What's happened?" Julie called. She was hunched down behind the rock, holding the AutoMag protectively to her chest.

"They're taking up positions," Bolan said, his hand automatically reaching down to count the number of extra clips in the webbing of the combat harness.

"What do we do?"

"I'm working on it." Whatever decision he made would have to come quickly. When the men on foot arrived at the scene they'd simply form a wide perimeter and close on them from the rocks around and above. If there was high ground to take, he'd have to be the one to take it.

He turned and looked at the rock face behind them. The laser was up there with two men to operate it, but it looked as if the climb up was neither impossible nor totally un-

protected. The cannon and its operators had gotten up
there, and so would they.

He hit the clip release and dumped the half-used magazine, shoving in a fresh one. "When I give the word," he
said, "stand up and dump the whole clip at them. Spray
the area, then follow me. Ready?"

She looked at him, her eyes trusting. "Okay," she said.
Bolan read her lips, unable to hear her above the blaring
sirens.

He took a breath. "Now!" he yelled, both of them
standing and opening up, sweeping a wide arc. The men in
front of them dived for cover when they fired, as Bolan
knew they would. They ran the clips dry in seconds. "Go!
Go!"

They turned and started up the rocks, quickly finding
the pathway between the boulders that led up the sandstone.

The troops on the ground began to return fire, but not
before Bolan had gained a small tactical advantage. As he
climbed, protected by rocks in front, he jammed a magazine into the Beretta and fired at the charging men.

Two men fell, short bursts from the Beretta taking them
out head high and throwing them to the steaming ground.
Once again the force retreated, Bolan lacing one of them
across the back as he ran, dropping him to sprawl face
forward in the dirt.

"Go!" Bolan yelled to Julie. "Gain some distance!"

They ran upward, a narrow passage winding its way
inexorably up the rock face to the cannon above. After
fifteen or twenty seconds, Bolan turned, panting, to look
at his enemy from a fifty-foot advantage.

The soldiers were wising up, spreading out a wide perimeter a hundred yards long and coming at the rocks individually or in tiny groups. He could have taken the time
to pick away at them, but it would have given the advantage to the others to gain ground. Instead, he opted to keep
moving higher, consolidating what he'd already gained.

A hundred feet from the laser, the going got a little tougher. They heard occasional fire behind them, but most of their assailants were busily climbing the rocks, in hot pursuit.

"What do we do when we get there?" Julie asked.

"We'll worry about that when the time comes," Bolan said. "Are you doing all right?"

"I'd walk on hot coals to get away from those bastards!" she yelled. "That laser..."

"What about it?"

"They'd need a generator the size of Rhode Island to run a cannon like that. We don't have things like this!"

"Remember who sent us here," Bolan said, turning to survey the situation. The valley floor was pitted with huge holes that from his position looked like dinosaur footprints. This was a manufacturing and test site.

Two men were following their path up. Bolan waited until he had a clear shot between two jagged rocks and squeezed off three shots, two of them drilling the first man through the gut. As the guy dropped to his knees, the other man hurried back to cover.

"The liquid electricity!" Julie yelled. "That's what they're using it for!"

He handed her another clip from the webbing. "Reload. Keep moving."

They picked their way up the steep face, Bolan occasionally laying down covering fire meant to buy them more time, more distance. Away from the bite of the floodlights and cloaked in darkness, they were free to pick out well-lit targets below.

But two men waited above them in the gloom, waiting to get off a clear shot.

Bolan looked up. The long barrel of the laser cannon poked out dark and ominous from the side of the rock face. He pulled three more clips from the webbing and grabbed Julie's arm to stop her ascent.

"Put it on single shot," he advised, handing her the clips. "Shoot at anything that moves."

"Where are you going?" Her eyes were wide in the darkness.

"I've got some business," he said, moving past her to take the lead. "I'll call you when it's safe."

She didn't protest this time, knowing to trust him in combat situations. He left her behind, following the path for another ten feet, then opting to climb the rocks instead.

He shinnied up the rock face, the Beretta back in its holster. Totally exposed to the ground, his dark clothes and the night itself kept him safe and unseen.

He crested just beneath the metal framework that supported the well-lit laser cannon. He crawled into the platform skeleton, inching along quietly, looking for the operators. He was dangling away from the rocks, two hundred feet above solid ground.

Then he saw them, M-16s at the ready, behind rocks on either side of the path that wound upward, ready to initiate a cross fire as soon as someone drew near. He and Julie had missed the ambush by no more than twenty feet.

Bolan wrapped his legs around one of the minigirders that anchored the platform to the rocks, then hooked his arm around it and tried to draw the Beretta. He had to twist his body to get at the gun, his legs slipping off the girder.

A groan twisted from his lips as his full weight swung from the arm still locked on the pole.

"Jake!" one of the ambushers screamed. "The platform!"

Searing pain tore through his shoulder as the men opened fire on him, his position barely protected by rigging and jutting boulders. Through waves of pain he cut loose with the Beretta, the girder sparking from ricochets.

One of the men screamed in agony, stumbling backward over the edge. His yelling stopped when he hit the rock face fifty feet down, his body continuing the tumble as deadweight.

The other man was protected, hiding.

Bolan struggled to get his legs around the girder. In doing so he was forced to wrap both arms around the structure, which made him defenseless. As he was hoisting himself back up, he saw the man run to the platform, then crouch to fire beneath the overhang. He had Bolan. He had him dead and buried.

Bolan locked eyes with the man, a huge grin spreading across his adversary's face. He brought the weapon up, shouldered it.

An automatic rattled loudly, and the grin was punched off the hardguy's face. He tumbled off the mountain, dead long before he hit bottom.

"Mack?"

"Under here!" he called, as he shinnied down the girder and climbed under the framework to the rock face. She was waiting for him beside the platform, smoke still curling from the barrel of the AutoMag.

"I didn't do what you told me," she said.

"I'll give you hell about it later," he said, then turned to look down the mountain.

As he feared, they were charging. The troops scurried up the rocks, about thirty of them spread out in a wide area. Soon they'd reach the safety of the darkness and the high ground.

He looked quickly around, his eyes finally resting on the cannon. "Can you figure out how to work this thing?" he asked, taking her hand and climbing the three metal stairs to the platform.

"I-I'll try."

The gun in many respects resembled the 130 mm heavy antiaircraft guns he'd seen the NVA using in Vietnam, but with a much wider mouth. It was bolted to the platform on a heavy tripod and automatic cranked for elevation and range. It was attached to a large gray box at the side of the platform by heavy cables.

Julie bent to the box, then followed the lines back, studying a small set of instruments attached to a panel be side the crude, manual sights.

"I don't know what good this will do," she said as she scanned the instrument panel. "We can't track low enough to make a go of it."

"Can you work it?" Bolan yelled, as the soldiers began to fire at them, forcing him back farther on the platform.

"Yes!" she shouted, and he ran to her side. She pointed to a dial. "You have to build up the charge to a certain level. Once you do, you can open it up, probably for eight or ten seconds before building the charge again."

"Is it ready to go?" he asked, bullets pinging against the platform.

She nodded. "It's your party! Just double-thumb these buttons once you've aimed."

"Got it!"

He grabbed the left-hand grip, using his right hand to track left on the auto-crank. He brought it all the way around until it was pointing at the mountain they were perched on. He took hold of the grips and thumbed the red buttons, the hum of the weapon shaking them violently.

Brilliant light shot from the barrel, etching into the mountain. And then it began to crumble.

Large slabs of sandstone began to be sheared from the cliff side, tumbling down the mountain, loosening other rocks as it went. The landslide was loud and devastating. The laser platform creaked, bending downward, even as the warrior cranked in the other direction, firing the rest of the charge into the rock face on the other side.

The mountain was collapsing all around them, rocks falling like huge, prehistoric animals, tons of stone dropping on the army that had exposed itself on the monstrous beast's flanks.

Julie grabbed Bolan, held on as the platform shook crazily, threatening to take them down, too. "Look," she said, pointing.

Through the ever-growing curtain of dust that was rising from the still-falling debris, he could see a Huey climbing from the ground behind the barracks, machine guns mounted in its open bays.

Bolan drew down on the chopper, the platform buckling forward as small rocks pelted them from above.

He checked the charge and thumbed the buttons, laser light deflecting through the dust particles, tiny lines of it zipping off in a thousand directions.

"Damn!" Bolan yelled, shutting down the big gun.

"It's coming!" Julie raised a hand to her face to wave away the thick dust.

The warrior ejected the magazine from the Beretta and shoved another into place. "Take cover!" he yelled, moving to brace himself against the end of the platform.

Dust choking his eyes, he switched to single shot, the chopper a specter slipping up and out of the dust fog. He heard the rattle from the open bays, recognizing the sound of a .50-caliber machine gun. As the bullets impacted all around him, he stood solidly, firing mechanically, aiming for the shadowy cockpit, his one good chance of taking the chopper out.

It closed in, a rampaging elephant charging a lone hunter, Bolan standing his ground to kill or die in the attempt. His concentration focused, he continued to fire, a sentient machine existing for a single purpose.

He could see the pilot's face, a mere fifteen feet away, chopper blades clearing the dust, the windshield pitted with bullet holes. The gunner drew down on him, screaming with battle fury as Bolan took one final shot at the pilot.

The shot drilled a hole right through the man's head, but he didn't move, didn't fall. He sat at the controls like an animated zombie, his hand moving on the stick. But the chopper knew the difference. It began to dip, then angled sideways, pitching the gunner out of the bay to his death. The machine danced crazily for fifteen seconds, then smashed into what was left of the mountain.

Bolan looked through the rapidly closing window in the dust the helicopter had made for him. He could see the building complex and distant figures of running men.

He juiced up the cannon, then thumbed the red buttons as he cranked the barrel and aimed at the huge coal oil storage tank.

The explosion was magnificent. Bolan stared in fascination as several hundred thousand gallons of fuel went up with the sound of a sonic boom, enveloping the entire complex in an incredible orange fireball. Thick black smoke rose in a majestic pillar, shot through with flames at its crown.

Bolan sagged against the laser, his arms cramped, locked onto the control pistols. He forced his hands loose, then turned, looking for Julie.

She stood behind him, a look of horror on her face, her arms limp at her side. She seemed in a state of shock, like a disaster victim.

"Are you all right?" he asked.

Her lower lip began to tremble and she ran to him, throwing herself into his arms and holding on with a death grip. She began to cry, violent, wrenching sobs.

They stayed that way for a moment, holding each other. Then they quietly picked their way down the side of the mountain and walked out of the valley of death.

They saw no one; they stopped for nothing. They didn't look behind them.

Chapter Twenty-One

Oscar Largent felt like a visitor to an insane asylum run by the inmates. He'd once heard someone say that each individual creates his own reality, and nowhere was it more apparent than in the underground control complex of Project GOG.

He walked quickly through level four, taking in the buttressed steel on the rock walls and the computer rooms, the personnel working madly to maintain and enhance the reality being created in this place.

Here was a system, an entire state of mind, based around the assumption of nuclear war with the Russians and the wonderful possibilities thereafter. From his casual conversation with Dick Bartello at dinner last night, he'd gleaned that much. How this nuclear war was to be initiated, the man didn't say, but Largent knew it somehow tied up directly with the space shuttle program, including the *Challenger* flight. Hal Brognola and his man, Bolan, had been right from the first.

His priority at the moment was in communicating with the outside. The beeper, useless four hundred feet underground, was back in his assigned room. He had lain awake the previous night trying to reach a decision about communicating, knowing that he ran the risk of blowing his cover. Oscar Largent, though dedicated and capable, was not one to risk his life foolishly. But this was worth it, and in the final analysis he had reached the only decision possible for him. And once it was made, he'd spent the rest of the night making peace with himself.

There had been a radio channel left open for him in case he had to try to make contact. They had played down that aspect, hoping to be able to track him more safely with the beeper. So much for safety.

The fourth level was the hub of the entire operation. There were emergency barracks, extra food services and recreation rooms. This was the command center, with all of the communication and control systems. These people simply sat here, anxiously awaiting the end of the world so they could take over. He had yet to hear anyone say exactly what it was that would be left to take over.

The ceilings were high to avoid feelings of claustrophobia, and the area was aglow with neon lighting. The architecture was minimal, but he guessed that a place designed to take a direct hit of twenty megatons had something other than interior decoration to recommend it.

The communications center was a glassed-in bunker set in the middle of the main chamber of level four. Largent walked quickly through a connecting passageway from the auxiliary barracks area, and made his way across the smooth concrete floor to stand in front of the booth.

Communications was capable of handling any kind of transmission known to man, from laser Morse pulse to shortwave to microwave satellite. In many senses it was the core of the operations center, for in an age of communication and information retrieval, GOG was set up to be the most sophisticated info in/info out system on the face of the planet. He couldn't help but wonder who had thought of all this—and what philosophy stood as its top end.

He paused at the glass door of the bunker and took a long breath. He had no way of giving a position to try to save himself. The best he could hope for was enough time to warn Brognola of exactly what was going on down here. After that, he figured he wouldn't be alive long enough to worry about anything else.

He pushed through the door, jets of compressed air blasting him from all sides to keep him clean in a dust-free environment. Then he passed through another door to stand inside a glassed-in half acre of communications gear. E-2s and E-3s moved busily around the room and on the catwalks that rose above the equipment. They were running condition-red system's checks.

The first thing he'd need would be a side arm, then ten minutes with a radio operator. He'd play it by ear after that. A second lieutenant stood near an open radar box, watching repairs. True to condition-red regulations, he was wearing combat gear, including a weapon. As Largent started toward the man, he saw Bartello walking across the chamber toward the booth with a general he didn't recognize. They were followed by a small party of SPs armed with M-16s.

Largent eased off. He couldn't fight them if he went for the side arm now, so he decided to try a bluff. He'd attempt to get through to the outside later.

The group approached the booth, Bartello and the general entering while the honor guard took up positions outside.

"Good morning." Largent saluted the men. "I've just been looking over the operation. Impressive."

"This is General Cronin," the colonel said, and Largent shook hands with the man. "He runs the show down here."

"Nice to meet you...Captain." Cronin smiled strangely at Largent. "Perhaps you can clear up a little problem we've been having."

"I'll do my best."

"Good." Cronin reached into his jacket pocket. The man was very tall and distinguished looking. He moved slowly, fluidly, with great authority, the expression on his face rock solid, never wavering.

He removed the transmitter pen from his pocket and held it up in front of Largent's face. "Our gear picked up a signal from within the compound, and we triangulated it to your pen, Captain. Can I call you Norm?"

Largent said nothing, refusing to play the game with him.

"Now, don't get all quiet and sullen," Cronin said, a darkness settling onto his face. "We've got quite a bit to talk about. You see, Dick here thinks we should just kill you and be done with it. But me, I think we should discuss this like gentlemen and get you to admit your error and help us out."

"You're making a mistake," Largent said, taking his best shot. "I brought that pen down here to test your security systems, and you've passed with flying colors."

Cronin and Bartello looked at each other, smiling, then Cronin turned back to the Fed. "Actually, your pen isn't the only problem. You see, Norm Michaels and I were stationed at the Pentagon together for three years. And partner, I've never seen you before in my life."

Largent stared at the man, drowning in the pulsating waves of darkness that emanated from his eyes.

THE AIRPORT AT PHOENIX was no more than a way station to Bolan, a pit stop during what was going to be a long and complicated journey. He and Julie strode through the busy terminal, feeling dirty and conspicuous as they worked to pick up the pieces of GOG's broken trail.

They had spent the morning driving back from Gila Bend. Bolan was tired, worn down both physically and emotionally. Looking out for himself *and* Julie was a taxing experience, made worse by the almost maniacal intensity of the opposition. This was no small operation they had stumbled upon. It was a huge and well-financed machine that seemed to be running on its own internal rhythms.

Julie had been quiet on the trip back, but not morose, as if something positive had happened at the test site. Perhaps she was still in shock, but it didn't seem that way. There was a lightness there, a playfulness. Didn't she understand that the problems were just beginning? Whatever the reason for her good mood, it was helping to keep him in gear, so he decided not to question it.

"I'd really like to find a ladies' room and freshen up a bit," she said, running a dirty hand through matted hair.

"Sure. We could probably stand something to eat, too."

They were passing a small coffee shop, with a bank of phones just outside and a duty-free shop butted up against it. "Look," he said, "I need to call Hal right away. I'll use one of these phones, then we'll grab a bite and some coffee."

"I'll go find a rest room and just meet you back here," she said.

"Great. Whoever finishes first orders the coffee." He dug through his wallet for the phone card. "You did good back there."

She kissed him quickly on the cheek. "We make a pretty good team," she said, then drifted off.

She found a bathroom a little farther down the hall. As she passed another bank of phones, it crossed her mind to call her people and tell them what had happened. It was obvious to her now that Bolan couldn't be what they feared he was. She and Bolan had found a secret base where research that had nothing to do with new jet engines was going on, research that was outside their knowledge.

She decided to wash up first, which she did, the whole time thinking about how to tell Bolan about her involvement in this whole business, once she contacted her people. She feared he'd be angry when he found out she was not quite as innocent as she'd pretended. But once she explained, she was sure he would understand.

She washed quickly, not bothering with makeup, then combed her hair, amazed at the number of burrs that came out on the brush. One thing she knew for sure: she'd had her fill of the great outdoors for a while.

When she came out, she stood in front of the phones for a minute, debating about placing the call. Then she realized she'd have to take care of it sooner or later and decided it might as well be sooner. She dropped a quarter in the slot and called the 800 number.

"This is Lady Madonna," she told the sleepy-sounding person who answered after three rings.

There was a slight pause, then the voice said to hold while they transferred the call. Thirty seconds later a voice she recognized as Reilly's came on the line. "Where have you been?" he demanded. "You were supposed to stay in regular contact."

"I—I didn't get the chance," she said, taken back by his tone. "Besides, I wanted to tell you that I'm sure Bolan is innocent. He—"

"Innocent, is he?" Reilly repeated derisively. "Well, I want to tell you that your boyfriend just destroyed a key government installation, and—"

"What do you mean? You told me that the only experiments being done using liquid electricity were with jet engines. And yet I saw, and operated, a laser cannon."

"Just who the hell do you think you are?" the man answered. "Should the government contact you every time it decides to work on a new secret project? Your orders were very simple. You were supposed to stay with Bolan and keep checking in . . . and those orders were sent down precisely to *avoid* what happened at Gila Bend this morning."

"You should have told me!"

"You're a security risk," he shot back. "Certainly you can understand why we couldn't tell you the whole story. Okay, so we've got it and the Russians are getting it while their man is busy destroying all the good work we've done. Obviously things have gotten out of hand on your end. Your usefulness as an undercover operative is about finished."

"Great with me," she said. "I never liked this stupid job anyway."

"Good," he snapped. "Your final assignment is to terminate your subject. Then we'll lose you in the witness-protection program somewhere."

She felt sick to her stomach. "I'm not sure I under-stand what you mean," she said softly. "I want you to spell out exactly what you want me to do."

"Kill Bolan," the man said without hesitation.

"I don't *want* to kill Bolan."

"Come on, Julie," Reilly cajoled. "This is business. The man's an enemy agent. Do it now before he does it to you. More to the point, perhaps, do it now before *we* do it to you."

"You're threatening me?"

"Honey," he answered, his voice controlled, cold, "you helped him last night. You're standing on the ragged edge of treason right now and if you've drawn your lines there, a great many people will be after you. Do I make myself clear?"

"Yes," she said quietly.

"You have a job to do. For ten years you've let the gov-ernment support you in luxury, and now we're calling in the chit. Just take care of the son of a bitch and get out of the way. We'll never ask you for anything again. Your country needs you, Julie. You can't deny that need."

"No," she practically whispered, "I guess I can't."

"That's the spirit. You've still got the pill?"

"Yes."

"Just put it in something he's going to eat or drink and stand out of the way. When it's done, simply walk out-side, get a cab and drive to a hotel. Contact us from there. Okay?"

There was no response.

"Okay?"

"Okay," she replied, choking slightly. "Will it work in coffee?"

"Quick as a wink."

"All right," she whispered. "I'll take care of it."

MORDECHAI LELAND SAT at the large, Pentagon confer-ence table and watched Mark Reilly talking on the phone. He appreciated the man's loyalty more than he could say, but found him untrustworthy on other levels. Reilly talked a lot, but seemed unable to deliver the goods when push came to shove. He had sworn to control the woman, which he didn't do, and had sworn to tie up the Washington loose ends, which he couldn't do. Everything the man became involved in seemed to leave a messy trail of bodies.

And now there was trouble. Michaels had been taken, probably on Brognola's orders, and had been replaced by a ringer from the Justice Department. It wasn't the end of the world, but it was more trouble than he wanted right now. He looked at his watch—900 hours, just a day away from success.

Reilly hung up the phone and smiled at Leland. "We've taken care of that end."

"What, exactly, did we do?" Leland asked.

"The woman is going to terminate Bolan."

"We can depend on that?"

The smile faded somewhat. "I'm ninety percent on that."

There was a knock on the door, Leland nodding to Reilly to answer it. Reilly opened the door to Kit Givan, who stood there with a cup of coffee in his hand.

"Morning, General. Mr. Reilly."

"Sit down, Kit," Leland said. "We've got some rethinking to do."

"What happened?" Givan asked, brows drawn.

"Michaels got snatched," Reilly informed him. "Probably those people in Justice. They sent an impostor, but Cronin fingered him."

"Will he talk?" Givan asked.

Leland shook his head firmly. "Norm would die first."

"What about the guy on our end?"

"We're interrogating him now," Reilly said. "He's not talking, either, but we figure we're hidden well enough down there in the Everglades that we won't be found."

"At least in the space of the next twenty-four hours," Leland said. "And that's the beauty of our operation. The computers are locked in at this point. It's go no matter what they try.''

, "Even if the computers are shut down?" Givan asked.

Leland nodded. "The missiles are set. The only thing that could stop them would be a legitimate access to the GOG program and a legitimate recall."

A slow smile spread across Givan's face. "So in other words, *we're* the only ones who can stop it."

"That's about it," Leland concurred. "If they got Michaels, I feel they must have us all under surveillance. I think you gentlemen should lose your tags and make your way down to Florida for the fireworks. Reilly can arrange it through his contacts."

"And what about you, sir?" Givan asked.

"They can't move on me without evidence," Leland said with confidence. "I'm too important. That's why they've maintained distance. We got their bugs out of my offices, so there's nothing to hear. The orders they've intercepted aren't complete enough to fill in details, so there's nothing there. I'm having lunch with the President this afternoon, at which time I'll see if he's got any suspicions, but frankly I doubt if he knows anything. No. They can't touch me without evidence, and there's no way for them to accumulate the evidence before the morning. We'll proceed with caution, but proceed we will. By tomorrow morning, gentlemen, we should be well on our way toward making this country strong and great again."

He watched them leave then, Reilly all worked up and excited, Givan with military stoicism, two old-fashioned throwbacks to patriotism and responsibility in a world of expediency and compromise. He had slowly watched the demise of America over the past twenty years, when art had somehow become pornography and relaxation meant drug-sodden orgies. America no longer had a heart. It seemed to have nothing to live for.

But America would live again. Oh, there'd no doubt be recriminations over the deaths, but eventually everyone would realize that the quick death of a few hundred million were nothing in comparison to the slow death that was already gutting the citizens of the country. And after he reconstructed what was left of the country, organizing this great land to once again thrive under solid Christian ethics and military leadership, he'd be a hero.

Maybe the greatest hero ever.

THE MAN'S EYES were open wide, his eyeballs like hard-boiled eggs with rosetta tattoos as he stared, upside down, at Hal Brognola from what had once been his dining room table.

"Project GOG is bad," the interrogator said into his ear. "It has to be stopped. General Leland—"

"The general's here?" Michaels said, his voice slurring through the effects of nearly twenty-four straight hours of questioning under sodium Amytal. "I want to see the general."

"You can," the interrogator said, keeping his voice even and nonthreatening, almost conspiratorial. "But before he comes here, he wants you to tell us the access code to Project GOG in the master computer. He wants to shut it off and can't remember the code."

"No, no, no, no, no," Michaels said, shaking his head violently. "GOG is good. GOG will make a new world...a better world."

"But we can't make it work without the code."

"No code. No, no, no. No code."

Brognola turned from the dining room, walking into the living area, where a squad manned the phones. A tired Bob Ito was nearly asleep at the computer terminal he had claimed for his own three days previously. Gunnar Greggson was moving around the table, talking quietly to the people on the phones and making notes on a pad.

Brognola sat at the table, taking a cigar out of his breast pocket to chew on. Greggson came and perched on the edge of the table. "Things are happening," he said. "Our quarry have flown the coop."

"All of them?"

The man nodded. "All the important ones. They've been managing to lose us and disappear."

The chief Fed ran a hand over his face. "That means they've got Oscar for sure. Dammit! I knew I shouldn't have sent him out there alone."

"What else were you going to do?" Greggson asked. "The opportunity presented itself. You had no choice. Oscar knew the odds when he went into this."

Brognola smiled grimly. It didn't help.

Loud, slurred singing came from the dining room.

"How about laughing boy?" Greggson asked. "Anything useful from him?"

Brognola shook his head. "We've tried pentathol, Amytal, lie detectors, you name it. God, late last night we even tried scopolamine. He won't budge."

"Everything but physical pain," Greggson replied.

"Believe me," Brognola said. "People like our Captain Michaels just *love* the pain. We'd be wasting our time."

"So, what now?"

Brognola rubbed his face again. He'd been dead tired for days, but every time he lay down to sleep, GOG haunted him. "We've got an appointment with General Ferris later today...."

"Head of the Joint Chiefs? Wow."

"Yeah, 'wow' if we can convince him. We've begun to build up an amount of circumstantial evidence against Leland. Enough, anyway, so that an intelligent, thoughtful person could read the situation."

"And you think that Ferris might be that person?"

"He's a good man, Greg, as long as he hasn't already gone over to the other side." He inclined his head toward Ito. "Anything from our hacks?"

Greggson tightened his lips. "They've walked right up to it, then backed off again," he replied. "Any further entry is going to take the password or the go-ahead from us that it's okay to experiment."

Brognola shook his head. "I'm not ready to take that chance yet. We'll sit on it for a while."

A phone rang at the other end of the table, one of the agents answering it. "A Mr. Bolan, for you, sir."

He nodded gratefully, then pulled a phone over in front of him. "Mack! I've been worried about you."

"You should've been," Bolan replied. "It got pretty hairy down there. GOG had a manufacturing plant just outside of Gila Bend."

"What were they manufacturing?"

"Laser weaponry," Bolan said, "using liquid electricity to run the damned things."

"The woman..."

"We're both all right—tired and sore—but still on two feet. I'm calling from the airport in Phoenix. What's happening in Wonderland?"

"I've got some news for you," Brognola replied. "Various pieces of it. We intercepted some GOG communication. The project is set to go at 900 hours tomorrow."

"Tomorrow!"

"We still don't know exactly what it is, but we substituted one of our own agents for the courier. He went to Florida, but is now presumed lost in the Everglades."

"Do you want me back down there?"

"I've already chartered you a flight," Brognola said. "I was just waiting to hear from you. We'll need you to coordinate our effort down there since you know the territory. Check with a firm there called Arizona Execu-air. They've got a Lear jet with your name on it."

"Anything else?"

"Yes." Brognola wasn't anxious to bring the next point up. "We finished our research on Grolier."

"What's wrong?" Bolan asked.

"Peg Ackerman. She wasn't working for the other side, Mack. She was one of ours."

"How's that possible?" Bolan said, his voice taut.

"Justice sent her down after the death of Jerry Butler," was the reply. "She was picked from a pool of applicants who had science degrees. It didn't look like anything really big, just a little deep cover, you know?"

"Then why the hell wasn't I told about her?" Bolan was angry, and the big Fed didn't blame him.

"She was small potatoes, Mack. Once they put her down there, they...forgot about her."

"Forgot her to death, you mean. And I helped."

Yeah, they forgot her. It was always the soldiers, the little people, who got forgotten in wartime. No wonder she'd been so mysterious; she'd been trying to check him out, a guppy investigating a shark.

"Mack..." Brognola said after a few seconds.

"I'm thinking," Bolan replied, because the information on Peg Ackerman had reshuffled his thought patterns. "Listen. If Peg isn't the one who turned us in down there, it has to be somebody else. Only four other people heard me shooting off my mouth that morning. Of the four, Ike Silver is dead, Fred Haines helped me fight the SPs and Yuri Bonner is a walking cardiac case. That only leaves Robbie Hampton, Hal. He set me up from the word go. If there's anything to find out down there, he's the one to ask."

"Go for it."

"How about that dog tag?" Bolan asked. He looked out the window of the booth, watching as Julie walked into the coffee shop, a sad smile on her face. She looked in his direction, waving listlessly when he waved at her. Perhaps the shock was beginning to wear off and she was dealing with the emotional exhaustion.

"LaMar Johnson had been assigned to General Albert Cronin's command at NASA at the Cape."

"Cronin again!"

"Yeah," Brognola replied. "We've made him positively as the head of Project GOG in Florida. When a routine check was run on the tag, Cronin's office said the man had lost his tag or it had been stolen."

"That's a story that can't hold up long."

"It only has to hold up, apparently, until tomorrow morning," Brognola said. "We've also tracked down Centurion Investments, the holding company that owns Baylor Goggle. Centurion has a paper board of directors, but the real owner is General Mordechai Leland. He bought the place about seven years ago. Once we've made all the connections, I think we'll find that the United States government provided the money to finance that operation."

"No wonder this whole thing seems so well-heeled," Bolan said, watching Julie get a table. He made a motion to her, a pantomime of a man drinking coffee. She nodded. "The country's taxpayers are footing the bill."

"And if this is anything like we think it is," Brognola said, "the bill that the taxpayers are footing is for their own funeral."

JULIE ARNOLD SAT in the coffee shop booth, watching as Bolan talked with his contact. The decor around her was all bright paint and phony plastic—flowers and wide bands of color meant to convey some sort of high-tech happy-face appeal to the endless chain of people moving past. She found it depressing.

Her mind was loose and freewheeling right now, disconnected from anything to do with her body, a disassociation just as complete as the one Bolan had been trying to attain with the rats in his lab at the institute.

An ultimate clash of values and ideals had rendered her senseless. The choice between love and duty—with life and death as the stakes—had finally stopped her from thinking altogether. Her problem was insoluble, her mind responding by going totally numb.

"Here you are, honey," the waitress said, putting down two cups of coffee. She was dressed in bright pastels and wore a flower-printed apron, a human being who looked just as plastic as the fixtures. "You'll be ordering food when your friend gets off the phone?"

"Yes," Julie answered mechanically, her eyes glued on Bolan.

The woman bent slightly, staring at Julie. "Are you all right?" she asked.

"Fine." Julie flashed the woman a mirthless smile and stirred sugar into her cup.

"Well . . . I'll come back for the rest of your order in a few minutes."

"Yes," Julie said again.

Mercifully the woman left, and Julie sat staring at the empty seat across from her and the steaming coffee. Mack Bolan, the Executioner. Mack Bolan, her love. The two forces seemed absolutely incongruous to her. She couldn't believe that he was taking her in, and yet the evidence came from what she considered a totally reputable source. She remembered Mark Reilly's words, which, loosely translated, were "Take care of him before we take care of you." Perhaps that was the bottom line, her survival. Everything else was just politics, was just—what did Mark call it?—business.

She pulled her purse onto her lap, digging through it until her hand wrapped around the small plastic bag containing the pill.

Despite the numbness, her hand was shaking as she surreptitiously opened the bag, the smell of bitter almonds assailing her. Cyanide. She knew the toxicology from years of working in college science departments. Cyanide binds up the person's breathing apparatus, the body unable to use the blood's oxygen. The victim suffocates—quickly. Despite her attempts at controlling her thoughts, she couldn't help but picture Bolan, choking, his skin turning pink, his eyes pleading with her in surprise and betrayal.

Suppressing those thoughts, she pulled his coffee closer to her and dropped the pellet into the dark brew with a shaking hand. She pushed the cup back in place then sat back, exhausted from the ordeal. At age thirty-three, she was getting ready to poison the only man she'd ever loved. The irony was more than she could bear.

Bolan hung up the phone. Even from this distance she could tell he was tired, though she knew he'd never admit it. He smiled at her and held up a finger, indicating he needed a minute more. Then he moved into the duty-free shop, and she knew he'd purchase a small suitcase to conceal his arsenal.

Her gaze returned to his coffee cup. So innocent, it was almost possible for her to think that nothing would happen when he drank it. It was just coffee with a little something extra, like sweetener, added. He'd drink it, they'd have a nice afternoon, and she could tell the people in Washington that she tried the stuff but nothing happened. It was just a tiny pill, for heaven's sake. How could it kill someone? How could it snuff out the life and the love of the man she had watched take on a small army in the Arizona desert, the man she had given herself to completely by the crackling light of a scrub oak fire? Unthinkable.

"Penny for your thoughts," came a voice, and she looked up. He was there, holding a small suitcase. "I guess we should have stopped at the campsite after all."

She smiled uneasily. "How are things in Washington?"

He sat down, looking around to make sure no one was listening. "Today's the day," he told her. "GOG is set for a go tomorrow. Whatever we do, it has to be done today."

"Are you okay?" he asked, his fingers tracing the rim of the cup.

She couldn't stand the tension. Couldn't he either drink it or leave it alone? "I . . . guess I'm just tired."

He nodded and picked up the cup, a slight plume of steam still rising from the surface of the liquid. "Hal has chartered us a plane to go back to Florida. Maybe you can grab some sleep on the flight."

"Maybe," she responded, trying to keep from screaming as he brought the cup to his lips. Every muscle in her body was tensed, her hands clenched into tight fists, her nails drawing blood.

"And do you know something else?" he said, lowering the cup slightly to speak. "Peg Ackerman wasn't the GOG plant at the institute. It was Robbie."

Words kept pouring from his lips, words that her mind wasn't even comprehending. He might as well be speaking Hindi. Then he stopped talking and she watched, in slow motion, as he brought the cup up, this time to drink.

She saw him tilt the cup to his lips and caught his eyes, the same eyes that had looked into hers with such vulnerability and honesty when they'd made love.

"No!" she shrieked, and she was on her feet, her arm swinging wildly, knocking the cup from his hands to crash loudly on the tiled floor.

"Julie!" he yelled, taking her shoulders. "What is it?"

She was crying, standing in the booth shaking, unable either to go to him or pull away. "P-poison," she choked out, panting. "I p-put it in . . . your c-coffee."

There was horror in his eyes as his gaze burned through her. "Who are you?" he demanded. "Just who the hell are you?"

Chapter Twenty-Two

Hal Brognola felt uncomfortable in the Marine Corps lieutenant's uniform he wore, watching General Ferris reading from the stack of documented evidence that was set before him. Greggson, dressed as an Army major, nervously puffed on a cigarette, his lawyer's brain no doubt upset by the lack of hard evidence in the case.

The disguises had been Brognola's idea, not so much to hide them in Leland's territory, though that was a consideration, but more to protect General Ferris in these circumstances. There was not a shred of doubt in the big Fed's mind that, at this point, Leland would do anything to protect his target date in the morning.

The office was large and comfortable. It was an imposing workplace for an imposing man, the second-highest ranking officer, beneath the commander in chief, of the armed forces. Brognola had gone to the top with his fears, and that move would either make or break their chances of stopping Leland.

The general put down the last page of the brief, his angular face hard, the expression revealing the depth of his concern.

"I've known Lee Leland for over thirty years," he said after a moment. "Ever since Korea. He might be the best field officer I've ever seen."

Brognola sat up straight, leaning forward to put an elbow on the general's desk. "I've only known him by reputation—" he pointed to the documentation "—and through this."

Ferris tightened his lips. "You're trying to draw me back to your evidence. It's not necessary."

"Yes, sir." Brognola backed off.

"You gentlemen have come to me with a great concern," Ferris said, and the phone on his desk rang. He picked it up. "Hold the calls. No . . . no, I don't care. Cancel it." He hung up and stared at each of them.

Ferris stood and walked to a small bar set at the side of the room. "Bourbon and water is what we drink in here, gentlemen. Is it all right with you?"

Both affirmed the drink. They would have agreed to anything at that point.

"Now," Ferris said as he settled behind his desk, "what exactly have you brought me?" He took a sip of the bourbon. "The existence of the GOG project is a fact. I can check that. I can call it up on my own screen using your methods if I want, though I can't physically get into the program. That Lee is the head of it is also a fact that can't be denied, as is the issuing of orders to implement the project. This is not outside the realm of standard operating procedure. At this point, everything is straightforward and on the up-and-up."

"But—" The general held up a hand to silence Brognola.

"Now we come to the other issues," Ferris continued, his face pained as he spoke. "The killing of your secretary. The attempts on your own life. The attack on your house. If I am to believe that these things really happened, it gives me a great deal of pause. But, in every one of these instances, your assailants remain unknown. And, Mr. Brognola, you are a man with a considerable number of enemies."

Ferris sat back, hands behind his head, and stared at the ceiling. "The physical evidence tying your secretary to Baylor Goggle and Optical is, in my opinion, relatively solid, as is your tying Leland to that company and your speculation about the nature of his funding. It smacks of illegality even if it's not what you claim it to be, and *that* gentlemen, is where I begin to part company with General Leland."

The man sipped his drink again, Brognola realizing that he was still holding a drink that had been forgotten in the excitement.

"Your man, Bolan," Ferris said, "has firsthand experience with Givan and others involved with this. Unfortunately I don't know how well evidence given by a renegade like him is going to help your case."

"Bolan's a good man."

"I'm not implying otherwise. I'm simply looking at what we're up against in trying to prove anything with this."

"Did you say, 'we'?" Greggson asked.

The man nodded. "Something damned dirty is going on here. And to me it all hinges on Captain Norman Michaels and his orders to assume command of the White House security forces. There's no way that orders of this nature could be implemented unless the entire command structure had broken down. The thought that the President's safety could be in the hands of traitors, gentlemen, frankly frightens me to death."

"Thank God." Brognola breathed a sigh of relief. "We were afraid—"

"I know what you were afraid of," the general said. "I don't blame you. This is all circumstantial. And now, thanks to both of you, it has become _my_ problem."

"What do we do now?" Greggson asked.

"From where I sit," Ferris said, "we do more of what we're already doing. I agree that we can't go public with this yet. It would do nothing to stop the project. We've got to take care of what we can, and hope to God that we find some way to stop the wheels that have been put in motion."

"Will you confide in the President?" Brognola asked.

The general shook his head. "The President and General Leland are extremely close friends. He would never believe this unless we had more solid proof. Besides, I don't know whether or not we have the right to involve the President in our own illegal intelligence gathering, and if I was to tell him, that's exactly what we'd be doing. Are you beginning to understand where I'm coming from?''

"Yes," Greg said, nodding slowly. "If this doesn't work out, all of us are going to jail for a long, long time."

"Precisely." Ferris stood. "Anyone care to join me in another drink?''

BOLAN SAT at the Bee Line toll booth in the rented T-Bird, waiting for his change, so he could take the ramp onto Interstate 4 and make the short jump into Orlando.

"No," Julie was saying, "my story about Harry and me is essentially true. I didn't like lying to you. I never wanted to."

"There you are," the young blonde said as she handed back the change. "Three dollars and twenty-five cents."

"Thanks," Bolan said, pocketing the money and driving on. He looked at Julie. "So, how did it happen?"

She took a breath. "Okay. The CIA had approached me when I was working as Harry's assistant. Harry had originally come from Germany, and they felt he was something of a security risk. All they wanted me to do was keep an eye on him and his research, just to make sure he was coming clean to the government about what he was doing."

"And you said yes." Bolan turned onto the I-4 ramp that skirted Disney World and headed north, inexorably closer to Robbie Hampton.

"It was the government, Mack. *Our* government."

"Plus they paid you," Bolan said.

"They paid me more money than I'd ever known existed. They were even nice enough to put it in a Swiss bank so I wouldn't have to pay taxes on it. God, I was twenty-two years old. I was going to be a spy and get paid for it. It was as exciting as hell."

"Then Harry asked you to marry him," Bolan stated.

She sank down in the seat. "Everything has a price tag, doesn't it? At the time I was too young to realize it. They pushed me to accept him and upped the ante to make it worthwhile. I hemmed and hawed, but in the final analysis, I wanted the money more than I wanted true love." She reached out a hand to touch his arm. "I've since realized what a prison money is.

"Maybe I thought I was doing the right thing," she continued. "I chose love this time around, but I've seen your record, Mack, and I think it's possible that this mistake is far larger than the last one."

He looked hard at her. "Don't believe everything you read."

They drove north, Bolan trying to digest the information that Julie had given him. He understood her predicament with the Company. Covert operations always carry the possibility of wrongdoing justified as a means to a noble end. Once the morality and ethics of the system were disregarded in covert operations, then anything became justifiable and everything became confused. It was a problem that veterans seasoned a lot harder than Julie had a tough time with. And he'd seen more than one man turn bad because of it.

They exited the highway at Orlovista, heading west, Bolan keeping an eye on the street signs in order to make the turnoff. He looked at his watch. It was nearly 6:30. The three-hour time lost on the flight back was critical.

"What makes you think that Robbie won't still be at the institute?" she asked.

"I called from the airport, and he'd already left for the day. I lifted everyone's address from the files while I was there, so hopefully, we'll catch him at home."

When they reached the intersection of Orlovista and Greenview Drive, Bolan took a left, then proceeded slowly down the tree-lined avenue. He stopped before a squared-off, flat-roofed building that looked like a miniature prison.

"Julie—"

"No," she interrupted, "I won't stay here."

The warrior shrugged, and they got out of the car. He briefly considered sneaking up on the place, but somehow Robbie didn't seem dangerous to that extent. He decided to walk right up to the front door and knock.

They passed through a bricked courtyard blazing with summer flowers, a well-kept place cared for by someone who intended to stay here. As usual, Robbie was an enigma.

Bolan rang the bell, and Robbie Hampton, dressed in Bermuda shorts and a Hawaiian shirt, opened the door. A can of beer was in his hand.

"David!" he said in surprise. "How wonderful to see you!"

"The name's Bolan." The big man pushed past Robbie and walked into his living room, Julie right on his heels. "Nice place you've got here."

"Thanks. With just me to care for, I'm able to indulge myself exclusively. You must be Mrs. Sparks, er, Bolan."

"The name's Julie Arnold, though I was Bernice Sparks for a little while."

"Can I offer either of you a drink? This is all so confusing, I—"

"Quiet," Bolan said tersely. "Sit down."

"I don't—"

"Now," Bolan interrupted. He pulled Big Thunder out of his webbing and laid it on a coffee table, which was a highly polished slab of wood. He sat on the sofa.

Robbie's face darkened. He took an easy chair across from the sofa. The place was tastefully decorated, various writing awards Robbie had won hanging on the wall. As in the man's office, incredible stacks of books filled wall-to-wall cases, as well as being piled around the room indiscriminately.

"So it's true what they said about you," Robbie said, taking a sip of his beer.

"What was that?" Julie asked.

"That he went crazy in his lab, killed people, caused havoc. There was so much damage up on Five, that they've simply shut it down. They transferred me to Four."

Julie looked at Bolan, her face tense.

Bolan looked at his watch again. There wasn't any time to play games with the man. He picked up the AutoMag and pointed it at Hampton. "You're going to tell me now about who you report to and everything you know about Project GOG."

Hampton's eyes opened wide. "I don't underst—"

Bolan fired once, a large ceramic lamp on the end table next to the man exploding, pieces flying everywhere.

"A-a-ah!" Robbie yelled, grabbing his temple, blood welling up between his fingers from ceramic shrapnel.

"Mack..." Julie pleaded, face drawn.

"If you don't like it, don't look." Bolan swung the gun back to Hampton. "Believe me, Robbie. If I don't get answers quick, you're a dead man where you sit."

The man put out his hands. "All right. But I don't see what all the fuss is about."

"Just say it."

"I report to the Air Force.... I think that GOG is probably the project name under which I'm filed."

"What do you report?"

"Everything that goes on up on the fifth floor. Sometimes, as you know, researchers get cold feet about sharing...."

"We've already talked about that," Bolan said. "Give me more."

"Jerry Butler was working on something big, something the Air Force wanted desperately. When it looked like he wasn't going to come through with the information, I got it for them. When you came along, I watched you, too. I was sure you were there to check up on Butler, so I fed you bits of information about him. When I saw your reaction to the news about Jerry's code, I was sure. I called and told them you were onto something, and I guess I was right."

"Why did the Air Force want Butler's project so much?"

Robbie took another sip of beer, then set down his can amid the rubble on the end table. "I think it was part of the hypothesis . . . the scenario."

"What scenario?"

"The takeover scenario."

"More," Bolan demanded.

"This goes back a few years, probably six or seven. I was invited to participate in a seminar in Washington . . . it must have been '81, '82, somewhere in there. Anyway, it was presided over by Air Force brass, mainly a general named Leland."

"Leland," Julie said, looking at Bolan. He put a finger to his lips in response.

"Anyway," Robbie continued, "it was one of those meetings of the minds sort of thing where hypothetical situations are tossed around. The theme of this particular retreat was, how to negotiate a coup d'état with as little financing and backing as possible."

This time it was Bolan who looked at Julie. A million apologies seeped from her eyes.

"Well," Robbie went on, "I presented my hypothetical scenario. I believe the name of it was 'Fire in the Sky.' It was quite well received, and all based on extrapolation from current scientific thought. It worked like this: the only way a major coup could be accomplished would be if the governmental structure had broken down completely, leaving the coup organizers in leadership positions, with the President of the United States in pocket to ensure a smooth transition of power. We were just getting into the shuttle program then, which gave me the idea for the means to accomplish the breakdown of government."

The man stopped and drank again, Bolan amazed at the information that was coming so casually from his lips.

"Where was I?" he asked.

"The shuttle program," Julie prompted.

"Ah, yes. I knew that the Pentagon had funds to work with, so setting up the systems could logically be done with the government's own money, with nothing having to come from the overthrow group, except for a top Pentagon officer who had access to the unreported funding. That was the key. All that had to be done, was to set up a dummy project and put it into the computers, giving all co-conspirators an existing communications system. Now, listen to this, this is really beautiful. At that point, I showed how the next major scientific advance would be in liquid electricity, the need for which is the only thing holding up the development of major laser weapons. So, you fund research in a big way, using, of course, government money."

"Of course," Bolan repeated, stunned by what he was hearing.

"Then, you get the laser weapons and send them up in the space shuttle, disguised as weather satellites or something equally innocuous. On the given day, you simply turn these weapons on, controlling them from a secret base in the Everglades."

"Why the Everglades?" Julie asked.

"You've obviously never been to the Everglades. You could hide a whole country down there. Anyway, you turn on the weapons. Maybe one goes to work on Moscow, just burning it to the ground, the others zeroing in on concentrations of missile silos."

"Then the Soviets have no choice but to hit back as their missiles explode in the silos," Bolan concluded.

"And the U.S. is the logical place to strike," Julie said.

"Beautiful, no?" Robbie sounded smug. "Action and reaction take place quickly, with our conspirators taking the President underground to wait it out while other key military leaders not in on the plans are assassinated by underlings."

"But doesn't the whole world get destroyed in your scenario?" Julie asked.

"Not really," Robbie replied. "You see, the lasers will still be up there working, using up trillions of volts of juice, just zapping Russian missiles on their own territory and burning down their cities. Oh sure, a lot of missiles will get through, but the point is, *they'll* be totally destroyed, while we will have taken away enough of their threat that large segments of our society will survive. We'll lose maybe a hundred million, a hundred and fifty million tops."

"This is insane!" Julie shouted.

"Take it easy," Robbie said, frowning. "For heaven's sake, it's just a scenario...just a story. Do you want to hear it, or not?"

"Go on," Julie said, agitated. "I want to hear it."

"You take your key people," Robbie said, excited by his own story, "and you don't need a lot. You put them underground, preferably in a deeply buried military compound from which you also control communications and your laser satellites. You make sure they're single, not attached to anything or anyone except your plan."

"What about all the people who've been running around doing all the dirty work for you?" Bolan asked.

The man shrugged. "Hired help. Screw them. When the dust settles, you have the President speak to what's left of the nation and tell them the Russians started a war and lost. You have the President put your man in charge of the cleanup, then you make sure the President never has any power again. Everything stays intact, nobody even knows what's happened. Martial law is in effect because of the war, and you make sure it stays in effect. All this because of the invention of liquid electricity, which has a world-shattering potential in the area of weaponry. Controlling it means that you could take over the country with no more than fifteen or twenty people who actually even know what the scenario is. Everybody else is just military and simply follow orders. And there you have a cheap, low-manpower plan for taking over the government of the United States of America. What do you think?"

"I think the world is going to end tomorrow morning," Bolan stated flatly.

"Oh, Mack," Julie said. "What are we going to do?"

"What's the problem?" Robbie seemed perplexed. "What are you guys so upset about?"

Bolan looked at the man. The mastermind of the destruction of the entire planet seemed so innocent, so guileless.

"Didn't it strike you as odd," the warrior asked, "that the shuttle blew up on the same day that Jerry Butler was killed?"

"Should it have?" Hampton replied. "History is full of strange juxtapositions. It was a coincidence."

"How about the attack on the institute?" Julie prodded. "Didn't it seem odd to you that the destruction happened on the same day that you reported Mack to your people?"

"I report to my people at least once a week."

Bolan stood. "This is getting us nowhere. Listen, Robbie, Project GOG is set to go tomorrow morning at 9:00 a.m. Do you understand that? Tomorrow morning, you, me, Florida and the rest of the world are going to be blown to bits, so General Leland can assume command."

"You're kidding." The man's face still did not register that he comprehended anything that was being said.

"And I'll tell you something else," Bolan continued. "You can play Mr. Innocent all day long, but there's only one way I figure that Jerry Butler could have found out about GOG—you fed him information the same way you fed it to me. Didn't you?" He moved to the man and stuck the barrel of the gun in his face. "Didn't you?"

Robbie shut his eyes. "Life gets so boring sometimes," he whispered.

"So you like to spice it up."

"Yes," the man said in agreement, easing back in the chair, Bolan relentlessly moving closer with the AutoMag.

"Well, at the very least, you are directly responsible for the deaths of Jerry Butler, Ike Silver and Peg Ackerman, who was wiped out because she was in the wrong place at the wrong time."

"I don't accept that." Robbie eased the gun barrel away from his face so he could take off his glasses to clean them.

"That's your deal, isn't it?" Bolan asked. "No responsibility for you. You owe nothing to your world or your fellow man or your country and its laws."

"Laws are all invented realities," Robbie told them, putting his glasses back on. "Everything's plastic, all is change. I take no responsibility for the actions or thoughts of others."

Bolan stared at him. "Are you ready to die, then, Robbie? Are you willing to abdicate responsibility for my actions in taking your life?"

"I've done nothing!" Hampton said, fear, finally, in his eyes. "I just tell stories!"

Bolan held up the gun. "And all I do is pull this little metal flange. I take no responsibility for the bullets that shoot out of the gun."

He put his hand around Robbie's throat. The man's eyes went wide. "Please don't kill me!" he begged. "Oh, God, please don't kill me!"

"I'm not going to kill you, Robbie," Bolan said. "I'm just going to see to it that you do for us what you did for Leland."

Chapter Twenty-Three

Bolan stood with the phone to his ear, watching Robbie Hampton, freed from the confines of reality, taking the situation in hand. He hurried around busily, happy as a lark, tacking a geological map of Florida on the wall that Julie held up for him.

"He says he can locate the base for us, Hal," Bolan said. "What I'm going to need from you is coordination and help."

"We're tied in to General Ferris of the Joint Chiefs," Brognola answered. "He says he can give us military backup if we can just locate the damned place."

Bolan looked at his watch. "Can we do it in time?"

"If anybody can do it, Ferris can. He's as married to this as we are."

"You got a good computer man?" Bolan asked.

"Yeah. Bob Ito's the best. And he's through up here, Mack. Project GOG was cut off the net a few hours ago."

"Get him on a jet. According to Robbie, *everything* of any value to the project is locked up in that Everglades compound. If we take it, I want someone here who'll know how to shut things down. Robbie says they've probably gone to automatic countdown on the satellite system, which means we'll have to go in cold and work our way into the system to shut it down."

"Got a problem with that, pard," Hal replied, his voice sounding incredibly tired. "We haven't been able to come up with the password yet, and we're too afraid of a tapeworm on the system to experiment around too much."

"We'll just have to work on that," Bolan said. "Let's get to the damned thing first."

"Okay...we're open. What have you got?"

"Hold on." Bolan laid the receiver down, as Robbie Hampton's living room rapidly changed around him into a junk pile of books, maps and professional journals. "Talk to me, Robbie!"

"Okay, look," Hampton said, excited, the way Bolan had seen him at the institute when he was heavily involved in a problem. "When I concocted my theory about the Everglades base, I went in with a real problem. Florida is mostly unstable swampland, absolutely no good for any kind of mining or underground work. So, I researched the geology of the area and found this."

He pointed to the map he had tacked on the wall. "There's a solid deep base core of sedimentary rock, called Osceola's Strata, after the Seminole chief who went to war against the United States government. It runs from the lower basin of Big Lostman's Bay on the southwest coast to the Mangrove Swamp on the southern tip."

He took a pen from behind his ear and circled an area solidly in the center of Mangrove Swamp. "Right here is the best bet," he said, pointing with the pen. "Far from any population centers, thick strata..."

"How could something like this be built without the government's knowing about it?" Bolan asked.

"That brings me to my next point. Go back through the computer records. Check with the Army Corps of Engineers, and with the GSA over bidding. See if the government has contracted for any work in the Everglades during the past six years. If they are truly working from the theory I invented, then they would very strictly use government funding for this project as a matter of policy. It's a fascinating thought. They could overthrow the government totally on taxpayer money."

Bolan ran and picked up the phone. "Hal..."

"We heard," Brognola said. "Bob's already working on it. Mack, we're putting a lot of eggs in this guy's basket. Are you sure we can depend on him?"

"If we can't, Hal, he dies with the rest of us tomorrow morning."

"Tomorrow morning," Brognola repeated. "Kind of gives you the creeps, doesn't it?"

"We've still got thirteen hours," Bolan said. "I'll stop for the creeps after this is over."

"Okay. We've got something on this end, and it looks good. The Army Corps of Engineers helped drain a swamp forty miles south of Florida City in the eastern Everglades, and bidding was accepted from a Dade Construction Company for the building of a research complex at that location, the financing charged against Project GOG."

Bolan looked up at Robbie. "Florida City?"

The man drew in his brows and looked at the map. "It's outside the Osceola Strata," he said. "It can't be there."

"My man doesn't like it."

"But he's making it up," Brognola replied, "taking it on the fly. This is solid—budgeted, for God's sake."

"Let's keep both options open," Bolan suggested, "and get the ball rolling. We'll make a decision when we have to."

"Fair enough. And Mack, ask your boy what, exactly, happened to the shuttle."

"He wants to know what happened to the shuttle," Bolan called to Robbie.

The man pursed his lips, then shrugged. "Simple enough. Just getting the thing launched on the shuttle wouldn't have been enough to silence Butler's objections. The satellite itself could still have been examined in space after the launch and before it was pushed out of the shuttle's cargo bay. A laser cannon could never have been disguised enough to fool someone who knew what he was looking for. And Butler wasn't just a crackpot. He was the *inventor* of liquid electricity. Someone would have believed him. It left absolutely no choice to the mission controller. To protect the three laser weapons he already had up there in space, he had to fire the laser on the fourth while it was still in *Challenger*'s cargo bay. A burst of a thousandth of a second right through the hull and into the solid fuel boosters and—'' the man made an explosive motion with his hands ''—powee!''

Bolan felt a chill ripple down his spine. He put the receiver up to his ear. ''Hal . . . ?''

''Yeah,'' the man said quietly, choked up. ''I heard.''

''We've got to move.''

''Proceed to Homestead Air Base,'' Brognola instructed. ''It's in Leisure City on the east coast of the Everglades. We'll have a plane chartered for you at Orlando Airport. We're arranging for troops and we'll vac Bob Ito directly there. Good luck to you, Mack, and Godspeed.''

''What do I do with Julie?''

''Mack, you can't let her out of your sight. Right now she's carrying around in her head the most important information in the world.''

''I see.''

''Do you?''

''Good luck on your end of it,'' Bolan replied.

There were several seconds of dead air, then Brognola said, ''Mack . . . I intend to see my wife and kids again.''

''Understood,'' Bolan returned, hanging up the phone.

He looked at Julie. ''Stay here. There's nothing more you can do.''

She rushed into the protective circle of his arms. ''If we're going to die, Mack, I want to die with you.''

He hugged her fiercely. Then the responsibility took over. He turned to Robbie Hampton. ''We're on the move.''

Hampton just stared at him, not wanting to comment. In the presence of a man of action, the man of words was totally outside of his element. He couldn't control the directions. "I really want you to know that I hope you succeed," he said finally.

"You should," the warrior replied. "Especially since you're going to be right there with us. This is your nightmare. It's all based on your thought processes. You're the only one who can crack it."

WITH THE BAY DOORS CLOSED, the four rotor blades of the Army Sikorsky S-70 Black Hawk sounded no louder than the average waterfall, no more grating on the nerves than a continuous jackhammer on concrete at five feet. The Black Hawk was designed primarily to carry an eleven-man assault squad, but now it held only four passengers, three of them unarmed.

Bolan and Julie Arnold sat beside each other, strapped into swing seats, and faced Bob Ito and Robbie Hampton in the near darkness of the bay. All of them were dressed in olive-drab coveralls, U.S. Army insignia over the heart. Beneath them, Florida swampland stretched out deep and inscrutable as far as they could see.

Bob Ito was writing furiously in a spiral notebook under the haze of a directional wink light. He looked up frowning. "If we don't come up with a password," he shouted above the continuous thrashing noise of the rotors, "I'm going to need four hours minimum to try to crack their system with a purge utility."

Bolan looked at his watch, the luminous dial confirming what he already acutely knew. "It's nearly 3:00 a.m.," he said. "It means we'd have to take the damned thing by 5:00."

"It's the safest method I can think of. I may be able to simply sneak in and look at the program without disturbing it. Any other method implies direct assault and, I fear, failure."

"Then we're lost," Hampton told them. "While we're all running around on a wild-goose chase looking for that research complex, the real thing will be slipping away from us."

"That's still undecided," Bolan argued.

"There's no question about it. They cannot have built an air raid bunker deeply enough to do them any good in Florida City. Hell, that was all reclaimed swamp. It's about a foot above sea level."

"We reach fail-safe pretty quick," Bolan said, "where we have to decide which target to go for." He looked out the bay window. On the road a hundred feet below, they were still being paced by the twenty-truck convoy, the four hundred fully armed airmen it carried thinking they were out on surprise maneuvers.

Julie looked at Hampton, shaking a finger. "How long before Jerry Butler's disappearance from Grolier did you tell him that the Air Force was watching him?"

"I never said that per se. We were arguing the outcomes of research one night, in which he took the stance that he'd never let anything he'd developed be used for military purposes. I laughed and told him that his reasoning was impossible, that once he had invented something on the government's nickel, it was theirs to do with as they chose. *Then* I told him that there was a project called GOG whose purpose was to make sure of that."

"How long before his disappearance?" Julie persisted.

"A year or so," the man replied. "He was anxious about it because he had just finished the prototype testing on a small engine and was worried about it. What are you getting at?"

"Something very simple," she said. "It was Jerry's code that put us onto the test site at Gila Bend. How could he have discovered that? Did you tell him?"

Robbie shook his head. "I don't even know what you're talking about."

"That's what I thought. Then, given a year, he had to come up with his own sources of information. I knew Jerry Butler pretty well. When he was onto something, he was like a bloodhound. You could never get him off the scent."

"You think that *he* cracked the computer?" Ito asked his tired eyes alight.

"I not only think he cracked it," she said, "I think he left us the information to crack it, too."

"What's she talking about?" Hampton asked.

"The code," Bolan answered. "The code was divided into three parts, two of which we were able to translate. The first phrase was Gila Bend, the second, Baylor Goggle and Optical. We weren't able to translate the third."

"What was it?" Ito asked.

"Seasonal Gift of God," Julie said.

Ito and Hampton looked at each other. "You think," Ito said, "that the password is hidden within that phrase?"

"It makes sense," Bolan replied. "Butler was a genius who left behind a gift. Smart enough to know his information was lethal, he left the code behind for anyone smart enough to crack. The first two clues were important links in the chain. From what I've seen, the only thing left would be the password, the same password *he* used to crack his way into the system."

"How did he come up with it?" Ito asked.

"Unfortunately," Julie said, "we may not figure that part out until *after* we've figured out the code. Remember, two years ago, Jerry didn't have anything to lose by experimenting with the codes."

The door separating the cockpit from the bay slammed open, the helmeted pilot leaning his body partway into their compartment.

"Mr. Bolan, Mr. Brognola is on the horn for you, sir." The man reached a hand around the divider and rapped on the wall. "You can take it here, sir."

"Thanks." Bolan grabbed the radio mike hanging on a spur on the wall, turning on the juice right next to the inset speaker. He listened to the static crackle loudly through the speaker, then pushed the call button on the side of the mike. "Bolan here. Over."

"You're nearing fail-safe," Brognola's voice staticked in response. "We've decided to go with the Florida City site. Over."

"No!" Hampton yelled. "That's nuts!"

Bolan pushed the button. "Hal, my man down here insists that can't be correct. Over."

"It's an executive decision. A known quantity versus unknown stabbing in the dark. Over."

"I know I can get us close!" Robbie shouted.

"What do you want me to do?"

The man leaned closer, his face intense in the semilight. "You're the one who told me that it was *my* nightmare. Well, listen to me. According to my nightmare, there is absolutely no way that we will do anything but waste valuable time going to that phony site. Hell, anything can go down on paper...that bedrock has been there for a couple of billion years!"

Bolan thought for a minute. "Can you get me coordinates on it?"

"Can I ever!" Robbie grabbed Ito's pad and wrote furiously.

"Mack, are you there?" came Brognola's voice.

Bolan pushed the button. "Hal, we're going to send the convoy on to Florida City while we check out the other possibility. If we're wrong, this baby does about two hundred miles an hour as the crow flies. We'll be able to hoof it back. Over."

Robbie ripped the page out of the notebook and handed it to Bolan.

"Roger. I'm not excited about it, but I guess a little insurance flight out there won't hurt. Over."

"Good enough. We'll work this out. Over."

"Or die trying. Over and out."

Bolan knocked on the dividing door, the pilot throwing it open immediately, his face bathed green in the glow of his instruments.

"Fly us to these coordinates," he called to the man, handing him the paper. "Put your foot to it. Let us know when you get there."

"Yes, sir!"

Bolan felt the pilot kick in the two big General Electric turboshafts, the chopper angling off in an almost forty-five-degree angle.

"You won't regret this," Robbie vowed.

"Oh, I don't know," Bolan replied. "There's plenty of regret to go around already."

They beat a heavy path above the treetops, the reference points giving them some idea of just how fast they were going. Bolan sat, tensing, a coiled spring desperate to loosen. He lived with his eye on his watch, the minutes dragging by to 3:00 a.m. and beyond, every click of the second hand another second off the life clock of the world.

Everything had gotten quiet in the bay, each person lost in thought, and when the pilot banged the door open fifteen minutes later, they jumped.

"We have reached the coordinates, sir!" he called through the opening.

"You got a spotlight?" Bolan yelled.

"Yes, sir!"

"Take us down as low as you can go and use the spot. We're looking for a cleared area, a military installation."

Robbie leaned forward. "There will probably be a lot of cleared area cemented in. Probably not too many surface buildings."

"Roger!"

Robbie shut the door. "Everybody strapped in?" he asked, and saw thumbs-up all around him. "Good."

He reached out and sprang the latch on the bay door, sliding it open. They were at treetop level, hovering.

"Just keep watching!" he said.

The door came open again. "Sir!" the pilot called. "I have just received word from the convoy outside of Florida City. They have found a large cleared and drained area, but no installation of any kind."

"I told you," Robbie said smugly.

"Tell them to proceed toward these coordinates," Bolan ordered. "Tell them—"

"Look!" Ito shouted, pointing south through the trees. "Something's there!"

"Circle back to the southeast," Bolan told the pilot.

"Yes, sir."

The bird angled again, and they came around quickly, the spotlight picking up the shining white concrete right away.

"My God," Julie said. "That's it!"

"Quick," Bolan called to the pilot. "Send these coor dinates to the convoy and tell them to hurry."

"Yes, sir."

The man shut the door, and Bolan turned to Robbie. "How many men do you think would be down there?"

He took off his glasses, playing with them as he gathered his thoughts. "You'd need enough to act as a small armed force, but not so many that it would make for too large an installation. The need for oxygen and water increases exponentially the larger the building and becomes infeasible. Plus you've got security problems with more people. I'd say, forty, fifty men tops."

"Oh-oh," Ito said. "Look down there on the perimeter. It appears to be—"

"A SAM site!" Bolan yelled, a small ground-to-air on radar track spewing fire as he spoke and screaming out of its portable launcher. "Hold on!"

At their altitude, the missile reached them in seconds, a huge explosion shaking the chopper violently, spinning it around. The cockpit door banged open, revealing nothing but open sky.

"We're going down!" Bolan yelled, as the world spun crazily around him. Trees blurred past and all they could do was ride it out, Julie somehow finding Bolan's hand in the writhing confusion and holding tight.

The ride down took only seconds, trees giving way to acres of concrete, and they stopped with a jolt as the tail smashed into a Quonset hut. The entire bay was smashed down into the structure with the rending of dying metal and the screams of human beings.

And then it was over.

Bolan, head giddy, lay within a tangle of twisted framework, staring up at the floor. His first conscious thought was that he was dead, the second was that he was alive but paralyzed, unable to move. Then someone groaned beside him. It was Julie, her body tangled up with his. They were lying on the ceiling of the bay, staring at Robbie and Bob Ito, who were still strapped, groaning, in their seats.

Bolan tried moving, but it was impossible. He and Julie were still strapped in their seats, which were broken and tangled with the jumble of their bodies.

"Mack...?" Julie spoke in a small, barely audible voice.

"Are you all right?" he asked.

"I—I think so. I just can't seem to move."

"We're tangled up together," he explained.

"O-oh." Ito groaned from above them.

"Are you all right?" Bolan called, as he moved his arms and legs, taking stock and trying to work himself free. They didn't have much time.

"I think my arm is broken."

"Robbie," Bolan called. "Robbie."

The man moaned loudly, as if coming out of a deep sleep.

"I think he's coming out of it," Ito said, pain in his voice.

All at once a beam of light etched through the jumble of their prison, then another from the other side. The warrior could hear voices and knew their troubles were just beginning. More light, flashlights, sliced into the chopper, sending crazy shadows into an already surreal landscape. Then Bolan heard a cutting torch being lit.

It took nearly thirty minutes to cut them out of the wreckage. They were pulled roughly from the remnants of the S-70, Bolan's combat harness stripped from him before he was led away, hands behind his head.

He was sore all over, but didn't think his body would have any surprises in store for him when the shock wore off. Julie was cut in three or four places, but seemed in decent shape, too, considering. Ito wasn't so lucky. His arm was badly broken, and he needed his free hand to hold it together.

They were led into a blockhouse of some kind, then down several flights of stairs, all sealed, that finally led them to an elevator.

They were herded inside the elevator, Julie working her way up to Bolan and whispering, "Did the pilot have time to radio our position to the convoy?"

He shook his head. "I don't know." He'd been wondering the same thing since his first coherent thought after the crash.

It was during the interminable ride down that Bolan realized why Robbie Hampton had been so insistent upon this location. There was no way that an installation like this could have been built in a drained swamp.

They were being guarded by Air Force personnel, E-4s and lower, all of them dressed in regular-issue fatigues, as if unprepared for real combat. It began to give him an idea about the basic attitude of the installation that might come in handy later—if there was to be a later.

The elevator finally stopped on the fourth level, and they walked out onto an area that seemed to be devoted to barracks and an armory, leading Bolan to suspect that this was the back door. They were pushed forward then led down corridors that were sculpted rock supported by titanium beams.

Airmen watched them from doorways of freestanding structures within the high-ceilinged chamber. The men were tensed, their eyes dark as they whistled and growled at Julie, the only woman in the compound.

Robbie, a hand to the back of his neck, was gazing around in wonder. "It's like watching one of my stories come to life."

"Quiet!" a squat E-4 barked, and pushed Robbie forward with the stock of his M-16.

They passed the open doorway of a gymnasium, several airmen in boxer shorts playing basketball on a full-size court, while others lifted weights off to the side. Everyone was awake, tensely waiting for the end of the world.

When the hallway branched off in two directions, their captors led them down the right fork, in the direction of an arrow that bore the message Food Services.

They walked the short hallway, then through double swing doors into a small, harshly lit cafeteria, its stainless-steel serving counter shut down except for the red light on a huge coffee urn. Several uniformed men and a civilian dressed in a suit were seated at the end of one of the long tables, drinking coffee and smoking. Bolan recognized one of the men, a face he'd never forget. It was Kit Givan, the man who was promoted for killing Julie's husband.

"The civilian," Julie whispered from beside him. "It's Mark Reilly, my Company contact."

A general stood slowly at the head of the table, a hard man going to fat. His face was pudgy and red, as if his collar was too tight for him, his stomach barely contained in his tight shirt—a proud man unwilling to accept the fact that he wasn't in the same shape as he once had been.

"You people are trespassing on government property," the general stated, "and are in violation of federal law."

"Cut the crap," Bolan said, taking several steps away from the group. "We know who you are and what you are."

"Well, aren't you the one." Mark Reilly stood, raising his cup of coffee. "You've sure caused me a lot of trouble this past week. I really take a great deal of pleasure in knowing that you've come to me so I can be the one to cut your throat."

"We don't need to be unpleasant, Mr. Reilly," the general admonished.

Bolan smiled, recognizing the man's voice from a tape recording. "General Cronin. The gang's all here." He turned to the others. "This is General Albert Cronin, the man who blew up the *Challenger* and destroyed those innocent people."

"You will be silent," the general ordered.

"It's a village idiots' convention," Bolan continued, "everybody gathered to bring on the end of the world because they don't like the way all the nasty people act. They want to make the world safe for all the maniacs like themselves."

Kit Givan laughed. "You sure have a way of glamorizing things, Mr. Bolan. I'll have to hand that to you."

"Recognize the man who shot your husband?" Bolan asked Julie.

"And where the hell were you?" Reilly demanded, pointing at Julie. "You were supposed to kill this bastard."

He got up and walked over to her, taking her face in his hand and smiling. "Maybe it's better this way." He reached out a hand slowly to unzip her flight suit.

Julie spit in the man's face, jerking away from him.

"Mr. Reilly..." Cronin began.

Reilly turned on him. "Don't mother-hen me. I'm not one of your soldier boys." He looked at Julie, laughed again, then walked away from her. "You know, General, we didn't plan on bringing any women down here, but it might be a fine idea to keep this one around to pass among the men. You know, four or five a day, keep a rotation going...."

"That's enough," Cronin shouted, face angry.

"At least he's honest about it," Bolan said, pointing at the man. "You're ready to destroy the country you've sworn to protect, while maintaining your sense of personal honor. You're just a killer, Cronin. A mass murderer."

"Sometimes lives must be expended in the search for the greater good."

"Greater good as determined by you," Bolan accused, "a crazy man, a killer."

"You will be silent!" Colonel Bartello ordered loudly. "We are remaking the world here, for the better. General

Cronin is our commanding officer and will be treated with respect."

"And who are you, Junior? Listen, I'm sick of you people. You've caused enough problems. Your little deal is over, all washed up. Your boss up in Washington is finished, your project finished. Give it up. And I demand medical care for my injured companions."

All the men at the table laughed; Reilly looked at Bolan with sparkling eyes. "You see that clock up on the wall, buddy? It shows that we have less than five hours until project start-up. It's going to happen. It's going to go through one way or the other. What if you have taken General Leland? Our program is large enough to absorb his loss. All we have to do is wait a few more hours and it will all be happening. We don't have to do anything."

"No," Robbie said. "That doesn't fit with the scenario. In order to take over, you must have the President and you must have a high-ranking Pentagon officer. The whole takeover is useless otherwise."

"You don't understand," Ito said, his face drawn with pain, his arm limp, supported by his good arm. "These men are animals. Through bitterness, or loss, or tragic stupidity they *want* to see the world end. It's the fallacy of your theory: the only people willing to sacrifice so much for a political ideal are ghouls like these. Unfortunately the military is rife with them. It's feedback from the combat mentality."

"The bottom line here, gentlemen . . . and lady," Reilly said, "is that we have you." He walked to the E-4 who had Bolan's harness slung over his shoulder. He took it from the man then slung it on his own arm.

"Before we finish up with you—though this has been very entertaining—we just need to ask you a few simple questions. Such as how did you find us?"

"Bedrock," Robbie said proudly. "We simply looked at the geological—"

"That's enough!" Bolan gritted.

"I'll say when it's enough!" Reilly screamed. He walked directly in front of Bolan. "It's time to take you down, big man."

He swung out hard at Bolan's stomach, the Executioner tightening his muscles and doubling over to take the power out of the punch. Reflexively he came up swinging, an uppercut to the jaw knocking Reilly off his feet.

Hands grabbed at Bolan as Reilly scrambled off the floor, coming hard at a now-restrained Mack Bolan.

"Enough!" Cronin ordered. "This is still a military installation."

Reilly stopped in midswing, wild eyes slowly coming back under control. "I want to see you cry," he rasped, then moved over to Robbie. "Does anyone else know you're here?"

The man looked at him, then at Bolan, his face a battleground of conflicting emotions. "No," he said after a moment. "We worked all this out on our own."

Reilly moved to Julie again, his hands gently rubbing her face, his fingers tangling in her hair, then jerking her head back hard.

"Leave her alone!" Bolan yelled.

"Fuck you!" Reilly suddenly had a knife in his hand, which he brought up to Julie's strained face. He rested the jagged blade against her cheek.

"Not here!" Cronin was appalled.

"Is your friend telling the truth?" he whispered to her, his mouth right up against her ear.

"Y-yes," she stammered through clenched teeth.

"Now don't you go cuttin' her up," Givan said genially. "She won't be much fun to any of us if she's all ugly and bloody."

Reilly turned and looked at him, a boyish grin cutting across his smooth face. "You've got a point there. Maybe we want to stab her with something a little less...sharp." The man wiggled his eyebrows. Bolan realized that Reilly was a total sociopath who suddenly found himself in control.

Reilly stepped away from them, going back to sit at the table. "My recommendation is that we cancel these gentlemen out immediately and save the woman for future reference."

"I wholeheartedly second that motion," Kit Givan concurred, smiling at Julie as if he were doing her a favor.

"I don't like it," Cronin said. "We are all gentlemen here, officers. Our purpose is to bring a new order to the land. Our behavior must be above reproach."

"There won't *be* anybody alive to reproach us," Reilly remarked. "It's our world to do with as we please. General Leland would understand that."

"He's got a point," Bartello said, and he was also looking at Julie. "We may have to stay down here for months maybe. Men without women in a closed-in environment will need some sort of... recreation."

Bolan was sick to his stomach, watching the animals divide the spoils. This kind had existed for ages, bringing a bad name to the military of all nations. The difference was, this time the animals had the power.

The double doors burst open at the far side of the cafeteria, a second lieutenant charging into the area. "General Cronin," he gasped, out of breath. "A large convoy is headed this way. We make it to be about twenty trucks."

"How far?" Cronin asked.

"Ten miles and closing, sir."

Cronin nodded, his face intent. "Go to alert. Break out the arms."

"Yes, sir!"

Reilly was on his feet, his eyes dark, smoldering. "You lied to me." The knife gleamed in his hand as he turned it around and around. "You're going to make me drag it out of you, aren't you?"

"Give it up," Bolan said. "You're no match for them. It's over."

"There's nothing you can do," Reilly taunted. "If we destroy the computer, the mission still continues."

"Don't destroy the computer unless we have to," Cronin said.

"Don't worry. I understand all that."

"We need anything they've got," Givan said. "But don't cut up the girl."

Reilly smiled widely at Bolan, then turned to the sergeant who had led them in from the surface. "Throw them in the brig. As soon as I take care of the computer, we'll set up for interrogation."

The Company traitor looked hard at Bolan. "I'll start with this one."

"But he'll never tell you anything," Bartello said.

"I know."

Chapter Twenty-Four

General Leland saluted the Marine guard at the east door of the White House, and moved into the building, checking his watch. It was six-thirty, the usual start of the work day for the President of the United States. He would be in his office, reading the early editions of the *New York Times* and the *Washington Post*, his mind turning toward his agenda for the day. Leland smiled. He was getting ready to present the President with an entirely new agenda.

He walked right past the manned appointment desk, winking at the detachment stationed there. "We'll be right down."

"Yes, sir," the young Marine answered.

He moved briskly along the lower hallway, just coming awake for the new day, minor diplomats and computer operators and clerks stumbling their way to the coffeepot.

Leland entered an elevator and pushed the button that would take him up to the President's suite of conference rooms. The chopper that would take them to the bunker at Camp David was warmed up and waiting on the pad.

This was it, the day he'd been planning for seven years. The restructuring of the world would begin today with no global threats, no organized crime, no illegal aliens, no mind-altering drugs. Today, he'd be doing God's work, the same work done at Sodom, the same work spoken of in Ezekiel.

As he stepped off the elevator, he felt a strange sense of calm and well-being. He had slept wonderfully last night, the rightness of what he was doing a soothing balm from the horrors that had plagued him since Milly had died back in 1978 in the car accident caused by the PCP-altered teenaged psycho. He would fix things now, set the record straight, take care of *all* of them.

It was good.

He moved down the carpeted hall, seeing no one, and tapped lightly on the door marked Private.

Hal Brognola, through the crack in the conference room door, watched the monster moving up on the Oval Office. Greggson and General Ferris stood behind him.

Brognola had never met Leland, knew him only through photos and the man's actions. When he finally got to see him in the flesh, actually bringing his horror unashamedly into the corridors of the White House, it made his neck hairs stand on end. He'd never before known what it felt like to want to rip a human being apart with his hands.

But he knew now.

As Leland knocked on the President's door, Brognola realized that his hands were clenched and cramping. He took a few deep breaths, trying to relax, and looked at his watch just as he had done every minute for the past three hours.

He heard the door to the Oval Office open, heard, but couldn't see the President.

"Good morning, Lee. This is an unexpected surprise. Come in."

"There's no time for that, Mr. President," Leland said. "We must go."

The President laughed. "Go where? There's nothing in my appointment book that—"

"Nuclear war usually doesn't show up in the appointment books, Mr. President."

"What are you talking about?"

"I have received information that the Soviets will launch an all-out attack by nine-fifteen this morning. We must proceed to the bunker at Camp David."

"Where did you get this information, Lee?" the President returned. "There's been nothing through the wire, or from NORAD, or—"

"You, sir, are the first to know."

That was enough for Brognola. He'd wanted to give Leland enough rope to hang himself if it ever came to trial, and the man had done everything but knot the noose around his own neck.

"Not quite the first," Brognola said, rushing into the hall, the others right behind.

"What's this all about, Hal?" the President asked, his face filled with confusion. He looked at Ferris. "What's going on, John?"

"I'm afraid you're the victim of a plot, Mr. President," Ferris informed him. "General Leland plans to start a nuclear war from which he can emerge the nation's leader."

"Lee?" The President stared at Leland. "What is he talking about?"

"The building is full of my Marines, gentlemen," Leland said. "I'm afraid the chase is over."

"Your men were all reassigned this morning, Lee," Ferris growled. "Now, please, let's stop this madness."

"Is it madness to want a better world?" Leland asked, his voice sincere. "Is it madness to try to stop the downward spiral of life on Earth?"

"No." Brognola's gaze locked with Leland's. "But to precipitate the deaths of four billion people is madness on a grand scale."

"How can he do this?"

"Believe us, Mr. President," Greggson said. "He can."

"Look, gentlemen," Leland said casually, "there is no way you can stop me at this point. Why don't we simply proceed to the shelter . . . all of us, and we can discuss it at leisure."

"I think that you've got half of a good idea." Brognola's rage, like a balloon within him, was ready to burst. "I think the President should, indeed, take to the shelter, but there's no way that you will go underground, you sick bastard. There's no way that you're going to survive if the rest of us go."

Leland laughed. "Oh, I understand now. You want to keep me out of the shelter so I'll give you the password. But I can assure you that will never happen. If I'm to die in the first wave, my dream will live on."

"Your complex in Florida is under attack right now," Greggson told him. "Give it over."

Leland turned to the President. "Listen to me. There's no way that this thing can be stopped. If you coordinate and launch a first strike at, say, 8:55, you can score an even more resounding victory."

"What are you saying, Lee?" the President replied. "I know things have been tough on you since Milly died—"

"Leave her out of this, sir," Leland snarled, drawing himself up. "The world has become a vile and godless place. It must be set aright. It will be set aright—" he checked his watch "—in exactly two hours and sixteen minutes."

The President looked at Ferris. "Should we hot-line to the Kremlin?"

"And tell them, what, Mr. President?" the general asked. "I fear that, knowing the situation, it will simply induce them to launch a first strike."

"Roll with it," Leland said. "History has dropped the imperative in your lap. Make the most of it."

The President turned to Brognola. "What do we do?"

"We pray for the success of our one hope, we go to red alert and we try to torture the information out of this maniac standing here with us."

THE BRIG WAS NEAT AND CLEAN. The size of a middle-class living room, it had freshly painted walls and six bunks with new mattresses poking out of the wall in three tiers of two each. Bolan had never been in a new jail before. The experience was just unique enough to be memorable.

They'd been taken down a long hallway of storerooms in two golf carts, Bolan memorizing the route, trying to figure out where the computers might be kept. They'd passed a holding area where the electric carts were recharged, then came to the brig. Out of options at this point, it was simply a question of where and when they'd be killed, and how messy it would be.

The cell was a sturdy one, its door sliding closed with a resounding clang once they'd been shoved inside. There was no light in the cell, other than what spilled in from the hallway. Four armed guards had escorted them there. Bad odds, but not impossible. It was time to regroup.

As soon as the golf carts sped silently off, Bolan took control.

"Robbie, tear a long strip off something and make a sling for Bob. We've got to free up his good arm."

"To what end?" Ito asked, his face pale and drained from the pain and the problems. "There's not enough time for me to break into the system."

"It's not over yet," Bolan said, as he watched Robbie struggle out of his flight suit and use his teeth to start a tear at the collar.

A moaning sound came from one of the bunks.

"There's somebody in here," Julie said, and moved through the half darkness to check, her progress noted by a sharp intake of breath and a whispered "Oh my God."

"What is it?" Bolan asked, moving to her side.

A man lay on a lower bunk, or what was left of a man. He was stripped to the waist, a mass of welts and bruises. The skin had been cut from his chest in long strips, and three fingers were missing from his left hand.

Bolan knelt beside him. "Are you conscious?"

The man groaned loudly through bloody lips, his swollen lids fluttering open.

"Oscar," Ito said from behind Bolan.

Oscar Largent spoke, his words rasping dryly from his throat. "Bob...Bob Ito?"

Ito approached him. "Oh, no. What did they do to you?" Ito's words were more a shocked exclamation than a question, and Largent wasted no strength attempting to reply.

"Who is he?" Bolan asked Ito.

"His name's Oscar Largent. He's a Justice Department operative. They sent him down here undercover."

Bolan put his mouth near Largent's ear, which was swollen and purple. The man had been beaten severely, and Bolan had no idea of what was keeping him alive.

"Can you talk? We don't have much time."

"A little," the man rasped. "W-water."

Bolan looked around. The place was equipped with the usual jailhouse plumbing, an exposed sink and toilet, each with totally enclosed plumbing so it couldn't be taken apart, each operating from a simple push button.

"Wet some cloth," Bolan instructed Julie. "Anything."

As she hurried to comply, Largent tried to sit up.

"No," Bolan said. "Just rest. I need to ask you a few questions."

Julie returned with the cloth, a piece of flight suit. Bolan took the sopping material and put it to the man's lips.

Largent worked hungrily on the cloth, turning his head away when he was through. "Ask," he said weakly.

"Do you know the layout in here?"

"Yes."

"Do you know where they keep the computer?"

"Y-yes...there's a...central hall at the...far end of the building. Com...puter is in a glassed-in booth...in the...center."

"Do you know the Project GOG password?"

"No."

"Okay. Thanks." Bolan stood. "You rest now."

"I-is it...over?"

"No. Not yet."

Bolan turned to Robbie, who had just finished fastening the improvised sling around Ito's arm and neck. Everyone was somber, nearly petrified after seeing what the Fates—and probably Mark Reilly—had in store for them.

"Okay, what's happening with them right now?"

Robbie frowned. "What dif—"

"Don't give me 'what difference,'" Bolan growled. "Just talk."

The man shrugged. "Well, they're probably pretty freaked out right now."

"Why?"

"Simple. This whole system, this whole...scenario, is based upon the concept that what people are doing down here is surviving a nuclear war. The place was built to keep out radiation and to be self-sufficient for a long time. But it wasn't built..."

"To defend itself against ground forces," Bolan finished.

"Right."

"That's what I thought." Bolan began to pace, his mind working furiously. "When we came in, I saw no real defenses except the SAM site."

"Right. Death from the air was a fear, but the entire point of my scenario was that ground forces would never be a problem."

"This place is a hell of a killing ground, too. Once in here, you've got nowhere to fall back to."

"That's why the scenario was so centered," Robbie replied. "Once someone breaches the elevator shaft, you're done for. They can come right down the pulley ropes if they want to, and the force here, just right for the scenario, is far too small to defend itself well against outside aggression."

"That's why they haven't killed us yet," Bolan said, and a plan was forming in his mind. "They're going to want exact information on troop strengths and weapons so they'll know what they're up against."

"Well, what are they waiting for?" Julie asked.

"The computer," Robbie answered. "They've got a real problem with that. They don't want to purge the program because it provides necessary control for the secondary stages of the laser operation, the target-spotting after the first stage. But they don't want it to fall into our hands, either. My guess is that they're rigging charges on the computer so they can blow it if they need to and the satellites will work on automatic timing."

"And remember," Ito said, "we still don't have the password even if we could save the computer."

"One thing at a time," Bolan advised. "The first thing we've got to do is get out of here."

"Impossible," Robbie said.

Bolan swung around, fire in his eyes. He'd had enough. "No!" he shouted. "Now you're going to hear *my* scenario, and it's real simple: we're not going to sit here and let those bastards destroy the world."

Julie took a step forward, her face set hard. "What do you want us to do?"

"Just listen to me," Bolan said, angered, so fired up that he felt he could tear through the rocks with his bare hands.

"Commitment is the key to the fighting man... commitment to action. The world is full of people trained, as you were, to behave in a civilized manner toward others of your kind. It's what makes you stop, hesitate before you give yourself over to hurting someone. It's what enables lone gunmen to commit mass murder with no one to stop them. It's what allows terrorism free rein in many societies. It's what holds civilization together. You have to forget about that. Every person in this installation is prepared to end civilization as we know it.

"They must be killed—immediately and without mercy, in order for life to continue. You must understand, there can be no hesitation, no human feelings attached to your actions.

"Very soon some men are going to come for us, and they'll kill us. We'll have to take the initiative and kill them. It's our only hope."

"But how can we do it?" Julie asked. "We're hurt . . . and they have the guns."

"And if you get to them quick enough," Bolan said, "they're your guns, your advantage. They won't be expecting anything because they've got everything going for them. If we move together as a unit, we have an excellent chance of taking them."

He walked over to Julie and positioned her hand out in front of her like a gun. "You know what I'm going to do," he said, moving five feet away. "I'm going to try and take that gun away. When I go for it, you yell pow! It's a simple as that."

"Okay. I'm ready."

He lunged.

"Pow!" she said, and he'd already sided her hand, the shot from the imaginary gun drilling into the wall.

"And follow through." Bolan brought an elbow up to her face, stopping just before smashing into her nose. "Commitment to action. When they come through that door, on my signal, we all go for them at once, for the closest one to us. They won't have a lot of men to spare for us. They're trying to organize their defenses."

"B-Bolan," Largent called weakly from the bunk. "I . . . think I can h-help you."

"How?" Bolan asked.

"M-move me over near the . . . door. I'll . . . yell to get . . . attention. . . ."

"Okay. When they turn to the sound, we take them."

"But he's hurt so bad," Julie objected.

"It won't matter in a few minutes," Bolan said with intensity. "They are taking us out to kill us. All of us. Remember . . . commitment to action. We have to take them first. We can have them before they even know it. These aren't seasoned troops. We can take them. We *will* take them."

All at once warning horns began to blare, and the lights in the hallway started to flash.

"The convoy," Bolan said. "It's started."

Chapter Twenty-Five

"They'll be coming for us any minute," Bolan said, watching the flashing lights play on the grim faces of his companions. "When the time comes, do whatever it takes. Go for eyes...go for the nose. With enough force the palm of the hand shoved straight up against the nose can jam the cartilage right into the brain. Do what you must to survive, then get to the computer and somehow secure it. There's a cart station just down the hall. Use the carts. This is our only chance...the world's only chance. It all comes down to us, right here, right now."

He looked at Robbie. "Can I depend on you?"

"The logic is irrefutable. I'm with you."

"Bob?"

Ito nodded grimly, his eyes dark pools, his jaw muscles tensed, the pain in his arm consigned to the back of his brain.

Bolan looked at Julie, but didn't ask for support. Her face was set in rock-solid determination. Her fate, should they fail, was perhaps worse than the death that awaited the others.

"Robbie," Bolan said. "Help me with Oscar."

They helped the broken man to his feet. "We're depending on you," Bolan said as they moved him into the shadows near the bars.

"C-count on it," the man rasped, groaning loudly as they helped him to the floor.

Bolan moved back to the others. "We will succeed. Bob, your arm's screwed, but a knee to the groin is still the best stopper around. Those with watches, move them to your knuckles or palm for a fist load. Use any advantage.''

"I hear something," Ito said. "Carts."

"They're coming. This will happen fast."

He turned to Julie, took her in his arms, their eyes meeting in the flashing darkness. "Julie, I—"

"Shh," she murmured, putting fingertips to his lips.

Two carts skidded to a stop outside the cell, Reilly jumping out of his just as soon as it stopped. He walked up to the bars, waiting for the man with the key.

"Well, here we all are," he said. "Isn't this cozy?"

Bolan gazed surreptitiously at the others. They were staring, trying to maintain the reality he had created for them. They were, at least for the moment, warriors.

The E-3 with the key unlocked the sliding bars.

"We don't have any time," Reilly announced. "I need troop strengths and ordnance counts quickly. We're going to take a little ride, and you're going to tell me the truth." He held up the knife. He smiled. "I'll start with your eyes."

The door slid open, Bolan tensing, wanting at least one of the airmen plus Reilly. The men lined up just outside the bars, their weapons held loosely at the ready.

Reilly swept his arm toward the carts in a broad gesture. "All aboard," he called in a conductor's voice.

The captives moved out in a line, Bolan last, positioning himself for a shot at Reilly. They were all close, within two feet of their captors. The tension was almost at the breaking point.

"Aaahh!" Oscar groaned loudly, just enough to make all heads turn, just for a second, in his direction.

The prisoners jumped.

It happened in flashes. Bolan came around with an incredible right, bone cracking on Reilly's jaw as he solidly connected, grabbed his harness and ripped it from the man as he fell. He completed the gesture, swinging out with the harness to smash the guard beside Reilly full in the face, the AutoMag, still holstered, snapping the man's head nearly around in a circle.

Ito had used his body to push his man back against a cart, then came up with his knee, catching the man's groin between his knee and the metal side of the cart. Robbie struggled with his man for the automatic.

Julie had pushed her airman's gun aside and jumped him, her legs wrapping around his waist as her fingernails clawed viciously at his face.

Bolan ran his man up against the bars, smashing his head hard, cracking his skull. He swung around to see Reilly struggling to his feet and staggering toward one of the carts. He was about to pursue him, when he saw that Julie's man had dislodged her and dropped her to the floor, his face streaming blood as he brought up the M-16 to finish her.

Bolan jumped for the airman, his flying tackle driving the guy backward into the bed of the cart. His back broke with a resounding crack.

Without a word, Bolan pulled the man's body off the cart and jumped into the driver's seat to go after Reilly, who'd taken advantage of the warrior's distraction to flee down the hall in the other cart.

Bolan hit reverse. His cart bounced over a body, then picked up speed. Reilly was going for the computer.

The man had a fifty-foot head start on Bolan. The vehicle had raced backward until it reached the cart station, where Reilly pulled a three-point turn and continued on.

Bolan pulled the same maneuver, both of them now charging full tilt toward the main chamber.

Reilly, still well ahead, screeched right as the corridor branched. Bolan gained the juncture within seconds, taking the turn too fast. He slid into the wall and bounced hard back on the track on two wheels, then jolted back to all four.

He put his foot to the floor. As both carts screamed through the hall, Bolan slipped the harness back on, then nearly lost everything on the next turn.

Smoke trickled through the corridor as soldiers ran in both directions. In the next hallway the smoke was thicker. Bolan figured that the attacking force aboveground was taking the shafts, covering their entry with smoke and patterned fire. He could hear explosions rumbling in the distance.

Suddenly the hallway widened to a huge open chamber, and the warrior could see the glassed-in booth across the room. Thick smoke poured through the elevator opening, followed by occasional explosions, making it impossible for Cronin's men to defend the shaft or get close to it. They were setting up defensive positions behind hastily erected barricades of office furniture and tables a good fifty feet from the shaft, giving the advantage to the intruders.

Reilly was already out of his cart and running for the door of the booth. Bolan sped toward him, pulling Big Thunder from its webbing as he closed in. But Reilly pulled a MAC-10 from a sling under his suit coat, sent a hail of stingers at Bolan.

The Executioner jumped from the speeding cart as 9 mm parabellums tore the front fender to shreds. He hit the ground hard, not ten feet from Reilly, and came up firing. A bullet ripped through the traitor's chest and knocked him backward.

Reilly reached for the door and squeezed through the opening, then through another. Bolan jumped to his feet in pursuit.

Jets of air hit Bolan as he erupted through the next door to find Reilly, bleeding profusely, trying to get to the C-4 charges that were stuck conspicuously to the side of a computer.

Bolan launched himself at the man, and he hit hard, both of them grunting as Reilly fell away from the machine. The charge ripped off in his hand and tumbled with him. Bolan heard the scream and rolled away, covering his head as the plastique went off beneath Reilly. The whole booth rocked violently with the force of the explosion.

The body of Mark Reilly had taken the brunt of the explosion. What was left of him was streaked in red on the walls and splattered all over the windows. A four-foot hole gaped in the floor. Bolan turned to the computer. It was still intact, still operational.

A huge explosion shook the booth. Bolan turned to see the elevator shaft one hundred feet away blown to shreds. The invading troops were swarming into the complex, using furniture they had dropped from the levels above as their cover.

Then he saw Julie, Robbie and Bob pull up.

He charged to the door. "Come on! Hurry!"

She raced across the smooth concrete floor, while a full-scale battle went on within the chamber, and skidded to a halt in front of the booth, all of them hurrying out.

"Bolan!" Robbie yelled. "I've got an idea about the passwor—"

He was cut off, a line of M-16 fire tearing through his torso to throw him violently against the outside of the booth.

Bolan had a second to look up and see Givan, Bartello and Cronin bearing down on them in a cart.

Julie and Ito dived behind their vehicle; Bolan was caught out in the open in the glass booth. Givan's face was frozen into a grin as he opened fire. The bullets hit the window, deep gouges of frosty white splintering across the surface. But the thick glass didn't break.

Julie came up firing an M-16 as Bolan darted around the doorframe, Big Thunder booming in his hand.

As the cart skidded by for another pass, he held it in his sight and squeezed once. Bartello grabbed at his throat and tumbled out of the vehicle. Cronin and Givan dived out as the cart veered, then rolled violently across the smooth floor.

"Take them alive!" Bolan yelled, as Givan, shaken up, crawled across the floor, blood dripping from his face. "We still need that password!"

Cronin had rolled to safety behind the wreck of Bolan's cart and was trying to make his way around the edge to come up on Julie's unprotected flank.

Just then Bolan saw Oscar Largent. Barely alive, he was behind the wheel of the cart on full throttle, bearing down on Cronin from across the chamber.

As Cronin stood to draw down on Julie, Largent rammed him, spinning him away. Cronin's M-16 flew across the floor.

Julie jumped up and ran for Givan, who was still dazed.

Largent stopped the cart and eased himself out, falling atop Cronin, who was broken and bloody, his hand still clawing for the .45 strapped to his side.

The two men fought for the gun, Largent winning. He straddled Cronin and jammed the barrel of the .45 into his mouth.

"P-password," he demanded, his body weaving.

Cronin's eyes were glazed, glassy nonhuman orbs staring up at Largent.

"Password!" Largent shouted. Cronin simply jerked his head up, pushing on the barrel. The gun went off by reflex and splattered his face all over the floor.

Julie had reached Givan, the toe of her foot kicking him over onto his back. Her brain was cold fire, her mission all encompassing.

Givan shook his head, a smile trying to find its way to his lips. "Should have got you on that Mississippi road."

"Keep your hands away from your body," she ordered.

"Hey...no problem," he said, wiping blood off his face and struggling to his knees. "I know when I'm licked. I don't want to die any more than the next fella."

"What's the password?" she demanded.

"I don't know."

"Password," she repeated.

"My orders always came down from Leland's office,"
he said. "Honest to God, I don't know the password."

"Then this is for Harry," she said coldly, "and God
knows how many others."

She pulled the trigger, tearing out the man's chest, his
body deadweight before it hit the ground. For crimes
against humanity, she had executed him. She felt no excitement or remorse. She had simply done a necessary job.

The defending troops had been broken by the convoy
personnel and were being chased through the building.
Bolan stood looking around at the death that littered the
area. His gaze stopped on Robbie.

Bob Ito was bent over the man, and it looked as if he
were still alive. Bolan hurried to him. Ito was holding
Robbie's head up, while blood streamed from the injured
man's nose and mouth.

"Let me," Bolan said, taking Robbie's head. "You go
in and fire up the computer. Go as far as you can."

"Right."

As Ito disappeared into the chamber, Bolan looked
down at the maker of realities who had dreamed up this
entire nightmare.

"I'm dead," he said to Bolan.

The big man nodded. "Before, you ..."

"Yes-s-s," Robbie hissed. "Listen to me, it's a good
story." The man coughed, his body nearly rising from the
floor with the waves of pain. "Gift of God," he said.
"Think about it as an acronym...the first letters...
GOG. GOG has no modern synonyms." He smiled. "It
had to stand alone."

He stopped speaking again. Bolan waited for him to
continue. But that was it. There were no more words, no
more stories.

He laid Hampton down and stood to walk into the
booth. He looked at his watch. Only ten more minutes
until project start-up.

"Seasonal," he said. "Seasonal GOG."

"I need the password now," Ito said, his hand flying across the computer keyboard. "I must have..."

"Seasonal... seasons..."

"What?" Julie said.

"Seasons," Bolan repeated. "Summer, autumn, winter, spring, March, April, May... May!"

"What?"

"May-GOG."

"Magog!" Julie said. "From the Bible. The land of Gog!"

Bolan pointed to Ito. "Try it."

"But..."

"Do it now!"

The man shrugged, his hand working the keys. He looked up, his eyes wide in astonishment. "I'm in!" he yelled. "I'm in! I'm trying the self-destruct. Watch those radar screens."

Bolan looked to a radar bay set cater-corner to the computer. There were four screens, one for each of the missiles, the fourth dead because of the *Challenger* flight.

A blip moved across each of the screens.

"Here we go," Ito said, a shaking finger reaching out to push Enter.

For a few seconds there was nothing, then one of the blips expanded on the screen, then disappeared, followed quickly by the other two.

Bolan and Ito shouted their victory, Julie looking oddly at them. "What's the big deal?" She pointed to her wristwatch. "We've still got five minutes to spare." Then the tears came, as Bolan knew they would. She had just realized that mankind was safe and that she was a killer.

He put an arm around her and led her out of the booth to one of the carts. Medics had already loaded Oscar Largent onto a stretcher and were wheeling him away. "Listen," he said quietly. "You did what you had to do."

"But, Mack, I... I..."

"I know," he said. "You just visited the place where I live all the time. I know how you feel, and I'm here to tell you that you can walk away from it."

"I'll never—"

"You may never forget," he agreed, "but you'll heal. You helped to save the world. You had to give up a little humanity to do it."

She looked at him, her eyes peering deeply into his, then turned to look at Robbie Hampton's body. "I don't know if I'm sorry he's dead or not."

"He was intelligence without restraints," Bolan replied. "Gentle himself, but dangerous to civilization. I don't know what I'd have done with him had he lived."

"There's no law against a probing mind. This isn't the Middle Ages."

He stared hard at the body, glad that the decision had been taken out of his hands. For there was no answer for Robbie Hampton, no way to pigeonhole his thoughts. America was, for all its problems, a free country. And that meant the freedom to have bad thoughts as well as good.

"Hey!" Bob Ito called from the booth doorway. "I've got Hal on the line in here. He wants to congratulate you."

Bolan climbed out of the cart. Julie slid over behind the wheel. He smiled at her. "You coming?"

She shook her head. "It's time for me to walk away from all this, to try to... forget." She patted the seat beside her. "You've done your duty. Come with me. Walk away."

He looked at her, then turned to stare at Bob Ito, at the telephone receiver he still held in his hand. He wanted to go, wanted to let others worry about the state of the world; but that was a reality he had dreamed of for a long time, a dream that was for others, not Mack Bolan. "You go on," he said. "I've got business."

She leaned out of the cart and kissed him then, a sad, lingering kiss. When she pulled away from him she said, "I couldn't live like this."

He took her face in his hands. "I wouldn't want you to. I wouldn't want anyone to."

She wiped a small tear from the corner of her eye, and turned on the ignition. "See you around," she said huskily.

"Yeah."

JAMES AXLER

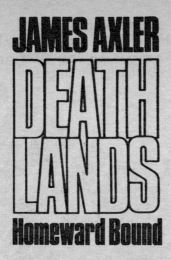

DEATHLANDS

Homeward Bound

**In the Deathlands,
honor and fair play are words of the past.
Vengeance is a word to live by . . .**

Throughout his travels he encountered mankind at its worst.
But nothing could be more vile than the remnants of Ryan's
own family—brutal murderers who indulge their every whim.

Now his journey has come full circle. Ryan Cawdor is about
to go home.

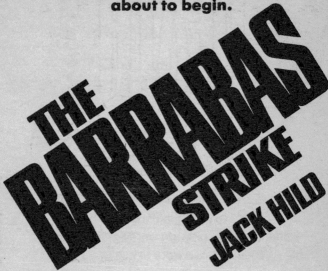

You don't know what NONSTOP HIGH-VOLTAGE ACTION is until you've read your 4 FREE GOLD EAGLE NOVELS

TAKE 'EM NOW

FOLDING SUNGLASSES FROM GOLD EAGLE

Mean up your act with these tough, street-smart shades. Practical, too, because they fold 3 times into a handy, zip-up polyurethane pouch that fits neatly into your pocket. Rugged metal frame. Scratch-resistant acrylic lenses. Best of all, they can be yours for only $6.99.

MAIL YOUR ORDER TODAY.

Send your name, address, and zip code, along with a check or money order for just $6.99 + .75¢ for postage and handling (for a total of $7.74) payable to Gold Eagle Reader Service. (New York and Iowa residents please add applicable sales tax.)

Remove from pouch...

unfold once...

unfold twice...

and they're ready to wear.

Gold Eagle Reader Service
901 Fuhrmann Blvd.
P.O. Box 1396
Buffalo, N.Y. 14240-1396

GES-1A

Offer not available in Canada.